razOr
bill

An Imprint of Penguin Random House
Penguin.com

ISBN: 978-1-59514-850-6

Printed in the United States of America

1 3 5 7 9 10 8 6 4 2

Book design by Anthony Elder

THE
Love
THAT
Split
THE
World

EMILY HENRY

razOr bill

An Imprint of Penguin Random House

For those who have loved me into the world: thank you;
And for those who have grown weary: you are well loved.

The night before my last official day of high school, she comes back. I feel her in my room before I even open my eyes. That's how it's always been.

"Wake up, Natalie," she whispers, but she knows I'm awake—if a fly buzzed in the hallway, I'd wake up—just like she knows the drooling, snoring rug of a Saint Bernard at the foot of my bed, the *watchdog* Mom and Dad got to help me sleep better, will keep drooling and snoring through our entire conversation.

I open my eyes on darkness, push back the covers, and sit up. The crickets are thrumming outside my window, and the blue-green moonlight shines through the foliage across my carpet.

There she is, sitting in the rocking chair in the corner, as she has every time she's visited me since I was a little girl. Her ancient features are shrouded in night, her thick, gray-black hair loose down her shoulders. She wears the same ash-colored clothes as always, and though it's been nearly three years, she looks no older than the last time I saw her, or even the first time I saw her. If anything, she might look a little younger. Probably because *I'm* older, and generally less terrified of wrinkles and age spots than I used to be.

I contemplate screaming—twisting the knob on the bedside lamp, doing anything my eighteen years have taught me will make Them disappear, just to teach her a lesson for leaving me for so long, for letting me think she was finally gone for good.

But despite my bitterness, I don't want her to vanish, so I stay still.

"Nice of you to stop by," I whisper. The words hurt my throat, which hasn't woken up yet. My vision's still settling too, piecing together the wrinkled details of her face, the laugh lines around her mouth, and the sweet crow's-feet at the corners of her dark eyes. "Where have you been?"

"I've been right here," she says. It's one of her typical, cryptic answers.

"It's been almost three years."

"Not for me it hasn't."

Again—for the thousandth time—I survey her tattered shawl and the threadbare dress hanging on her bony body. "No," I say, "you're outside of time, aren't you?"

Her right shoulder shifts in a shrug. "Your words, not mine. Have any *others* come to see you?"

I rub the heels of my hands over my eye sockets, stalling for time. I'm ashamed to admit that no one's come and that I know exactly why. Though I want to be mad at her for abandoning me, it's my fault I haven't seen her in three years. *I* caused her disappearance. But it doesn't matter whether I admit it or not—she already knows everything anyway. As if to prove that point, she says, "I think Gus farted."

I lean over the bed and look down at the shaggy dog. His tongue is lolling in his sleep, and his perpetually oozing nose is busily sniffing. One of his back legs starts to kick in response to a dream, and the horrible smell she must've been referring to hits me.

I cover my nose with my forearm. "Ugh, *Gus*. You're a monster, and I love you, and you're disgusting."

I wait for the worst of the odor to pass before I answer her question. "There haven't been others. They're all gone. Dr. Langdon thought the EMDR therapy worked. She said that's why you stopped coming. Apparently any trauma I had was resolved. I'm a lucky girl. Or I was until five seconds ago."

EMDR: eye movement desensitization and reprocessing. It's a type of psychotherapy used to treat the effects of post-traumatic stress disorder and, in my case, to shut out the woman in front of me and the various others who've appeared at my bedside over the years.

She thinks for a moment. "You know, just a moment ago—a moment for me, that is, three years for you—I told you something about Dr. Langdon. Did you pass it along?"

I keep staring hard at her.

"Do you remember what I told you, Natalie?" she presses.

I nod once. "You said she would die in a fire."

"And?"

"She's still alive," I supply. "She also suggested I try Ativan, though of course Mom didn't approve. Apparently this is just a stressful time in a teenager's life."

God—the private name I gave her years ago, though she insists I call her Grandmother—laughs and looks down at her weathered hands, folded in her lap. "Girl, you have no idea."

"Were you ever my age?" I ask.

Her thick eyebrows rise up over her cloudy dark eyes. "Yes," she says quietly.

"And it was stressful?"

She jams her mouth shut. "When I was your age, I knew nothing. Nothing about myself, nothing about the universe or about heartbreak. I remember being terrified to grow up, afraid of losing my friends, sure I'd lose my mind. Life felt like a blender that wanted to eat me. But the things that happened to me when I was just a little bit older than you are—those things made the blender feeling seem like a bubble bath."

I look down at the tear in my quilt. Mom made this blanket from a pattern while my birth mother was pregnant with me. It was going to belong to a different baby, from an adoption that fell through. Instead, it became mine when I became my parents'. "I missed you," I tell Grandmother.

"I missed you too."

"I thought you said it was only a minute for you."

"It was."

For a while we're both silent, staring at one another. Then she asks, "How are the twins?"

"Good," I tell her. "Coco's transferring to a performing arts high school next year. Jack's still playing football. Mom's *so proud* of us all that she's liable to explode any day now, so that's good. At the end of summer she and Dad are taking us to San Francisco then up to Seattle." The trip is a tradition they've had since they got married. Mom had never really traveled anywhere before, and her only reservation about marrying Dad was that she knew he loved Kentucky so much he'd never leave. They were poor then, but Dad still promised they'd see the world, or, at the very least, the continental U.S. Thus the annual Cleary Family Road Trip was born.

Grandmother closes her eyes for a long moment, and their corners crinkle prettily when they open. "I thought this year was Boulder down through Denver and into Mesa Verde," she says. "Jack gets food poisoning, and Coco won't eat anywhere that's not a chain after that."

"That was last year," I say. "This year it's all Highway 101. Probably a good time to buy stock in Dramamine, if you're looking for a hot tip."

"And you? How are you?"

"I'm great. Moving to Rhode Island in August, to go to Brown—but you probably already knew that."

She nods, and again we fall into stillness and silence. I've missed this feeling, of sitting awake at night with her while the rest of the world dreams. The last three years have felt chaotic without these moments of quiet.

"Is it true that God leaves you when you grow up?" I ask. "Is that why I haven't seen you?"

"I've never said I was God."

It's true—she's avoided the question of *what* exactly she is since she first appeared when I was six, and not for lack of my asking, guessing, and hypothesizing.

Before Grandmother, the hallucinations had all been terrifying: black orbs floating a foot over my nose, grizzled men in green jackets with eyes like endless pits, women painted like clowns posing at my bedside. When they came, I'd scream, reach for the light, but by the time my parents came running to my bedroom door, the things would be gone, evaporated into the walls as though they'd never come at all.

"It was just a nightmare," Mom would assure me, running her long fingers through the tangles in my hair. Then Dad would get blankets from the hall closet and make a nest on the floor beside their bed, and I'd finish the night in their room.

But when Grandmother appeared beside me that first time in the dead of night, things felt different. It's not like I had an extensive vocabulary for the spiritual or metaphysical—my family is the "church twice a year" type, and those biannual visits have never done anything for me—but I also never had any aversion to the concept of God Itself, just to the idea that we could possibly nail down all Its details.

God is a thing I think I see in glimmers all over: an enormous and vague warmth I sometimes catch pulsing around me, giving me shivers and making tears prick my eyes; a mysterious and limitless Thing threaded through all the world and refusing to be reduced to a name or a set of rules and instead winding itself through millions of stories, true and made up, connecting all breathing things.

And I'd given Grandmother that nickname not because I thought she *was* that Thing but because I saw It in her, and knew she belonged to It. I had no other word at my disposal that could encompass a being who came out of the walls to protect me from the dark.

While *The Shining*-esque visitations hadn't been enough to make my parents take me to a shrink, an elderly American Indian celestial being showing up to tell me creation stories had. When I'd mentioned *Grandmother* over breakfast, Mom immediately left the kitchen to call Dad. It was obvious I'd done something wrong—I just didn't know *what* until a week later, when Mom got home from her meet-and-greet with a child psychologist and had her first *talk* with me.

"It's only natural to wonder about your heritage, honey," she'd said, voice shaking. It sounded like a line from one of the *You Were a Special Gift* books she read to me as a toddler, in lieu of the more devastating "You're adopted" speech some other kids I knew got later. "It's okay to explore your identity."

"My eyes were open," I told her then. "I wasn't dreaming. Grandmother's real."

I couldn't convince Mom or Dad or Dr. Langdon, but I still knew: Grandmother was real. And she may have never admitted to being God, but I knew she was something, or a part of something, sublime.

"Fine," I say, "the Great Spirit, the Above Old Man, the Earth Maker, or Holitopa Ishki, or whatever exactly you are or call yourself—just answer the question. Are you going to leave me now that I'm an adult or . . . whatever it is I am?"

Grandmother's mouth tightens. She stands, and my heart starts to pound—she's never stood before, in all the dozens of nights she's come to me. She crosses the room, perches on the edge of my bed, and takes my hands in hers. Her skin is impossibly soft, like velvet, like powdered sediments or antique silk.

"This," she says, "may be the last time you'll see me, Natalie. But I'll *always* be with you."

I blink back tears and shake my head. My oldest friend in the world, someone who doesn't exist according to all the experts, who is only and fully mine. It shouldn't be much of a surprise. I'm leaving for Brown in three months. Soon, that rocking chair, this bedroom, the rolling blue hills of Kentucky will all be things of the past. Did I really think she'd come with me? Still, I hear myself ask her, "Why?"

She smooths my hair back from my forehead, the same way Mom always does. "Lie down, girl. I'm going to tell you one last story, and I want you to listen well. It's important."

"It's always important."

"It *is* always important." She returns to the rocking chair, stopping to scratch behind Gus's ear when he lets out an unconscious whimper. She sits and clears her throat. "This is the story of the beginning of the world, and the woman who fell from the sky."

"I've heard that one before," I remind her. "Actually, I'm pretty sure it was the first story you ever told me."

She nods. "It was the first, and so it'll be the last, because now you've learned to listen."

Learn to listen, listen with your bones, let the story fill you. Things she's always saying. Honestly, I have next to no clue what she's talking about, partly because I only ever see her in the middle of the night when my brain's full of fog, and partly because her voice is the phonic equivalent of a music box playing "Clair de Lune," so soothing that the words get lost in the blanket of the sound. I lie back and close my eyes, letting that voice wash over me now.

"There was an old world that came before ours," she begins, "a world that had never before seen death. And in that world there was a young woman who was very strong and very strange. The woman's father was the first person to die in the world, and even after he did, she would speak with his spirit often. Death had opened her father's eyes to all sorts of secrets the woman could not yet see, and because of this, his spirit told her to marry a stranger in a distant land whom he had chosen for her. So against her mother's wishes, the young woman trusted her father's spirit and journeyed to that distant land and presented herself to the stranger. This man was a powerful sorcerer, and he received the woman's marriage proposal skeptically, since she was still very young and he would need a wife with strength and resolve. He decided that he would give her three tests, and if she should pass, then he would marry her.

"First, he took her into his lodge and gave her corn. 'Grind this corn,' he told her. And she took it and barely boiled it, and though there were many mounds of it, she ground it against the stone very quickly, and the sorcerer was amazed.

"For the second test, he ordered her to take off her clothing and to cook the corn over the fire. As she did, it popped and splattered on her, the mush burning her skin where it landed, but she didn't flinch. She stood, unmoving, as the corn burned her until the mush was finished.

"For her final test, the sorcerer opened the door to his lodge and called to his beast servants, who came running, and he invited them to eat the mush from off her bare skin. And though their sharp teeth and tongues sliced and cut and repulsed her, she still remained serene and steadfast. So the sorcerer agreed to marry her.

"For four nights, the wed couple slept with the soles of their feet touching, and then the husband sent his wife back to her village with a great gift of meat for all her kin. He told her to divide it evenly among all the people in the village. He also told her that they should peel back their roofs so that he could bless them with a rain of white corn that night, and so she did, and it was so.

"When she returned, his lodge became her home too, and she began to spend her days with one particular tree that grew there. It was a tree with blossoms made of light so bright that they illuminated all of his land. The woman loved the tree—it made her feel less strange, less out of place—and she would sit under it and talk with all the spirits and with her dead father too. She loved it so much that once, late at night when everyone was sleeping, she went out and lay with it and became pregnant.

"Around that time, her husband grew sick, and none of the medicine people could heal him, but they all told him that the illness had been caused by his wife. He knew they were right; he'd never met a person as powerful as her. He asked them what he should do. Divorce didn't exist there. The only death that had occurred was her father's, and no one yet understood it. But the medicine people were wise, and they found a solution.

" 'Uproot the light tree,' they told him, 'and call her over to it, and trick her into falling into it. Then replace the tree, and your power will be restored.'

"That same day the sorcerer dug up the tree of light, but when he looked into the hole beneath it, he saw a whole other world below. He called to his wife, and when she came he said,

'Look, lean over, there's another world below us.' She knelt beside the tree and peered down through the emptiness where the roots had been. At first she saw only darkness, but then, far below that, she saw blue, a shimmering bright blue that was *beautiful*. Full of hope and joy and dreams and the same kind of light that grew all through her tree. Here was the very source of all the light that had comforted her when she was lonely. She looked at her husband, smiling, and said, 'Who ever would have guessed that the light tree was growing right over such a beautiful place?'

"He nodded. Then, carefully, he suggested, 'I wonder what it's like down there.'

"She said, 'I wonder too.'

"He said, 'Maybe someone could go down there and find out.'

"But his wife was shocked. 'How could anyone do that?' she asked.

"'Jump,' he said.

"'Jump?' she said, leaning over the hole again. She tried to guess how far below the new world was, but she had no idea. She'd never seen such a great distance, she was sure.

"'Someone as brave as you could easily do it,' her husband said. 'Become a gentle breeze, or a petal or blossom from the light tree, or any number of things, and jump lightly and float down, or dive like a hawk, to that beautiful world below.'

"For a long minute she stared down into that glimmering blue, that endless blue of things she'd never seen, dreams she'd never dreamed. 'I could jump,' she said. 'I could float. I could fall into the shining blue.'

"'Yes, you could,' her husband said. For another long

minute, she stayed there, kneeling and gazing and meditating. Then she stood and flexed her hard muscles, bent her knees, raised her arms up high over her head, and dove down through the hole in her world into the beautiful blue.

"For a long while, the sorcerer—for he was no longer her husband now—watched her body tumble through the darkness. The medicine people who had advised him made their way toward his lodge and the hole where he stood. 'She jumped,' he told them, and then they all lifted the tree back into place and covered the hole that led to the new world.

"And because she jumped, our world began," Grandmother concludes.

"Depending on who you ask," I say, sitting up.

Grandmother tips her head. "Depending on who you ask." About a third of the stories she's told me are creation stories of some type, and no two are identical. I don't know who all the stories belong to, precisely, although I can usually make a decent guess when the names are Squirrel and Corn Woman or Abraham and Isaac. "You know . . ." Grandmother takes a deep breath and glances down at her hands. "There's a reason I've told you all these stories, Natalie."

I sit up again. It's not like I haven't asked her *a million times*: Why do you show up in my room in the middle of the night to tell me these things? "You said the stories *were* the reasons."

She sighs, and her voice becomes weaker, gruffer. "The stories matter. Separate from us, they matter. We are part of them, Natalie. We're much smaller than them. But there's another reason too."

I see tears lining her dark lashes, and suddenly she seems

so much younger. "What's wrong?" I say. "Grandmother, what's wrong?"

"I don't want to scare you," she says. "But you need to be prepared for what's coming."

Goose bumps prickle up along my arms as Grandmother buries her face in her hands, and I get out of bed to crouch in front of her. I've never seen her like this. I've only ever seen her the one way. She grips my hands hard, and her eyes find mine. "The stories," she says. "It's all in the stories."

"What is?"

"Everything. The truth. The whole world, Natalie," she says brusquely. "That girl jumped through the hole, not knowing what would happen, and the whole world got born. You understand that, right? The *whole world*."

"I understand," I lie, to calm her. Because I *am* scared now, and I need her to be the Grandmother I know, so I can be the child who's soothed from her own fear of the dark.

"Good." Her hand grazes my cheek. "Good. Because you have only three months."

"What are you talking about—"

"Three months to save him, Natalie."

"Save? Save *who*?"

Her eyes, immense and milky all of a sudden, dart over my shoulder, and her mouth drops open. "*You*," she breathes. "Already—*you're already here.*"

I look over my shoulder, neck alive with tingles, but no one's there.

"Don't be afraid, Natalie. Alice will help you," Grandmother says. "Find Alice Chan."

When I turn back, the rocking chair is empty, still nodding back and forth as though the ancient woman has just stood from it.

I'm alone again. I'm no longer the girl who talks to God.

I tumble out of bed and hurry to stop the shriek of my phone alarm. I don't know how I got back to sleep after last night's events, but apparently I did. The moonlight has faded, and the dim streetlights lining our cul-de-sac have popped on, sprinkling yellowy glares throughout the purple-blue of my dew-dampened windowpanes. The earliest birds and backfiring pickup engines are waking up, but the chirping crickets haven't gotten the memo that this hellish hour is technically considered "morning."

I flick the light switch of my walk-in closet, and Gus moos unappreciatively before turning over and going right back to sleep. I'm so jealous I throw a pillow at him, and would have immediately felt horribly guilty if not for the fact that he just lets out a snore and covers his eyes with one paw.

As exhausted as I am, I still can't shake the fear left over from last night. For as long as I can remember, Grandmother's been a force of calm in my life. I mean, her stories don't tend to be happy or calming by any means, but her presence has always made me feel safe. Until last night.

What could she have been talking about?

My late-night Google trail of "Alice Chan" led to a dead end. It would seem that half the human population is composed of Alice Chans, each one less obviously significant than the last.

Three months to save him. I shake my head as if to clear the words.

I slip on a fitted black T-shirt dress and pull a denim jacket from a hanger on the top rack. It may be eighty degrees and ninety-nine percent humidity outside, but with Principal Grant in menopause, the school's temperature is completely unpredictable. It's best to be prepared. I survey the neat rows of heels that used to do something for me but now seem about as necessary as a pubic wig, and instead grab a pair of boots before walking back into my room.

Two of my walls are painted a ghastly orange, the other two a high-gloss black: Ryle High School's colors. If that weren't bad enough, one of the black walls has our mascot—the Raider, a one-eyed pirate with two swords crossed behind his head—taking up its majority. My bedding is white, and so are the tea-candle lantern and antique lamp on my desk. When I have headaches those are the three focal points I have to choose from, unless I feel like lying down inside my closet.

Mom and Dad decorated the room for me while I was away at dance camp the summer before seventh grade and already zealously looking forward to high school. Obviously the garish school-spirit color scheme was the best thing ever, until about a year ago, when I realized I had eyeballs, and it became just about the worst thing ever. With a better sound system and a few more Black Eyed Peas albums, my bedroom could give Guantanamo Bay a run for its money.

In the years since the original Makeover from Hell, I've also added my own touches: corkboards covered in notes from friends, shadow boxes full of dance team ribbons and medals, black-and-orange pompoms stuffed behind both my desk and my dresser, a dozen or so picture frames capturing carnivals and football games and dances.

There I am, a million times over, smiling back at myself: same coarse dark hair, deep brown eyes, and dark skin; same square face and high cheekbones. There I am kissing Matt Kincaid, for the four consecutive years I kissed Matt Kincaid. Standing in the gymnasium in the dead center of the dance team's middle row, with all the other girls of perfectly average height. Hugging Megan and making that godforsaken *Charlie's Angels* pose, in a completely nonironic way that can never be undone, all over Gray Middle School.

Since Grandmother disappeared, I've felt less and less like the girl in the photos, and more and more like I needed to get out of here. I quit the dance team, quit Matt, and ever since getting in to Brown, have started to quit Kentucky altogether. And now, three months away from my grand escape and new start, Grandmother's visit has everything feeling messy again.

"NAT—JACK—COCO—BREAKFAST!" Mom shouts up from the kitchen, and my stomach flip-flops as I pass the rocking chair and head downstairs.

I'm usually the last one out of my room in the morning. Coco, being the very definition of efficiency, is always first to the breakfast table, doubling back upstairs a few minutes later to hurry Jack along as she sounds off a checklist of things he needs for school, while simultaneously texting, braiding her hair, or applying mascara. Without her, Jack would probably routinely walk out of the house without pants, and honestly, he'd also probably manage to have a pretty good day.

Downstairs, Jack has a plate full of only bacon, which he's shoveling into his mouth with a fork. I'm pretty sure his eyes are closed. Across from him, Coco is texting over a bowl of fruit, her pretty blue eyes lined perfectly in clean layers of eyeliner and eye shadow. She looks exactly like Mom, except for her angular nose, which comes from Dad. I've always wondered what that must be like, to look like our parents.

One excellent thing about being adopted is that you always get to worry you'll end up accidentally dating someone you share a gene pool with. If I were fully Native American, I wouldn't have to think about that in a mostly white town like Union, but they tell me my biological father was white, so that complicates things.

Mom looks up from the stove, and she clamps a hand over her mouth and gasps like her sleeve's just caught on fire. "Oh, honey. Look at you. You're so beautiful." She starts shaking out her loose strawberry blond waves as if it helps to fight back emotion, then holds out her arms. I shuffle forward reluctantly into the hug. "I can't believe it's your last day of high school! I remember the day we brought you home like it was yesterday."

"Yeah, I was a real crybaby."

"Oh, stop it, you were not. You were so quiet and so curious. That whole first night we just stayed awake looking at you, and you just looked back at us and didn't make a sound—"

"Mom," Jack says from the table.

"We knew you were special, and now look at what a smart, talented—"

"Mom, I think something's on fire," Coco says, without glancing up from her phone.

"What?" Mom spins back to the stove, immediately harried by the blackening omelet caked to her cast-iron skillet. *"Shit."*

"I didn't know you spoke French, Mom," I say.

"Did you hear Mom say 'shit'?" Jack asks Coco, his mouth full of more bacon.

"Yeah, she's so weird," Coco answers flatly. They're polar opposites—Coco the goal-oriented perfectionist type and Jack the goofy, go-with-the-flow jock—and yet they've always been inseparable. I guess that's what cohabitation in a womb for nine months does.

Mom waves a dishrag at the smoke plume. "Give me five minutes. I'll make you another one."

I pour myself a mug of coffee and step through the glass-paneled door onto the deck, where Dad stands, drinking coffee in his long-sleeved denim shirt, despite the hot morning mist. "Morning," I say.

He flinches in surprise before turning back to me and ruffling my hair. "How you doin', sugar cube?" I shrug, and Dad sets his mug down on the railing, folding his arms. "Nightmares?"

Dad has this way of knowing things, at least when it comes to me and horses, without understanding the nitty-gritty of *how* or *why,* but he won't pry. I want to tell him everything, but I can't speak, and I suddenly realize why: I'm terrified it's him—what if it's Dad I'm supposed to save?

I shake my head and lean out over the shadowy yard. Dad takes a long sip. "You remember those tantrums you used to have? I don't know why, but I was just thinking about those. You'd lie down and scream and kick and bite and sob, no matter where we were."

I sigh. "Some things never change."

The sun peeks through the woods beyond our yard, turning everything golden at the fringes, even Dad's brown eyes. It used to make me so happy when people who didn't know any better would tell me I had his eyes. When I was little I thought maybe mine were the same shade as his because I really did belong so wholly with and to Dad.

"You know, when a horse bucks or bites, it's just frustrated communication."

I raise an eyebrow. "Is that so?"

He rubs the back of my neck like I'm a filly. "If you need to talk, I'll always listen." He kisses the crown of my head, then turns to go inside.

"Dad?"

He turns back. "Yeah?"

It would be a relief to tell him about Grandmother's warning, but I can't get the words out. Sometimes it's so hard to speak, scary even. My heart rate goes up, my hands shake, and it feels easier to keep things in the dark than to drag them into the light. "Be careful," I manage.

Though he furrows his thick chestnut eyebrows, he doesn't

ask any questions. "For you, sugar cube, always."

Three months to save him, and I don't even know who. I've got to find Alice Chan.

I skip lunch and slip off to the bathroom, where I plug in my dying phone and resume my frantic Googling. I click through every result I can (Alice Chan the Local Dentist, Alice Chan the Criminal Lawyer Two Towns Over, Alice Chan the Professor at NKU) until the bell rings, then run back to my locker. I'm getting my things for class when I feel a pair of hands slide down around my eyes. "Guess who."

"Harry Styles?"

"So close it's insane."

"Okay, give me a clue."

"I'm one of your biggest fans."

"I'm having a hard time, because the only thing that's coming to mind other than Harry Styles is the ghost of River Phoenix, and I wouldn't be able to feel his hands."

Matt uncovers my eyes and leans against the locker beside mine, smiling that perfect golden-boy smile that not even the best orthodontist could've faked. His sandy hair's pushed up off his forehead, and he's sporting his football jersey. "Natalie Cleary, has anyone ever told you you're really weird?"

"I think at some point that assessment even became Kentucky state law, which is partly why I'm going to college in Rhode Island."

He sticks out his bottom lip. "I'm going to miss your weird."

"Only because you were born without any."

"Probably." He holds my gaze for a little too long, and his fair skin starts to flush. We've been broken up for nearly a year, and we've both done our fair share of exploring since, but sometimes those old feelings seem ready to resurface.

As if prompted by my subconscious, which definitely knows I do *not* want to end up married to Matt Kincaid, living on his farm in Union, Kentucky, I break the silence with "Although your mom only eats beige food. That's pretty weird."

His forehead creases. "What are you talking about?"

"She told me she hates anything that's green. She also once said the sentence 'I don't like fruit.'"

"Lots of people feel that way."

"Yeah, people under the age of ten."

"And, like, lots of people in general."

I shrug.

"Anyway," he continues, "I was just gonna see if you were going to Senior Night."

"I am, in fact, a senior."

"But you're not on any teams anymore."

"Yeah . . . ?"

"And you and I broke up."

"Wait—what? When?"

He rolls his eyes. "So you're coming?"

"I'm coming."

"Okay, cool," he says, smiling. "We should do something after. For old times' sake."

"Old times?" I say suspiciously. It's not like Matt and I totally stopped hanging out when we broke up, but ever since we relapsed into old habits six months ago, for the third time,

I've made it my solemn duty never to be alone with him outside school walls. The kiss itself had been fine, but the bottom line was, no matter how much I didn't want to ruin our friendship, I did *not* want to keep dating Matt, and I was pretty sure he *did* want to keep dating me.

"I'm not sure 'old times' is what we should aim for, Matt."

"*Old*, old times," he clarifies.

Ah. That would put us squarely back in fifth grade, the dark ages before Matt Kincaid picked me to be his girlfriend and popular-girl counterpart. Even back then he was socially magnetic, the kid everyone wanted to be around, and his attention made me feel like the funniest, most interesting human on the planet.

Megan was already close with Matt, and soon he and I were friends too. By seventh grade, his glances became bashful, lingering, and that made me feel like the sun. It was another year before he kissed me, and four more until we broke up. By then, Grandmother had left, and I felt like a supernova mid–gravitational collapse, all the things I'd thought made me *me* falling away rapidly.

Matt tried to understand why I was withdrawing, why dance and popularity and school spirit had started to nauseate me. Truthfully, it wasn't any of those things in and of themselves, and it wasn't Matt himself either; it was what all those things brought out in me—the way that for years I did things I didn't want to do, laughed at things that bothered me, went to parties I had no interest in because the thing that seemed most essential for my survival and happiness was being seen as Like Everyone Else in Union. Once I stopped fighting to be that person,

Matt and I started fracturing. I ended things before they could get any worse, thus sentencing us to a life of perpetual though tolerable limbo.

He blushes at my lengthy silence. "You know, me, you, Megan. Everyone."

"Okay, it's a date, then."

"A date?"

Why do I do that? Why do things like that just come out every time it feels like Matt and I are on the verge of moving forward? I try to make my voice light, teasing. "Yeah. You, me, Meghan, and the ghost of River Phoenix."

"Who's River Phoenix?"

I tilt my head at him. "Do you even *have* the Internet up on that farm of yours, Matty? What keeps you warm at night if not angst-ridden male celebrities who died before we were born?"

"Football, Nat."

"Well, I don't know for sure, but I suspect there are whole websites devoted to football too."

"Duly noted," he says. "Anyway, why do you care so much about this Phoenix guy when there's a ghost haunting our very own Ryle High School band room?"

I gasp and grab his sleeve. "Wait—do you think River could be the Band Room Phantom?"

Matt rolls his eyes and opens his mouth, but before he can speak, I feel my stomach somehow rise up in my abdomen, and I double over, fighting against the sensation that I'm falling. The overhead lights cut out. The entire hall falls dark and silent. I swear under my breath and reach out for him, finding nothing but empty air. "Matt?"

The back of my neck prickles as the swarms of color fade, allowing my eyes to adjust. My heart starts hammering in my chest as my eyes try to tell me something impossible: Everyone has vanished. I'm *alone* in the nearly pitch-black hallway.

There's a current in the air I've felt only in very specific moments of my life: the quivering charge of a dream breaking into reality, the same way the man in the green coat and the other hallucinations did before Grandmother came.

I'm dreaming. This is some new brand of hallucination, and, like always, it all feels too real, impossible and yet undeniable. I try to swallow but my throat's too dry, and my arms are shaking as I shuffle forward, one palm sliding along the cool metal of the lockers. "Matt?" I call loudly. My voice echoes against the scuffed tile.

Something brushes my arm, and I stifle a half-choked scream as, all at once, the overhead fluorescents blink back on and everyone reappears.

"Oh, *God*." I clutch my chest and try to ease my hyperventilation back into even breaths as my eyes register Matt's faint freckles, his hand on my arm. His eyebrows pull together, and he glances over his shoulder, as if expecting to see a tornado barreling toward us.

"Nat?" He shakes my arm lightly. "You okay?"

"Power," I pant. Matt tilts his head. "The lights just cut out." *And everyone disappeared.*

"Huh." He shrugs. "I must've missed it."

I force my sandpaper throat to swallow. "Guess so."

Matt looks around and lowers his mouth to my ear. "What's going on, Nat?" he presses. "You can tell me."

I take a step back from him, folding all my fear back down into the pit of my stomach. "Nothing. I'm fine."

He sighs. "See you tonight."

As he walks away, bumping his shoulder into Derek Dillhorn's, I turn my eyes up to the light panels in the ceiling, watching, waiting. *I don't want to scare you,* Grandmother said, *but you need to be prepared for what's coming.*

3

After dinner, Jack and Coco ride back to Ryle with me in the Jeep, which is making a sound like there's a cat stuck in the engine. "God, what do you think that is?" I ask them.

"I dunno," Jack says. "Your radiator?"

"He doesn't have a clue," Coco says without looking up. "Hey, are you and Matt getting back together?"

"Why would you ask that?"

"Abby said he asked you on a date, and you said yes. I think that's great."

"Really? Because you sound like Stephen Hawking when *he* thinks something's great."

"That's really mean, Nat," Coco says flatly. "He can't help that he sounds like that."

"*He* doesn't sound like that. His machine sounds like that.

He could choose any voice he wants. It could sound like Morgan Freeman, if he wanted it to."

"Could Matt get me on varsity if you guys got back together?" Jack says.

"Would you come home from college more often?" Coco says.

"That's not how football tryouts work, Jack. More importantly, I'm not getting back together with Matt, and what the *hell* is making that sound?"

"The carburetor," Jack says.

"He has no idea," Coco says.

We park at the edge of the lot and make our way across the asphalt. There's a slight breeze, but the humidity still has my hair and my dress clinging to every inch of me, and I'm hoping this night goes quickly so I can get back to the air conditioning.

I used to dream about this night.

We make our way down to the football field, whose bright white stadium lights beckon us like holy bug zappers. Parents have turned out in too-nice clothes, their formal wear too stifling for the heat, and have compensated for their inevitable body odor with too much cheeriness and zeal. I spot Rachel and the rest of the dance team just inside the chain link fence along the upper level, and they shriek and point and wave until I wave back and head over to them. Jack and Coco split off to find some of the freshmen from the football team and their popular girl friends and girlfriends to sit with.

"You guys look great," I tell the Raiderettes. They're performing tonight, so they're dressed in full uniform and shimmering makeup, their hair slicked back in neat ponytails, their eyelashes impossibly long.

Rachel sticks out her bottom lip. "I wish you were dancing with us tonight. It's still so weird to see you here out of uniform."

"Yeah," I stammer. "Pretty weird, but I needed the time to focus on school, and somehow you guys managed to plod on even without me in your back row. Anyway, good luck. Or break a leg. Or *merde*. Or just . . . whatever. Do some stuff, and do it well."

I turn and make my way down the metal bleachers, and warm relief fills me when I spot Megan sitting at the edge of the girls' soccer team. I go perch beside her. "Hi."

"Hiiiiiiii," she says, giving me a hug. "How are you?"

"Grandma's in town."

Her mouth drops open. "No way."

I nod. I can trust Megan with Grandmother, because she's the only one who really believes. More than anyone I've ever met, she believes in God and always has. And while God doesn't talk to Megan quite how Grandmother talks to me, and our ideas of what God is aren't identical, Megan didn't bat an eye when I first told her my secret, because she believes in things that can't be seen, and she loves me enough to think that if God were to appear on Earth, her best friend would obviously be the one It would appear to.

"Wow." She gives me another quick squeeze. "Okay, you have to tell me everything."

I nod again. The dance team is descending the bleachers in an even row, their poms behind their backs, elbows out to their sides, and chins held high. "I will," I promise, "after Rachel shimmies us the meaning of life."

And even as she does, there's something magical hanging thick in the air tonight right alongside the humidity.

Maybe it's the glow of the lights on the yellowing field or their glare on the bleachers. Maybe it's the marching band in their white-feathered hats, all lined up to the left of the bright orange end zone, blaring out the fight song. They're moving through the choreography like they're all a little bit tipsy—not in a bad way. Like when Mom has a glass of red wine, how she walks with that sway. Normally she moves with perfectly upright posture, straight and aligned, as if she's Miss October in the University of Kentucky Dance Team Calendar again, her pretty strawberry hair blown out around her by an off-camera fan.

But the wine makes her forget how to walk like that, or maybe she becomes just un-self-conscious enough to *want* to sway her hips. Either way, it's nice, and the way the marching band's playing the fight song, to no one but the home team, is kind of like that.

And all those feelings I forgot to feel today while I was at school, hugging people I've known forever and saying goodbye and promising to keep in touch, I'm feeling them now.

And then I think about Grandmother and how I may never see her again.

And I think about my front porch, and how many nights Megan and I sat out there when we were little, summer nights when we were sticky and dirty from playing, when Gus was just a puppy. All those evenings we played Ghosts in the Graveyard and tag with the neighborhood kids who went to St. Henry and St. Paul—and sometimes Matty, when his dad dropped him off after chores—until the sun dropped abruptly into the night.

And now I see fireflies in the grass down by the track that runs around the football field, and hovering around the hill sloping up the left side of the marching band—the very hill where I got my first kiss from Matt Kincaid, the quarterback himself, when we were in the eighth grade.

My eyelids are heavy, and the fight song is growing slower and slower, until suddenly, I must drift off, because there's that abrupt *falling* sensation right through my middle, and then everything is gone.

Not the stadium or the field—but the sound, the band, the people. Even Megan.

Everything and everyone, except me and the crickets and those holy stadium lights.

As if another light is blipping into view, a person appears, out in the middle of the field. A boy, standing with his back to me, tall with broad shoulders, and long, kind of dirty dark hair. He's holding a paper bag in his right hand, and he brings it up to his mouth, takes a swig of whatever's inside, then tips his head back and looks up.

The silence is so big it makes the world swell, and the boy feels farther away than he possibly could be.

I follow his gaze upward, and the Kentucky sky seems miles higher than it ever has. There's a waning crescent moon tonight, with a fair mix of clouds and a smattering of stars. I look back down at the boy's shaggy hair, and his back and butt, trying to place him, but I can't.

I'm dreaming about a stranger. I guess that's not so strange, really. I'm reminded of that first time Grandmother appeared at my bedside, the way I should've been afraid and wasn't, the way I knew to trust her and felt that I knew her, unlike all the visitors that came before her.

I stand and lean against the rail in the aisle between bleachers. I want to go down to the field, to stand with this boy between the sky and the grass until every part of me touches every layer of the world. It feels important, but even though I'm so sure this is a dream, I feel a little shy and embarrassed, like I won't know what to say when I get down there.

But my need to get out there outweighs everything else. I go down one step, and the metal creaks under my foot.

The boy on the field must hear it, because he starts to turn around, but before I can see his face, everything snaps back into place: The fight song is ending; the crowd is shouting, clapping, cheering.

And he's gone.

"Nat?" Megan shouts over the noise.

I'm standing in the aisle, holding on to the railing.

"You okay?"

"I don't know."

"Do you want to leave?" she asks. "We can go."

"No," I answer honestly, sitting back down beside her. I don't want to take my eyes off that field. Something's happening here, and I'm afraid to miss it.

"Are you sure?"

I nod. What I need is to stay, and to watch. I need to figure this out.

Besides, I may not be on any teams, but Megan is, and this night matters for her and for all the girls we're sitting with.

After the dance team's performance come senior awards for softball and baseball, followed by the cheerleading team's performance, then senior awards for soccer, at which point I'm forced to elbow Megan in the rib cage because Brian Walters's icy blue eyes are so blatantly staring at her. "He wants to have your glorious, blue-eyed babies," I whisper.

"So as long as no one tells him he doesn't have a uterus, I have a chance?" she murmurs back.

The next award is for archery, which is when Megan and I first discover Ryle has an archery team. Then comes basketball, and then a color guard performance, and then, finally, it's time for the football awards.

Coach Gibbons approaches the podium to call the seniors down, and the crowd bursts into whistles and foot stomping. Matty stands at the far end, looking both handsome and sheepish, and all around like a Disney prince come to life in his neat jersey and nice jeans.

"Most of y'all know I'm a man of few words," Coach starts off into the microphone. "But I say them slowly, and that helps." An appreciative chuckle rumbles through the bleachers, and, true to form, Coach slowly, methodically starts speaking about each of the seniors and the ways they've contributed to the team.

I've always loved watching Matt play. He has a grace that most athletes just don't have. You can be good at a sport without it—good, but not great. Mom says Dad had that grace with basketball, before he tore his ACL his first semester of college; he was on track for the NBA when it happened, Mom says. That's always been hard for me to picture, since I've never known him as anything but a horse doctor and trainer. Honestly, he's so good at *that,* it doesn't seem possible or fair he could've ever had another talent of that caliber. Right now, all Jack cares about is football, but a part of me wonders what secret talents he might discover if he couldn't play anymore—and then I try to cast that horrible thought from my mind so I don't accidentally will an accident on my baby brother.

Getting lost in Matty's big moment almost makes me forget about the dream, but then it happens again: a flicker on the field, right beside the eight seniors lined up next to Coach. Suddenly, at the end of the row, there's a ninth. Only that's not quite right, because every time he flashes into view, the others vanish, leaving only him.

Tall, broad-shouldered, full mouth, long dark hair, and serious hazel eyes.

The two images flicker alternatingly four or five times rapidly, as though two giant invisible hands are taking turns covering first the team, then the other boy. When the glimmering stops, it's the team that remains in sight.

I look around the crowd, searching for signs that anyone else saw the ninth boy appear on the field, but everyone remains riveted by Coach's speech, totally unbothered by the way the world just shuddered.

"Nat?" Megan whispers.

"Did you see him?" I ask.

"Who?"

"That guy on the field?"

Her blue eyes dart over to Coach, and she maneuvers her posture to see around either side of the podium, but when I look back to the field, the boy's already gone.

"I'm going crazy."

"You are not," she whispers back. "You said Grandmother's in town. Couldn't it be one of her friends?"

"I don't know if she *has* friends."

"Of course she has friends. What do you think angels are?"

"I'm not sure she's like *that* God."

"She tells you stories from the Bible, doesn't she?" Megan's always acted like Grandmother is Jesus in a mask. I, on the other hand, have never known *what* to think about where her God ends and where mine begins. Sometimes when Megan talks about her faith, I think *yes, exactly*, but Grandmother's stories have made me feel like the concept of God is too big for a book or a group of bodies lined up in pews or even a world religion. God is a thing I know when I see, and I see It all over, in Megan, in the night sky and the morning sun, and especially in Grandmother.

"Yeah . . . sometimes. But she also tells me stories about people named Squirrel and Chipmunk. Are those people from the Bible? Did Grandmother Spider steal fire in the Old Testament or New, because I thought that was a Choctaw story."

Megan knocks her elbow into mine. "Fine, I don't know how all this stuff fits together, but the point is, I know you. You're not crazy. Grandmother's real, and whatever's happening to you now isn't just a figment of your imagination. We'll figure all this out, okay?"

I dig my teeth into my lip and nod. I slide my phone out of my purse to pick up where I left off on the ongoing Google search, and the battery icon onscreen practically frowns at me. Just then I remember the charger I left in my locker, with the rest of the stuff I planned to clean out next week.

I'm about to tell Megan I'm going to run up to the school and plug my phone in when Coach finishes his awards and the crowd erupts into applause. As soon as the football players start filing back up to the bleachers, everyone else stands to fan themselves and shake out their sweaty shirts. Matt bounds up the steps to us and hooks an arm around our necks, kissing the sides of both of our heads, though I can't help but notice how long his friendly forehead kiss lingers on mine.

"Ew, you're sweaty," Megan says, pushing him off.

Ignoring her, he says, "You guys wanna go get food?"

"Sure," I say. "I just need to get something from my locker first."

"Better hurry; they're gonna lock up as soon as they've got the podium back in the gym."

Mom and Dad have made their way down the steps to us now, and they're hugging Megan and Matt. "Oh, how fun to see the three of you together again," Mom says, squeezing Megan's elbow and putting on that smile that earned her the real estate license. "Isn't that fun, Patrick?"

Dad nods, says nothing. Coach thinks *he's* a man of few words, but I'd like to see him spend a day at the stables with Dad. Mom turns to me and assumes an expression filled with so much empathy I think her soul must hurt to make it: "Was that hard for you, to watch the dance team perform?"

"It was hard for me," Dad interrupts quietly. "I thought Rachel Hanson's eyeballs were going to pop out of her head. What do they call that stuff she does with her face?"

"Facials?" Megan says.

"I think they call that particular facial 'sharting while doing a *grand jeté*,'" I say.

"*Natalie*," Mom says.

"When a horse makes that face, you know she's in fight-or-flight," Dad muses.

"When Rachel dances, everyone's in fight-or-flight," Megan agrees thoughtfully.

Mom buries her face in her hands. "She comes from a broken home."

"Yeah, so did War Horse and Seabiscuit, Mom. That's no excuse."

The school's pitch-dark and cool, though still heavy with humidity. I look over the balcony down to the cafeteria and the wall of windows overlooking the lawn, and then, remembering this afternoon, I do a quick once-over of the shadowy foyer before taking off through the too-dark halls.

The farther I get from the doors, the more terrified I am to be alone in the dark. Grandmother's voice echoes in my head with every step. *You need to be prepared for what's coming.*

I spin through my locker combination, dig through the obsessively ordered rows of binders and memorabilia still left in there, stuff the phone charger into my purse, and turn to leave before the inevitable axe murderer arrives.

Something stops me.

Beautiful music, spilling down the dark hall from the band room.

I've been hearing the myth about the Band Room Phantom for the past four years, but whenever I'd thought about what I would do if confronted by its siren song, I certainly hadn't pictured myself venturing toward it.

But there's no ghost, I remind myself. There's just a sneaky senior, whom I must know, and a hauntingly beautiful song trailing un-self-consciously across the keys of a piano.

I creep down the hall and stand outside the wooden doors, just listening for a while. The song is sad, heartbreaking even, and I'm overcome with frustration that I don't have a better word to describe it. It occurs to me then that Grandmother would. She'd have a whole story that would sound exactly like this song. I open the door as quietly as I can and slip inside.

The black grand piano sits in the far corner, heavily scuffed but still elegant. The person playing it hasn't turned on a single light, which makes him hard to see. But if the broad shoulders and long, slightly dirty hair didn't give him away, the paper bag sitting on top of the piano definitely would have.

Who the hell is this guy? Maybe he really *is* a being like Grandmother. Either way, I don't want to interrupt the song. I stay close to the door with my head tipped back against its dewy surface as I listen and watch. His too-big hands travel gracefully over the keys, his too-big shoulders tensing under his worn-out T-shirt, and the image—a grizzly-bear-sized boy hunched over a piano, who shouldn't be able to make the keys sing like that, so tenderly, so gratefully—would be funny if the song weren't so arresting.

I close my eyes and think about all of Grandmother's stories, finding the one that feels the most like this song.

"This story is true, girl," Grandmother said. "So listen well."

"You say that about all of them," I argued. I was nine, and, so far, none of the stories had seemed true.

"They *have* all been true," Grandmother said. "But you'll think this one is truer than the rest."

"So you mean it actually happened."

"No story is truer than any other story that has the truth in its heart."

"What are you even talking about?" I asked.

"Stories are born from our consciousness," she said, lacing her fingers in her lap. "They come from the things we already know. They come from the things we learn from our ancestors and our kin. We all learn different things, depending on where we're born, so the stories you hear will be different. So too the things your kin decide to do will be different. So too the things *you* decide to do will be different. The way to make the best decisions is to listen to all the stories and to know them by heart and to feel them in your bones. You need to know, Natalie, that no story is truer than truth itself. All good stories and all our lives are born from that knowledge."

"So, what's the truth?"

"It's hard to say. That's why it's so important to listen and to look both backward and forward at the threads that Grandmother Spider spins between things. You understand?"

"I never understand a word you say," I told her.

She shrugged. "Well, anyway, you'll like this one, because it happened, and a white guy in a frilly hat wrote it down and stamped it with wax to prove it. It starts in a place called Nee-ah-ga-rah, or if you like to say things in a stupid and wrong way just for the hell of it, you could pronounce it Niagara—like Viagra. It means *thundering waters*."

"The waterfall?"

"The very same," Grandmother said. "Nee-ah-ga-rah was a sacred place to the Seneca tribe, who believed the falls were a doorway to the spirit world, the Happy Hunting Grounds. When they went there, they could hear the roaring of a mighty spirit that dwelt in the waters."

"You mean they could hear the water," I said.

"Maybe," Grandmother said.

"Definitely."

"How do you know?"

"Because there are no spirits," I said.

"How do you know?" she asked.

"Because my mom told me."

"And what did your mom tell you about me?" she asked, and when I didn't answer, she went on, with a touch of smugness. "Every year, the Seneca offered a sacrifice—a young maiden from within the tribe—to the great spirit of the falls, and it was considered a great honor to be chosen. The women would compete for the chance to be the one to lie in a white canoe that would pass over the falls into the spirit world. There, she would be with the rest of her kin and honored for her sacrifice.

"In 1679, there was a beautiful and strong woman named Lela-wala who wished to be chosen for that year's sacrifice. Lela-wala was the daughter of the Seneca's Chief Eagle Eye, and though his wife and other children had died years before, he blessed her decision, and Lela-wala was chosen for the sacrifice. There was also a French explorer named La Salle, who had been living among the Seneca for some time, working to convert them to Christianity, as was the custom of the time. When he learned of the tribe's plans to sacrifice Lela-wala, he went to Chief Eagle Eye and the other leaders to beg them to withhold their sacrifice.

"But they would not be persuaded. One of the tribal leaders answered him, 'Your words witness against you. You say that Christ sets us an example. We will follow it. Why should one sacrifice be great, and our sacrifice be terrible?'

"And so LaSalle went away, devastated and furious with Chief Eagle Eye. But he did not understand the Seneca or their ways. He did not see Chief Eagle Eye's grief at his daughter's decision, as the chief was a very brave man who had to honor his daughter and his tribe, despite how precious Lela-wala was to him. While he was part of the great web of life and kin, both human and inhuman, she was the thing most dear to his heart that remained alive.

"On the day of sacrifice, the Seneca gathered on the river-bank to celebrate, feasting and singing and dancing, playing games and honoring ritual. When the time finally came for the white canoe to round the corner, everyone fell silent and watched as the little boat came into sight, decorated with fruits and flowers to honor Lela-wala's life and her death, and the role both played in the tribe's story.

"But when the boat entered the rush of the current, the tribe saw a second white canoe skirt out from beneath the trees on the far side of the river. Chief Eagle Eye's grief had been so great that he had decided to join Lela-wala in her sacrifice. The current carried him swiftly toward the falls, and soon he was beside her.

"They looked at one another, their hands reaching out across the water that separated them, and the tribe lost their perfect serenity, a cry of both despair and gratitude rising up through them. Together, the two white canoes dropped over the falls, and the maiden and the chief slipped into the Happy Hunting Grounds, where they were changed into pure spirit, made whole and clean and strong.

"From then on, they lived beneath the falls, where the roaring sounds like quiet music."

"You were wrong," I said after a long silence.

Grandmother's dark eyebrows flicked up, and her eyes brightened. "About what?"

"I didn't like that story."

"And you thought I was *never* wrong."

I thought hard for a long minute. "Did Lela-wala and Eagle Eye *really* go to the Happy Hunting Grounds?"

She thought hard for a long minute. "I believe they did."

"I'm scared to die," I said.

"Even Jesus was scared to die, honey."

"How do you know that?"

"I know everything."

"Not *everything*."

"Fine. I read it in a book, and I felt that it was true. Happy now?"

"And the girl who fell from the sky, she was scared when she jumped, wasn't she?" I said, and Grandmother nodded.

"None of us is alone, Natalie. Her story is my story is your story."

That's what the song makes me think of, and I'm so deep in that memory that it takes me a second to surface when he stops playing, reaches for the bagged bottle on the piano, and takes another swig.

"That was beautiful," I say, crossing the room, and he spins on the bench and spits out his mouthful across the carpet.

He drags one thick, suntanned arm across his mouth and says, "Who're you?"

"Me?" I laugh. "Are you serious?"

Laughter comes spilling down the hall, and the boy grabs my arm and pulls me toward the back of the room. "Hey!" I object, trying to shake him off. "What are you doing?"

He whips back one of the curtains that cover two deep

window bays and an alcove full of stacks of chairs and metal music stands. He pushes me behind the curtain and steps in after me, just as I hear the doors creak open and the laughter spill inward. I recognize the voices immediately: Matt, Megan, Rachel, and Derek Dillhorn.

"Tonight's the night," Rachel says triumphantly. "We're going to find that ghost."

"Or we could go back out to the parking lot. Nat's probably waiting for us by now," Matt says.

"Let her wait," Rachel says. "*I'm* not graduating without a good Band Room Ghost story."

"Woo-*ooo-ooo-ooo*," Derek says. "The ghost of a nerd—what could be scarier?"

"Okay, say what you will," Rachel says, "but last summer at Matty's birthday, I accidentally got drunk on Cinnabon Vodka with Kelly Schweitzer, and I made out with Wade Gordon, and I am *not* kidding—he was a really good kisser for someone who spends all his time with his mouth on a trombone."

"As if you even remember," Derek shoots back. "You threw up on him, and he still probably counts that as the best night of his life."

"Omigod, I forgot about that." Rachel breaks into hysterical laughter.

I look up at the boy, standing between the curtain and me. With the moonlight spilling in from the big window behind us, I can see him clearly now. He's definitely the same guy from the field. As his eyes shift down to mine he lifts a finger to his lips, then lowers his mouth beside my ear and just barely whispers, *"Don't wanna ruin their ghost."*

He has the smile of a shy little kid, completely at odds with his serious hazel eyes, which are hard to imagine looking any way but mildly concerned. When he pulls back, I nod understanding.

Matt, Megan, and the others are still moving around the room, and the non-ghost and I seem to realize what's going to give us away at the same time, because he points down to our feet. The curtain hangs almost to the floor, but not quite, and if my friends explore the room much longer, the myth of the Band Room Phantom is bound to get debunked.

He reaches over my shoulder to set his bottle down in the concave bay window behind me. His eyes meet mine, and his hands hover over my hips, silently offering to lift me into the bay. I nod, but when he picks me up, I feel myself blushing, my heart rushing from being so close to a stranger. And not just because he's a stranger, but because about an hour ago I watched him looking up at the moon and I then listened to him playing that song, and now I'm close to *that* person.

His skin and shirt are warm, damp with perspiration, his hair soft on the side of my neck. His scent is a nice mix of grass and sweat and the sweet liquor in the bag.

He sets me down, and I shift silently until my back is flush against one side of the deep window bay. I mess with my ponytail just so I have something to do as he lifts himself up into the bay and leans back against the wall right across from me, his head tipped back and full lips parted.

For a while I try not to look at him, and every time I give in and do, he's got that shy-kid smile, which makes me smile like an idiot in turn. It's so embarrassing I look away, but when I look back, it happens again, only worse. Eventually I give up and just let myself sit in the window well, staring at this complete stranger, smiling with all my teeth showing while my friends are talking behind a red curtain on the other side of the world.

The boy holds out his paper-bag-wrapped bottle, and I take it and sip, even though for all I know, he may have herpes or at least never brush his teeth. Whatever's in the bottle, it's syrupy and sour and makes me wince to swallow. When I open my eyes again, I see the boy's big shoulders sort of shrug in a silent laugh. He takes the bottle back and holds it in his lap.

"Where do you think Natalie went?" The sound of Matt saying my name pulls me back to the conversation on the other side of the curtain.

"Natalie, Natalie, Natalie," Rachel groans. "Seriously, Matty, don't you know that ever since that girl got into Brown, she's been waaaaay too good for all us little people in Union?"

"Oh, shut up," Megan says. "Matt, she's probably back out at her car by now."

"Try calling her again," Matt suggests.

My heart hammers in my chest as I dig through my purse. I manage to find my phone and set it to silent before Sheryl Crow and Stevie Nicks can give away my hideout by demanding to know, in sonorous volume, whether the whole world's "strong enough to be my man."

But my phone never lights up with a call alert, and Megan says, "Straight to voice mail."

I look down at the screen, expecting to see that I don't have service, but according to the little bar icons, I do. Piece of junk.

"Maybe rather than waste another minute with us, she just started *walking* to Rhode Island," Rachel says. "Maybe she's so smart she already built a hover car to take her."

"Or she could've summoned a horse spirit," Derek says.

"You guys suck," Megan says. "Let's go back to the parking lot, Matt."

"Oh, we're just kidding," Derek says. "You know we love Natalie."

They're still talking, but the door has creaked open, and I hear it swinging shut again over their voices. I listen as their conversation recedes down the hall, and, for a long moment, the boy and I don't move or speak. I have a hard time even looking up at him. I don't really care what Rachel or Derek say about me, but I'm a little embarrassed that they said it in front of a stranger I now have to talk to.

Finally I meet his eyes again, and after a long moment of silence, he dips his chin and says, "Hi."

I laugh, but it comes out a little quiet and a little strange. Maybe that's just because it's dark and we're still sitting pretty close together. "Hi."

He holds the bottle out to me again, and I take it even though whatever's inside it tastes disgusting. I down another sip with difficulty that I try to hide but surely don't. His thick eyebrows quirk, and the corner of his mouth shifts up, amused, and I pass the bottle back to him.

"Keep it," he says, leaving his hands loose in his lap. "I think you like it more than I do."

"Oh, I doubt that," I wheeze.

He laughs again and takes the bottle, looking at it as though trying to read the label through the paper bag. "Yeah, it's pretty bad."

"That's what Satan's pee tastes like when he has a urinary tract infection. What *is* that?"

"I have no idea," he says. His voice is low and kind of slow, but in a nice way. He sounds like July to me, and I wonder where his family's from that his accent's a little thicker than that of most people around here. "It was a gift."

"Ah," I say. "Thus the wrapping paper, I guess."

"You like that? That's my dad—he thinks of everything."

"Your dad gave you Satan Pee as a present? Do you want me to call child services? I have the world's worst cell phone with me."

He does another one of those inward laughs, where his shoulders lift and his heavy eyelids dip but he doesn't make any real sound, and then he takes another swig.

"That really was a beautiful song. What was it?"

"I dunno," he says, staring down at his hands with a faint grin. "Think I heard it in a Gary's Used Auto Parts commercial or something."

"Oh, right," I say. "That must be where I've heard it too. Their commercials always move me to tears."

The left corner of his mouth inches up, and his eyes lift up to mine, and I ignore an inclination to look away. "What were you doin' in here anyway?" he asks.

"I happen to go to school here," I tell him. "Or I did until today. What were *you* doing here?"

"Haunting," he says, holding his arms out to his sides. The Satan Pee sloshes over the mouth of the bottle, running down his hand onto the window bay, and we both laugh and reach for the puddle, our hands fighting and failing to mop it up. "I'm sorry," he says, looking up at me through the strands of dark hair that have fallen around his face. "I spilled whiskey all over your school. That was rude of me."

"It's fine," I tell him. "Really, today was my last day. I don't need this school anymore. Feel free to spill all over it."

"But you've got it all over your hand too," he says, and when he looks down to where my hand rests beside his, I feel my forehead and cheeks flushing. There are times I really appreciate my complexion, and this is one of them.

His gaze comes back to mine, and I straighten up, putting a more natural amount of space between us. "My friends are waiting for me," I tell him. "I should get back."

He nods. I hop down from the window, pulling the curtains back along their track to let the moonlight unfurl across the room. I look back at him and hesitate for a second. "Okay," I say again, pulling at my ponytail, then head for the door.

"Hey," he says, stopping me.

"Yeah?"

"Natalie—that's your name?"

I nod. His face is etched with shadows, but I can still see the corners of his smile. "Natalie Cleary," I say.

"Nice to meet you, Natalie Cleary," he says.

"Nice to meet you too, . . . ?"

"Beau," he tells me.

"Beau."

He nods.

Beau.

"See you around."

When I get back out to the parking lot, Matt Kincaid is saying the words "How 'bout Hooters?" and that's how I know it's time to go to bed.

"I think I'm just going to go home," I say, and all four of them jump.

"*Jesus,* Natalie." Rachel clutches her chest, and her eyelids flutter dramatically.

"Yeah, seriously, did you *float* here?" Derek says.

"Where were you?" Matt asks, and immediately I feel guilty. For hiding from them, for letting them look for me, and, if I'm being honest, for flirting with someone who isn't him.

"At my locker." I lift up my purse like it's evidence.

"We went to your locker," Rachel says, digging her hand into her hip. "You weren't there, and by the way, you missed out on seeing the Band Room Ghost."

"I stopped at the bathroom." Now I'm outright lying, and I can tell by the arch in Megan's thin blond eyebrows she knows it. That's fine—I plan on telling her everything, but I'm not going to ruin everyone's ghost story, and I'm *not* going to talk about boys with Matt Kincaid.

"We don't have to go to Hooters," he offers. "We could go to BW3's."

"What's wrong with Hooters?" Rachel says.

"Literally everything," I say.

She gives a harsh laugh. "You honestly think you're too good to eat at Hooters."

"Rachel, anything with functioning taste buds is too good to eat at Hooters," I say. "Their food is gross, and I'm tired."

"Or Barleycorn's," Matt suggests. "We haven't been there

in a while." Matt was the type of boyfriend to accommodate me, or to at least stand by my side in public. The *I don't get why you couldn't just go along with it/were offended by that/don't want to do the things we used to do* would always come later, when we were alone, but I got the feeling he genuinely wanted to understand.

"I'm suddenly feeling exhausted too," Megan says.

"Let's just go drink at Rachel's," Derek tosses out.

"I don't really feel like drinking," Matt says.

"Since when, man?" Derek says.

"You used to eat at Hooters," Rachel says, still on me. "Before you went all uptight feminazi Ivy Leaguer."

"And *you* used to wear blue mascara," I throw back. "People grow up."

"Yeah, you know, I remember that blue mascara. My slut sister got that for me—the one who works at Hooters."

"Rachel," I snap, "I don't care if Janelle wants to work at Hooters. I don't care if you and the rest of the world want to go spend your money on dried-out chicken and ketchup-based sauces. And least of all—less than almost anything else I can imagine—I don't care how much sex your sister is or isn't having. That's kind of the deal with the whole *uptight feminazi* thing—we don't care when other women want to wear stupid orange Soffe shorts with white tennis shoes and have a lot of sex, or when they want to wear habits and live in a convent, or if they want to walk around in pasties and never French kiss, so long as they're allowed to do what *they* want. And right now, all *I* want is to go to bed. Okay?"

She crosses her arms and glowers silently, so I turn and stomp across the parking lot back to my car. I don't know what's come over her lately, but Rachel never lets anything I say go without a fight anymore.

"Call me later," Megan shouts after me.

I climb into the Jeep and look back to where they're standing under the bright white floodlight at the back of the lot a few rows over. "Tomorrow," I call back.

Tonight I need to find answers.

I speed out of the parking lot, past Matt's farm, past whitewashed churches, over dark narrow roads lined in lush foliage that roll and curve as determined by the buffalo herds that shaped them long ago. I think about Beau and his song, whose sounds I can't remember but I can still *feel*.

I spilled whiskey all over your school.

I said like *ah*. I think about him all the way home.

Nice to meet you, Natalie Cleary.

Nice said like *nahs*. I think about him until I fall asleep.

Three months.

I spend all weekend sorting through Alice Chans, without any conclusive results. By Sunday night, I'm still uselessly tossing and turning in my bed, mulling over every last word Grandmother spoke, and replaying the disappearance of Matt and everyone else at school and the appearance of Beau on the football field, in an attempt to make sense of it.

Before the eye movement desensitization reprocessing therapy, I'd had horrible nightmares, several recurring. The worst one involved a vast, shapeless darkness that chased me and Mom down a country road, eventually slamming into us so hard the car spun off the pavement and careened into a tree, folding in half. That dream woke me up gasping for breath sometimes, but it still wasn't the worst part of nighttime. That would be the hallucinations. I'd had two different kinds, hypnopompic and hypnagogic, but I don't see how what happened with Matt in the hallway or Beau on the field could be one of those.

Hypnopompic hallucinations happen when you're sleeping: Your body wakes up—eyes and vision included—before your mind fully does. Thus you may see your bedroom, exactly as it is, except there's a torrent of spiders crawling all over you, or blood pouring down your walls, or an ancient American Indian woman sitting in your rocking chair. These hallucinations can be a sight, a smell, even a sound or sensation.

Hypnagogic hallucinations are nearly the same as hypnopompic—but hypnagogia occurs when you're falling asleep instead of when you're waking up: Your body, eyes, and vision remain awake though your brain's already dreaming.

You know when you're drifting off, when you're nearly there, and suddenly your bed gets yanked out from under you, and you're falling? You jerk awake and realize you're safe—you were in bed the whole time.

Congratulations, you've just had the most common nighttime hallucination.

You don't need treatment if you wake yourself up with the sensation that you're falling. You *do* need treatment, apparently, if you have insomnia, anxiety, night terrors, and tri-annual visitations from a seemingly omnipotent deity.

The EMDR had put a stop to all that, almost making me believe Grandmother *had* been a dream.

For the first time ever, I wish she were. Then her warning wouldn't mean anything. Then I wouldn't be chasing down one of apparently five billion local Alice Chans. I shove Gus's snoring snout aside so I can roll over for the millionth time. Tonight even the partial sleep of a hallucination would be welcome, but it doesn't come.

At two in the morning, I give up on sleeping altogether and reach for my phone on my bedside table, rattling off a few more search word combinations. With a stroke of inspiration, I type a new one into the search bar: *Alice Chan Kentucky hypnopompic hallucination.*

I hit ENTER, and my heart stops when I see the first result.

Visitations: Premonitions and Other Psychic Phenomena Surrounding Hypnopompia and Hygnagogia by Alice Chan, Professor of Psychology at Northern Kentucky University.

I open the abstract and know right away: I've found Grandmother's Alice.

The first Spirit Week event is the Superlative Parade, the one I'm least excited about, but after last night's success, I'm jittery with excitement and nerves. The lack of sleep and excess of caffeine surely aren't helping. When we get to the school, it's drizzling and thundering. I drop Jack and Coco off at the front doors, then pull around to the back lot, where the Spirit Week Committee is lining up the "floats"—which is, apparently, what you call a pickup truck once you hang a black-and-orange banner on it.

When I spot my assigned float and co-rider, I park as far away from both as I can and wait for Megan, reading and rereading Alice Chan's abstract over and over again as if I haven't memorized every word. A minute later, Megan's black Civic pulls up beside me, and she hops out of her car and into mine, shaking the warm rain out of her hair and hood. "Okay, let's see it."

I pass my phone to Megan right away.

"Why does your phone look like it passed through the heavens to fall to Earth?"

"Um, maybe because I was on it for the last forty-eight straight hours, during which I was also making little sandwiches out of spray-can whipped cream and Lay's potato chips."

"Ah, brain food." Megan turns her eyes down and scans the text. "So this is like a light, fluffy, beach read, right?"

I tap the portrait of the severe-looking woman with a bob and a thin-lipped scowl in the top right corner of the screen. "Alice Chan's the head of the Psychology Department at NKU."

"And you think she's *Grandmother's* Alice why?"

"Because." I free the phone from her hands again. "Look here. This is exactly the kind of weird sleep stuff I was going through all those years. Hypnopompic and hypnagogic hallucinations are basically just dreams, but you have them while your body's technically awake. Maybe that's what happened to me the other day in the hallway—and at senior night. Anyway, that's what Dr. Langdon always thought Grandmother was: a nighttime hallucination."

Megan purses her lips. "But she's not. She knows way too freaking much to be a product of your subconscious—no offense."

"Thanks for knowing that. But the point is, Alice Chan isn't a counselor. She's a researcher. She says herself these hallucinations are really 'visitations and psychic phenomena.' Maybe she knows how to induce them. If she can bring Grandmother back . . ." I trail off, and Megan reaches across the middle console to squeeze my hand. She's trying to calm me down, but her own features are obviously torqued with worry. I shouldn't have told her about Grandmother's warning. I'm freaking out enough for both of us. "Grandmother told me to find this woman for *some* reason," I say. "She can help."

Megan's thin lips scrunch up as she thinks. "Have you called this illustrious Dr. Chan yet?"

"Not yet. I'm going to, right after my wedding."

Megan grimaces out the window in the direction of my float. Its banner reads MR. AND MRS. MATT KINCAID, our names surrounded by orange and black hearts. Matt's standing in the truck bed in his letterman jacket, his sweatshirt hood pulled up from underneath to keep the rain off his neck and face. A girl couldn't ask for a classier processional.

"Do you think this is the first time in history that the couple voted Most Likely to Get Married weren't even a couple when they were nominated?" I ask.

"People suck," she replies.

"That *banner* sucks."

"You didn't even get a *first* name, let alone a last name."

"My husband's name is all I need now," I say. "Unlike people like you, who are crowned Most Athletic."

"True," Megan says.

"Are you ready?"

"*I* am," Megan says. "*You're* not. I saw the thrift-store wedding dress Rachel and the Spirit Week Committee got for you."

"Oh God."

"That's right. You'd better pray. By the way, what the hell is that sound?"

"I think it's the carburetor."

"What's a carburetor?"

"It's a thing inside a car that sometimes makes that noise when you're about to commit your life to the wrong person in the back of a pickup truck."

"Ooooh, gotcha," she says. Then, "He still loves you, you know."

"I love *him*. But not like that, I don't think."

Megan nods. *That's* how it should be. Two people who are right for each other should get one another, trust one another. I should've known I could tell Matt about Grandmother and he'd actually listen, but I never genuinely *felt* that, so I never did. We spent every minute together, but still I kept so much of myself from him—everything he wouldn't understand. It only made it harder for me that he always seemed so perfect, so un-shakably sane and normal. When we broke up he must've felt totally blindsided, though to me, looking back on it now, it had been coming for ages.

Megan and I get out of the car and jog through the rain toward the floats.

"Nice of y'all to show," Rachel shouts across the parking lot. "It's not like the rest of us are just standing here in the rain." She only joined the Spirit Week Committee as an alternative to summer school (which was an alternative to all her detentions), but you'd think we just interrupted her wedding. She plants one hand on her hip then points her other hand sharply, first toward my float, then Megan's.

I make my way along the long line of trucks and convert-ibles toward Derek's cherry-red pickup. The whole senior class is invited to participate in the parade, but those of us who "won" a superlative lead the way. It's just a few laps around the school, the underclassmen watching through the classroom windows, followed by a pancake breakfast in the cafeteria. Pretty unremarkable, but it's a tradition I've always looked forward to. We all have, I guess.

"If it's not my beautiful bride," Matt proclaims from the truck bed.

"Hi," I say stiffly. I don't want to be cold, but frigidity seems like the best course of action when you're standing with your ex whose heart you'd rather not keep shredding, on a float devoted to your relationship, just like all the "Matt &Nat" carvings in all the trees and bathroom stalls around the middle school. Even his letterman jacket proclaims our "undying" love: Matt Kincaid, QB1, has been #4 since age twelve, when he chose his jersey number in honor of my birthday, April fourth.

As he offers me a hand and helps pull me up, my eyes land on a hideous monstrosity of white taffeta and lace draped over one side of the truck bed. "My gown," I say. "It's just how I imagined it."

Matt laughs, swipes the dress up, and lifts the immense amounts of fabric over my head for me to put on.

"Don't you have to wear a tux or something?" I grumble, forcing my head and arms through the respective holes.

"Rachel gave me a suit jacket," he says. "It's under my coat."

"Oh, how convenient," I say, then a whiff of something sweet hits me. "Is that whiskey on your breath?"

He glances down at his feet, scratches the back of his head, and then eyes me. "Maybe."

"Since when do you drink whiskey at eight in the morning?"

"Well, I guess you wouldn't know, would you, Nat? You're not exactly blowing up my phone these days."

"Fair enough," I say. By the time we broke up, I already found Matt's burgeoning party boy persona a little annoying. At first, I'd just assumed that he was being absorbed into the many-headed monstrosity that the football team can be, while forsaking his true self. But when his drinking became more and more regular, I knew that wasn't it.

"You want some?" Matt says, patting a flask-shaped lump in his pocket.

"A flask?" He nods. "What is this, Atlantic City in the 1920s?"

"Do you want any or not?"

"Hold on, I'm about to make a joke about the little teeto-taling town from *Footloose*."

"Nat," he says. "Yes or no."

"No thanks," I say. "I don't want to fall off the stage onto the mob bosses while I'm doing the Charleston."

He laughs again and shakes my shoulders. "So, what do you think? Are you ready?"

"To debut my flapper dress to a bunch of bootleggers?"

"To get married," he says.

"Ah." I look up at the cement-and-faded-redbrick school, the cropped green grass and trees, the columns of dark clouds forming overhead. Thunder booms in the distance, and this secondhand dress is soaking through, growing heavier with rain every second.

And suddenly, it happens again.

I feel my stomach rise as though I'm on a roller coaster.

Matt, Megan, Rachel, and all the others, Derek's truck, the school itself—everything—is gone.

I'm alone in a field of rolling blue-green hills, standing in a cool breath of wind beneath a brewing storm, my hair and dress dripping. Thunder booms again, closer this time, and rain rushes down my eyelashes, blurring my vision. On the hill in front of me, where the school should be, I see a herd of buffalo.

I can hear them eating the grass. It's a thick, breathy, crunching sound, and puffs of mist expulse around their velvety nostrils. Their great heads swivel back and forth as they eat; their large brown eyes with impossibly long and curled lashes are watching me, though they don't seem concerned.

And then it ends, as quickly as it started.

My stomach drops back down. The school flickers back into place. The buffalo wink out of existence. Matt's in front of me again, the corrugated truck bed firm beneath my feet. The sounds of the world rush back in, my classmates hooting and laughing and talking all around me, leaning on their horns and driving Rachel insane as she tries to get everyone moving. "SCREW YOU," she's screaming. "Seriously, Tony, *screw you!*"

"Nat?" Matt says. "It was just a joke. I don't really think we're getting married. You know that, right?"

I nod, distracted.

"I mean, unless you *want* to get married, in which case—"

"Matt," I warn, immediately alert again.

"Don't do that, Nat. Don't say my name like you're about to deliver crushing news. It was just a joke."

"I care about you," I tell him. "You're a good person."

"But," he says flatly.

But I'm still reeling from the fact that you disappeared a second ago.

But I'm too busy trying to figure out what's happening to me to have this conversation again.

But I'm worried that I started liking you because you made me feel normal, in the most Union sense of the word.

But you can't stop trying to turn me back into the Natalie you fell in love with, the one who tried desperately to be the quintessential prom queen instead of the girl with two mothers, two fathers, and two nations.

"But I'm moving to Rhode Island, for one thing," I settle on.

"Why does it have to be Rhode Island?" he says.

"I don't know. Maybe it just can't be Kentucky."

He laughs harshly. "What, you need to make sure there's nothing else better out there?"

"I'm not going to college to look for a boyfriend, Matt. I'm going to figure out who I am and what I want to do. Why are *you* allowed to figure those things out, and I'm not?"

"Oh, right, I'm sexist. I forgot," he throws back.

"Well, I didn't hear *you* offering to go to school in Rhode Island," I shout. "You're so convinced you know exactly how your perfect life should unfold that you haven't noticed it's not what I want and that *I'm* not who you want. You like me *despite* the things I care about—can you imagine how bad that feels?"

For a moment we're both silent, staring. I wonder if either of us really sees the other clearly anymore or if we're stuck looking at the frozen images of who we used to be. It's the only explanation I can think of for why Matt would still want to be with me when we've grown to disagree on approximately everything.

The Rachel and Tony disagreement has been resolved, and the front truck has jolted to life, to the applause of all except for us.

But while everyone else is cheering and hollering, flipping off younger teammates and shouting proclamations of love at a disapproving Ms. Perez, I'm watching Matt turn away from me toward the place where minutes ago I watched buffalo grazing.

I'm feeling cold and lonely, and still I'm looking at a puzzle whose pieces don't make sense.

Buffalo and unlit hallways, mysterious boys on the football field, and Grandmother's stories. A warning and a ticking clock. A painful hollow in my stomach. What is Grandmother trying to tell me?

At eight P.M. on Thursday night, we arrive at the school in our pajamas. We check in at the front doors where Mr. Jackson, Officer Delvin, and a slew of parents glance in our bags and make sure we've brought our signed waivers before sending us downstairs to the cafeteria, where pizza and pop await.

At ten o'clock, they project a Nicholas Sparks movie in the gym, which seems like asking someone in a nostalgic, sensitive, emotionally heightened state to get impregnated in a bathroom stall, but hell! It's only rated PG-13, and we're graduating! I spend those two hours like I spend every hour lately: miserably checking for e-mails or missed calls from Dr. Alice Chan.

After the movie, it's back to the cafeteria for more sugar, in the form of an ice cream sundae bar. While Megan and I are in line to make our ice cream mountains, she nudges me and points to the corner table where Matt and Rachel are waiting for Derek to get back with the bathroom pass. Rachel, Matt, and Derek are among a coterie who have clearly had a few too many tiny, smuggled-in tequila bottles, and the bathroom passes have become a hot commodity as the football players and their girlfriends start to fall like dominoes to Jose Cuervo.

Rachel's slumped against Matt's shoulder, her mouth smushed open and her head dropping as she nods off every few seconds. As his glossy eyes find mine, I see that Matt doesn't look so great himself.

"You're going to have to talk to him eventually," Megan says, as if reading my mind.

"I know," I say. We haven't shared a single word since our fight on the float, which might make this the longest stretch we've ever gone without talking. My chest feels like it's tied into knots. Even when I'm *not* thinking about it, my body feels the wrongness of being at odds with him. I never wanted it to be like this—half the point of breaking up was avoiding getting to a point where we hate each other, and now it feels like we're teetering on that line.

"Sooner might be better," Megan says.

"Maybe."

"Like, ideally by Saturday night."

"Ugh, his birthday party," I groan, remembering. "I was thinking I might skip it and do something fun, like dust my entire house, instead."

"Nat," she says gently. "I leave for training at Georgetown in, like, sixteen days. I don't want you to be alone all summer."

"How dare you initiate a countdown," I say sullenly. "I'm

doing my best to stay in denial."

She frowns and gives me a hug. "Me too."

"Maybe we can stay in denial together forever?" I suggest.

"I think I'll notice the Nat-shaped hole that will form in my heart when I'm not seeing you every day," she says.

"No, I mean, maybe there's a town called Denial, and we can literally move there and forget about college."

"Okay," she says, pulling free. "That sounds nice. We'll move to Denial."

At one A.M., the boys are sent to set up their sleeping bags in the gym, and the girls are banished to the library, where our respective chaperones check off our names and very definitely lock us in. At first the room bubbles with conversation and laughter, but soon we fall into whispers and hushed giggles, until a chorus of deep, measured breathing takes over. One by one, the stragglers drop off into sleep too, and still I lie awake, staring up at the ceiling.

Tonight marks one full week since I last saw Grandmother. That's one less week I have to save whoever's in danger, and I haven't gotten so much as an out-of-office automatic reply from Dr. Alice Chan. I toss and turn all night, worrying about Grandmother and where she went, about who might be in danger and what life will be like without Megan, and Matt, and even Rachel and Derek and everyone else I know.

Finally, hours after the last set of lungs slips into a steady rhythm, I feel myself drifting toward sleep, and my mind swirls away from everything dark and unsettling toward all that is warm and magical. That night on the football field with Beau, and all the enchanting nights that came on that field before it, when the crowd bristled with excitement, voices going hoarse from screaming into the wind as the sun slid down and the stars slid up to replace it on the far side of the sky.

I see the purple of twilight, hear the chorus of cheers punctuated by the whistling of fanatical parents, feel the buzz of people falling in love with each other, with the field full of gnats and lightning bugs, with the nighttime itself.

I'm almost asleep, flat on my back, when my stomach lifts up toward my throat and the world is rearranged once again. The walls, the bookshelves, the ceiling disappear, leaving behind only a wide night sky.

I sit bolt upright and stare up into the deep blue and the sparkling stars overhead. I look around and find myself alone on top of a grassy hill surrounded by forest. I know where the parking lot should be, where the golf course should begin just beyond a thin range of trees, but neither exists in this place. Instead, at the bottom of the hill, I see a few buffalo lying stretched out in the grass, their thick eyelids soft in sleep. Some are clumped together in twos so that their enormous heads rest on one another; others slumber a few yards off on their own. I hear myself laugh.

It sounds a little bit like I'm being strangled, probably because all the air has left my lungs. I stand and turn in place as all of me is filled with simultaneous dread and awe. My stomach settles and, like that, the library's back, as if the whole thing never happened. Except that now I'm alone in it. The other girls aren't there. Neither are the chaperones, the sleeping bags, or any of the duffel bags except for mine.

"What's happening to me?" I whisper to the empty room.

The clock above the doors reads 4:34 A.M. The library is too dark, too quiet. I'd take the sleeping buffalo over this any day. For a few minutes, I just turn circles, waiting for everyone to snap back into place. Eventually, though, I'm too anxious to sit still any longer. I need to think. I need to figure out what's going on. I grab my duffel bag and dig through it. Megan had planned on running this morning around six, and I'd brought a sports bra, shorts, and running shoes on the off chance she could convince me to get up with her. Good sleep is so rare for me that, when it comes, it trumps everything. Especially early morning exercise.

I dress as quickly as I can, conscious the whole time that the building could disappear or the people in it could reappear without any notice. Then I slip into the hallway and wander through its emptiness, my footsteps echoing. The front doors are locked from the inside, but Officer Delvin is nowhere in sight, and, squinting through the darkness, I see the parking lot's empty too. I let myself out, prop open the door with a stopper, and sweep my hair up into a ponytail as I make my way across the asphalt. At the edge of the lot, I break into a jog and turn down the sidewalk toward the football stadium and field houses, momentum carrying me fast past them to the intersecting street beyond. I don't know where I'm going—whether I'm going to run the six miles home or turn back to the school at some point—but moving has always let me get out of my head a little bit, and when I return, it's usually clearer.

Dance used to do that for me too: a place where there was nothing to do but *be me* and let everything else fall away. For a lot of the girls on the team, it was all about the performance, but for me, I think it was always about communication. I know I was supposedly too young to remember those tantrums Dad brought up the other day, but I do. I remember feeling like my throat was closing up. I remember feelings so big and unnamable that all I could do was cry, or sometimes scream. The smallest thing could set me off, anything I thought was unfair or intimidating. When I was a little bit older, I remember fighting to hold those unfocused emotions inside, and sometimes feeling so aimlessly frustrated that I'd shriek into my pillow at night. And then I remember taking my first dance class, a ballet-inspired workshop for kindergarteners, and how everything changed.

For one hour each week, I'd toddle around in a ruffly black leotard and pink tights, skipping across the floor in pre-*chassés,* spinning around in preludes to *chaînés.* We imitated animals and growing trees and whirlybirds falling from branches, pantomimed holding beach balls and swimming. We made ourselves as big as we could, and then as small as possible.

But most of all, I remember the great bodily relief I felt as I sank into the passenger seat on the drive home after my first class. I felt empty, in a good way. Like the things I couldn't find words for had found a way out, and now I could relax. Now I could enjoy the warm, cozy silence between me and Mom.

Probably my favorite thing about that class, and dance in general, was seeing the way the same movements could look so different when performed by different bodies. When I joined the dance team in middle school, I learned how to manipulate my natural inclinations so that I could be exactly in sync with everyone else, but when I lost Grandmother, my talent for blending in began to make me sick. It felt more like hiding than syncing.

As I run, I pass through the fog of memory and back into the sweltering heat and still-dark morning, turning right along the white fence lining Matt's family's property and picking up my pace. As my limbs loosen, my muscles heat, my heart rate increases, and my mind slips into its sweet spot: the unequaled silent peace you get from exercise. Somehow I skip the horrible middle part of any workout when my body's usually screaming and my mind can't stop repeating *I hate this, this sucks, I hate this*, and dive straight into the nirvana of being soaked in sweat. Unbothered by the thick clouds of mosquitoes riding the grass around my ankles. Moved by the intense thumbnail of sunrise visible beyond the hills.

I run across the tumbling fields, down to the Kincaids' big white farmhouse and their junky rental property adjacent, then turn and start climbing back toward the stadium and track as the sun crests the trees. The gates are locked, but I climb the chain-link fence pretty easily and make my way down the bleachers toward the field just as the world—my world— is bathed in rosy light. Except it's not *just* my world anymore. Someone else is down there, running on the track.

I lean out over the railing and watch the boy circling the field. He's tall and broad but fast, too—a football player for sure, I'd guess a running back. At the far end of the field, he curves around the track, and I feel myself smiling involuntarily when he notices me.

"What are you doing, sweating all over my track?" I shout down to him.

He comes to a stop in front of me, resting his hands on his hips as he catches his breath. "Well, nice to see you too, Natalie Cleary."

"Do you live around here?" I ask.

He walks forward to the bleachers and reaches his hands up through the chain link separating me from him. His white T-shirt is worn out and horribly mud- and grass-stained, the sleeves cut off to reveal long stripes of tan skin on either side of his rib cage and stomach. "Not too far," he says. "What about you?"

"Down off Wetherington," I tell him. He nods but doesn't say anything, and his smile is unnerving. I nudge the fencing with my foot. "What's that look for?"

"Nothin'," he says. "Those are nice houses."

"And?"

He looks out across the field, the intense yellow of the rising sun catching his hazel eyes and painting caramel highlights at the tips of his hair. "You dress real nice. I bet you come from a nice family."

It occurs to me that maybe my calling in life is just to make Beau say *nahs* as many times as possible. "They're nice," I say. The elaborately strapped gray sports bra and moisture-wicking running shorts are also probably the nicest clothes I own. My mom thinks workout gear is sacred, and thus is constantly throwing out my old stained stuff and replenishing my supply. "What about you? You play the piano like Mozart—your family must be all right."

Beau lets go of the chain link, walks around to the steps, and comes to stand beside me. When he leans out over the railing he eases his arm up against mine, and I'm careful not to move at all, so he won't either. I want to stay there, touching him. "I live with my brother, Mason, and sometimes my mom," he says. "She made me take lessons when I was little because she wanted to date the teacher, and now when I wanna play, I come over to the high school."

"I see."

"Which one of those guys from the other night was your boyfriend?" he asks.

"Neither." I feel my blush worsening, and when it's at peak severity and my whole head might actually be on fire, I add, "I don't have a boyfriend." I risk a glance at him. He's looking at the field, but the corners of his mouth are turned up, and I like the way his eyelids dip when he smiles.

"So now I know why you haunt the band room," I say, breaking the silent tension between us. "But why do you run on our track?"

"*Our* track?" he says. "I thought this was *your* track."

"Well, I'm really good at sharing, especially things I hate using."

His eyes rove over me. "You're here right now."

"Yeah," I say, because *I had a vision of you* might come off a little too strong.

He pushes his hair back from his face. "Do you wanna come over?"

"What—right now?"

He shrugs. "Whenever. Now. We have cereal."

I laugh. "What about milk? Do you have milk, Beau?"

"Mason usually just uses beer, but yeah, if you want milk, I can get you milk, Natalie. There's a gas station right up the road."

"You know what? I'd try it with beer," I tell him.

"So you do?" he says. "Wanna come over?"

"I can't right now." I wave vaguely toward the school. Beau nods, and I hurry to add, "But some other time, later in the day, would be good."

"Okay."

"Do you have your phone with you? I could give you my number."

He feels his shorts pockets. "Nah."

I realize then that I left *my* phone in the school, although I *did* manage to bring the pepper-spray can Mom attached to my keys, which I self-consciously remember I'm wearing on a wristband. "You could find me online," I offer helplessly.

"Okay."

"Or you could find me here again."

"On your track," he agrees.

"Yeah."

"That you never use."

"Well, it's a small town," I say. "How hard could it be?" A little voice in my head points out that I'd never seen Beau until a week ago.

"I'll find you," he says.

"I hope so." I turn to go, chest fluttering and abdomen incongruently cramping inward from the run.

When I get back to the parking lot, it's still empty, but as I'm standing there, there's a flicker of color and form across the asphalt as the cars—mine included—appear for the breadth of a blink. I stand there watching until it happens once more, this time for three whole seconds. That seems like a good sign, so I go inside. As far as I can tell, the school's still empty, but after my conversation with Beau nothing feels as eerie as it did before my run, and I'm not as anxious either. Perhaps misguidedly, I'm totally confident the world *will* go back to normal soon, just like it has all week. So I go down to the locker rooms and rinse off as quickly as possible before I head back up to the library, crossing my fingers that I can get in without any trouble.

When I get there, it's the same as I left it: void of everything except bookshelves and one lone sleeping bag and duffel. The clock on the wall reads 6:01, and, because I have no clue what else to do, I get in my sleeping bag and lie back down, watching and waiting for the world to right itself.

Next thing I know, someone is shaking me awake. My eyes pop open onto a pair of round blue ones, framed with sheets of straight blond hair. "Good news or bad news first?" Megan says.

"Bad news," I croak.

"Okay, well, that's the wrong order, and the good news is: I know you very well, and I didn't even bother trying to get you up to go running with me this morning, so you're welcome."

"Thanks," I say, though my mind is still sorting through the fog of knowing that I absolutely *did* go running this morning.

"The bad news is, you have to get up right now, because breakfast started ten minutes ago, and everything's obviously super greasy and everyone's obviously super hungover so it's sort of a fly-to-bug-zapper situation."

"Rachel's going to eat all my bacon," I whine, running my hand over my face.

"No one wants to see that happen. Please get up."

"I left," I tell her.

"What do you mean?"

"I mean, it happened again. First, the school disappeared and I was lying in a field. Then the school was back, but everyone else was gone, and I left. I went for a run, and I saw Beau down at the stadium."

"Oh my God. Natalie Cleary is dreaming about a boy who isn't Matt Kincaid. I'm so happy I think might explode."

I shake my head. "It wasn't a dream. Beau was one hundred percent real. And the other stuff, it was like the other times, like when I see Grandmother. I can't really explain it."

"That's so weird." Megan sits down beside me. "So . . . did anything *happen*? With Beau, I mean."

"He invited me over."

"In what way?"

"There are multiple ways someone can come over?"

"So many ways," Megan assures me.

"Are these ways, like, the front door, the back door, the bedroom window, et cetera?"

"Sometimes," she says. "What was his energy like?"

I bury my face in my hands because I know exactly what she means, and I know the answer, and I don't want to tell her. "Please don't make me say these words aloud."

She breaks into giggles and lies down beside me. "What does he look like?"

"Well, his biceps are roughly the size of my head, and his eyes look like summer incarnate, and he has two little dark freckles on the side of his nose, and a mouth that somehow manages to look like a shy kid's one minute and a virile Greek god's the next. So I guess you could say, pretty decent."

"Oh my God," Megan says. "I'm shaking I'm so giddy right now. I feel like this is happening to me. Where did he come from?"

"No idea," I say.

"You're going to make out with him," she says knowingly.

I roll over and bury my face in my pillow. "What if you just jinxed me?"

"No way. I love you too much. My psychic energy is literally incapable of jinxing you. If anything, I'm willing you into this make-out."

"Hey, perhaps you'd like to react to the fact that an entire building and the many people within it vanished before my eyes too? Or no, not really of much interest to you?"

"Of quite a bit of interest," she says. "Slightly less interest than your incomparably soft and beautiful heart opening like a flower to Beau, but yes, I'm interested." Her smile fades, and she squeezes my hand. "You know, I like to think of myself as somewhat of an expert on my best friend, but the truth is I have no idea how to help with all of this. So tell me, okay? Tell me what you need, and tell me every single time you need it, and I'll be there."

I squeeze her hand back and swallow a lump. "You are the best person," I tell her. "But I don't know what I need either."

But by the time the last Spirit Week activity, the Seeing Off, is over, and we've walked through the halls saying goodbyes and giving out hugs to teachers and underclassmen, I've figured out the only thing I really can do.

"Are you sure you don't want me to come with you?" Megan asks as we walk out to our cars. "I can make sure Dr. Chan knows you're not crazy."

"Good thinking. I'll just bring a friend to see a psychologist I don't have an appointment with, and you can open with 'She's not crazy!' So she'll know I'm not crazy."

"I can wait in the car."

"No, you can wait at Steak 'n Shake with the soccer team, where I know you were planning on going before I sprung this on you."

She sighs. "Call me after the Cleary Family Celebration Dinner and let me know how things went?"

"Sure. Or maybe, like, while I'm still on Dr. Chan's couch. If she questions my sanity, I can demand we conference you in."

"Sounds good. I'll put you on speaker with the soccer team. We can have them vote on whether they think you're crazy."

"Perfect. Thank you."

We exchange a parting hug and climb into our cars. A few minutes later, I'm cruising on 275 East, a wide and rarely congested highway that winds out from the suburbs through a scrubby, rural valley occasionally punctuated by towns even slower and smaller than Union, pretty much until you get to the college. Though I've driven to NKU a couple of times for friends' games and friends of friends' parties, once I make it to campus, it takes me a while of aimlessly circling until I spot the psychology building: an enormous, gray-brown cement block with tiny windows grouped in twos that remind me of coin slots in an arcade game, and a faded red roof slanting up from the three narrow towers separating the two wings. The parking lot's mostly empty, and I take a spot near the front and slip inside.

The building is chilly, if out of date and poorly lit, and I find Dr. Chan's name posted outside a yellowed wooden door at the end of a narrow corridor. The door is cracked open but I knock anyway.

When I hear no reply, I push the door open, and it whines on its hinges. The little office is packed. A chocolate-brown desk and a whiteboard are wedged between two bookshelves, an office chair just barely squeezes in between the desk and the window beyond, which overlooks a long yellow lawn and a little blue pond. On my side of the desk, there's another chair and a small couch, both of which are completely covered in stacks of stuffed filing folders and loose papers and books.

"Can I help you?" someone says behind me, and I spin to find Dr. Chan in the doorway. She has a short, blunt bob and a dappling of freckles across her nose. Without makeup or the structured blazer from her portrait, she's barely recognizable. She looks about twenty years younger than the austere middle-aged woman I was expecting, and not quite old enough to be the person who holds the keys to unlocking Grandmother's secrets.

"God, I hope so."

Dr. Chan sits in the chair on my side of the desk, chewing the back of her pen, apparently deep in thought. The piles of displaced files surround her ankles like eager puppies; meanwhile my tailbone's been balanced on one corner of the paper-strewn black sofa for the length of my life—with Grandmother—story.

"Fascinating," Dr. Chan says finally, leaning down to dig through a stack of notepads on the ground. She chooses one and flips to a clean page. "I've never heard of anyone having such long conversations with Them—the Others—before. And I've sure as hell never heard of a full-on scenery change." She scribbles at the paper until the ink starts flowing.

"So there are more than just the ones I've seen?" I stammer. "What are they? Ghosts?"

She laughs and splays her hands out. "Oh God, we're so far from knowing that."

"Well, have you seen any of them?" I ask. "Do you know Grandmother?"

"No," Dr. Chan replies. "But I saw Others, when I was a kid. The black orb you described? That's very common for people like us, Natalie. I've been calling that orb 'the Opening.' I think that's sort of what it is: the beginning of the encounters with the Others. I can call it whatever I want, because no one else wants to touch this kind of stuff. Not in my field, at least.

Anyway, there's the Opening, and then there's what I call the Closing. The equal and opposite event."

"So it will stop?"

She tips her head back and forth. "For me, yes. For you? No idea. The research is all so new. I hate to think how long I'll be dead by the time anyone figures this stuff out. But . . . well, you've described some very unique things." She leans forward, elbows on her knees, and drums her nail-bitten fingers against her mouth. "Okay, so typically people who have these encounters are sensitive types—they tend to be somewhere between INFJ and ENFJ."

"I'm not tracking," I say.

"They're different personality types," she explains. "The Myers-Briggs Type Indicator—have you taken it before? Do you know where you fall on the spectrum?"

"My mom's obsessed with that kind of stuff, and I try to avoid anything she might someday use to psychoanalyze me over breakfast."

She waves a hand flippantly. "The *I* stands for introvert, someone who gets energized by alone time. Its counterpart is *E*, extrovert, a person who gets energy from being around people. The *N* stands for intuition, meaning you take your cues from internal sensations or sudden knowledge rather than concrete, observable facts. The *F*, feeling, indicates people who tend to make decisions based on emotion rather than thought. It's an important trait, but so is the *J*, which stands for judging. A person who's judging prefers to know what to expect at all times, to work with a schedule or outline or checklist, to make plans ahead of time rather than going with the flow.

"The combination of intuition, feeling, and judging creates people who are sensitive yet structured. They prefer boundaries and expectations, which is rarer for the intuitive, feeling type. It's an odd mix of personality traits in and of itself, but then you throw in a little trauma, and bam! You've got someone with a disposition toward creative symbolic modes of thinking—e.g., vivid dreaming—and somewhat unique stress triggers and responses. Usually these responses manifest as nothing but brief flashes. Usually, but not with you. In other words, you're super open, Natalie Cleary. You're like the goddamn Florence Walmart on Black Friday."

"Open to what?" I say.

"That's the question you and I are going to try to answer. So this Grandmother person told you to come to me—any idea why?"

"I was hoping you would know," I say. "I figured maybe . . . she'd come to you too, that she knew you'd be able to help me bring her back. *Can* you?"

"Probably not," she says. "In fact, that last visit may have been your Closing."

"Then what about what happened at school and at the football stadium—when everyone disappeared?"

She tilts her head back and forth again like she's weighing a few internal arguments. "Okay, second theory: Your Closing happens in three months. Grandmother knows that something will happen, possibly within that time frame or possibly not, but you only have three months left to gather information and prepare."

"So you think she's sending me these visions?" I shake my

head. "Why not just *tell* me what's going on?"

"Who knows? But look at every single religion in this world: They leave room for visions and prophecies when, presumably, their deities could make things a hell of a lot easier."

"Listen, Dr. Chan," I say. "I appreciate your theories, but I really think the best thing would be to get Grandmother back. She can explain everything."

She nods fervently. "Call me Alice, and believe me, I'd love to. So let's think about this. You did EMDR. Tell me a little bit about that—what was the memory you used?"

I feel suddenly naked, if not totally transparent, as I grudgingly launch into the story. "My birth mother showed up when I was three," I tell her. "I was sitting on my mom's bed while she was in the bathroom, drying her hair, and I heard the doorbell ring. I went downstairs and opened the door, and a woman leaned down and held her hand out to me." The memory's foggy, even now. I can't even see my birth mother's face, just a blur where it should be. "She asked if I wanted to go for a walk. I said yes. So we went down the sidewalk."

I remember asking, *What's your name?*

She smiled and said, *You can always call me Ishki.*

Ishki. I whispered it once aloud. We didn't talk any more; we just were. I wonder if some part of me understood who she was. If I knew even then, years before Grandmother came, years before I'd pore over the Internet for clues about my past and find that word associated with at least two different tribes, that *ishki* means *mother*.

"According to the reports, we walked for twenty minutes. By the time I returned, after she pointed me back toward my house and got into her car a few blocks away, there was a swarm of police cars with flashing blue and red lights crowded in and around my driveway." I was afraid—terrified, actually. "And when I ran down the street to meet my mom, she was crying." I felt so ashamed, so utterly guilty for scaring her like that. She scooped me up and held me tight, whispering, *Baby, baby, I was so scared she was going to take you.*

Before the therapy I hated to think about that memory. It made my stomach tense and my skin crawl. Whenever my mind wandered toward it, I distracted myself.

Alice looks up from her furious scribbling. "So how did the process itself go?"

"The therapist made me choose a negative self-belief, something that might explain why Grandmother had showed up." *I'm not wanted. I don't belong.* I didn't bother telling Dr. Langdon I didn't really believe those things. Counseling always went better if I nodded my head a lot. Back then, I'd thought she was a total hack. "Then she made me choose a positive self-belief to replace it with. She made me sit on the couch, and she sat across from me. She moved two fingers in front of my face, side to side, up and down. She said I didn't need to understand it—I just needed to let my eyes follow her fingers all the way to my right peripheral, left peripheral, up and down, without moving my head.

"While her fingers moved, she asked me questions. About the negative self-belief, the positive self-belief, other things like that. I answered her, repeated after her when she told me to"—feeling incredibly stupid the whole time—"and when she was done, she told me to go back to that memory, and *feel* it fully. Before we'd started, she'd asked me to score how anxious the memory made me feel. I'd said a seven out of ten. After the process, I said five." I'd surprised myself. "Then she sat forward and repeated the process again. The fingers, the questions, the scoring. We did it three times, and when she asked me to go back to that memory the last time, I told her, honestly, I only felt about a one on the anxiety scale."

Recalling it now, it sounded like hocus-pocus. And yet, afterward, Grandmother, the man in the green jacket, all the flickers in my bedroom had been shut out for nearly three years. And, still, when I think about that memory—no anxiety. "I don't know how, but it worked."

Alice's eyes glitter with excitement. She leans forward, touching the back of her head. "There's a part of the brain called the amygdala. It stores things that you're unable to pro-cess—like trauma. Before we're eight years old, our minds have very few cognitive processing skills. So everything we're un-able to work through at that young age gets stored up in the amygdala, as general associations or a roughly pieced-together idea of cause and effect—a warning for future events. When we dream, our eye movements signal to the amygdala that it's time to work through that backlog.

"Now, the emotions and sensations of an event are stored al-most exactly as they were experienced. Strangely, the same chem-icals that imprint them on the amygdala can actually impede the formation of memory in the hippocampus. You might have no conscious recollection of what happened, but that won't stop it from messing with your brain. When those stored connections are triggered, you revert to the childlike mentality in which you first experienced them. That's essentially what a panic attack is—

the full experience of fear without the tools to reason through it.

"EMDR allows you to access those connections while you're awake. The eye movement triggers the amygdala, while the questions trigger the memory. It allows your adult self to have a conversation, of sorts, with your child self. You explain things to your child self so that the unhealthy thought pattern, or cause-effect association, can be corrected."

"But why *that* memory? I mean, nothing happened. I took a walk."

"The separation of an infant from a parent can be traumatizing, in and of itself, even if you continue receiving the appropriate love and care from a new relationship. During infancy, all we know are our biological mothers. They're our entire world, our whole sense of stability."

Alice's gaze makes me feel like I'm being X-rayed. I sometimes think the whole world knows my history, and I'm the only one who can't see it.

I sometimes think they all know, and all I'll ever get is what Mom told me, a logistical play-by-play of how the adoption went: She and Dad tried to get pregnant for a long time. Once, they thought they had. She miscarried; they were heartbroken.

Down in Alabama, on a reservation, an eighteen-year-old girl found out she was pregnant. Before anyone noticed her growing baby bump, she ran away, up to Kentucky, where her boyfriend's family lived.

Meanwhile, Mom and Dad got a call from a friend of a friend, who'd gotten a call from a friend of a friend, whose nephew's girlfriend was having a baby.

That baby was me.

Did they want her, the friend of a friend wanted to know.

They needed time to think about it, Mom said.

They had ten days and not one more, the friend of a friend said. The mother-to-be, my *ishki*, didn't want her baby to grow up on the reservation. She'd never been happy there, had very little money, no real hope for a career, and an abusive father she didn't want anywhere near her baby, near *me*. But she needed to find me a family soon, or she would have to take me back to the reservation with her.

Mom and Dad always say they were never terrified to take me; they were terrified to lose me—they thought that logic showed my *ishki* wasn't sure, that she was ready to change her mind.

When Mom and Dad spoke to their lawyer, he brought up the Indian Child Welfare Act, a protective measure put into place in the 1970s, in response to the nearly one-third of all Native children who were being forcibly removed from their homes and put into non-Native boarding schools and foster homes. To protect babies like me and parents like my biological ones from being coerced into adopting to non-Native families, the act added a few extra hoops to the adoption process, one being that I couldn't be adopted within the first ten days of my life.

Ten days during which my birth mother looked at me, rocked me, maybe even whispered or sang to me, and held fast to her decision to give me away. I wonder if in that time she ever stopped to think that people could be unhappy, lonely, weary anywhere; that in a town like Union, there would still be parents who hit their kids and kids who stared up at the night sky, whispering that they'd like a better life, a gentler place. Did she ever, in those ten days, want to be the one to soften the world for me?

Mom and Dad's lawyer was unconcerned by the rest of the ICWA's stipulations—Alabama was apparently notoriously unfriendly toward the act, and my biological mother's extended trip to Kentucky was just one more way to ensure Alabama's courts saw me as *not Indian enough* to fall into the category of *all Indian children*, to which ICWA was supposed to apply.

I knew she could never regret me, but Mom always told me that last part with guilt in her eyes, like she was pretty sure she'd done something wrong by adopting me, by playing into a system that made exceptions for people like her and Dad.

If at any point in the first two years my birth mother *had* changed her mind about the adoption and could prove she'd been under duress when she'd decided to give me up, legally the state was supposed to rescind the adoption. After Ishki's neighborhood walk with me, Mom was terrified Ishki was going to try to regain custody, though of course by then the two years were up.

And it's not like I wanted to leave my family—I never did. But sometimes, after that walk, I used to lie awake and cry, because it hurt so bad that Mom had thought my birth mother wanted me back, and it hurt so bad when it turned out she didn't.

Even if I wouldn't have wanted to go with her. She should have wanted me to.

Funny thing about belonging to two worlds: Sometimes you feel like you belong in zero.

"An EMDR therapist might say these manifestations are a coping mechanism," Alice says, pulling me back to the office. "You needed a continuation of your original world—a time when there was stability with your biological mother—so your mind created one. When you're under duress and returning to a precognitive state, Grandmother resurfaces. An EMDR therapist might think your dream states are triggering suppressed memories, which were in turn triggering a PTSD response. A hallucination."

"Well, what would *you* say is happening?"

She grins. "*I'd* say it's pretty hard to prove whether something's real or a hallucination."

"What do you mean?"

"I mean, *all* of my subjects have post-traumatic stress disorder, but not *all* PTSD patients have seen the orb. I mean, your PTSD may be real, but that doesn't mean Grandmother isn't. I mean, maybe the EMDR banished her because the trauma really is at the root of your ability to see her—perhaps it stimulates your dream life so thoroughly that it causes you to tap into something else entirely. And the fact that you're having the visions again indicates there's something else—a remnant of the anxiety attached to the memory or some forgotten bit of it, another negative self-belief you haven't dealt with, or even another cataclysmic event you haven't processed—allowing a tenuous connection to continue."

I shake my head. "I went over this with Dr. Langdon. There's nothing else, just that one memory."

Alice looks skeptical, but she lets it drop. She turns toward her desk and digs a calendar out from under a leaning stack of notepads. "Okay, Natalie," she says. "I think, unfortunately, the way we'll be most productive is to go by the book. Start with twice-weekly sessions and see how we do. It'll be important that you talk about whatever you want to talk about, at least at first, because later you might have to talk about some stuff you *don't* want to talk about. I'd also like you to write down all the stories Grandmother told you, as well as you can remember them, so we don't lose any of the details. Sound good?"

I shake my head. "I can't."

"Can't what? Do twice-weekly?" she says.

"No, I mean, I can't write the stories down. Grandmother didn't want me to."

"She . . . didn't want you to?"

"She wanted me to remember them," I explain. "And she wanted me to *hear* them."

One dark eyebrow arches over one of Alice's green eyes, demanding more of an explanation. This is the exact sort of thing I dread talking about—or, rather, I guess I dread the rolling eyes, the uninterested shrugs, the blank looks that might follow. Despite how much I used to tease and hassle Grandmother, I've always held the things she's taught me close to my heart. They are a part of me I keep, and nothing makes you more vulnerable than sharing something you care about. "Most of them are stories from the First Nations. They've been shared orally for generations and generations. She wanted me to experience them like that, how they always have been. "

Grandmother wanted me to love the stories, to take them into my heart through my ears and let them become a part of me, connecting me to all the people who told them before. It feels disrespectful just to give them away on a sheet of notebook paper. It feels wrong not to be able to include or incorporate the way she said certain words, and where she paused, in her retellings.

My retellings should be wrapped in my voice, cradled as carefully as water so that no word spills. "If you want Grandmother's stories, they should be told how she told them. They're sort of hers, you know?"

They're yours too, Natalie, Grandmother used to tell me.

Alice considers me for a long moment before her head does that wobbling thing again. "Well, what if I send a voice recorder with you? You could tell the stories and record them."

I think it over. "Yeah, I think I could do that," I say. "But don't write them down. Just listen. That's how you're supposed to experience them."

"You've got yourself a deal—we don't want to piss off the person we're trying to find. Will Tuesdays and Thursdays at nine work for you?"

"Yes." I'll be dropping Jack off for early morning conditioning every day of the week anyway. That's the deal with Mom and Dad paying for my car insurance and gas—while they're at work, I'm the twins' chauffeur.

"In the meantime, try to get as stressed as possible. Reeeeally get your trauma to the surface—know what I mean?"

"Oh, I think so," I tell her.

Maybe that's why I agree to go to Matt's birthday-slash-graduation party with Megan the next night. Or maybe I'm a masochist when it comes to Matt Kincaid. Maybe, even though it doesn't feel right to be with him, I'm too scared to let him stop loving me, lest cutting that last tether sends me floating away.

8

"Remember: You were going to have to talk to him eventually," Megan says gently. With the Jeep in its geriatric state, we decided to take her Civic instead, and it's rumbling from the little Presbyterian church's parking lot to the Kincaids' connected gravel driveway, the one they open to visitors every fall for their corn maze, and when they host weddings. "It's not like you and Matt have never fought before."

"We've *argued* before," I correct her. "And even that was mostly just us sighing back and forth until someone gave up. This was different. More like he verbally poked me in the rib cage a couple of times and then I verbally beheaded him."

Megan rolls her eyes. "You could've nonverbally castrated him, and he'd still want you here."

"The point of breaking up was to not have to fight anymore."

"You mean *argue*," she teases. "And I thought the point of breaking up was so you guys didn't drag things out until you ended up hating each other. The point was saving your friendship."

I shrug. "Maybe it would've been better to let him hate me."

"Then you should've tried getting a worse personality and an uglier face." She reaches over and squeezes my hand in the dark. "Everything's going to be okay."

The lot beside the barn is already full, so we park just off to the side of the gravel drive instead, where we can hear music blaring from the house. Matt's parents are out of town this weekend, ensuring 1) this party will get out of control and 2) I won't have to hear the phrase *I'm so heartbroken my grandbabies won't have your coloring* from Joyce Who Only Eats Beige.

"This will be fun," Megan insists. We get out of the car, climb the last few yards of the upward sloping drive, cross the lot, and are met by a cheer rising up from the people perched along the edge of Derek's truck bed. Even Rachel seems genuinely happy to see us, like old times.

"Happy birthday, Matt. We come bearing Heaven Hill," Megan says, holding up a bottle of bourbon.

Matt stands up, grinning and swaying like a stalk in a stiff wind. "Whoa there, cowboy," Rachel says, grabbing a fistful of his shirt to steady him. "Try not to break your neck on your birthday."

"Come up, come up," Matt says to us, waving his arms wildly. I've never seen him quite this drunk before, and I'm not sure what to think about it. Still, after our fight, I'm just relieved he's happy to see me.

"You're in rare form," I say, trying to sound lighthearted.

Derek guffaws. "Rare? This is classic Matty Kincaid. Now

he's off your leash, boy likes to party."

"Oh, shuttup," Matt says, clumsily slugging Derek's arm. "Come up here, girls."

"Is there room?" I say, scanning the packed truck.

"Course there's room, Nat," Matt says. "Come 'ere."

"You two," Rachel says, pointing to two juniors. "Get out. Sorry, birthday boy's wishes."

The girls exchange affronted looks but ultimately obey, and Matt helps pull us up—or at least, he's sloppy enough to think he's helping.

"Can't believe it," Derek says. "Baby Matty's eighteen. We're all grown up."

"Are you kidding me?" Rachel says. "Five minutes ago you asked me to take a picture of your bare butt with Matt's donkey."

"Oh yeahhh," Derek says, hopping up. "I almost forgot about that. Come on, let's do it."

"Dude, no."

"Why not?"

"*Why not?* Because I'm not an ass photographer, and all you're gonna do with that is send it to some poor freshmen girls and scar them for life."

He lifts her hand up and gives it a courtier's kiss. "My beautiful, wonderful Rachel. Would you please make me the luckiest man on Earth by taking a picture of my ass with that ass?"

"Fine," she groans. As they serpentine toward the barn, I see Jack and Coco standing off to one side with a semicircle of freshmen and sophomore girls. As usual, the group's unanimous attention is fixed on Coco and her best friend, Abby, and Jack's just goofily grinning along. He's always been able to run with the girls as well as Coco's been able to run with the boys, and, being four minutes younger, he's always let her call the shots on where, how, and with whom they spend their time. The second I became a big sister my job as such was already obsolete. Watching from afar has always been my M.O.

Megan lies down in the truck bed beside me, and I realize the rest of the group has split off. It's just the two of us and Matt now, how it used to be. I lie back too, then Matt does, and the three of us look up at the sky.

"Look," Megan says, "the Big Dipper."

"What's a *dipper*?" Matt slurs. "I mean, think about it."

"It's a ladle," Megan says.

"It's a boat," I disagree. At least that was my favorite of the explanations Grandmother gave. "It carries the souls of good people across the Milky Way, the *so-lo-pi he-ni,* to the City in the West when they die."

"So-lo-pi he-ni," Megan repeats dreamily.

"Sssolopahennu," Matt says.

"Hey." A new voice comes from the foot of the truck. I look down toward my feet and see Brian Walters, of varsity soccer fame, with his pretty blue eyes fixed on Megan.

Megan sits up quickly, pulling the strap of her tank top back up her shoulder and brushing her bangs aside. "Hi."

"Did you go see the animals yet?" he asks, awkwardly shifting his weight between his feet.

"No, not yet," Megan says, as if we haven't all seen Matty's cows and goats and donkey a thousand times.

"Me neither," he says, nodding.

I look back up at the sky, cringing. "Well, what are you

two waiting for?" I say. "If you hurry, you might get to see the extra ass that's in the barn right now."

Megan scoots to the end of the truck and hops off, hiking her jeans up by the waistband and brushing stray bits of hay from her clothes. "Can't miss out on that."

I watch them make their way toward the open barn doors, the golden light spilling out over the soft wispy grass and the gravel lot, suddenly wholly conscious of the fact that Matt and I are alone. "Well, that made me want to scratch my face off," I say. "Since when is Brian so shy?"

Matt doesn't answer, and we lie there for a while longer, contemplating the stars and all their stories in utter silence.

"It wasn't all bad, was it, Nat?" he says finally.

"What wasn't all bad?"

"*Us.*"

"Of course not," I say. "Hardly any of it was bad."

"Thasss what I thought too," he slurs. "I donwanyou to think I love you despite things. I hate that I made you feel like that."

"Matt," I say. "You were a great boyfriend. That wasn't the problem."

"You always looked so cute over on the sidelines with that little ponytail," he murmurs. "Made me wanna win to make you proud."

"I always was proud," I tell him. It's the truth. "You play football like it's a science. You made me love the game."

He laughs. "You don't love the game."

"Fine, tolerate it," I amend. "Sometimes even enjoy it." It's true I've never loved, and probably *will* never love, football. But watching Matt play—and Jack too—always fascinated me.

The thing about football is once you get past the point system and general cultishness, it's exactly like any other hobby or skill: There's a generally agreed-upon technique, and then there's personal style. The latter, for those who look, is a window to a person's soul. Personal style is my mom, after some red wine, walking like she intends to restore order and beauty to the world with her posture alone. It's Rachel dancing like she's fighting her way out of quicksand, Megan running across the field like she's floating on her back in the ocean. And it's Matt Kincaid playing football tidily, like he's checking off boxes.

He's always in the right place at the right time, rarely too fast or too slow. He runs, looks up, finds the open teammate, and sends the ball soaring toward him at the exact right moment; he doesn't have to speed up or slow down or backtrack, even when he sneaks it forward. He just clutches the ball like it's a brick of gold as he dodges beefy linemen and jumps over fallen bodies as if they're narrow streams and he's a gazelle. He breezes through tackle attempts and scores as the last buzzer sounds. Practically every play he makes resembles the hundredth take of a choreographed sword-fight scene.

"I was thinking," he mumbles, and his unfocused eyes wander over to me. "Do you remember the firsssong we danced to?"

I sift through my memory. "It doesn't even feel like we *had* firsts sometimes. I don't think I even realized we were dating for, like, the first six months."

"Well, I remember it," he tells me.

"You do not."

"Yeah-*huh*."

"Sing it," I say.

He starts humming something that sounds like a few different songs mashed together, and I start cracking up beside him, until I feel the back of his hand graze mine. We both fall silent, and after a second, he slides his fingers through mine. I'm so shocked I freeze.

"Why did you push me away, Nat?" he asks. "You were everything to me. I loved you *so* much."

"It's not that simple," I say shakily. My heart is pounding as if I'm sprinting, and I'm just praying someone interrupts us fast, because I don't want this to happen. I don't want to keep putting him through this.

"I love you," he says. "It's so hard, Nat, not being able to talk to you about everything. I don't even feel like myself lately. It's so hard, and I love you."

I love him too. I don't think I could know a person as well as I know Matt and not love him. "Matt," I plead.

"I could be better," he says. "I could make you happy, if you told me what you needed."

"Matt, you can't make everyone happy. You can't be everything everyone expects you to be, and you especially can't be what I need *and* what everyone else needs, because what I need is to stop trying to make myself fit here and go somewhere new."

"You'll find someone else," he says quietly, "at school. I know you will. But I won't."

"Of course you will, Matt."

"I don't want to."

"Eventually you will."

"No one will be you," he says.

"We have to move on, Matt. It's only going to get harder."

"It doesn't have to," he says. His eyes are soft on me, much too close to my face. The next thing I know, he's kissing me. Still, my brain is caught in a panicked frenzy in which part of me almost thinks it would be wrong or rude to stop him, while the rest of me knows I don't want this. It must feel like kissing a dead fish to him, but he doesn't seem deterred.

Finally I push lightly against his chest, but he either doesn't feel it or ignores it, and now I'm freaking out. "Matt," I say, but my voice is mostly lost in his mouth. I push harder, and this time I know he feels it, but he just keeps kissing me. I say it again—push again—and he pulls me closer, one hand skimming the hem of my shirt much too aggressively.

"Matt," I snarl, but then he pins my hip down when I try to sit up. I shove him backward, hard, and he rolls away from me and sits up, blinking at me in the dark.

"I—" I don't know what I'm going to say, but I don't have time to figure it out before he half-falls off the truck and storms toward his house.

My whole body is shaking, my mind throbbing and reeling with waves of hurt and confusion.

Why did I do that?

I don't know how long I sit there shaking, caught fast in a cycle of unanswerable questions, before I finally snap out of it and realize that *I* did nothing. And now I'm mad.

It's only the second time I've ever been truly angry with Matt. All I want to do is go home, but there's this voice in my head that says, *no. You can't let him get away with that.* Because it wasn't my fault, and he shouldn't have kissed me, and most of all he shouldn't have made me afraid. I shouldn't have felt afraid in the arms of my first love.

The angry tears begin again as I scramble out of the truck and start toward the house. I vaguely hear Jack call after me, but I ignore him. There are people in Joyce's cutesy-country-crafty kitchen, a few lounging on the soft floral couch in the living room, but Matt's not with them. I head down the hallway toward his room, trying to keep myself from crying as I knock on his door.

He doesn't answer, but he didn't respect my space—why should I respect his? Matt Kincaid hurt me, and this night can't get any worse.

So I throw open the door, and oh my God do things get worse.

My eyes land on Rachel as she shrieks in surprise and scrambles sideways off Matt, halfway off the bed. She bounces back onto her feet quickly, clutching her arms around herself self-consciously, but Matt's still sprawled out on the comforter unconcerned, and I wish I had turned away as soon as my eyes registered them, but there was something so impossible about the situation that I'm completely frozen.

"Jesus, Natalie!" Rachel yelps, face flushed and eyes wide and white-rimmed. "Ever hear of *knocking*?"

The look on Matt's face is the worst part. He looks pissed but sort of happy about it, like he couldn't have planned this any better. I turn and run back down the hall, and this time, unlike all the rest, Matt doesn't follow me.

I run through the living room and kitchen and burst back out into the lot, sobs breaking out of me like splintering wood.

I have to get out of here.

I spin, searching for Megan, someone to hold on to. But

everything's suddenly different, and I can't get my bearings. The old red barn I've always known is gone, and in its place there's a looming, powder blue and white storehouse that looks brand new. There are still people here, but the details are completely wrong. Derek's in the cab of his truck making out with Molly Haines, a girl who's loathed him since I misguidedly set them up in the ninth grade, and if that weren't strange enough, he's parked in a different spot. I run toward the mouth of the gravel driveway, but I can't find Megan's Civic anywhere. Everything's wrong, in a nightmarish way where it's not so wrong that I can be sure I'm sleeping. In fact, I'm sure I'm awake, but I'm also sure the world isn't right, and the people and parked cars and music are closing in on me, and I can't breathe. I'm no longer in control of my body, and I'm turning in search of help, then running, trying to put as much distance as possible between me and that sinister blue storehouse.

I take off down the slope of the gravel path, and at the bottom of the hill, I make my way toward the little bridge in the woods that connects the Kincaid farm with the church. *Please let this stop right now. Please let this whole night be undone. Please get me to a place where everything's how it's always been and the world is stable, and I'm safe.*

Bright headlights swing around the road. I hurry to the side of the path as a junker truck drives past, then reverses to stop beside me. The glare of the headlights is blinding, but I can see the door swing open and someone squinting through the darkness at me.

"Natalie?"

Beau swings his legs out of his truck and comes toward me.

"What happened?" he says. "Are you okay?"

I bite my bottom lip and nod. If I speak now, it'll only lead to sobbing. He stands in front of me, his hands resting on his hips. "Natalie, what happened?"

I drop my face into my hands and try to press back the tears. "I can't" is all I offer up. When I look back up at him, he gently grabs my shoulders and pulls me against him, wrapping his arms around me and cupping the back of my head with one of his big hands.

"Are you hurt?" His low voice rumbles through me, and I shake my head. "Do you need a ride home?"

"Mm-hm," I manage. Neither of us releases the other right away. I feel a terrible sadness sweep over me, the last cleaving of myself from the world I thought I knew.

Beau's hands lift to gently hold the sides of my face, and he pulls back to look me in the eyes. "Let's get you home," he says softly.

I follow him to the truck and climb in on the passenger side. It's not like Derek's Ford; it's boxy and sits low to the ground, the interior a rough fabric covered in spills and burns, and the windows the kind you have to crank by hand. "What were you doing here?" I ask him.

He starts the engine. "Friend of mine invited me to a party."

"Oh." I run my hands over my cheeks to wipe them dry. "I'm sorry—you should go. I can find another ride." The thought of calling my parents to come pick me up from this disaster makes me nauseous.

"Heard it was pretty close to your track," Beau continues. "And I figured you might still be waiting for me to find you."

I'm not really sure how to respond, but then he smiles, and my mouth follows his lead.

I tear my gaze from his and pull my phone from my pocket. "I should let someone know where I'm going." I was supposed to stay the night at Megan's; her parents are way less strict about knowing where she is or enforcing a curfew. But when I press Megan's name the call won't go through, and I get an automated message informing me that the line isn't in service. I press END and text her instead, cursing my carrier under my breath.

"Ready?" Beau says.

I nod because I'm not sure what else to do. He stretches his arm across the back of the seat as he cranes his neck to check for traffic behind us. We rumble backward over the gravel and onto the bridge, through the strip of forest to the parking lot beyond.

Then he takes the truck out of reverse and pulls up by the church.

That's when I realize the church is wrong. "Oh my God."

He looks over at me then ducks his head to follow my gaze. It's not the wrong color or in the wrong place, but it is much too big. There's a whole wing that shouldn't be there—that *wasn't* there when Megan and I arrived. "Do you see that?" I ask.

"See what?"

"That wing right there." I roll down the window to get a better look and point at it. "When did that get there?'

"The Kincaid family donated that," he says. "Or the money for it, I guess."

"You know the Kincaids?" I say, confused.

"No," he says after a pause. "My mom used to go out with a guy from the church. Real nice guy. They were gonna get married for sure, just as soon as he and his wife got divorced."

"The Kincaids don't even *go* to that church," I say.

He just shrugs and pulls onto the road, cranking his window down to match mine. For a while we don't talk, but it's not awkward despite the obvious tension between us. At least I think it's obvious. I only have experiences with Matt to compare things to, and this feels like something else entirely.

Matt. Thinking about him makes my stomach roil.

"I don't want to go home," I admit. If I go home, I'll be sad and lonely, upset about Matt and endlessly fixated on Grandmother's warning and the way the world keeps changing. Sitting with Beau, I don't feel like those things can get at me as easily.

"Where do you wanna go, then, Natalie Cleary?" Beau says. "You want beer and cereal?"

His hazel eyes flash from the road to me, and I feel an instant flush of heat from my chest out through my shoulders and neck. He gives me that smile that makes his eyelids look heavy, and the wind whipping through his window blows a piece of his hair against his mouth.

As if to prove our thoughts are in sync, he moves his hand from the headrest and tucks a stray wisp of my own hair behind my ear, then sets his hand down behind my head and turns back to the road.

The thought of going to Beau's house makes me feel like my veins are full of butterflies. But I turn cold as everything that happened tonight pushes to the forefront of my mind. I don't think I could handle it if something real happened between me and Beau tonight. "I think I want to be outside for a little bit, if that's okay."

"Sure." He draws up to a stoplight, scans the abandoned intersection, and turns us back the way we came. When we pull onto the driveway to the high school, we pass the side of Matt's property, and I can vaguely make out the sounds of the party in the distance. My stomach turns sour, and I close my eyes, focusing on the warm breeze rippling over me to stave off tears.

Beau pulls around the street behind the field house on the far side of the football stadium and turns the truck off.

"I knew it," I say.

"Knew what?"

"Let me guess," I say. "Fullback."

"What makes you so sure I play?" He climbs out of the truck, and I follow him around to the back.

"Don't you?" I ask.

He pulls aside a tarp in the truck bed, lifts up a six-pack of

Miller High Life, and rests the cans on the tailgate.

"Come on. You're *such* a football player." I glance down, and sure enough there's a battered, battle-weary football lying there in the bed. I hold it up.

He stares at me for a long moment, then finally says through a smile, "No idea how that got there."

He reaches for the ball, and I pull it back, out of his reach. "I knew it!"

He turns and leads the way to the fence around the field, calling back to me, "Bring that with you, Cleary." He climbs the chain link first, still holding the beer with his left hand, and I toss the ball over then follow. When I'm on the other side but still holding on to the fence, still a few feet off the ground, I jump, and he catches my waist as I land. He doesn't let go even as I turn to face him.

"Halfback," he says.

His fingers graze over me as I walk out of his grip, laughing as I reach to grab the football. "Okay, let's see it," I say. "Show me the money. Or whatever."

He pulls a beer from the plastic rings and hands it to me, and I probably take it only so my hand can brush his. He cracks a can open for himself as he walks backward across the dark field. "Whenever you're ready," he calls.

I tuck the ball under my arm, open my beer, and take one bitter gulp before setting it down in the grass. I throw the football, which spirals up beautifully, then hits the ground ridiculously close to me. Beau tips his head in an almost reproachful gesture.

"Hey, that looked great," I protest.

"I'll give you that," he says, going to retrieve the ball. "It looked real pretty for those two seconds it was in the air."

He backs up again and throws the ball my way. It arcs high between us, and I turn and run as I watch the little blur of darkness streak over the starlight before plummeting down to the field. It falls into my open arms as I reach the end zone, and I slam it against the ground. Beau claps. "You're fast, Cleary," he calls, his voice reaching me only dimly.

"And you can throw." I snatch the ball and cross back toward him as he bends to pick up his can. "Ready?"

He nods, takes another swig, and I toss the ball back his way. He runs forward, catching it neatly with his free hand. "That was better," he says.

"You're a liar," I say.

"Yeah, it sucked."

"But I'm *fast*," I say. "In case you forgot."

He shakes his head, grinning. "I didn't." He walks backward and throws the ball again, but this time as it soars overhead, he takes off running toward me, and I break into a full-out sprint toward the falling ball and end zone, feeling him gaining on me.

I start to laugh and I can't keep my pace. It's like being tickled, when you suddenly lose control of your hands and feet. As I see Beau come into my peripheral vision, I veer right, biting back laughter as I fight to keep my lead on him. He catches me around the waist, and I let out a half-screamed laugh as he spins me in place, the ball falling between my arms to the ground. He sets me back down, his arms still locked loosely around me, his chin over my shoulder. We just stand there like that, swaying back and forth, my back warm with his heat, the side of my face barely touching the side of his. I've never liked the smell of sweat so much. His is nice, warm and earthy, soft.

I turn in his arms to face him. "Thanks for finding me to-night," I say quietly.

"It's fine," he says, shaking his head.

"*Fahn.*"

A smile crooks up the side of his mouth, his forehead lowering against mine. "Do I sound like that?"

I nod against him. I could kiss him right now, but I barely know him, and then there's Matt . . .

I move out of Beau's arms, my cheeks still burning. I pick up the football again, jogging the few remaining yards to drop it in the end zone. Beau throws his arms out to his sides in mock disgust. "You little snake. I should've known you were just distracting me."

"The oldest trick in the book," I say.

"The one where the other team makes you think you're about to make out," he agrees. "Usually doesn't work quite that well."

"Well, I'm *really* good."

We sit down on the grass together beside our beer cans, and a few minutes pass silently, but I still don't feel uncomfortable. In the least creepy way possible, this reminds me of when I used to go to the stables with my dad. We could easily spend the whole day in silence and not even notice until we were greeted at home by Mom, the extreme extrovert, who'd fire off a million questions and demand stories from our time away. I like being around people, most of the time, and I certainly wouldn't call myself shy, but there are certain people you can just be silent with—like Dad, and Megan—and it's every bit as good as a long heart-to-heart. That's how sitting with Beau feels.

He lies back on the field. "Natalie Cleary, you are pretty," he says quietly.

I laugh and lie down beside him, letting my head rest in the dip between his shoulder and collarbone. I feel his lips and nose against the top of my head, and I know if I looked up at him right now we would kiss. I can imagine exactly how it would feel. "Where are you from?" I ask instead.

"Here," he says, and I don't think he's going to say any more. His eyes are closed, his forehead serious. "But when we were kids, I went to live with my dad for a while in Alabama and then Texas."

"Why'd you come back?"

His shoulder shrugs under me. "My dad got sober and then he remarried, and then his wife got pregnant. They decided it didn't make sense for me to stay. He still cares about the important stuff, though. Course, he *misses* all that stuff, but he makes sure to mail me a fifth of whiskey every few months in his place."

I sit up on my elbow and look at him until his hazel eyes open. "I'm so sorry."

"It's *fahn*," he says. "This is home anyway."

I wonder what that must feel like, to know that for sure. *This is home.* I look around the field, up at the stars, back down to Beau's hazel eyes. I listen to the crickets sing and watch the sparkle of lightning bugs around us. When the world is quiet and no one else is around, Union still feels like home. I don't think that feeling ever left me, really. It's the noise and eyes of other people here that make me feel stilted and caged, like I'm onstage and everyone is watching for *signs* that I don't belong in everything I do. I'd like to think I'm self-aware enough to know that thought is both narcissistic and ridiculous, but at the same time, I can't make myself stop acting like it's true. Being around people is exhausting. Being around Beau is like a really good version of being alone, as easy but more fun.

I lie back down, and Beau's arm wraps around me, his fingers soft on my shoulder. "I don't know my birth parents," I tell him. "I was adopted when I was eleven days old, and I've always lived here, but I don't really know where home-*home* is."

"I bet your mom was a doctor," he says.

"Oh yeah? What makes you think that?"

"Same reason you knew I played football, probably."

"My muscular body and worn-out T-shirt," I say.

"Tell me you're not going away to some fancy college to become a doctor or a lawyer or something like that," he says.

"Actually, no," I say.

He looks down the plane of his face at me. "So you're staying here."

"Well, no." I'm unable to meet his eyes. "I *am* going away to some fancy college, but I think I'm going to study history."

"History." His thick eyebrows rise. "Well, aren't you full of surprises."

"Are you surprised by how boring my future sounds?"

"It was never my favorite subject," he says.

"What was?"

"Probably gym," he teases.

"Well, that was my second choice," I say. "I'm just not sure Brown offers degrees in classes that are named for the room they take place in."

"Their loss." He sits up enough to take another sip of beer. "Really, though, Beau. Gym?"

His eyes scan the starry sky. "I don't know," he says. "Maybe woodshop."

I consider pointing out that's another class named after its location. Instead I watch his breath raise and lower his chest slowly and imagine his hands working over wood with the same tenderness and exhilaration with which they traveled across the piano that night in the band room. Of course it makes perfect sense that the same hands that pulled those notes from those keys could make beautiful objects too. Physical incarnations of his music. His serious eyes slide down to mine. "Really, though, Natalie," he imitates me. *"History?"*

"History," I confirm. "That, or women's studies."

"Women's studies. Is that, like . . ." He hesitates, then sort of shrugs and shakes his head like he can't even come up with one guess as to what that might mean. "Gynecology?"

I stare at him, trying to judge how serious he is, until he cracks a smile. "I'm gonna be honest with you, Natalie," he says, "I wasn't much of a reader in school, and I would've failed history the *second* time I took it, except my teacher didn't want me gettin' suspended from the football team. But, yes, I've heard of women's studies."

"So you're at least as familiar as I am with woodshop."

"I am." He nods. "So why history or women's studies?"

"I like understanding how things fit together: who influenced whom, how one event affects another or how one little thing can change everything. I guess I feel like . . ." I hesitate, trying to put into words an amorphous thought I've had a million times since Grandmother left but have never said aloud. "I guess I feel like someone forgot to write down my beginning, and I just showed up in the middle of things, in time for this." I hold my arms up in the sticky night air as if hugging the sky. "And I don't really get what I'm supposed to do with the present because I can't see the whole picture. But until I can figure out my own place in all of this, I want to hear other people's stories. Knowing stories that have been around forever and have almost been lost a hundred times already, it feels important."

After a beat of silence he says, "I do remember one story from history."

"Yeah, what's that?"

"When they tested the atomic bomb and it worked," he begins, "everyone involved knew the world would never be the same. One of the guys who invented it said, 'I am become Death, the Destroyer of Worlds.'"

"I can't imagine how that must have felt." I roll onto my side to look at him, and his eyes are still fixated on the stars, thoughts hiding behind the wrinkles in his forehead. "So tell me this: How does someone who *wasn't much of a reader* remember a verbatim quote from the inventor of the atomic bomb?"

"Oh, I'm *real* good at watching movies." Once again, he grins and it's contagious, and even though my cheeks are starting to ache, I can't make them relax.

"Really now?"

He nods. "Yeah, coulda gone pro."

"So what you're really saying is you're a good listener."

"Oh yeah, Natalie Cleary," he says soberly. "The best."

"Now you're just trying to impress me."

"Yeah," he says. "But it's true. Tell me one of your stories."

"And afterward you'll be able to quote it?" I challenge.

"If you're any good," he says, only breaking into a smile when I scoff. He reaches over to flip my hair back over my shoulder then slowly kisses the side of my neck. A wave of warmth and tingles passes through me, like Beau's mouth is the moon pulling tides through my veins.

"What kind of story do you want to hear?" I say, quietly, to hide the shake in my voice.

"Somethin' happy," he says.

There've been plenty of stories Grandmother's called "happy,"
but there's only one I remember actually making me *feel* happy.
I was ten and I'd woken up from a nightmare to find Grandmother in my room.

"Why are you crying, honey?" she asked, and I told her
about the dream. It was one of the recurring ones, where I'm
in the car with Mom, talking and laughing as she drives us
through the countryside. In the nightmare, it's bright outside
and the sky is pale blue and cloudless, the creeks lining the
road sparkling. But suddenly, a dark orb appears ahead, rising
up over us and flinging us sideways off the road. We spin across
a ditch, the front of the car smashing into a thick tree, and the
world goes dark, as thunder breaks the sky, sending rain pouring over us. Gradually, the car begins to fill, not with water but

with blood, though neither Mom nor I is cut. I'd never told anyone about the dream before. I was too afraid it would come true, but telling Grandmother felt different.

"I used to have a dream just like that," she told me. "It seemed like it would never go away. But it did, Natalie. Everything but the truth goes away in the end. Now, lie down and let me tell you a story."

And she did, and this is how it went.

In the very beginning, Moon, Sun, Wind, Rainbow, Thunder, Fire, and Water lived on the earth. They simply awoke there, not knowing how they had arrived, and that was okay. They lived happily on their earth, until one day they met a very Old Man. This Old Man turned out to be their leader, the Great Spirit Chief. He had just formed people to cover the earth in all the spaces between Moon, Sun, Wind, Rainbow, Thunder, Fire, and Water.

"Old Man," Thunder said, "can you make the people my children?"

And Old Man said, "No, Thunder. They cannot be your children, but they can be your grandchildren."

Then, hearing this, Sun asked, "Old Man, can you make the people of the world my children, then?"

And Old Man replied, "No, Sun. They are not your children. They can be your friends. They will be your grandchildren. But your main purpose is to cover them in light, and to make them warm."

Moon asked next, "Old Man, if not Sun's, can you make the people my children?"

"No, I cannot give you the people of the world, Moon,"

Old Man said. "You will be their uncle and their friend, light-
ing their way at night while giving them rest."

"Old Man, please make the people of the world my children," Fire said.

"I cannot do that, Fire," Old Man answered. "They will be
your grandchildren. I have made you to keep them warm in winter
and at night. You will cook their food so they can fill their bellies."

Wind asked next, but Old Man's answer was the same. "No,
dear friend Wind. But they will be your grandchildren, and you
will clean the air for them and keep them healthy and strong."

"Old Man, might I have the people as my children?" Rainbow asked.

"They cannot be your children," Old Man explained. "You
will always be busy preventing the rains from falling too hard and
the floods from rising, and painting the sky for their eyes to enjoy."

"What about me, Old Man?" Water said.

"No," Old Man said. "The people of the world can never be
your children, Water. But you will clean them and quench their
thirst, and let them live long lives on the earth."

Moon, Sun, Wind, Rainbow, Thunder, Fire, and Water
looked at one another in confusion. Then Old Man continued,
"You are well made, and I have told you the best way to live to
help the people of the world. But you must always remember that
these, the children of the human race, they are my children."

And that, Grandmother told me, was the truth.

Tonight, with Beau, the story makes me feel the same way
it did the first time I heard it: freed from a nightmare by a hug
from the world.

Beau's quiet for a long moment when I finish, staring up

into the sky thoughtfully before he says, "You *are* good."

"At telling stories?" I say.

He nods. "That, and in general."

"At everything," I agree.

"Except football."

"Nah, I'm pretty good. Just not compared to you."

He tells me about his first game, when he scored on the wrong end zone, and about his job changing tires and replacing brakes, how he much prefers construction work but can't seem to get enough hours. He'd like to build his own house someday, and I tell him he should build mine too, and that it has to have a porch, and he agrees, because a house isn't a home without a porch. He tells me how his mother sometimes leaves for months when she thinks she's met The One, only to turn up a few months later, so devastated she can't get out of bed for a week, and refuses to say what happened. I tell him about Mom's ability to turn everything I do or feel into some metaphor about my "adoption journey."

"Do you think she's right?" he asks.

"I don't know," I answer honestly. "I sometimes think I wouldn't feel so lost if she didn't try so hard to make me feel okay about looking for myself. I mean, I *always* knew I was different from my family, but I didn't feel the need to justify it until I started school. Every time my parents dropped me off at a birthday party or took me to school or the neighborhood pool, all my classmates would ask me why I didn't look like them. And, I mean, my mom had prepared me for that. But then one day, this neighbor kid asked me what my real name was. I had no idea what he was talking about, and he was like,

You know, your Indian *name. Like, Running Deer.* So then I asked my parents if I had an Indian name, and they kind of laughed, but when I told them why I was asking, Mom was *super* upset, so she started doing all this research, trying to prepare me for any and all potentially offensive inquiries, while also being like, *Remember, sweetie, you don't have to answer anyone's questions if you don't want to. It's no one's business but yours.*"

"Wow," Beau says. "Didn't know six-year-olds had business."

"Exactly," I say. "Oh, and then she started buying me these early reader books about Native American history and culture. She'd leave them in my room, and then very casually tell me I should be proud of every part of who I was, but I guess that made me feel even more different than I already did. Then, one year, when I was six, I think, I wanted to be Pocahontas for Halloween—the Disney version, of course—and she acted so weird about it, sort of tried to talk me out of it, but I wouldn't budge, and in the end she ended up making my costume. But then a few years later, she read this article about racist depictions of Native Americans in popular culture and how harmful they are. That somehow led her to an essay that appeared right after some designer was in the news for sending his models out on the runway in Navajo headdresses, about the way modern American culture abuses and appropriates Native culture. Mom felt so bad she came to my room and apologized to me. She was crying, and I didn't even understand why, but she wasn't acting like she was my mom. More like I was a complete stranger to her."

Beau shrugs. "Aren't you?"

"What do you mean?" I say, taken aback.

"Just seems like all parents start out thinking their kids are a part of them, another mouth they've gotta make sure eats, another body they've gotta get dressed. And then one day, our parents look at us and notice we're whole people. We're *not* a part of them anymore, even if they're a part of us. And for the ones who never really wanted to be parents anyway, that's probably a relief. But for a mom like yours—I don't know, she must've been sad when she realized your life was gonna be different than hers. She must've been scared when she realized she wasn't gonna be able to protect you, and that you were gonna deal with things she never did."

"Yeah," I murmur. "I guess, but as a kid it still felt horrible to be different from her. It didn't feel normal. I think I, subconsciously, spent the majority of my childhood trying to make that feeling go away. I joined the dance team, learned to laugh off jokes about me talking to wolves or catching fish with my bare hands. Made a point to insert myself in the middle of the social scene, and started dating this really popular guy . . ." I trail off, thinking of the time after Grandmother left, when it was just me, alone in a world I was obsessed with fitting into. No more quiet moments when the rest of Union had fallen asleep and I'd lie awake listening to her stories wash over me in her gravelly voice, filling me up with drops of truth and color. Pieces of myself. I realized then I didn't know where the fake me ended and the real me began.

"I don't know. It's hard being surrounded by people— generally good people—who don't get it, who think I'm uptight and weird whenever things bother me. I mean, sometimes it's like people assume I'm like them in ways I'm not, and that sucks, but other times they think I'm different in ways I don't feel different, and that sucks too."

Beau thinks it over for a long moment, then says softly, "That why you're leaving for your fancy school?"

"Maybe," I admit. "It's hard to feel like you belong when you don't know who you are, and it's hard to know who you are when you don't know where you come from."

"Maybe you're just lucky."

"Lucky? How?" I ask. "You can't imagine how hard it is to not see yourself in anyone around you. Or to be constantly encouraged to look."

His shoulder shrugs under me. "And you don't know what it's like to see yourself in people you don't like. You're just you— no deadbeat dad, no alcoholic mom, no family curse."

"Or maybe I'm still made up of all those things, and I'm just good at pretending."

"You know what I think?" he says.

"Football?" I guess, and he laughs silently.

"That," he says, "and I think you belong here more than anyone I've met."

"Whaaaaat?" I say, sitting up again. "Why?"

"I just do."

"You just do."

"I do," he insists.

"Well, *fahn*."

"*Fahn*." After a minute, he says, "You got any more stories, Natalie Cleary?"

I tell him about the Girl Who Fell from the Sky. Then I drink the last beer and tell him about the Vampire Skeleton and the Ghost of the Tetons and the Ghost House Under the Ground.

I'm just finishing the story of Brother Black and Brother Red, when my phone vibrates in the grass beside me. "Hold on a second," I tell Beau.

When I sit up to answer Megan's call I realize the sun is starting to rise, the sky fading to a deep blue. We've stayed out all night, and I can't decide whether it's felt like minutes or days. "Hello?" I say.

"Oh my God, I'm so sorry," Megan whispers.

"Why are you whispering?" I ask.

"Brian and I fell asleep at Matt's. I'm leaving now. Where are you? Are you okay?"

"I'm fine—I'm at the football field."

I hear a door close, and she resumes her normal volume. "Oh my God, Nat. I'm so sorry. I'm so, so, so, so, so sorry. I'm on my way. Don't move."

"I can take you home," Beau says beside me.

"Who was that?" Megan squeals. "Was that *him*? He sounds like a subwoofer!"

I cup my hand over the phone. "It's Megan. She's still at Matt's," I tell Beau. "It'll only take her a second to come get me." He nods, and I uncover the phone. "See you in a minute," I say.

Beau and I gather the cans and toss them over the fence with the football, then climb back over. Again he catches me on the far side, but this time there's no hesitation. He eases me back against the fence and kisses the corner of my mouth, his hands tightening on my hips. Light sifts through the trees, yellowing with the dawn, accentuating the golden-brown ring around his greenish irises.

Even though this has been all night coming, when Beau pulls back, I still feel shy and dumbstruck. "Thank you," I'm horrified to hear myself say.

He laughs and touches my hair. "Anytime."

In the quiet of morning, I can hear Megan's car pulling onto the street that runs behind the far side of the field and leads to the parking lot. I release Beau and look back. Megan parks at the top of the hill beyond the stadium, lowers her window, and waves.

"You wanna ride up there?" Beau asks.

"That's okay. It'll feel good to walk."

He pulls out his phone, which is two models older than mine and looks like it got caught in a lawn mower, and passes it to me without a word. I type my number in, save it, and pass it back. "Thanks again," I say, then hurry to add, "for saving me from that party. I'm sorry you missed it."

"I told you why I went," he says.

Neither of us speaks for a minute, then I awkwardly say goodbye and turn to walk up the hill to Megan's car.

"Bye, Natalie," Beau says, and I turn around one last time and wave.

As soon as I get in, Megan begins to apologize again, but as we turn around and drive off, she falls silent then says, "Okay, so he was pretty faraway and tiny from where I was parked, but wow."

"I know."

"Wow," she says again. "I can't imagine what Summer Incarnate looks like up close."

"You really can't."

"Oh my God," Megan says. "I'm shaking I'm so giddy right now."

"And what about you and Brian?" I demand.

"Eh," she says. "We kissed. Then I fell asleep. Bad sign?"

"Not necessarily."

"I didn't say bye to him this morning. What about that?"

"That doesn't mean anything," I say. "You probably just felt awkward."

"I guess." She looks over at me, scrunches her nose up. "He tasted like Cheetos."

"Ugh, I'm going to be sick."

"I know," she groans.

"The literal kiss of death."

"Exactly," she says. "I'm dead. My body just hasn't gotten the memo."

"Those Cheetos probably had some kind of reanimation spell on them," I suggest.

She drops her forehead against the steering wheel for a second. "I liked him *so* much. There, I said it. How could this happen?"

"Is it possible he just, I don't know, ate Cheetos?"

"I mean, I'm no forensic investigator, but I would say there's roughly a one hundred percent chance that's exactly what happened."

"I'm sorry."

"*You're* sorry? I abandoned you to make out with a Frito-Lay product."

"Honestly, Meg, if I needed you, I would've found you, mid-cheese-powder make-out or not."

"I die," she says. "I die a thousand deaths every time I think about it."

"I think you should give him another chance."

She looks at me, utterly aghast. "That's just because you're all moony! Because you *obviously* just kissed someone who didn't taste like the floor at Derek Dillhorn's fourth-grade birthday party!"

"I would bet money Brian's mouth doesn't always taste like that."

"We'll see," she says. "I may just be too scarred. Hey, do you want Waffle House? I'm starving. Starving for details. Starving for waffles and starving for details."

"That sounds good, but I think I need to sleep for ten hours first. Maybe reconvene for dinner?" We're driving past the Presbyterian church now, which is back to normal—the additional wing vanished, and the parking lot too big for the small Sunday crowds. "Hey, does anything about that building seem different to you?" I ask.

Megan peers out the window. "Just the haze of flaky, cheese-flavored orange hanging over everything, but that could be my imagination."

We pull up to the curb in front of my house, and Megan presses the heels of her hands into her eye sockets and drops her head back into the headrest, groaning again for good measure.

I pat her arm. "This too shall pass."

She straightens up and sighs. "From your mouth to Grandmother's ears."

I get out of the car, legs wobbling from fatigue, and wave goodbye as Megan pulls away. I turn back to the house just as Gus comes running through the front door and across the yard. "Jack!" I shout, annoyed. He's always leaving the front door unlocked, and half the time it pops open and Gus takes a jaunt around the neighborhood. I lunge to grab hold of his collar before he can take off, but as my fingers curl around the leather, it happens again.

One second Gus is there, the next he's gone, and I nearly let out a shriek as the collar drops limp in my hand. I turn in circles, searching the abandoned block. "Gus?" My dog is gone, and I don't know what to do. I turn in circles, calling his name more loudly. "Gus! *Gus!*"

And then he's back. Like it never happened, wearing his collar and trying to pull me up the street to where a decidedly terrifying standard poodle lives. I dig my feet in and try to yank him back toward the front door.

My mind is reeling. My stomach roils. I drag Gus across the yard and run up onto the porch, but I come up short. It feels like my heart just slammed into a wall. And now Gus is gone again. The door and the shutters are red, not green like they should be. I'm so freaked out that for some reason, I still try to jam my house key into the lock, but it won't work. My insides are screaming, I can barely breathe, and I fumble with the key, panic filling me up like a flood of acid. "Gus," I say again. Then, "Grandmother. Grandmother! Are you there? Please!"

The key finally slips into the lock as the door turns green again before my eyes, and Gus reappears in the same moment.

I run inside, hauling Gus in after me, and lock the door behind us. I slump against it and slide to the ground, wrap my arms around Gus's neck as tears stream down my cheeks. I nuzzle into his fur and wait for the fit of trembling to pass.

My first session with Alice is eerily similar to every appointment I've had with real therapists, as long as you completely ignore the *Hoarders*-esque state of her office and the way she keeps snapping her gum and the fact that she occasionally rolls her eyes when I say something she disagrees with. I have this sense that she's assuming the pose, role-playing the whole thing like we had to do in A.P. Psychology.

It's like we're playing doctor until we get to the bits that might actually be useful, when she sits forward abruptly, drums her lips, then jots something down haphazardly in her notebook.

"Are you sure there's no faster way to do this?" I ask. "Maybe if you told me what you're writing down."

"There's no faster way," she says, scribbling furiously. "I'm following my gut. Some things may seem mundane to you, but they might hold the key. Other things may seem really big and have nothing to do with it. I just want you to keep talking."

And I do. For ninety-five straight minutes, and I don't leave a single second empty. And I feel productive, like I'm getting something done and need to keep plowing ahead.

I tell her about my tantrums and how dance seemed to get them out of me, and how Mom thought that meant maybe I'd had ADHD. I tell her the night terrors started out as dreams, then spread to the visitors at my bedside and I'd scream until they disappeared and Dad would come running in with the baseball bat he kept under the bed. I tell her things I've never said aloud, not even to the other counselors, because the words themselves make me feel weak, and when I feel weak, I cry, and when I cry, I feel out of control. I tell her how, when I was little, I thought Debra Messing and Isla Fisher and Amy Adams were the very definition of beauty and how, when the twins turned three and their baby-blond hair started darkening toward Mom's reddish color, I was secretly heartbroken, as if I'd lost something, no matter how stupid or self-absorbed that sounds. They were going to look like our parents, and I was going to keep looking like a stranger.

But I tell Alice the truth, because for the first time, I want the counseling to work more than I want to hide the parts of me I'm scared of.

At some point we bounce toward the present. "The Wrong Things," Alice says. "The changes or flickers. Tell me about those again."

So I talk, telling her about the most recent events with Gus and the buffalo and the renovated church. But the more I talk, the more the piercing headache behind my eye swells. "I don't understand what's happening," I gasp.

"You've come to the right place," Alice says, without looking up from her notebook. She has the voice recorder I traded her this morning balanced on her lap. "I mean, maybe. Hopefully. In an ideal world, yes, this is the right place. Look, you may have been having these extended conversations with one of Them for your entire life, but what you're experiencing now is much more common. I mean, typically they'd only be happening on your way in or out of a dream state, but the gist is the same."

"Well, what are they?" I ask.

"Too soon to say. What I do know is that most people only experience very brief visitations, like the flashes you describe. You wake up and you're not in your room, but as soon as you scream you're back. You fall asleep on the bus and when your eyes open someone's staring at you—you jump up and they're gone. You hear someone talking downstairs, so you go see a couple having dinner at your table. When you flip on the light, they vanish. Usually, they don't even see you. When they do, witnesses describe the Others as seeming just as surprised as they were. I don't think they're fully aware of us."

"Grandmother is."

"Grandmother, like you, my dear Natalie, is different. And that's why this is so important."

"She *is* God, isn't she?" I say.

Alice exhales. "I'm a scientist who studies nighttime hallucinations under the primary assumption that there's something supernatural about them. I'm the last person prepared to make a statement about what God is and if it exists. I personally have never really bought the idea of a higher power, but then again, as far as the rest of the faculty's concerned, I might as well be the chairperson of Leprechaun Studies. All I know is that Grandmother and all the visions that came before her are *something*. God, ghost, or something in between, we're going to find out who Grandmother is. I believe that, Natalie."

The next morning Jack and I are walking out to the Jeep when it happens again. The shutters and door flash red. The basketball hoop in the driveway and my baby brother vanish. I stand in the middle of the front yard, the whole world frozen and congealed, feeling like I'd have to cut through gelatin to move another step.

Just as quickly, though, a blast of sound tears through the stillness, and I jump.

"Hurry up!" Jack calls from the car. He's leaned across the seat to hit the horn, which wouldn't be so alarming if I had any idea how he got there. I shake myself out of it and climb in beside him.

"Sorry," I say. "Thought I forgot my phone."

Jack chortles then tries to play it off like he's clearing his throat, a trick Dad frequently employs when Mom disapproves of whatever he's laughing at. "Nothing," Jack hurries, before I even get a chance to glare. "You just checked it, like, three times between the kitchen and the porch."

My cheeks burn at his observation, and I start the car, devotedly pretending not to have heard. It's been four days since Matt's party. I'm still actively fuming over what happened with Matt that night, but it's Beau who has me wavering between giddiness and obsessive, all-consuming overthinking. It seems like the Wrong Thing incidents and the thought of Megan leaving for Georgetown in a couple of days are the only things that make me stop wondering why he hasn't called.

As I drive toward the school, I do what I've done every time I didn't want to deal with or think about something for the past two years: I imagine myself at Brown, with new friends who don't know about Matt or care about why I quit the dance team, a place where I can start over. But the daydream gives me no relief. I'm too angry at Matt, too embarrassed about whatever happened with Beau. It felt right while it was happening, sweet and genuine and so intense that I'd been sure he was feeling the same thing. Now I'm forced to replay all the highly personal details I shared with him and cringe at my own vulnerability.

When we pull up to the gate outside the field house, Jack springs out of the car, calling, "Later!" but I don't drive off right away. Instead I watch my brother sprint across the field. He's blipping in and out of view—just like Beau did at Senior Night—and then I see his teammates in the distance buzzing with the same strobe-light effect. Only those guys aren't disappearing like Jack is. They're shifting, rearranging with impossible speed, on the left side of the field one second and the right the next; mid jumping jack one instant and jogging along the far side of the track the next. I watch one boy in particular, T.J. Bishop, whose hairstyle keeps oscillating between a close shave and a pathetically short ponytail, his body bulking up and slimming down in steady, alternating beats.

"The Wrong Things," I say aloud to myself. I still have no idea what they mean.

Thunder crackles overhead, but it's distant and soft, like a bass drum covered by a towel. Megan and I are sitting in my garage with the door cranked open so we can watch the thick spray of rain slap the driveway and the blue-green foliage framing the yard.

We've storm-watched like this for as long as I can remember, and it's always given me a sense of peace. We don't need to talk to feel happy or understood. The rain flooding the cul-de-sac is enough. Our eleven years of friendship tell me so. We may be different, but in this moment we're feeling the exact same thing: the sad kind of bliss where you realize, suddenly, how perfect your life really has been all along. So perfect it hurts, and you could let yourself weep if you wanted. So perfect that even though everything you know is ending, you truly believe life will continue to be beautiful, even—or maybe especially—in those pure moments of loss.

We sit there for hours. When the rain finally lets up, we stand, brushing the dirt and leaked car oil smears off the backs of our thighs.

Goodbyes have always been as natural for us as silence, unspoken agreements between us nine times out of ten. There's no *I should go* or *look at the time*. Megan just smiles and squeezes me tight in a hug. "Love you," she says.

"Love you back," I say. "Get home safe. Get to school safe."

"I'll see you so soon, Nat," she says, and I nod, unwilling to doubt her. She pulls up the hood of her thin sweatshirt and darts through the drizzle back to her black Civic parked at the curb.

The headlights flick on, and Megan pulls away. As soon as I shut myself in my room, I see the cardboard boxes spread around the room and break down and cry. When the tears are all used up, I pull out Alice's recorder and tell another story about love and pain.

"There once was a young man who believed he was in love with a beautiful woman," Grandmother said. "So he went to the woman's father, who was the Chief, and told him that he wished to marry his daughter.

"'Bring me many horses,' the Chief answered, 'and you may marry my daughter.' So the young man set out into the wild in search of horses to please the Chief.

"While the man was away, the tribe moved on, and though the man caught several beautiful horses for the Chief, when he returned his tribe was gone. The man planned to go in search of his lost tribe, but the sun was very low in the sky, so first he decided to rest. He went to a lodge nearby but could find no doors, no matter how many times he circled it. Finally, he dug his way through the sod surrounding the lodge and made his way inside, where he found a burial bed supported by four high posts.

"On the burial bed lay a young woman in clothes decorated with the teeth of elk. The woman turned and looked at him. He recognized her right away as a member of his tribe, who must have died while he was away. But the woman sat up and greeted him by name, for she remembered him, too, from her life.

"The man stayed with the Ghost Woman for many nights. As time passed, he thought less and less of the Chief's daughter and more and more of the Ghost Woman bound to her burial bed, until finally she became his wife.

"Though the man loved his wife and their lodge and the land where they lived, he awoke one morning, hungering for a buffalo hunt, something of which he had not taken part since before he left to find the Chief's horses. He said nothing aloud of the hunt, but the Ghost Woman knew his thoughts. She told him, 'Mount your horse and ride to the bluffs. There, the buffalo await you. When you see the herd, rush into the center and kill the fattest bull to bring home. Roast the meat and bring me a share before you eat yours.'

"The man followed her commands. When he brought the roasted meat to her, he found her standing in the lodge, which startled him. 'Please don't be afraid of me, my husband,' she said, because she knew his thoughts.

"His heart was calmed, and he knew his wife better than he had before he saw her ghostly form standing there. They shared the meat and spoke freely of everything, living and dead, making plans for the things they would like to do. 'Let us pitch our tent by day and travel by night,' the Ghost Woman said. 'In this way we can see the world.'

"And it was as she said: The Ghost Woman floated ahead of her husband, her head covered and her mouth silent. Whenever the man thought something, the Ghost Woman heard it clearly, until eventually, the man became a Ghost as well. Then they passed their thoughts back and forth to one another like water poured between bowls with no drops spilled, and they knew each other as they knew themselves. Their tribe never found them again, and the Chief's daughter often wondered what had become of her young love, though in the end she married someone else.

"The Ghost Woman gave up her rest, and the brave gave up the world of the living, and they loved one another well. And that, Natalie, is your happy ending."

"But he died," I protested.

"It's a condition of living," she said. "Besides, judging a story by the ending alone, or a life by its death alone, is as pointless as judging a long hike through the mountains by the fact that when you get back to where you parked your car, there's a pit toilet full of you-know-what and beer cans."

"Exactly," I said. "Why not stay out in the woods forever?"

"Because," she said. "You need that car to get to the next hike. I want you to understand something, Natalie. No matter how hard it feels, you don't need to be afraid to move on, and you don't need to be afraid to stay either. There's always more to see and feel."

"You really think so?" I said.

"I know so."

Alice closes her notebook thirty minutes early, while I'm mid-sentence. "You're not stressed, Natalie. You're sad. I can't do anything for you if you're sad."

"It's a little bit hard to control that," I reply edgily. It's been a week since Megan left. The Wrong Things have all but vanished. It probably doesn't help that I've barely left my house in the past three days.

"It shouldn't be. Stress starts to overshadow, *transform* sadness when you're overcommitting your time, keeping yourself awake all night, spending time with people when you need to rest and be alone."

"You're the worst therapist in the world."

"Then it's a good thing I'm a research psychologist, not a therapist. Look, I'm starting to see some threads forming in your history, and I agree with what your last doctor said—there's some other trauma there, something you haven't worked through. All of your behaviors, your decisions and habits suggest so."

"*What* behaviors—?"

"The fact that you can't pinpoint a new aspect of the memory," she cuts me off, "or recall any other event indicates that either you've suppressed the memory or it's something that seemed really mundane to you at the time. I once read a case about a girl who was abandoned by her father, who went through EMDR and recovered a memory of opening the mailbox on her birthday. It wasn't her parents' fights or the memory of the day he walked out. It was the absence of a stupid birthday card. We've got to find *your* missing birthday card."

"What if I don't have one?"

"You do," she says. "I feel it. I'm going to start bringing in a colleague to do hypnotherapy on Thursdays. We'll keep having our normal one-on-one Tuesday sessions. Meanwhile, you need to push yourself. Do things that make you uncomfortable; overextend yourself. In the long run it'll be good for you, and in the short run it will overrun you."

Mom gets back from a run looking like a Nike advertisement, dressed in her sleek pink and gray workout clothes and only dewy and bright with sweat. "Hey, honey," she says, ruffling my hair from behind the couch. She takes a long swig from her matching pink water bottle then comes to sit beside me. "Everything okay?"

The tone of her voice tells me she knows it's not. "Yep," I lie.

She nods, her eyes intense on mine. "It must feel really weird around here with Megan gone, huh?"

"Yeah." I want to be in my room, waiting for Megan to get done with practice so I can call, but thanks to Alice, I'm down here instead.

Mom puts her arm around me and squeezes me. "College goes by so fast," she says. "I honestly felt like I blinked, and it was over. These are going to be some of the best years of your life, and when they're done, you can go anywhere, you know?"

"I know."

"Hey, I have an idea. Why don't we go see a movie tonight?"

The thought of going somewhere I'd likely run into classmates makes me feel sick and anxious. I don't know who knows about Matt and Rachel, but I'd bet money the answer is everyone, which of course makes me feel embarrassed. And angry. It makes it look like *he* rejected *me*, completely hides the fact that he practically forced himself on me then ran off to hook up with Rachel for revenge.

"A movie sounds fun," I tell Mom.

"Really? You don't *have* to," she says hesitantly. "If you already have plans. I would just love to spend some time with my girl."

"No, no plans," I say, as if she didn't already know.

"Great! I'll just take a quick shower and then we can go." She kisses the side of my head and walks off.

An hour later, we're heading over to the theater. Following Alice's orders, I chose the movie that looks the most disturbing: a drama about a girl who was kidnapped and forced into the sex trade for ten years, until she manages to escape.

"Are you sure about this one?" Mom says, trying and failing to not look horrified. "This kind of thing usually upsets you, doesn't it?"

"It has a happy ending, I think," I say.

Mom pays for the tickets and we go into the theater. "Let's use the bathroom first," she says. She'll have to go again in the middle of the movie regardless. It's the Davidson family curse, apparently, which she inherited from her father. I wouldn't know what that's like since I don't have any Davidson blood. I could probably hold my bladder if a tornado picked me up.

I pee anyway and wash my hands, waiting a minute in the bathroom for Mom to come out. "I'll meet you in the lobby, okay?" I say finally. When she doesn't answer, I bend over to look under the stall but her feet aren't in there. "Mom?" I'm alone in the bathroom. She must've already slipped out.

I turn and push through the door, immediately colliding with someone in the lobby. I stumble backward, apologizing, until I see who it is. All the blood drains from my face. "Matt."

He looks confused, glancing almost impatiently between me and the ticket-taker. "I'm so sorry," he says, clasping his hands in front of his chest. "We've met before, haven't we? I'm horrible with names."

"Are you serious?" I say, fuming.

His gaze cuts across the lobby again. "I'm really sorry. My girlfriend's waiting for me inside. It was great to run into you."

Girlfriend.

He jogs toward the bright red podium and stretch of velvet ropes leading to the theaters, and I'm left staring at his back, my whole body on fire yet tingling with chills. On the one hand, I can't believe I ever loved him, someone capable of *convincingly* pretending I'm a complete stranger to him. On the other, I'm legitimately freaked out. Matt's familiar blue eyes looked blank—no recognition behind them at all—as if really and truly his brain had erased me from its archives. This has "bad dream" written so vehemently all over it that I open and close my eyes hard a few times, hoping I'll wake up in my bed.

"Ready?"

I turn to find Mom emerging from the bathroom, and more chills rush down my arms.

"Where'd you go?" I ask, biting back the remnants of angry tears.

"I was in the bathroom," she says. She grabs my chin. "Honey, what happened? Are you okay?"

"Nothing," I say. "I just ran into Matt. He has a new girlfriend." It's an easier explanation than the whole truth.

"Oh, baby." She pulls me into her arms, and we stand there until a woman approaches the bathroom and we realize we're blocking the way. We step aside and head into the concessions line. "We don't have to stay," Mom says. "If you want to go home, that's fine."

I shake my head. "I need a distraction."

She nods. "Okay. But if you change your mind, just say the word."

We pay for our popcorn and head into our movie. Within five minutes, I know I've made a horrible mistake. This movie's the most upsetting thing I've ever seen, and there's no escaping it. My insides are in alarming turmoil, and I'm fairly sure I'm going to have diarrhea for days. I close my eyes and shut out the sounds.

But when I steer my mind away from the awful plot unfolding in front of me, another gruesome image resurfaces with a vengeance. I think of the boy I fell in love with as we sat on a hillside, swarmed in fireflies, and of how, on the night I broke his heart years later, he promised he could never hate me. Then I think of the guy who just treated me like a stranger. I think of the two different Matts my mind can't reconcile, and then I think of a story Grandmother told me.

"This is the story of Brother Black and Brother Red," Grandmother said. "There once was a brother and sister who lived in a lodge deep in a forest. They rarely saw any visitors. The brother was different from other people, in that one half of him was red and one half of him was black.

"One day, he went away to hunt, but no sooner had he left than his sister saw him coming back down the path toward their lodge. 'I thought you went to hunt,' she said, following him inside.

"'I changed my mind,' he told her and went to sit by her on the bed. He seemed different to her, and when he tried to embrace her, she became afraid and fought him off.

"'Why do you act as my husband when you are my brother?' she said angrily, but again he tried to hold her as a lover, and she fought him off again, and this time he left.

"The next day the brother returned home, but his sister would not speak to him, though usually they spent many hours talking. 'My sister,' the brother said, 'Why do you treat me as one hated? What have I done to deserve such a change in your love toward me?'

"'You know what you've done,' the sister answered. 'You harmed me and broke our bond.' But the brother insisted he didn't know what she was talking about, so the sister told him plainly, 'Yesterday you embraced me as a lover, and today I can't look at you.'

"'My precious sister,' the brother said, 'I was not here yesterday. I was hunting. You must have met my friend, who looks like me in every way.' The sister was angry that her brother had given such an outlandish excuse. 'Do not treat me in that way again,' she said, and for many days he seemed to be his old self.

"Finally the brother went away to hunt again, and as before, the sister saw someone who looked just like her brother and wore his clothes, hiding in the brush near their home. He followed her back inside, and this time when he tried to hold her, she tore at his face with her nails until he fled.

"Three days passed and her brother returned again with a deer he had hunted. Again she refused to speak to him, and again he spoke gently to her, saying, 'Sister, you're very angry with me. Has my friend been here again?'

"She did not answer him, but he repeated the question, and she broke down and wept. 'How could you attack me again, when I had come to trust you? I see my nail marks on your face. I know it was you, brother.'

"But the brother denied it. 'My face was scratched by thorns as I hunted,' he told her, 'but if you scratched my friend, that is why my face is scratched—whatever happens to one of us then happens to the other.' But she didn't believe him. She avoided him as much as possible until he left again to hunt, and this time when he returned and attacked her, she tore his hunting shirt from his throat to his belly button and threw hot grease on his stomach, burning him and causing him to flee.

"As before, her brother returned, and as before he denied having been there though his shirt was torn and his stomach was burned just as his sister remembered it. 'I tore my shirt while climbing a tree, and I burned myself while cooking the meat I hunted,' he tried to tell her, but she would not believe him, and he saw what had to be done. 'Sister, I will find my double and bring him here to prove to you it was not me who hurt you, and for what he's done to you, I'll kill him, though it may kill me too. That is how important it is to me that you know my heart and my brotherly love for you.'

"The sister did not believe him, and the brother left to find his double. He wasn't gone long in the woods before he returned, dragging with him a man who looked exactly like him and whose clothes were torn in just the same way. 'You've betrayed me by hurting my sister,' the brother said to his double, 'and now you must die.' He lifted his bow and arrow and shot his double through the heart. The sister looked on as blood poured from the identical man's chest and he slumped to his knees. Then she heard a second noise behind her—a battle cry—and when she turned, she saw her brother fall, an identical wound over his heart, blood spreading out through his shirt.

"The sister knew then she was safe, but her heart was broken."

The story had upset me when I first heard it, but now it takes on a whole new meaning. I'm sure Grandmother knew what was going to happen today, how Matt's feelings toward me would change so violently that he'd seem like a different person, one who saw me as a stranger. She had to have—why else would she have told me that story? And how many of her other stories contain hidden warnings too?

When Mom and I get home from the movie, I go to my room and record the story of Brother Black and Brother Red for Alice. I'm in the middle of it when someone knocks on my door.

"Yeah," I answer, and Coco pokes her strawberry blond head in the door, looking worried.

"Can I come in?"

I sit up and pat the bed. "What's going on?"

She perches on the edge of the mattress and crosses her legs. She looks more and more like Mom every day, and while not on the school's dance team, she takes ballet and jazz, and she definitely inherited Mom's dignified grace. "Mom told me about the movies. That Matt has a girlfriend?"

"Oh," I say. "Yeah."

"So weird—I've heard nothing about it." Her pretty, deep blue eyes come up to mine. "Is it Rachel Hanson?"

I avoid her gaze, pulling a stray thread in my quilt. "I don't know."

Coco twirls her loose waves around her finger. "Abby told me what happened at Matt's birthday—that they hooked up. I thought Matt was better than that. I *definitely* didn't think they'd date."

Of course Coco knows. "Matt and I were broken up," I say. "I told him I didn't want to date him. He's free to be with anyone he likes."

"Still," Coco says. "Rachel? You guys are, like, friends. Or at least in the same friend *group*. And I know you were upset. Everyone's talking about how you snuck away from the party after."

Ouch. So she hasn't mastered Mom's sensitivity training yet, but at least I know she cares. "Believe it or not, that was about something else. Or at least, it wasn't *just* about him and Rachel. There was more to it."

She scrunches up her mouth in thought. "It's okay to be mad at her. I would be."

"I'm not mad at her," I insist, but I have no idea if I'm lying. "Rachel and I haven't been close in a long time. It'd be weird if I expected her to choose me over Matt."

Coco rolls her eyes. "Whatever. She used to come over all the time. Girl code stands."

The strange thing is, that sounds like something Rachel would've said a couple of years ago. She's always been tough and blunt—the type of teammate who wouldn't hesitate to tell you you "sucked" at turns in second, or leapt like a grandma in need of a hip replacement—but she also has this enviably commanding confidence and fierce loyalty to her few select friends.

When Matt and I first broke up and Kara Van Vleck expressed interest in dating him, Rachel told Matt that Kara was being treated for a contagious flesh-eating bacteria. It was a completely appalling thing to do to Kara, and I doubt Matt believed it, but that was the sort of messed-up way Rachel showed love, even after she'd been so pissed at me for quitting dance, accusing me of being too good for anything other than the Ivy League. When I found out she was the source of that particular rumor, I'd felt a similar pain to the one I felt the night I broke up with Matt: like I'd realized how much I'd always love someone at the same moment I realized that person and I might never fit together again.

Maybe that's why I'm not mad at Rachel. Because Rachel can't help but make it known when she's trying to hurt you, just like she makes it known when she cares about you. The look on her face, in that horrible moment at Matt's house, told me she was horrified that I had walked in, upset that I had seen them together, distressed that she'd been caught with Matt Kincaid. She hadn't meant to hurt me, but that almost hurt worse. Rachel, it seemed, still had the inclination to protect me. Matt did not.

"I don't know what Rachel and I are anymore," I tell Coco, "but we're not enemies."

Coco nods silently for a few seconds, then stands. "Anyway, I wanted you to know I'm on your side. About the whole Matt thing."

"Thanks." I manage a weak smile, and she turns to go. "Hey, Coco?"

"Yeah?"

I'm not sure how to say this without it getting back to Mom and her putting the pieces together, which I don't feel ready for, but I want Coco to hear it. "Sometimes you change your mind about a person," I tell her. "Or your feelings for them change, or *they* change, or, I don't know, you just want to make a different decision. And that's always okay. You don't owe anyone anything. You know that, don't you?"

"What do you mean?" she says.

"I mean, like with Matt. I wanted to date him, and then I didn't want to anymore, and some people made me feel guilty for that. As if he just deserved whatever he wanted, and I was being selfish for not giving it to him."

"Are you talking about sex?" she asks matter-of-factly.

"No," I say. "Yes. Kind of. I'm talking about everything: dating, kissing, sex. All of it. You never owe another person something, no matter how nice they are to you. Relationships aren't transactions."

"Mom already covered all this," she says, "in the grossest, most uncomfortable way you could imagine. I thought I was prepared for it, but you honestly can't imagine how bad it was."

"Oh, trust me," I say. "I can. I got that talk immediately after my first date with Matt."

Coco scrunches up her dainty eyebrows and crosses her arms. "I guess you get more of it than me and Jack, huh?"

"More of what?"

"That Mom-the-psychoanalyst crap."

"I hate to break this to you, but I'm pretty sure I'm the *origin* of that particular alter ego."

Coco glances over her shoulder at the door then lowers her voice. "You mean 'cause of Grandmother."

Wow, right there, out in the open. It's the first time Coco's ever brought my alleged hallucinations up to me. "Yeah, her," I say. "And just the whole adoption thing. Perhaps you've noticed our expansive library on that topic."

Coco rolls her eyes. "Sometimes I think Mom just cares too much."

"We're lucky," I reply, thinking about Megan's obscenely rich but virtually absent parents, Rachel's single mom who's worked the night shift as long as I can remember, Matt's dad screaming at him from the sidelines during football practice despite Coach's pleas for him to leave.

"I know," Coco relents, turning back toward the door. "But *still*. Like, give us some room once in a while. Maybe don't try to tell me about sex while I'm eating a bagel."

I laugh. "Hey," I say, stopping her again. "Thanks again. For being on my side."

"We're sisters," she says. "I know you'd be on mine."

14

"You look horrible," Alice greets me the following Tuesday.

"Thanks," I say. "I wanted to fit in with your interior decorating scheme."

"Have you been sleeping?"

"No," I tell her. Having still not heard from Beau, I've had a particularly easy time occupying my mind with things other than sleep at night.

"Good girl," she says.

I tell her about Mom's feet disappearing in the bathroom, and a slew of littler things—flickers of changing colors, flashes of trees where they shouldn't be and construction sites where there should be buildings. I also tell her about Brother Black and Brother Red, and how it was all I could think of after Matt acted like a completely different person at the movie theater, even going so far as to pretend he didn't know me. Not to mention the terrifying feeling I have that maybe he actually *had* forgotten me. "I mean, could he have a split-personality disorder or something?"

Alice wobbles her head uncertainly. "Without more information, I couldn't guess. But, like you said, it could be that Grandmother knows something about Matt, or about your future, events that are going to happen to you. Or the story could be a complete coincidence. We're getting closer, though. I can feel it."

Thursday brings my first hypnotherapy session. I'm both nervous and hopeful. I can't help feeling that if there's something dark hidden in my past, there's probably a reason I've forgotten it. I guess that's the point, though. Once I find and face this hidden memory, Alice expects there to be some sort of reaction—the exact kick in the proverbial pants that I need to get Grandmother back. I've been sleeping more and more during the day, staying awake all night, waiting for a flash of her face, her wrinkled hands, her gray shawl in the rocking chair, but I've had no luck.

When I step into Alice's office that morning, the first thing I see is Dr. Wolfgang, a white-haired hypnotherapist who's been living in the area for three decades but still has a German accent so thick he might as well be speaking without using his tongue. Alice seems to catch every syllable, but I have to use context clues as he prepares for the session. When Dr. Wolfgang says something that sounds like *"Gerrfansittanonze-curch,"* Alice's eyes flick forcefully toward the leather sofa, and I take the combination to mean "Go sit on the couch."

I shuffle a bunch of papers aside and plop down. Dr. Wolfgang drags a stool toward me and sits down, leaning over his own belly. His scratchy voice, speaking words I rarely catch, quickly lulls me toward something like sleep, but next thing I know, I'm coming to, feeling like someone just spritzed me with cold water. Alice looks annoyed, and Dr. Wolfgang looks bored.

"How'd I do?" I ask.

"Ve vill hahv to try hotta," he says. "Zis may take some time."

Alice says her mantra for the end of our sessions: "Just keep doing what you're doing."

Grandmother or the Universe seems willing to oblige me: On my way home, the clanking in the front of my car reaches new heights, and the gas pedal seems to stop working. I'm lucky to manage to get to the shoulder of the highway, but I'm down in a valley surrounded by scrubby hills and fairly light traffic. I pull my phone out to call my parents, and while I see that I have service, when I press Mom's name I hear that same infuriating message I got when I called Megan the night of the party. *We're sorry. The number you have dialed is not in service. Please hang up and dial again.*

I get out of my car and slam the door, stress mounting so fast a headache starts to spin behind my skull. It's eighty-five degrees out with ninety percent humidity. I flip open the hood, knowing this will do me exactly no good, then call my dad. "Come on, come on, come on."

"We're sorry. The number you have dialed is not in serv—" I hang up and run my hands through my hair, weighing my options.

I don't want to get in a car with a stranger. Under no circumstances will I get into a car with a stranger, no way in hell
after seeing that abduction movie.

I can walk up to the next exit, two miles off, or I can flag
someone down and try to borrow a working phone. I turn back
to the road and wave my arms at a truck coming my way.

The driver pulls off onto the gravelly shoulder right behind the Jeep, and my stomach drops to the ground as Beau
opens his door and gets out.

The Universe has to be kidding me right now.

"Hi," he says, smiling. It's the same smile he gave me that
night in the band room, all night on the football field, and I
don't understand why he thinks it's okay to smile at me like
that after ignoring my phone number for three weeks.

He shouldn't be making my heart speed up. He shouldn't
be looking at me like he wants to kiss me, because if he's wanted to, he would have called me.

"Can I borrow your phone?" I shout over to him. "I mean,
I assume you still have a phone, right? I need to call my parents
to come get me."

He leaves the truck door open and comes over to me, looking me up and down before turning his eyes to the open hood.
"You want me to take a look at it?"

"No thanks," I say. "I just want to call my parents."

"I can give you a ride," he says. "I was on my way back to
Union anyway."

"That's okay. I'll just call them."

The space between his eyebrows knits together, and he
passes me his phone. I walk off a few yards and call my mom first.

"We're sorry. The number—"

I try my dad, Jack, and Coco, and get the same thing. I pace along the shoulder, outwardly sighing and inwardly groaning as I try to come up with a plan that doesn't involve Beau.

"Natalie, let me take you home."

I look back. Beau's leaning against the Jeep, arms crossed over his chest. He wears worn-out jeans and a white T-shirt, like a Calvin Klein model, which infuriates me. I toss him his phone and stalk back to his truck.

I climb in without a word, and he watches then follows, wordlessly starting the truck up again and pulling back into the lane. For a while we both remain silent, but not in the comfortable way we were the night of the party. "You should let me look at your car," he says finally. "I might be stupid, but I know cars."

"You're not stupid," I say begrudgingly.

"So just not your type," he says. "You're more into golden boys like Matt Kincaid."

"I am *not* into Matt Kincaid," I snap. "Not now, not ever again." Beau looks over at me for a second, and I fight a stutter in my chest. His eyes drop down to the space between us before trailing back to the road. After a long silence, I gather my courage and say, "You didn't have to ask for my number."

"Oh, that's real nice, Natalie," he says. "Thanks for that. You know what? I have some advice for you too. Next time someone asks for your number and you don't wanna give it to him, say so instead of giving him a fake one."

"What? I didn't give you a fake number," I almost shout. "What kind of bullshit excuse is that?"

He slides his phone out of his pocket, messing with it

while he drives, then holds it out to me. The screen says "Calling Natalie . . ."

"And?" I say.

"Go ahead," he says, pushing the phone closer to me. "While we're callin' bullshit."

I take the phone and hold it up to my ear just as the ringing stops. "*We're sorry. The—*"

"You have to be kidding me," I say, looking down at the screen. I double-check the contact info. "Beau, this is the right number. I don't know what's going on with my phone."

He looks over at me again then back to the road, and says nothing.

"I promise," I say. He glances over at me again, face grave. Per usual, I feel near to tears, maybe because I'm relieved Beau tried to call or maybe because I'm worried he won't believe me. "Really, I promise."

We stare at each other for a few seconds, and when he looks back at the road, he starts to smile. "So no QB1 for Natalie Cleary?"

"A quarterback is literally half of a halfback, Beau," I say. "It's simple math."

"Simple for you, maybe," he says. "You should probably know it took me five years to graduate from high school before you start overestimating me."

"You should probably know I couldn't possibly care less."

A full, bright smile breaks across his face, and I look out the window, feeling my own grin spreading. We're about five minutes from my house when I see something that makes my smile falter. "Can you pull over?" I ask.

He looks hesitantly over at me then to the parking lot on our right. "Sure," he says, pulling off. As soon as he stops the car, I get out and walk toward the building on the far side.

"You okay?" he calls after me.

I turn back to face him. "It's a daycare."

"I can read," he says. "That much, I got down."

"No, I mean, it used to be a nursery."

"What's the difference?"

"A plant nursery," I say. "Lindenbergers' Nursery. My mom brokered the deal when the Lindenbergers bought the land."

He scratches the back of his head and looks around. "Someone else must've bought it since then."

"What happened to all the greenhouses?"

He shrugs. "Bulldozed them, probably."

"Since yesterday?"

"I don't know, Natalie."

"You are seeing this, though, aren't you? I'm not imagining it."

He laughs and crosses his arms. "No, it's there. What's your point?"

"Nothing," I lie. "Sorry, it's just weird. My mom is friends with Rhonda Lindenberger. I feel bad that they went out of business."

Beau looks almost suspicious, but he doesn't ask any questions, and we get back in his pickup. Five minutes later we pull up to my house, and everything looks how it should, but I'm eager to talk to Alice again. It's the last day of June, and time is speeding past.

"Thanks for the ride."

"Anytime," Beau says.

"So I guess you'll just find me next time I need you?" I say.

"Or *you* could call *me*."

I take out my phone and hand it to him. I'm going to have to get a new one, but at least I'll have Beau's number. He saves it in my phone then passes it back to me.

"When should I call?" I ask.

"I don't know," he says. "Whenever you want me to come pick you up next. So maybe in, like, five minutes."

I laugh, and he rests his forehead against mine, his hand on the back of my neck. "Okay, five minutes." Our mouths are almost touching when I hear the porch door open, and I scoot backward abruptly.

"Nat?" Dad calls from the doorway. "Where's your car?"

"Thanks again for the ride," I tell Beau, climbing out of the truck.

"Five minutes," he mouths through the glass, holding up as many fingers, and I nod.

My parents get the Jeep towed to the house on Thursday afternoon, but they make no motion to take it into a shop until Saturday morning, after Dad's spent a few hours tinkering and swearing at it. When he's convinced *no one's gonna be able to fix the piece of sh-junk*, he skips right over the possibility of taking it to an actual mechanic and starts talking about all his friends and colleagues who might be able to cut us a deal on a new car.

Mom stands in the kitchen, one hand on her hip, making this face of patient disapproval that is the closest she ever gets to glowering. When Dad's done rifling through the pantry for the healthy potato chips he hates but Mom insists on buying, she says calmly, "I want to have it looked at first."

Before I even know what I'm doing, I say, "I have a friend."

Dad's stony frustration cracks into a smile. "Well, that's great, sugar. Always knew you had it in you."

"A friend who does car things," I amend.

"Car things?" Dad repeats skeptically.

"Yeah, you know, drag racing and assembling historically accurate plastic models." Mom misses the joke and starts to gently explain that those things don't qualify a person to work on her teenage daughter's potential death trap. "I'm kidding, Mom. My friend Beau—the one who picked me up when I broke down—he does tires and brakes and that sort of thing mostly, but he offered to look at the Jeep."

Dad shrugs, as if to say *if I can't fix it, no one can!* Mom sets a hand on his shoulder and says, "Sure. Call your friend," then smiles as if to say *and I will also call a mechanic regardless of whether your friend appears to fix the problem.*

That night, during the early Sunday morning hours, I've finally gathered the courage to call Beau and ask him if he's still willing to help with the car. But while I'm staring at his pre-entered name, my phone starts buzzing in my hand, and Matt's name appears onscreen. Immediately, there's a pressure on my chest like a teenage elephant is sitting on me as I stare and blink and stare some more at my phone, making the snap decision to answer on the final ring.

"Hello?" I feel like I'm swirling around in a toilet, preparing to go down the drain.

"Natalie," Matt says.

"What do you want?"

There's a long pause before he says, "I just missed you."

"Leave me alone."

"Please let me say something." I don't answer. "Natalie?"

"Yeah."

"I'm sorry," he says. "I'm sorry and I'm embarrassed and I hate myself."

"Yeah." I swallow the knot of emotion in my throat. "That's pretty much how I feel too."

"Nat," he says gently. I can tell he's been crying, and I don't care. "Nat, please. I'll do anything."

"What do you want from me, Matt?"

He sighs. "I don't know. I just want to make it right. Tell me how to make it right."

"I don't think you can. I don't think *we* can. Matt . . . we're broken." I hang up, and despite all the promises we've both made, I think it's finally true.

When an hour has passed, I'm still staring at the ceiling, eyes burning and chest heavy. By now I'm thoroughly self-conscious again but I steel myself and call Beau anyway, holding my breath and hoping that the call will go through. It seems to be working, but with every ring, my heart sinks further. I just want to hear his voice right now. The line clicks, and noise fills my ear, music and shouting. "Hello?" I half-whisper, not wanting to wake Coco in the next room over.

The music fades into the background until it's all but gone. "Hi," Beau says, his voice even slower than usual.

"You're busy," I say.

"No," he says.

"No?"

"I'm just out with my brother. It's fine. I'm glad you called."

"I'm glad my call went through."

"Hey, you wanna come over?"

"Tonight?"

"Right now."

"I'm already in bed," I tell him.

"Is that a maybe?"

I briefly contemplate sneaking out. "I think it's a rain check."

"You *think*, Cleary?" he says.

"Hey, what's your last name?"

"Wilkes, why?"

"No way," I say. "You're kidding."

"I'm not."

"Beau Wilkes. The exact same name of Ashley Wilkes's son in *Gone with the Wind*, and you're not kidding."

"Pretty sure the whole reason my mom slept with my dad a second time was so she could give that name to a baby," he says.

"Beau Wilkes."

"Natalie Cleary, what can I do for you? It's late and you don't wanna come over, so what? Do you have another emergency you need me to pick you up from?"

"Would you come if I did?"

"I would."

"What if you had to travel by carriage through a dangerous shantytown?"

"I have no idea what you're talkin' about," he says. "Did you call for any reason?"

"Yeah, actually. I'm wondering if you still want to take a look at my car, before I take it in."

"You want to use me?" he teases. "I've never been used for my brain before."

I laugh. "How's it feel?"

"Fine."

"Fahn."

"And now you're making fun of the way I talk. You're heartless."

"I'm sorry, Beau Wilkes. I like the way you talk. And this is probably obvious, but I'm using you *equally* for your mind and body." He's silent for a long second, and I almost think he's hung up. "Hello?"

"Yeah," he says.

"You're still there?"

"I was just picturing you," he says softly.

"Oh" is all I can manage.

"You look real pretty."

I cover my face with my hand, smiling stupidly into my palm. "Thanks, Beau."

"I'd love to take a look at your car."

"You would?"

"I would."

"When's good for you?"

"I'm working all weekend," he says. "I have Tuesday morning off."

So maybe I'll have to miss one session with Alice after all, or maybe she can push it back to later in the day. "That sounds perfect," I say.

"What time?"

"Whenever," I say.

"So, like, one or two?" he says.

"Is it at all possible you could do nine?"

He laughs. "Yeah, I'll just park my truck on your street and sleep there the night before."

"If that's too early—"

"Nine's fine."

"Thanks, Beau."

There's a pause before he says, "Goodnight, Natalie."

"Goodnight, Beau."

Monday night brings the Promenade for Independence downtown, a parade complete with high-stepping horses in costumes, followed by the annual fireworks display at Luke Schwartz's mini-mansion. I used to love the Fourth of July—marching with the dance team in our sequined blue and orange leotards with their little spandex skirts, going to Luke's to see the illegal fireworks his dad's assistant drove out to Indiana to buy for us. The irony of celebrating Independence Day as an indigenous person was lost on me only until I was about seven years old, but last year was the first time I felt grated enough by the idea to skip the parade. Mom knew how excited I used to get about the Fourth and was understandably confused, and for some inexplicable reason, I decided the best way to *casually, lightly* explain my growing discomfort was to compare my participation in the parade to cartwheeling down the Trail of Tears.

It landed about as successfully as you'd expect any joke about genocide to land. That is to say, I made myself feel sick and my mom sob. She and Dad had of course skipped the parade in solidarity, which is why I'm not surprised when I hear a light knock on my door frame and look up to see Mom, smiling tentatively. "Thought you, your dad, and I could have a game night tonight while Jack and Coco are out?" she says.

"Dad hates games," I point out.

She waves the notion away with a manicured hand then crosses her arms over her stomach and glides into my room. "Your father loves games. He hates losing."

I don't bother pointing out that I actually *do* hate games, and anything with a semblance of competition for that matter, because I know the point of Mom's offer is to pretend today is just like any other day, and not a holiday she used to love.

"I was actually thinking about going to the parade," I lie.

She studies me. "Really?"

"No," I admit. "But only because I don't want to see Matt." As soon as I say it I realize it's true. Convictions aside, I really, really, really wish I could be at that parade tonight. I wish I could sit on a quilt surrounded by friends on Luke's front lawn, watching explosions of glittering light fill up the sky. I wish Megan and I would get to take pictures of one another writing each other's names in the air with sparklers, and that we'd drink bottles of Ale-8-One with sneaky quarter-shots of vodka we can't taste or feel but enjoy just for the sake of rebelliousness and summer and friendship and all the parts of the Fourth of July I still love. I wish that change weren't so hard, or that I didn't feel so thoroughly that I needed it to make room in my life to live and space in my brain to think. "I would go," I say again, "if things were different."

"Oh, honey." Mom releases a sigh and sits down beside me, pulling me against her chest and lightly circling her fingernails against my scalp. She squeezes me tight. "It won't always feel like this," she says. "Time heals all."

And by the end of our conversation, after Mom and Dad have finally accepted that I'll be fine staying home while they go out after all, I start to think she's right. Last July I made Mom cry, and now she's going to a cookout. Maybe by this time next year, when I look at or think about Matt Kincaid, my heart won't start to break. Maybe I'll be able to think of him as my friend again.

For tonight, though, I wander barefoot through an empty house, catching the dust of years on the bottom of my feet and memorizing the walls I'm leaving behind soon. When the sun sets, I go up to my room and watch my cul-de-sac's private show of fireworks from my bedroom window.

When the last of our neighbors sets off the last grand finale, I fall into bed and text Megan:

Miss you so much it hurts.

Seconds later, she texts back, *The feeling is mushrooms,* followed by a second text reading, *Yes, autocorrect, I meant to say mushrooms, not mutual. Good catch.*

Life without you does feel a little bit like fungus, I reply. *But definitely less tasty.*

I mean, both mushrooms and my tears taste a little bit salty? Megan says.

How do you have fluid left for tears with all the soccer sexting you're doing? I answer, *Btw I tried to type soccer sweating, but my phone simply wasn't having it.*

Your phone's right, she replies. *Soccer sexting. Fave competitive sport. Considering trying out for Olympic team.*

You're a shut-in, I say. **Shoe-in*. SHOO-IN**.*

You're a beautiful and wonderful and sensual and strong golden fawn, she says, followed by, *That was supposed to say "my best friend," but my phone . . .*

The feeling is mushrooms, I tell her. I fall asleep feeling a happy kind of sad.

Beau never shows up. When I call him, his phone goes straight to voice mail. I call a handful of times and leave one message, but soon it's noon and it's clear he's not coming.

Dad decided to take a half-day, so he gets home around one, drops his bag in the kitchen, and starts digging through the refrigerator for a beer. "Where's your friend?" he calls over his shoulder.

"Something came up," I lie. "He couldn't come." Dad glances back at me suspiciously. I am, after all, sitting at the kitchen table in the middle of the day like I've been waiting, but he doesn't call me out. I've never been sure if it's more annoying when Mom tries to help me process my emotions aloud or when Dad looks at me with X-ray, horse-whisperer eyes but keeps what he sees to himself.

He looks down at the bottle in his hands and gives it an apologetic sigh before stuffing it back in the fridge and clearing his throat. "Well, your mom's right. We probably oughta get a second opinion on it before shellin' out a few thousand bucks on something new, and I'd feel better if we took it in to a professional anyway. Don't want my baby girl in a car some kid duct-taped together."

My first inclination is to defend Beau, but then, with disappointment sinking in my stomach, I remember that Beau's supposed to be here, and he isn't. I don't really know who he is; maybe he is just some kid. "If you really loved me, you'd forget the car and buy me an airplane," I say, steering the conversation away from the absence of Beau.

"Kiddo, if you really loved me, you'd get a bike." Dad swipes his phone off the counter and shoots the refrigerator one last mournful glance. "Come on. Let's get that sucker towed in."

"What about this one?" Coco spritzes another purple bottle identical to the last hundred into the air beside my nose. We've been in Bath & Body Works for thirty minutes, and by now I've entirely lost my sense of smell.

"It's nice," I lie, scrambling to check my phone when I feel it buzz in my pocket. My mounting nerves skyrocket when instead of the apology from Beau I'd been hoping for, I see a mass text from Derek Dillhorn, alerting us to a party he's throwing while his parents are out of town. I haven't tried calling Beau since yesterday afternoon, and he hasn't called me either. Four days have passed since we talked about him coming to look at the car, four weeks since Grandmother gave me her *three months'* warning, and this shopping trip isn't proving to be the distraction from either situation I had hoped it would be.

"That's what you said about the last six," Coco complains.

"They were all nice."

"Then why are you making that face?"

"Because my brain is full of fumes, and I'm about to pass out," I say. "It's unrelated to all that toxic gas you keep spraying into my eyes."

Coco groans. "Why did you even come?"

"Because I wanted to hang out with you." And because Mom was too tired when she got home from work and asked me to. And because while the Jeep's in the shop, my only opportunities to get out of the neighborhood are going to come in the form of running errands in Mom's car. And because I needed to do *something* that required me to stop staring at my impossibly silent phone.

Coco sighs and clasps her hands together. "Can't you, like, wait outside or something? You're making me anxious."

"Are you serious?"

She widens her eyes and nods sharply.

"Can't you just get Abby a gift card? She's turning fifteen, not getting a Nobel Prize."

"I need to show her we're going to stay friends after I transfer," Coco shoots back. "Her love language is gifts! This needs to be perfect."

"Am I supposed to know what you're talking about right now?"

"You're only making this take longer."

"Fine," I say, "I'll be in the food court with my face buried inside a pizza until my nose stops stinging."

"Great," Coco says, spraying the air with a pale green bottle for emphasis.

I fight a sneeze as I leave the store and make my way over to the food court. I spot Rachel sitting across the room at a table in front of Sbarro, her hair freshly dyed an unnatural shade of blond as opposed to her usual unnatural dark brown, and my stomach sinks. I still wouldn't say I'm mad at her, but I *had* resolved not to see her or Matt again until our ten-year high school reunion.

The sinking sensation goes from bad to worse when I see who's sitting across from her.

Beau. Slumped back in his chair, hands resting on his legs, and Rachel has her foot hooked around his calf under the table. At the exact moment I register all of this, his eyes shift up to me. I look away as fast as I can and turn sharply toward the bathroom hallway, picking up my speed and praying he didn't see me. I know he did.

God, I'm so tired of avoiding everyone and everything.

Maybe I should just be grateful. It's going to be so easy to leave here after all. Maybe I needed my hometown to turn on me so I could let it go.

"Natalie," Beau calls after me.

I don't turn around. I'm in the hallway now, virtually running to the women's restroom.

"Natalie, wait," he calls again.

I bolt through the door and pull it closed behind me, starting to pace along the sink as I wonder how long I'm going to have to stay hidden in the bathroom. Everything about this is so humiliating. I should've just said "hi" to them, acted normal, but instead I ran away and hid, and now there's no pretending I'm not upset.

"Natalie," Beau calls through the door. "Natalie, I'm coming in."

My eyes sweep over the bathroom for any other exit as I hurry to hold the door shut, but I'm too slow. Beau's already in, and we're alone together, and I'm so embarrassed I want to die.

"This is the ladies' room, Beau."

He walks me up to the edge of the sink, grabs me around the waist, and kisses me. For a second I'm so surprised, so overwhelmed by both how frustrated and how attracted to him I am, that I kiss him back. When he lifts me up and sets me on the sink, I abruptly come to my senses and shove him back.

"What's wrong with you?" I shout. I jump down and stalk past him to the door. "Stay away from me."

I storm back toward Bath & Body Works, noting that Rachel is no longer in the food court when I pass. I weave through the clouds of sugary-sweet scents, march up to Coco, and drag her toward the faux-wooden checkout counter. "Whatever you're holding in your hand right now is what Abby's getting."

I wake with a start in the middle of the night, and my first thought is that Grandmother's here. I sit up and stare into the rocking chair, but it's empty. I turn on the paper lamp next to my bed, and Gus lets out a frustrated moo. Maybe he was barking in his sleep again—that's been known to wake me up.

Just then something clinks against the window in the

walk-in closet, the wind, probably. But a second later, I hear the same sound, only a little louder. I get out of bed, creep toward the window, and pull the drapes aside.

I look down past the porch roof to the front lawn, where Beau's standing. He drops a fistful of pebbles and holds a hand up to wave. I hesitate for a second, then shut the closet door behind me before sliding open the window.

"Hi," Beau says. He's swaying a little bit where he stands, his clothes rumpled and hair messy.

"What are you doing here?" I hiss.

He looks down at his feet then back up at me. "Can I come up?"

"Are you *drunk*?" I ask. That's when I notice how rough his face looks, faintly bruised like he's come straight from a brawl.

He glances away, running a hand over his mouth. His silence answers my question.

"Go home, Beau."

"I need to tell you something," he says.

"Then come back when you're sober."

He looks up the street. "I know what's happening to you, Natalie."

I give a frustrated laugh. "What, that I'm being jerked around by someone who's dating one of my former best friends?"

He shakes his head. "I'm not dating her."

I don't care what he says. I'm not body-language illiterate—that was a date. "Beau, go home."

"I'm sorry about the other day," he says. "I messed up. I should've been here."

"No." I half-laugh in disbelief. "Actually, you shouldn't have,

Beau. You also shouldn't have asked for my number or kissed me in a public restroom while you were on a date with another girl, but, I don't know, maybe you were just drunk then too!"

He stares up at me, fingertips resting on his hips. He runs one hand over his mouth again as he turns back toward his truck. As I watch him walk away, my heart starts to pound in my chest. "Beau, wait," I whisper-shout as I climb through the window onto the porch roof.

He looks back up at me. "You're right, Natalie," he says. "That's what kind of person I am. You got me nailed."

He opens his truck door, and I walk to the edge of the roof. "You shouldn't drive right now," I say, scanning the neighbors' windows in anticipation of flicked-on lights that will lead to phone calls that will get me busted.

For a long moment, he stares up at me, and then he gets in his truck. Furious, I climb down onto the porch railing, drop into the yard, and cross toward him, jerking the passenger door open. "Get out."

"It's my car," he says. "You get out."

"Why did you come here, Beau?" I say. "Why are you doing this to me?"

"Get out, Natalie," he says again.

I don't budge, so he clambers out of the truck and storms around it, pulling me out of the cab and closing the door. He starts to make his way back to the driver's side, and I chase him, cutting between him and the door. "You can't drive like this."

He grabs me suddenly by the waist. I grab him back, kissing him as he lifts me against the truck. He burrows his mouth against my neck, tightens his arms around me. We move sideways and he pulls the door open, lifting me into the cab and stepping closer until our stomachs are locked together, my legs wrapped around him, his hands roaming across my neck as he kisses me over and over again.

What the hell am I doing? My anger floods back into me, and I push him away.

He staggers back into the street. "Fine. You want to know why, Natalie?" he says. "Because my whole life I've thought I was crazy, but now I know I'm not the only one. And that would be real nice, except the other person—the only other person in the world who sees what I see—is the love of my best friend's life, and I'm not quite sure how the hell to handle that."

My heart seems to stop in my chest. I stare up through the darkness into Beau's eyes. They're serious and stern, the inside corners of his eyebrows creased. "What are you talking about?"

"The two different versions of Union," he says. "I know you can see them both."

"How do you know about that?" I breathe.

"Because," he says. "I can see them too."

When I finally invite Beau up, I almost regret it. He's far past tipsy and has a difficult time climbing on top of the porch. The whole time he's struggling up over the railing to the roof, I'm picturing him falling, an ambulance waking my parents up to find a drunk boy they've never met passed out below my bedroom window.

As soon as he's up, I reach back through the window to help pull him through. He hops down into the closet and pulls me against him, wrapping his arms around my shoulders.

His body is warm and tense around me, his heartbeat palpable all down my rib cage and stomach. He buries his face into my neck, and there's a part of me that knows I should push him away—that every second I spend with him makes me want *more* time, and, even if I weren't leaving in a few weeks, a boy who doesn't show up when he says he will but then shows up, drunk, when you're not expecting him probably isn't someone I should let myself feel anything for.

Short term, I want nothing more than to stand against him like this. Long term, I know letting this happen will make things hurt worse later.

I pull back and sit down on the floor, folding my knees up against my chest. He sits down across from me. "Tell me every-thing," I say.

He looks down at his hands and nods. "It started hap-pening when I was five," he says. "My mom and Mason would disappear for an hour or so, and then they'd be back, acting like they'd never gone anywhere. It got bigger fast. Sometimes whole buildings changed. There were two different versions of my house. There was the one we lived in, but sometimes while I was outside playing, I'd look back and the place would be all overgrown, the windows busted, that kind of thing. Then it was people. I met a version of Kincaid who didn't know me."

"Matt?" I say.

Beau nods. "We've lived on his rental property my whole life. Kincaid and I grew up playin' together, then one day, I went over to his yard, and he introduced himself to me, like we'd never met. He took me into his house, and his dad didn't know me either. Nicest Raymond Kincaid ever treated me," he says with the hint of a smile.

"No one lives in Matt's rental property," I say.

"Not in your version," Beau says. I stare blankly at him and he goes on. "When I was ten, my mom sent me to take piano lessons. It never happened while the teacher was watching, but if I played alone, sometimes things would disappear from the room. Little changes, nothing big. When I stopped playing, everything would go back to normal.

"It got worse and worse. My mom would've thought I was going crazy if she was around enough. Instead she figured it was just a phase and sent me to live with my dad. It happened less while I was there, but when it did, it was bad. One time my dad didn't even know who I was, chased me out of the house with a baseball bat in the middle of the night, but when I came back an hour later, he acted totally normal. Anyway, he'd had enough after a year and a half, and when I got back here, it was worse than before.

"I was a freshman when I figured out I could go between them when I wanted. Especially when I was playing piano, or listening to it, or even if I was just thinking about a song. Alcohol makes it easier too. And sometimes, I could go forward."

"Forward?"

His hazel eyes flash up to mine. "In time."

"That's impossible," I say, breathless.

He laughs. "It's all impossible, Natalie."

"Good point," I say, massaging my forehead. "So are there two futures?"

He shakes his head. "I don't know. When I'm going forward, I can't slow it down. It's like . . ." He thinks for a second. "It's like I'm standing in one place and makin' the world go past me, but as soon as I try to freeze it, live in it, I fall back into now, either my version or yours."

"None of this makes any sense."

"It doesn't," he admits. "That's why I didn't tell anyone

about it. There's no visible proof. It doesn't matter if other people are around when time starts moving; when it stops, I return right back into the present. For them it's like nothing happened, like I just blanked out for a second, no matter how long it felt like to me. I managed to take Mason's hamster with me once when I was a kid, but that didn't do me any good, and I could never replicate that with actual people, so I gave up. I'd go to the school at night to play piano, and I'd pass over to your version of the world, and then when the janitor came running in, I'd stop playing and let myself fall back into my version."

"The Band Room Ghost," I say.

He shrugs his shoulders. "The night I met you, I tried to go back to my version, but I couldn't. I thought it was just like it was with everyone else—like I was tuning in to where you were supposed to be, and that was what grounded me in your world. But then, after that night, you kept seeing flickers of *my* version of things. You saw the church with the extra wing, and you saw me and Rachel at the mall today."

I stare down at the carpet. "*Your* version of Rachel, though," I say, trying to sound natural.

He nods. "Rachel's pretty much Rachel, no matter where she is."

"She's your . . ."

"Nothing," he says, shaking his head.

"Your ex?" I guess.

He looks at me for a long moment. "Something like that."

"What about that night on the football field? Was she your ex then?"

His eyes dart sideways toward the window then back down to the ground. "Not quite." My stomach turns, and I cover my face, massaging my temples. "Natalie," he says.

I shake my head and let my hands fall. "It doesn't matter," I say. "There are more important things to worry about."

He stares at me, eyes heavy, as if he's asking me for something, and the inside of my chest feels like tearing paper. "That's why I didn't show up," he says finally. "When we first met I didn't even know who you were, where you fit in. But when you saw all that stuff—my version of stuff—the way you acted, I didn't know what to think about it at first. Then your phone number didn't work in my world, and I started putting it together. So I got this." He holds up a crappy flip phone.

"What, is that a burner for calling drug dealers?" I say dryly.

He gives me a mock-reproachful look. "Sort of," he says. "It's to call you. I bought it in your version, so when you called my number, it'd actually go through. The other night I wanted to see you. Thought you'd be at Schwartz's Fourth of July party, so I went, but I couldn't get to your version. Happens once in a while. Drank too much, and I still couldn't get through. Still couldn't the next day. Anyway, after I saw you today, I decided to try again."

I pull anxiously at the carpet. "Alcohol really helps you pass between them?"

He shrugs one shoulder. "Maybe. I thought so, anyway."

"Seems like a pretty convenient excuse for alcoholism. Takes the concept of social lubrication to a whole new level."

When I look up, Beau gives me one of those heavy smiles: summer in mouth form. "Well, Natalie Cleary, how 'bout you figure out how to pass back and forth, and then I won't have to drink to find you."

I laugh. "If you stop drinking beer, then what are you going to pour over your cereal?"

"Beer doesn't count as *drinking*."

I laugh again. "Oh, another convenient view."

"Fine," he says. "I'll cut out beer too, get into scrambled eggs or something. You just figure out how to get to my Union, okay?"

"Okay," I say, fighting a smile. Then something important occurs to me. "I think I'm looking for someone in your version. Or maybe she's in both versions, or in a third altogether. I'm not really sure. She's an old woman with gray hair and dark skin, and she calls herself Grandmother. Have you seen anyone like that?"

He hesitates, pushing his hair back and down his neck. "Natalie."

"What?"

"As far as I know, we have all the same people you have," he says. "There's two of everyone."

"Everyone?" I say.

He holds my eyes for a long moment. "Except us."

"Seriously?"

He nods. "I'd never seen you before that night in the school."

"I saw you on the field that night," I say. "I was at Senior Night, and right in the middle of everything, everyone disappeared. It was just us."

He looks up at me, the corner of his mouth lifting. "Our Senior Night was the week before yours. I was there alone that night." He looks at me until I can't hold his gaze anymore. "Can I show you something?"

I nod, and he gets to his feet. "Stand up," he says. "Give me your hands."

I do and climb to my feet. We stand there, holding hands, heat spreading from his fingers down my arms to my stomach. He reaches over my shoulder to flick off the closet light and presses his forehead against mine. "Close your eyes for a second," he whispers against my mouth, and I do, feeling him all around me, in all the spaces where we're not quite touching.

There's a drop in my stomach, like my center of gravity is sinking into wet sand, and light flickers against my eyelids—red, yellow, blue, purple—like a movie reel. "Now open them," Beau whispers.

My eyes flutter open. The dim light spilling across Beau's face is a silvery blue, but as I look into his eyes, the light beyond the window changes, rapidly intensifying through a hundred shades of pink into burning purple and then a blinding gold that slants through his irises like coppery spears. Within seconds the closet is lit up with daylight. Just as quickly, the daylight's waning, the gold swarming back in to color Beau's cheekbones and eyes and mouth as the sun falls down the western side of the house. Soon that turns to orange, then purple, deepening finally into a blue so dark it stretches out toward black.

The cycle repeats, the colors washing over us in new variations of the same shades, moving faster and faster until it's like we're standing in the center of the solar system, and it's the sun that circles us. Rising east of us and setting west of us. But somehow it also feels like we're moving, walking through chin-high water that pushes gently back against us.

The whole world is changing, and I gasp as another version of me moves between the closet and the room so fast I can barely see her. The closet empties, refilling with organized plastic bins I've never seen before, shadows of people I don't know blurring past, moving right through us. Those boxes disappear too, replaced by racks of clothes, and all the time the sun is rising and setting and Beau's hands are on mine.

Everything is changing, except Beau and me. We're the same.

"It's beautiful," I whisper.

He nods, never looking away from me.

"Do you think they hear us?"

The walls and floor are aging now, the light still juddering through its phases like a movie from a projector, until the drywall starts crumbling, spiderwebbed with vines and weeds. From those vines, flowers blossom and wither and grow back and die again. Seasons stretch into years stretch into decades stretch into centuries, all in moments, while I can hear Beau's breath, make out his edges through the millisecond of dark before another morning comes.

"I don't think there's anyone left to hear us," Beau says.

He's right. I laugh because I don't know what else to do. We're standing at the end of the world, light looping over us.

He moves closer to me, and the pressure in my stomach disappears, the light falling away to leave us together in my closet in the dark. My breathing feels shallow now. I can barely see Beau towering over me, but I can feel him. I can still feel his kiss on my lips, and I'm acutely aware of the distance from his mouth to mine.

And then there's no distance. My back is against the closet door, and Beau's kissing me slowly, softly, his roughened hands on my stomach, mine tangling in his hair. His hands glide up to my neck, his fingers burrowing into my skin then sliding gently down the sides of my throat to my collarbones. As before, the light passes over us, but this time my stomach lifts like I'm falling through space and the sun is rising up in the west, just outside the closet window and falling down behind the house, full night cycling into sunset then midday and morning.

When the kiss ends, we stay there for a while, my heart still thundering as the sun cycles west to east again and again, a Ferris wheel of color twirling around us. An earlier version of me moves backward between the closet and the bedroom, an impossibly fast blur of brown. The sensation of being pulled backward through water works against my legs and back.

Down in the cul-de-sac, sparks of light rise off the ground, drawing together high in the sky to form a blossom of colorful fire—*fireworks.*

We've reached the fourth of July, and when all the fireworks have been undone, full night swallows us again. Our breath the only sound in the dark, his hands on mine the only thing grounding me.

"Show me how to do that," I whisper.

He looks out the window. "I think you *are* doing that."

He kisses me again, lifting me up against the door, and the world speeds forward once more. This time when it reaches the age of crumbling walls and reaching vines, I try to hold it there around us. I try to hold *us* there, at the end of the world.

"A long time ago, there was a drought," I tell Beau. We're lying in the closet on our sides, his arm draped over my waist, hand resting on the back of my thigh. "And all the water dried up, every creek and stream, every river and lake, and the ocean surrounding America.

"The people became hungry and thirsty, so they wandered the world, looking for anything they could eat or drink. But when they found dead fish and animals where the water had been, they became angry. They blamed the animals for the drought, and they began to hack at their dead bodies, pulling them into pieces and flinging them around in their rage.

"This went on for some time, until a strong wind passed over them, and the people froze and looked up. They saw a man, carried by the wind, coming down to them. When he touched the earth, he spoke. 'You've acted as fools,' he told them. 'You've abused me and each other and all that I created for you to enjoy and care for.'

"Then the man held out a leaf, and four drops of water fell from it to the earth. The water spread out from there, covering all the land in a flood. The man then chose several people to follow him up a mountain, and as the water continued to rise, the man spoke to the mountain and made it rise too, carrying the people to safety.

"They stayed on the mountain for four days before the floods retreated, leaving all the earth green again where it had gone dry. The man led the people back down from the mountain and they saw that the people who had stayed below the water had not drowned, but had been reborn as fish and alligators and other animals, so great in number that the empty earth was filled again.

"In this way the man remade the world, righting every wrong."

"The end?" Beau says, running his hand down my side.

"Or the beginning," I say, "depending on how you look at it. That's what Grandmother used to say, anyway."

He turns onto his back and I lay my head on his shoulder, resting my hand on his chest and feeling every breath pass through his lungs. "I'll help you any way I can," he says. "Finding her before you go, I mean."

Right now the thought of leaving makes me want to dig my hands into Beau and freeze time around us. I turn to burrow into his T-shirt and breathe him in.

"I would've drowned in that flood," he says, and I sit up abruptly.

"What are you talking about?"

"In my version, Kincaid's not doing good," he says. "He was always happier in your version. Probably 'cause he's had you."

"Matt and I are over," I say. "Regardless of this . . . you."

A faint smile crosses his face, but it quickly fades back into a serious, thoughtful look as his fingers skim down my arm. "He wouldn't do this to me."

"You don't know what he'd do," I say. "You don't know the same Matt I know." After what happened at his party, I'm not sure I do either.

"And you don't know the one I'm friends with," he says.

"Exactly. They're two different people," I say. "You don't need to feel bad about this."

He gives a humorless laugh and shakes his head. "It wouldn't matter," he says. "If we were in the same world, the one where Kincaid was in love with you, I'd still be here. If you wanted me, I'd be here."

"Why?" I ask.

He hides a grin and runs his thumb over my lips. "I'm not sure the world and me are as complicated as you think, Natalie. I didn't mean to choose you or anything. I just know if I only get to build one porch in my life, I'd like it to be yours, and if there's one person I never have to hurt or disappoint, I'd want that to be you too."

I grab the sides of his face and kiss him again, slowly, deeply, his hands coming around me and lifting me over and on top of him. I fold over him to whisper, "I would still want you here too. In every version of the world, I would."

Beau tightens his arms around me and kisses the top of my head. "Tell me one more and then I'll go."

"You don't have to leave," I say. "You could just disappear if someone came in."

"And then I'd wind up in someone else's closet," he points out. "The first time I threw rocks at your window, an old man came outside, screaming about calling the cops."

"Then you could stay in my version and just climb out the window."

He looks down at me, smoothing the hair away from my face. "I'll stay as long as you want me to."

Forever, I think. This moment, forever. I'm self-aware enough, if only barely, to know that I've always had a hard time focusing on the present. I mean, for months leading up to Megan leaving all I could think about was the time we spent together and how it was going to feel to be without her. Once,

Dad caught me crying about it when he brought a stack of laundry into my room. At first he apologized and turned to go, but then I assume the haloed Little Mom on his shoulder told him to stay and comfort me. When I told him why I was upset, that I already missed Megan even though she hadn't gone, he fought a smile, cleared his throat, and said, "You've gotta enjoy the moment, sugar cube. You'll miss your whole life looking forward and backward if you're not careful."

People say that kind of thing all the time, and I believe them. The problem is I can't stop it. I can't make my brain forget the past, or my heart disregard what might come in the future.

But right now, sitting on the floor with Beau, I don't want to retreat to the past or fast-forward to the future. I don't want to be alone so I can think or try to figure out how things between us will end before I ever let them start. Time stands oddly still, is maybe absent altogether, when I'm with Beau, like there really is only this moment and nothing else. I wonder if he has this calming effect on everyone or if it's possible that out of all the people in the world, in two different universes, Beau and I are uniquely equipped to fit together.

I don't believe in love at first sight but maybe this is as close as it gets: seeing someone, a person you have no business loving, on a football field one night and thinking, *I want you to be mine and I want to be yours*. Lying on a closet floor with someone and thinking, *I shouldn't know you but I do*. Recognizing someone as a part of you before they've even become that person in your life, and knowing, without a doubt, that neither of you will ever be who are you in this exact moment ever again and believing, against all odds, you will continue to belong to one another despite that.

I don't love Beau yet, I don't think. But being with him feels like a better version of being alone, and in that way, I think we are each other's.

I look up at the ceiling and wait for another story to come to me, feeling the threads pass through my mind like the light of knowledge Grandmother Spider wove through the first humans.

"What do you think it all means?" Beau murmurs against my ear. "All those stories she told you."

"I don't know. Maybe she just didn't want them to be lost."

But as I say it, I remember what she said the last time I saw her, how she gripped my hands and said, *It's all in the stories. Everything. The truth. The whole world, Natalie. That girl jumped through the hole, not knowing what would happen, and the whole world got born.*

"Before the flood, there were the Yamasee," I tell him. "The world had gotten so dark and violent that no one could survive without fighting back. And the Yamasee's hearts were broken, because they didn't want to kill to live. They couldn't justify it. So when the water started to rise, rather than wasting their time fighting, they walked deep into the flood, singing as they went. And that was how they were lost."

17

I wake up in the closet and Beau's gone, his sweatshirt still draped over me and the windowpane slid shut but unlocked, catching drops of rain and purring with distant thunder. For a while, I just stare up at the ceiling, wondering if last night was only a dream.

If Beau is a dream. If Grandmother was a dream.

I sit up and a tiny white flower falls out of my hair. I pick it up, twirling it between two fingers: one of the blossoms that will someday grow in my wall, years and years and years from now. Holding it, I feel Beau's mouth against mine, a simultaneous flush of heat and a rush of confusing guilt.

It's not just Rachel, though that's definitely part of it. Beau has a whole other world he's cheating on with me. Another Matt Kincaid who's his best friend. Another Rachel Hanson, who's his Not-Girlfriend-but-Something. Another Union, where I don't exist.

That's when I remember it's Thursday.

I jump up and run into my room, nearly tripping over Gus, who moved to sleep against the closet door in the middle of the night. I catch myself and step over him, then throw on jean cut-offs and a tank top and lunge for my phone to check the time.

Eight-thirty. With the Jeep in the shop, Jack's carpooling with teammates, but I'd still meant to call Alice as early as possible to beg her to come get me for our meeting. I scroll through my phone until I find her name, but the call won't go through, and when I look up I see why: Gus is gone, the walls are covered in pale pink floral wallpaper, and a single bed sits in the far corner, its tan quilts neatly folded. *Oh God. No, no, no.*

I'm in someone else's room. I take a deep breath, poke my head into the hallway, and check that the coast is clear before running toward the stairs. I open and close my eyes, hard, like I used to do when I realized I was having a nightmare and wanted to wake up. I spin around the corner and fly down the steps.

Thank Grandmother. I'm back in my world. Coco's standing in the foyer, front door open, and I draw up short when I see Matt on the porch. "Hi," he says tentatively over her shoulder.

Coco turns back to me and mouths *sorry*. "I was just about to come see if you were up yet," she says aloud, glancing back and forth between us. "I'm going to go eat breakfast," she stammers, then slips down the hall toward the kitchen.

"What are you doing here?" I ask, guilt twisting my insides. This Matt doesn't know Beau, I remind myself, but part of my mind is still reasoning that I've just stayed up all night making out with my ex-boyfriend's best friend, and thinking that Matt is better off in the version of Union where he didn't waste all his energy on me.

He runs a hand up the back of his neck and over his sandy hair. "I'm not sleeping," he says, and it shows in his red-rimmed eyes and rumpled clothes, the tang of beer on his breath. "I can't think straight. I needed to see you."

"I'm late." I look over to where the Jeep's usually parked and groan at the realization of what I'm about to do. "Fine, you need to see me? I need a ride to NKU. You can take me."

"Okay," he says eagerly. "Sure."

"This doesn't mean we're friends again."

"That's fine."

"I probably won't even speak to you."

"That'll give me a chance to talk, for once," he says, smiling meekly. It's the kind of joke that would've made me laugh a few weeks ago. Right now it just makes me feel sad and empty. I want Matt to be happy. I want him to be happy somewhere else, because I want to be happy too, and right now, seeing him doesn't bring back memories of our years of friendship. It only brings back memories of one night.

Matt leads the way to his car and opens the passenger door for me. "You look beautiful, Nat."

"I don't care," I tell him.

We drive in silence, and I can feel his anguish filling up the air like a cloud of hornets, which only irritates me more. "I was really drunk, you know," he says finally.

"If that's how you act when you're drunk, you shouldn't drink," I say.

"You're right," he says. "I'm not going to anymore."

"Oh, really? Because you sort of smell like you spilled a keg on yourself five minutes ago."

"Last night was rough," he admits sharply. "But that was the last time. I'm done with that."

"You haven't even started college yet."

"So?" he says. "I mean it."

I don't argue, but I don't believe him either. A part of me wonders if he's still drunk right now, whether I should really be in the car with him while his eyes look like that and his clothes smell like that.

I think about the Other Matt Kincaid as we drive, the one who's best friends with Beau, a slow-talking, whiskey-drinking Super Senior. I can't imagine it, but then again it outwardly makes more sense than the idea of *me* with Beau.

Beau and Rachel. *That* makes sense, but the thought drives me crazy.

"What are you going to NKU for anyway?" Matt asks as we're getting off the exit.

"Counseling," I tell him.

His eyebrows flick up. "Is everything okay?"

"Not really, no."

"Do you want to talk about it?" he says.

"No." The silence swells between us, unspoken words burbling up under my chest until I feel like I'm going to burst if I don't say them. "You really hurt me, Matt."

"I was a jerk."

"You were supposed to be better than that."

"Believe me," he says. "I thought so too."

As soon as he pulls into the parking lot, I jump out of the car even though we're still on the opposite side of campus from Alice's office and it's pouring rain. I can't sit next to him any longer. Everything Beau said itches under my skin. Beau is under my skin, and Matt doesn't even know he exists. As I march toward the building, Matt drives alongside me, rolling the window down. "How will you get home?" he asks, clearly worried, and I look up, wiping raindrops free from my lashes.

"I'll figure it out," I tell him. "Please leave, Matt."

He opens and closes his mouth a few times, like he's trying to supply his tongue with words. "You know, this isn't all my fault," he says, anger ebbing into his voice.

"What isn't? You forcing yourself on me and then hooking up with a girl who used to be one of my best friends?"

"God, Natalie," he snaps. "I made a mistake. You don't need to keep rubbing my nose in it like I'm a dog who pissed on the carpet."

"I'm sorry if I can't forget about something like that in the course of a few days, Matt," I shout back. "You *scared* me—don't you get that? I didn't feel safe. I thought you were going to . . ." I trail off, unable to even say it aloud.

Matt scoffs, cheeks turning livid. "Just say it, Natalie," he almost screams. "That's what you really think of me. You think I would *rape* you."

"I didn't say that," I say, shaking badly now.

"You might as well have."

"I was *scared*," I answer. "I told you to stop, and you didn't listen. You'd never acted like that before. What was I supposed to think?"

"Sometimes," he says, shaking his head at the steering

wheel, "I can't even believe what a raging bitch you can be."

My mouth falls open, the retorts I'd prepared slipping from my mind, leaving me empty and trembling. "Don't ever talk to me again," I say. "Don't call me. Don't come to my house. We're done, Matt."

"No problem," he spits. He rolls up his window and speeds off.

I close my eyes, letting the rain soak me through, and my stomach floats upward within me, the sensation that lets me know the world's changing around me. When I open my eyes again, the buildings are gone, replaced by rolling hills and thick thriving woods that shimmer and shake in the rain, but I set off toward where Alice's building should be anyway.

With the buildings gone, it's like Matt doesn't exist. Like no one exists and so nothing bad can happen. The whole world feels safer and more tender, but I can't stop crying and shaking.

I just need to keep going. Don't think about Matt. Don't think about the countdown or even about Beau. I'm getting closer to understanding everything. The whole world, and my place in letting it be born. If I just keep going, everything and everyone will be okay.

With a jerk in my center, Alice's building pops back into view. I go inside, climb the stairs, and wind down the hallway to her office. "Cancel the rest of your appointments today," I say when she and Dr. Wolfgang, the hypnotherapist, look up from her untamed desk.

"No can do," she says, turning the page in her notebook. "It's your responsibility to get here on time, and if you can't manage that—"

"I know who the Others are."

Alice pales. "Dr. Wolfgang, I think we're going to have to reschedule."

"Alternate realities occupying the same physical space," Alice says, drumming her fingers on her mouth. "I've never seen concrete evidence before, but it makes sense." She scribbles in her notebook, stops writing for a moment, and starts drawing tight circles with her pen as she *hmmm*s.

"Hmm?" I say.

"So, say your Closing comes in three months," Alice says. "Maybe you only have three more months before you're shut out of these alternate realities, which are sort of like lunar eclipses. Multiple worlds overlapping, but it's temporary."

"Okay." I already feel panic coursing through my veins at the thought of being shut out of Beau's world.

"In that case," Alice continues, "it's possible Grandmother wants you to do something in the *other* world. Maybe that's what the time limit's for."

"Maybe," I agree. "There's only one way to know for sure, though. I have to find her."

"And your friend—Beau—has he ever encountered her?"

I shake my head. "No, but he says he'll help me find her."

"You think he can?" she asks, one dark eyebrow arching.

"I don't know. But he has a lot better control over this. He's been going between the two worlds since he was little."

"Bring him here next time," Alice says. "We'll see what parallels we can draw between the two of you."

"I'll try," I say noncommittally. I can't imagine Beau agreeing to be cross-examined by Alice, especially not after spending his whole life thinking he was losing his mind.

"In the meantime," Alice says, "I still think we're heading in the right direction. I feel it. The key to getting Grandmother back is in your mind. Dr. Wolfgang just has to find a way to get at it. Your brain's like Alcatraz in its heyday."

"I thought it was a Walmart."

"A maximum-security Walmart," she says. "One where otherworldly visions and teenage football players are welcome, and hypnotherapists panning for trauma are most definitely not. We'll bulldoze your brain if we have to—we're getting in there."

"Speaking of getting somewhere," I say, "I need a ride home."

She glances at her watch, then throws up her hands. "Who am I kidding? I'll make time." She squeezes between her desk and her bookshelf and grabs her keys off a tray balanced precariously on a stack of papers. Suddenly she freezes and grabs my arm. "Brother Black and Brother Red," she gasps.

"What?"

"Brother Black and Brother Red—the story you recorded for me last week. Holy dear freaking Grandmother."

"Alice—*use your words.*"

"Two different versions of the same person," she breathes. "The answer was in the story."

Goose bumps prickle up along my skin beneath my still-damp clothes.

It's all in the stories. Everything. The truth. The whole world, *Natalie. That girl jumped through the hole, not knowing what would happen, and the whole* world *got born.*

18

I tell Megan everything that's happened since Beau showed up outside my house, leaving very little out. Every few words bring a new gasp from her mouth, and when I'm finished, the first thing she blurts out is "Grandmother is *so* God. Or a spirit. Or an angel. Or the missing link—ooh, an alien. No, wait, I think God."

"I don't know what she is," I say. "But she's not like us. I know that. She's something different, and she's helping me."

"So do you think it's Beau?" Megan asks. She's panting as she talks, feet audibly pounding against the treadmill in her dormitory basement. "The guy you have to save, I mean."

"I don't know," I say. "There's only one Beau. If Alice is right, if the story of Brother Black and Brother Red has something to do with all this, I'd guess I'm looking for someone there's two of."

"Oh my God," Megan gasps. "What do you think the other

me's like? That is so freaking freaky."

"Not nearly as pretty," I joke. "Probably a real bitch."

"Probably," Megan agrees. "Do you think she's at Georgetown?"

"I guess? I don't see why not."

"This sort of makes me feel like I'm going to puke."

"Could that be the torture device you're running on?"

"It's certainly not helping."

"Hey, so tell me about things there," I say.

"Intense," she says. "The girls are nice. Some like to party. Some never do anything except work out. There's a sophomore named Camila who's pretty cool, kind of moderate."

"Don't you mean horrible and hideous and nothing like me?"

"I mean, if I were speaking comparatively, yes," Megan says. "But without my soul mate standing next to her, Camila seems all right."

"I'm glad you're making friends," I say, despite the pang in my chest.

"You don't have to be," she says. "I won't feel bad if you loathe them on principle."

"Honestly, I kind of do."

"And I promise to feel the same insane, possibly unhealthy jealousy when you go to Brown and all your friends are genius history buffs with gender-ambiguous names like Kai and Fern and The Letter Q."

"Does it make you feel better to know that Kai's legal name is Jamantha?"

"I would pay the Universe and Grandmother big money if they could put a new friend in your path named Jamantha."

"I would pay them big bucks to be at Georgetown with you."

Megan sighs. "Listen, I'm not saying this to put any pressure on you, but you know there's always transferring. If you don't like Brown or I don't like Georgetown, no problem, we're back together."

"I know," I say, and I almost hope that's what happens. I'm honestly more worried that I *will* love Brown, that Megan *will* fit Georgetown like fuzzy lime-green socks on a pair of cold feet, that we'll go off down our separate paths, loving our lives but getting further apart with every new turn. "Kentucky's beautiful tonight," I tell her, staring down past my porch to the houses across the street. The setting sun casts deep shadows along the surrounding foliage, painting everything in streaks of yellow and blue. It's raining, but in a mist so light it's barely palpable.

"Kentucky is always beautiful," Megan says.

My heart aches, an internal acknowledgment that what she said is true.

You belong here more than anyone I've met, Beau said.

Three months, Grandmother said.

"Anyway, you know what I'm going to ask next," Megan says.

"I do."

"How was kissing him?" she says. "No Cheetos breath, I hope."

"He tasted like cheap beer and he smelled like football practice, and somehow it was perfect."

Mom and I are in the car, talking and laughing as we drive down a winding country road that meanders through the woods. It's bright outside, the sky a pale blue, completely absent of clouds, and sunlight sparkles over the creek that runs along the right side of the narrow road.

The dark orb appears overhead, an inky blemish blotting out the sun, but Mom doesn't see it. She keeps driving, talking, laughing. She doesn't hear me start to scream. She's waving her hand to emphasize what she's saying, and suddenly the darkness shoots upward like a tower made of oil. It arcs over itself and pounds the side of the car.

Mom starts screaming now too, and all of a sudden it's night. The car spins off the road, plummeting down into a ditch like a falling star, the side of the car wrapped around a gnarled old tree trunk. Thunder crackles in the sky and rain pours down on us. The car begins to fill, not with rain but with blood.

"Mom? Mom, are you okay?" I plead.

She's staring, dazed, at the steering wheel. I grab her hand and search her for cuts, her arms, her head, her neck. I find none, and none on me either, yet the car is still flooding with blood.

The world had gotten so dark and violent that no one could survive without fighting back, I hear Grandmother say in my mind. *And the Yamasee's hearts were broken, because they didn't want to kill to live. They couldn't justify it. So when the water started to rise, rather than wasting their time fighting, they walked deep into the flood, singing as they went. And that was how they were lost.*

I start to sing, but my voice trembles with tears of terror. The blood rises higher, up my neck, toward my chin, and my singing breaks into a shriek.

"Natalie," someone is saying, and it occurs to me now that I'm dreaming. That the voice is coming from beyond. *"Natalie."*

I close then open my eyes as hard as I can. My vision swims then adjusts as I sit upright in bed.

"Honey, you were having a dream," Dad says, kneeling beside me. "It was just a dream."

I'm still gasping for breath, tears streaming down my face, and I throw my arms around Dad's neck, waiting for the pounding in my chest to subside.

"Shh," he says, stroking my hair. "It's okay, honey."

"Did I wake you up?" I ask tearfully.

He sits back on his heels. "Actually, no. I got a call from Raymond Kincaid. Their mare's in labor. I thought I'd see if you wanted to go over to the farm with me."

I glance around the dark room, eyes darting to the rocking chair, then turn on the lamp. "What time is it?"

" 'Bout two," Dad says.

I barely slept last night, and I know I need the rest, but there's no chance I'm going to fall back to sleep now, not without Grandmother here.

"Matthew's not home," he volunteers, anticipating my concern.

"You asked?" I whisper.

"Wanted to make sure Raymond wasn't on his own tonight, in case it took me a while to get over there," Dad lies. "Matthew's out and Joyce is home, but you know how she gets around blood."

"Well, blood's not very *Country Home & Garden*," I say, and Dad's head tilts. "Never mind. I'll get dressed."

I grab socks, boots, and a sweatshirt from my closet and meet Dad on the porch. He's smoking a cigarette, which I haven't seen him do since I was tiny, and he stubs it against the railing before tossing it in the bushes. "Helps me wake up," he says. "Don't tell Mom."

I pantomime zipping my mouth and follow him out to his car. The air is peculiarly cool tonight, and Dad drives with the windows down. No one's out on the road, and we pull up to Matt's barn within a handful of minutes.

Dad gets his bag out of the trunk and leads the way up to the foaling stable, a special double stall a hundred yards past the main barn where the Kincaids keep the pregnant mare. The lights are on, and the door's slid back. Dad knocks lightly against the frame. "Hey, Raymond."

"Patrick," Mr. Kincaid says, standing up beside the mare, who's lying on her side. "Natalie, good to see you."

"You too," I say. It's half true. Raymond's way less awkward than Joyce, but as kind as he's always been to me, the way he used to flip out on Matt at games and practices has always made me cautious around him.

Dad moves into the warmth of the stall and crouches in the hay near the mare's back legs. Normally it's best to keep observers away when a horse is in labor—they're nervous and restless enough as it is—but horses don't respond to Dad the same way they respond to other people. "How long ago did the hooves pass through?" he asks as he puts on gloves.

"'Bout twenty minutes," Raymond says. "I called you soon as she lay down and the alarm went off. She's been struggling on her own this time."

Dad gives a gentle tug on the foal's hooves, but he doesn't have to do much. The mare is groaning and snorting against the hay, and her foal's legs are passing quickly through her. "Good girl," Dad says gently. "Good mama, good job, keep pushing."

The mare snorts again fiercely as Dad pulls on the upper portion of the foal's back legs, leaning back against the stall wall. Her sounds become more worried, sharp.

"Is she okay?" I ask from the doorway.

"Mama's fine," Dad coos. "She just wants this damn thing out, don't you?"

I come a few steps closer, torn between repulsion and amazement as the slimy, knobby bundle of fluff strains through the mare's body onto the hay. Within ten minutes, all four legs are through and the foal's head slides clear, plopping softly against the hay, bleating. "You got a nice little colt, Raymond," Dad says.

The mare is curling around herself, licking the filmy amniotic sac first from her baby's back haunch then up toward its mane, and I inch closer, steadying myself against an old support column. The foal's four legs stick out in four different directions, and it turns its head in toward its mother, nuzzling against her neck as she licks him beneath the soft glow of the lamplight. She's a horse and she knows how to love her child.

She can't help it. It wasn't a decision. No one explained her pregnancy to her, but when she sees the foal, she knows: *You are mine, and I am yours.*

"Just gonna make sure she passes the rest of the placenta," Dad says.

But the mare's licking and nuzzling has slowed. She looks exhausted, and suddenly her head drops to the ground, a low whine wheezing through her nostrils.

That's when I see the blood pooling in the hay. "Dad," I say.

"Damn," he says under his breath. "Nat, honey, go wait outside."

"Is she okay?"

His eyes flick up to mine. "Outside, baby," he says.

"Dad."

Raymond hurries back to Dad's side, kneeling in the hay.

"Now," Dad says.

I turn and leave the foaling stable, but I can still hear their voices from out here. The sound travels with the lamplight out along the grass, and I know it's just a horse, but it's also a mother, and I'm breathing fast, trembling.

I take off through the field. When I get to the edge I turn and keep walking. In the distance I can see the rental property, a trashed mobile home on a long gravel driveway. The Kincaids—my version of them—have had renters before, but none had stayed long. There'd always been something strange about the house. Everyone could feel it.

I break into a run toward it now, begging the world to change for me. "Grandmother, help me," I say as I run. I'm nearly there when my stomach drops and I hear the crackle of tires on gravel behind me. I turn to see headlights cutting toward me and run off into the grass as the truck goes chugging past, stopping in front of the house.

Only it's not quite the same house it was a minute ago. Solid glass replaces cracked windowpanes. The overgrown yard is still filled with weeds and clover, but it's cut short, the vines hacked off where they were trying to grow up the vinyl siding. Beau gets out of the truck and squints through the darkness at me. "Natalie Cleary?"

"Beau," I say.

Just then, someone practically pours out the passenger side of the truck and falls straight to the ground. In a momentary flash of panic I worry it's Beau's version of Rachel, but I quickly realize it's a man, mid-twenties though prematurely gray and beer-gutted. "Dammit, hold on a second," Beau says, walking casually to the other side of the truck and hauling the man to his feet.

He sort of mumble-slurs something as Beau pulls his arm around his shoulder and starts dragging him toward the front door. "I can walk," he protests.

"Fine," Beau says, dropping him. "Walk."

The man takes one swaggering step before collapsing on the front step. Beau lifts him back up and ushers him through the doorway. A minute later, Beau comes back out, and I cross the lawn to him, throwing myself against his chest. He wraps his arms around me tightly. "You okay?"

"I think I just saw a horse die."

He pulls back and ducks his head to look into my eyes, a smile tweaking the corner of his mouth. "Are you serious?"

"Why are you laughing?" I say, angry.

"I'm relieved."

"Relieved?"

"Hell, Natalie. You showed up at my house in the middle of the night in a panic. What was I supposed to think?"

"Sorry."

"Come inside."

I glance back to the barn on the hill beyond the cornfield.

"My dad's back there with Mr. Kincaid," I say. "I shouldn't be gone too long."

"No, not too long," he says, scooping me up in his arms. I'm still tingling with shock, but I'm laughing as he kicks the screen door open.

"If you carry me in like this, we're technically married," I tell him.

"That so?" he says, lids heavy, smile wide, as he takes me inside. "I can live with that."

He sets me down on my feet, the floorboards creaking in the dark space, and he walks me up against the wall to kiss me.

A deep snore shakes the wall. "So nice you finally got to meet my brother, Natalie Cleary," Beau says, smiling.

"Real *nahs*. I wish he weren't so uptight and formal, though. How will I ever feel comfortable here?"

"Yeah," Beau says, tightening his arms around my waist and lifting me up, squeezing a squeal and a laugh out of me. "It's sorta like living in the White House." He carries me like that, laughing, down the hall to a partially open doorway and into his tiny room, setting me down onto his single mattress on the floor and lying down beside me.

I've never seen a room that managed to be both so bare and so messy. His blue flannel sheets are rumpled, his clothes all over the floor. Crumpled water bottles spill over the trash can, and the outdated lamp sitting on the floor beside the mattress sprays yellow light across the wood laminate walls. There's one thing, though, that's completely out of place. Along the far wall there's a long smooth credenza made of bright reddish-gold walnut, its natural finish showing a slice of blond curving through the center and a darker grain on either side, thin stainless steel spindles holding it up a few inches off the floor. It looks like it was made from the most beautiful tree in a Japanese forest. It's the kind of thing that begs to be touched. Beau's eyes follow mine to the lone piece of artwork. "That actually belongs in the White House," I tell him. "During Jackie's reign, of course."

"Right, President Jackie," he says, then after a pause adds, "I made that."

"You did not."

"What, you think I couldn't make a pretty thing, Natalie Cleary?"

"I've heard you play; I know you can make pretty things," I say. "I guess I didn't expect them to be quite as pretty without a piano."

"No piano," he says. "That used to be a beat-up armoire the Kincaids threw out. I used the inside of the doors for the front." A strand of hair falls across Beau's cheek to the corner of his mouth, making me think about riding in his truck that first night we spent together, when the wind trailed his hair across his face and I wanted so badly to move it.

"I should go," I say.

He kisses me, sliding a hand down my thigh and lifting it over his hip. "You should stay."

"My dad might be waiting for me." I'm dizzy with his closeness, pulsing with warmth everywhere he touches me. I shift my leg off him, and he sits up, but I don't move.

He's silent for a long moment. "What are you doing tomorrow?"

"Nothing, why?"

"You wanna go to Derek's party with me?"

I groan as I remember the mass text invitation. "My version or yours?"

"Whichever," he says with a shrug.

"Whichever I want or whichever we can get to?"

"Either."

Thinking it over gives me a little thrill. This is a chance to meet the Others, to be around people without any of the pressure. It's a chance to practice moving between the worlds too, which might bring me closer to finding Grandmother. "Okay," I say. "Let's go. To your version." He nods, but then something occurs to me. "What if I slip? What if I can't stay in your world?"

"Then I'll come find you," he says.

"What if you can't?"

He cups the side of my neck. "I'll find you, Natalie. I promise."

Maybe it shouldn't be enough, but it is.

Beau walks me to the front door and kisses me goodbye. When I look back at the house, he's gone, the windows broken and yard overgrown. I'm slipping back and forth between the two worlds and I don't even know how. I walk back to the barn and find Dad sitting in his car, staring at the steering wheel.

"Dad?" I say, getting in across from him.

"Foal made it," he says quietly then starts the car. "Foal made it."

I touch his elbow. "I'm sorry."

"That's life," he says. "It's all right, sugar. It's all right."

We start to crackle over the driveway. I'm thinking about Grandmother and her warning, about Megan being so far away, about my blowout fight with Matt, and everything else there is to fear in the world. I can get swept away in those things, drown in them for hours, fixate on something like the death of a horse until standing up feels like climbing a volcano I know is about to erupt. "Sometimes the whole world feels like that horse to me," I say aloud. "Does that make sense? Like everyone's just groaning and screaming through the pain, hoping something better comes out."

Dad nods. "It makes sense." He reaches over and stretches an arm around my shoulders, kissing the top of my head. "I feel that too."

"The bad things get exhausting," I say. "Sometimes I just want to be somewhere else." I can't explain what I mean, but I imagine a place like outer space. Where nothing exists.

Dad's eyes soften as we pull onto the road. "Honey, you're a smart kid, and you're sensitive too. That's not a bad thing, but it is a hard thing. For you, the dark's going to feel a whole lot darker, and you won't be able to hide from it." He pauses for a second then goes on. "But I want you to listen to me. Listen good."

It sounds like something Grandmother would say.

"You don't know everything," he says softly. "Not yet you don't. And when you see those good things—and I promise you, there are so many good things—they're going to be so much brighter for you than they are for other people, just like the abyss seems deeper and bigger when you stare at it. If you stick it out, it's all going to feel worth it in the end. Every moment you live, every darkness you face, they'll all feel worth it when you're staring light in the face. Okay?"

I swallow the knot in my throat. "How do you know?"

He smiles and rustles my hair. "Because you're like me. And when you came home with us, everything changed. I saw my whole life for what it had really been, and even though I was goddam *terrified* of all the things that could happen to you, when I looked at you it was like all the bad things had been a dream, and I was finally waking up. That's how I know, sugar cube. This is only the beginning. If you want the good, you can't give up."

19

"I think it's *great* that you're going to Derek's party," Mom says from the doorway as she slips on her dangling earrings.

"Really? Great?" I say. "Have you met Derek?"

She purses her lips. "Admittedly, he's not my favorite of your friends. But I know how hard it's been for you being apart from Megan, and growing apart from Matt. You only have a couple more weeks here before vacation, and then you're pretty much off to Brown." Mom looks wistful despite her best attempts at tranquility. The summer trip always has this effect on her. It's the one time of year where everyone's happy and connected and engaged simultaneously, and that's because she carefully plans it that way. This year, with Brown looming, the trip feels different, like we're planning one last hurrah before our family splinters. "You should take advantage of that time," Mom says.

"You want me to get wasted."

"*Natalie,*" Mom says, touching her hand to her chest. "That's not what I'm saying."

"Kidding," I say.

"Will there be drinking at the party?" she says, suddenly worried.

"No," I lie, trying to keep my eyes from flicking sideways.

Mom grabs a pump of hand lotion from the bottle on the top of my desk and rubs her palms together. "If you need a ride home, you know you can call, right? I'd always rather you were safe."

"Okay, now you're *definitely* telling me to get wasted."

"I am not," Mom protests. "I just recognize that you're becoming an adult. You're going to make your own decisions, and I know you're a smart girl, but everyone makes *some* mistakes. I want you to know you've got me, no matter what. You can always count on your dad and me."

"So you want me to get pregnant, or . . . ?"

Mom crosses her arms and gives me a stern look. "Be good," she says, turning down the hallway.

Beau picks me up at nine, about an hour after Mom and Dad take off for their date night and twenty minutes after Abby's mom picks up Jack and Coco to drop all of them off at the movies. He honks from the driveway, and I run out to find him looking unbearably good in worn-out jeans and an equally aged plaid shirt.

"Ready?" he asks when I climb in.

"As I'll ever be." Truthfully, just about the second we parted ways last night I started worrying that we'd get separated again, but now that we're together that seems impossible. I feel like we're anchored together.

We drive out past the high school to the Dillhorns' fancy neighborhood of mini-mansions, with its own golf course and country club. The party's already going full force, music blaring and cars parked all the way around the circular driveway at the top of the hill. "My version or yours?" I ask Beau. I felt that sinking sensation in my stomach awhile back, but it had been so subtle I'd thought I imagined it.

He closes his eyes for a second. "Mine."

"How do you know?"

"I told you, you belong here more than anyone else," he says softly.

"You did."

"Your version of the world feels different," he says. "It feels like you."

I laugh. "When did it change?"

Beau shrugs. "They're so alike sometimes it's hard to tell."

"I guess I'm holding up my end of the deal so far," I say. "I came to your Union."

"So I shouldn't drink tonight?"

"Only beer," I say. "Beer doesn't count."

I hop out of the car, following him around the expansive lawn to the glowing blue pool and patio behind the house. The back doors are open to the kitchen, people spilling from the keg on the counter inside all down either side of the pool to the deep backyard, moths fluttering around the mounted lights, their fragile wings vibrating with the music.

Beau's hand slides around mine, and he leads the way through the crowd toward the patio furniture on the far side of the pool, where half the football team is crowded around, drinking and sharing joints, their girlfriends perched in their laps.

Beau clamps a hand on one of their shoulders, and my heart nearly stops when Matt turns around, the blond girl in his lap jumping up to let him stand. I'm doubly stunned when I recognize the blonde as Megan.

Oh my God. They're together. In a parallel universe, my best friend and my ex are together. That had to have been who Matt was at the theater with that day.

"Hey, man," Matt says, clapping Beau on the back, and I desperately fight to get my facial muscles, heart rate, and nausea under control. Seeing Matt with Rachel was one thing, but this is something else entirely.

"Wanted you to meet someone," Beau says. Matt's and Megan's eyes both wander over to me. Megan's hair is cut short, her eye makeup more generous than usual and her hoop earrings bigger, but she's undeniably the double of the Megan I've known for years. And this Matt looks identical to the one who gave me a ride to NKU a few days ago.

"Hi," I say, holding a shaky hand out to Megan first. "I'm Natalie."

I don't know what I'm expecting. Some flicker of recognition maybe, some sign that she's aware we were born to be best friends, but I don't get it, and I feel like my heart's collapsing. Megan smiles politely. "Meg."

I turn to Matt next, trying to compose myself. When our eyes meet, his soften immediately and his mouth drops open, a blush spreading rapidly up his neck as his gaze roves over me. "Hey," he says, taking my hand.

When his eyes drift back up to me, I'm stunned by what I see in them: not recognition, exactly, but something that shouldn't be there, not in *this* Matt Kincaid: softness, connection.

Beside me I'm aware of Beau's eyes dropping to the ground, and I let go of Matt's hand as fast I can. Megan's noticed Matt eye-fondling me too: She crosses her arms and lifts her eyebrows as she looks out across the yard. "Excuse me," she says. "I think I need to pee. Or take a shower. Puke. Something in the bathroom."

I want to go after her, to apologize, but at the same time I feel betrayed, no matter how illogical that is. How could Matt and Megan be together? And why isn't she at Georgetown? It shouldn't matter—they're not *my* Megan and Matt. It's hypocritical and I know it. How can I tell Beau he doesn't need to feel bad about what's going on with us when *I* feel bad about what's going on between them?

"How do you and Wilkes know each other?" Matt asks, his voice tight and awkward. This whole thing is too weird.

I open my mouth to answer, but I'm cut off by someone drunkenly shouting from across the pool.

"SCREW YOU, BEAU WILKES." I turn to find Rachel and some of the dance team girls huddled together on a couple of Derek's plastic chaise lounges, Solo cups in hand. She smiles aggressively and lifts her cup to wave at me. "Enjoy it while it lasts," she calls.

The crowd sort of *ooh*s, and Beau sets a hand on my back. "You want that beer yet?"

"Or fifteen consecutive tequila shots, whichever you find first." Beau's version of the world or not, tonight might be harder to get through than I had realized. I glance at Matt. "You want a drink too?" Beau stiffens beside me.

Matt just shakes his head. "Nah, I shouldn't."

Beau relaxes again. "Be right back, then."

I watch him slip off into the crowded kitchen, until I feel Matt's stare on me. "We've met before," he says.

"We have?"

"At the movie theater. And at some point before that, right?"

"Oh." I peel my hair off my neck and pull it over my shoulder. "That's right. I think maybe we met at a party last summer, or something."

"Huh." Matt digs his hands into his pockets and looks down at his shoes. "Are you from around here?"

"Rhode Island," I lie, as quickly as my brain allows. "I'm just here visiting family."

Matt laughs. "Rhode Island? What's in Rhode Island?"

"Brown University, for one thing."

"You go to Brown?"

"I start in the fall."

He glances over his shoulder to the kitchen, where Beau's filling a couple of cups from the keg. "Don't take this the wrong way, but you're not Wilkes's usual type."

"And what would that be?"

Matt looks back again. I follow his eyes to the girl leaning across the counter, death-glaring at Beau. "Rachel Hanson," Matt says. "Crazy girls in general."

"I wouldn't call Rachel *crazy*," I say. Matt looks confused, and I backtrack. "I mean, she doesn't strike me as crazy. It's sort of admirable how she just screams whatever she's thinking at the top of her lungs."

"Even if what she's thinking is that she'd like to shave your head?"

"That would be her mistake," I say. "I'd look great with a shaved head."

"Probably so," Matt says, blushing. The joking, the flirting, the feeling that it *means* something to be wanted by Matt Kincaid. God, this feels so familiar. But he's also different from my Matt, more relaxed. Definitely less animated or affected, though just as friendly.

I look over his shoulder into the kitchen. Rachel's gone, but Beau's been hijacked by Derek and some of the other players. He's leaned up against the pantry door, staring straight past everyone to me, and when I meet his gaze, he just barely smiles. It's such a small, quiet expression, but it lights him up, makes me flood with heat until I have to look away.

"So is he any good?" I ask Matt.

"No, he's pure evil," Matt jokes.

"I mean at football," I clarify.

"Yeah, he's good. Really good, but lazy. He could be great if he wanted."

"You don't think he wants to be great?"

"Nah, not really. I don't think he'd know how to handle it if the world found out how good he was. He can barely handle having *us* rely on him, and most of us have played together since we were ten." Matt pauses and scratches the back of his head anxiously. "It was the same way with Rachel, you know."

"Oh."

It feels like a slap in the face, and he must notice because he hurries to say, "Not as *you* and him. I mean, he was the same way with her that he is with football."

"I don't get it. What do you mean?"

"I don't know. It's hard to explain," Matt says, staring out over the pool. "They only lasted as long as they did because she kept settling for less and less. She'd cheat on him and he wouldn't even care, but every time she got in a fight with her mom or got pushed around by some other guy, he'd be there for her and they'd slip back into it."

I find myself thinking about my Matt, how many times I let things drift on because I couldn't parse out loving him from just wanting to be with him.

"When it comes down to it, Wilkes can't help himself," Matt says. "He's a martyr. A self-sabotaging martyr, actually, which in my opinion is the worst kind."

I laugh. "What a monster."

"Exactly," Matt says, smiling at the ground. "It's probably what makes him so good at the game, but it's also why he took all the blame when we both accidentally burned down my family's barn when we were thirteen. And now I'm forever in that dick's debt."

"Do you want me to trip him or something so you can catch him?"

"Would you? That'd be great." After a second he adds, "He's a good guy. Remember that . . . if he starts to push you away."

He holds my eyes, and a strange ache passes through me. This is more like the Matt I know than the Other Matt has been in weeks. This is what it would be like if we'd managed to stay friends instead of falling into a relationship. I miss him, I realize. I miss a Matt Kincaid I'll never have again. "I should go save him from the team," I say, tipping my head toward the kitchen, "before anyone *needs* anything from him."

"Yeah." Matt's voice carries a hint of regret only someone who knows him well would catch. "Definitely."

I squeeze between the Other Brian Walters and the Other Skylar Gunn and make my way inside. Beau straightens up as I approach him, setting his cup on the counter and sliding his arms around my waist to pull me in close to him. "No tequila shots?" I ask over the music.

He shakes his head.

"Who's your friend, Wilkes?" Derek shouts. "You know her name, Four?"

"You better get it before Rachel assaults her and you have to make a statement to the police," Other Luke Schwartz says.

"Four?" I stand on tiptoe so Beau can hear me.

"Football number," he says.

"That's Matt's number," I say. My birthday.

He shakes his head. "Kincaid's nineteen."

Giddiness and nostalgia flutter through me simultaneously. There's a whole world where Matt *didn't* build his life around me, didn't plan a forever with me that I couldn't give him, where no one thought we were headed down the aisle. Here's a world where I am nothing but myself, where, by coincidence or chance or fate, Beau is number four.

My birthday.

Luke and Derek are still carrying on, trying to one-up each other in their game of making me uncomfortable, completely unaware that I've seen them get pantsed, hammered, dressed in Buzz Lightyear and Woody Halloween costumes, and spanked by their parents on field trips. Beau's ignoring them completely, his eyes heavy on me.

"Let's go outside," I say.

He follows me back out to the patio. We walk along the illuminated pool and sit down at the edge, ignoring the flurry of mosquitos circling the warm surface. Rachel's left the kitchen, but she and her friends aren't out in the yard anymore either, and I feel a momentary flash of guilt that I might've chased her away, the same way seeing her and Matt together sent me running.

It occurs to me then that it wouldn't matter. Just like Beau said, if we'd all been born into the same world—if Matt and Beau were best friends and Beau and Rachel were exes— it wouldn't change anything for me. I can't undo everything that's happened between me and Matt; I can never go back to just being his friend, but I can move forward from the past I have.

"You okay?" Beau asks, bumping his shoulder into mine.

"Yeah," I say, shaking my head clear. "Hey, guess what I heard."

"What?"

"That you're really good at football."

He studies the electric blue glow of the pool, nods but doesn't answer.

"Are you going to keep playing?"

He shakes his head then tips it back to look up at the stars. "Nah."

"What—why not?"

"Where would I play, Natalie? You think the tire shop has a league?"

"Didn't anyone scout you?" I ask. He's silent for a beat. "They did, didn't they?"

He takes a deep breath, and his eyes fall down to me. "I don't wanna talk about football."

I struggle for a moment, caught between my need to understand him and my desire to clear away that look in his eyes. "Okay," I say.

He leans over to kiss me, but before he can, someone shoves him hard from behind. He drops forward into the pool, surprised shrieks rising up all around the patio as water splashes up onto legs and feet. I look back in time to see Rachel smugly storming away, and when I turn back to Beau, he's laughing in disbelief, pushing his wet hair back and wading toward me. I can't help laughing too as I grab the sides of his dripping face.

"You think that's funny, Natalie Cleary?" he says, smiling.

"I'm so sorry," I say, but I can't stop laughing. "That's awful."

"Yeah, I can tell you feel real bad."

"I do. I feel terrible."

"Me too." He slips his arms around my waist and kisses me, then pulls me off the ledge and into the heated water, my dress trying to rise around my thighs and sandals trying to swim clear of my feet.

"*Beau*," I chastise him halfheartedly. More screams erupt as Derek and Luke and Lauren Peterson jump into the pool around us. "I can't believe you did that."

"I'm *so* sorry," Beau parrots. I splash him and he grabs my arms, pins them to my sides, and kisses me, my stomach fluttering. He eases back enough to look into my eyes. "Do you forgive me?"

I'm about to answer when I see Matt over Beau's shoulder. He's standing at the edge of the patio staring at me, slack-jawed, drunk, and devastated. Not Beau's Matt.

My Matt. I'm sure of it.

"I need to talk to you," he shouts over the noise.

Everything's exactly as it was a second and ago, and yet completely different. The dance team are gathered on the chaise lounges, Rachel among them as if she never left, her hair its usual glossy brown. We're back in my world now.

Beau turns to look at Matt and must make the same realization because he doesn't say anything. He looks back to me. "I'll just be a minute," I tell him, surprising myself with my decision.

He nods once. I make my way to the steps and climb out of the pool, dripping and shivering in the slight hint of breeze. Matt takes off toward the driveway without a word, and I follow him, my face hot from embarrassment and anxiety.

The Dillhorns' floodlights are on out front, illuminating the elaborate planter-covered mound in the center of the grandiose driveway. Matt stalks halfway to the street before he turns back to me. He opens his mouth but no sound comes out, and he angrily spins away again. When he faces me again, his eyes are watery, and my chest clenches with guilt. "Why are you doing this?" he says.

I take a deep breath and try to stay calm, unemotional. "Doing what?"

He thrusts an arm out in the direction of the backyard. "Who is that guy? Why would you bring him here, when you knew I was going to be here? Why would you—" He cuts himself off and takes a few more stumbling steps down the slope toward his car.

"I thought you were going to stop drinking," I say quietly.

"I thought you loved me," he throws back.

"Really?" I shout. "Did you also think *you* loved *me*?"

"I *do* love you," he growls. "I love you, and you're ruining my life. You threw me out like trash, and I still don't even know why. Do *you* even know why? Because one day you loved me, and the next you didn't want me anymore, and you've *never* given me a straight answer why. And you know the worst part? I've *still* loved you this whole time, even though it's killing me, and then you show up here with some random guy and kiss him right in front of me."

"Matt, please," I sob, lunging for his hand. "I'm sorry. I didn't know you were going to be here, I swear. I wouldn't do that to you."

"It's my best friend's party!"

"I know, but—"

"*Stop!*" he yells, shaking me off. "You were all I wanted. You're all I've *ever* wanted, and I'm nothing to you."

I shake my head. "That's not true." The tears are breaking loose harder, faster, warping my voice worse with each syllable. "I love you, Matt. You know I love you."

"I don't know that," he says, shaking his head. He turns and heads for his car, throwing the door open.

I chase after him. "Matt, I'll leave. You shouldn't drive right now."

I almost scream when he grabs my upper arms and shoves me

against the side of the car. "Stop pretending you care what I do."

"You don't have to leave," I say, breathless, trying to touch his shoulders, to calm him, though he keeps knocking my hands away. "I'll go. I'll leave. I'm sorry."

His fingers dig in deeper, and his eyes are unfocused as he slams my back against the car door again. "How could you do this to me?" he shouts. "Tell me why you ruined us."

"Matt, please." His hands are shaking, or I'm shaking, or both, and tears blur my vision. "You're hurting me."

"Tell me *why.*" He slams me backward again. Hard, too hard. Stars swirl behind my eyelids. I'm not hurt, but I'm shocked, scared, shivering madly. His mouth is an inch from mine, and I'm terrified he might try to kiss me, when suddenly someone rips him backward into the street.

He staggers to gain his balance and moves toward Beau, who throws a punch to Matt's cheek and sends him reeling back again. Next thing I know, there's an all-out brawl in the middle of the street, and kids come running down the side of the lawn to see. *"Stop!"* I shriek, but they ignore me.

Beau has his arms locked around Matt's neck, and then he's kneeing him in the stomach. I try to haul Beau off Matt, screaming all the time. "Beau, *stop,*" I'm sobbing over and over again. Matt trips backward and lands on the ground, breathing hard as Beau advances on him. *"Beau,"* I plead.

He stops, turns to face me, and wipes the back of his hand across his mouth.

Matt scrambles up, blood dripping from his lips and the split across his check, and stumbles toward his car. The whole time he's staring at me, furious, shaking his head. He gets in his car and pulls away, his tires squealing.

I don't know how long I stand there. I don't know which version I'm in anymore. Does it even matter?

I finally turn to head back, finding Beau and a hushed crowd of my classmates watching me.

"Take me home."

Beau walks over to his truck and gets in without a word. I follow, my legs wobbling like Jell-O in an earthquake and my eyes desperately avoiding everyone staring after us as we back down the driveway.

"You didn't have to do that," I say.

"Yes, I did." His voice is low and he's driving fast, won't look at me.

"You should've stayed out of it." He laughs harshly. "I'm serious, Beau. You really hurt him."

He shakes his head. "You mean like he was gonna do to you?"

"He wouldn't have hurt me," I insist, though I'm still shaking, still seeing the unfocused, almost bloodthirsty look in Matt's eye.

"Natalie, you really don't get it, do you?"

"Get *what*?"

"Forget it," he says. Neither of us speaks for the rest of the drive, and when we pull up in front of my house, he turns the car off, and we continue to sit in silence. Finally, Beau speaks, without looking up from the steering wheel. "I may drink too much and get into fights now and then, but I would *never* hurt you, or anyone else I care about. You don't deserve that. No one does. You shouldn't be scared of someone you love, Natalie."

"I have to go." I get out of the car and run inside before he can see the tears really start to fall.

I wake up in the middle of the night again, and this time I know right away: I'm not alone. My eyes focus on the rocking chair.

Grandmother is there, but for once she's wearing different clothes: an open pink robe over a faded blue nightgown. Her skin is less wrinkled, her hair swept into a neat bun.

"Grandmother," I say, sitting up.

She seems blind, the way her eyes move across the room. "Don't be afraid, Natalie," she says, and then she's gone.

"Grandmother," I say into the night. "Grandmother."

No response. I try to think about the song Beau played in the band room that night, the feeling it gave me. I try to tune in to my own anxiety. That part's easy—there's a lump in my chest and a weight in my stomach, that indescribable feeling that something's wrong.

I hear Gus whining at the door. I get out of bed to let him into the hall, and he trots right to the stairs, thumping clumsily down to the foyer. A light from down in the kitchen reaches the fringes of the stairs, and hushed voices drift along it.

I creep down the steps and follow the hallway to the kitchen. Mom and Dad are sitting at the table across from one another, and when Mom notices me standing in the doorway I see that her eyes are red and puffy. Dad turns around and looks at me, revealing his own sunken and dark gaze. "Hey, sugar cube," he says softly.

"What's wrong?"

They exchange a look and Mom starts to cry, covering her mouth with her thin hand. Dad tips his head toward the yellow wooden chair beside him, but I can't move. My feet weigh a thousand pounds, and my heartrate's like I'm in the middle of a sprint. "Dad?" I urge, my voice little more than a squeak.

He sighs and stands, setting a hand on Mom's shoulder as her slim frame shakes with silent tears. "Honey, he's alive," Dad starts, "but Matt Kincaid's been in a car accident."

20

When we get to the hospital waiting room, everything happens at once. Joyce Kincaid grabs me in a hug and cries into my hair. Raymond shakes Dad's hand but can't say a word. But the worst thing, the hardest thing, is the drop in my stomach, the flicker in the blue chair in the corner, under the mounted TV.

The flicker during which, for a split second, I see Beau, sitting hunched over his knees, his hands pressed together and resting against his mouth, his eyes on the gray speckled floor. Sitting a few seats away from him are different versions of Joyce and Raymond, both silent. Joyce looks over at Beau, and I swear her lip curls hatefully in blame.

They don't see me, but I see them over my Joyce's shoulder as she death-grips me and sobs beside my ear.

I see them, and I know what it means. Both Matts are here.

Oh my God.

The doctor comes through the swinging gray doors. He's a young, skinny blond guy with wire-frame glasses and a too-big white jacket.

"Mr. and Mrs. Kincaid, would you come with me?" he says. His expression is grave, devastating, and he barely looks away from the wall he's chosen to focus on. Joyce breaks down further, and Mom gently rubs her back.

"Come on, Joyce," Raymond whispers as he tries to free his wife from my arms. He leads her closer to those gray doors, toward bad news, and I take a few steps after them.

"I'm sorry, Miss," the doctor says to me. "Family only."

"She can come," Joyce says. "She's Matty's girlfriend. She can come."

I don't correct her, but my whole body pinches at the mistake. The doctor nods and takes us inside. I don't catch most of his words over the noise in my brain, the two sides of me screaming two different versions of the same story.

He was drunk. He wouldn't listen. There was nothing you could do. He'll be fine.

You let him drive away. You could've called the cops. He's going to die. He's going to die twice over, and you ruined his life.

Suddenly I become aware of Joyce's escalated whimpers beside me, and I return to the sound of the doctor's falsely calm voice. ". . . induced a coma," he's saying. "We'll need to operate, and then we'll have to let the swelling go down. It's possible he'll suffer from brain damage, but we can't say how severe."

"*Possible*," Raymond repeats as he rubs Joyce's shoulders. "*Possible*, Joyce, not *absolute*."

She's shaking her head, her eyes closed tight against her tears, her ears closed off from his words, and I can't feel my legs.

Can't feel my legs, or my heart, only the hollow in my stomach.

I'm backing away, but it's like someone else is controlling my body with a remote. I don't mean to leave them, but I do. I turn. I run.

I am running away.

I'm running through the horrible gray doors back into the horrible blue-gray waiting room, where everything's different—the Other Joyce and Raymond sitting somberly in their chairs, far away from Beau, my own parents gone. I keep running.

I run out of the hospital, and then the hospital's gone. The busy intersection of two highways gone. The Steak 'n Shake, the Christmas Tree Shop, the Check-into-Cash, gone. Everything gone but the trees and rolling blue-green hills, which crash like waves under my feet, threatening to pull me under.

But they can't, I think.

As long as I keep moving, they can't pull me under.

And I run. I run hard, feeling flecks of moisture—not-quite rain—dampen my skin.

Grandmother, where are you?

I'm afraid.

Help me.

Help me.

"Please." The word tears out of me, wrenched sideways and tattered to shreds by my gasping lungs. *"PLEASE!"* I scream.

A bright white light explodes in front of me and, for a split second, I think, *she's coming for me. She'll pull me out of this. I'll leave it all behind.*

In the next instant, my feet make sense of an abrupt change in the earth's texture, from soft and malleable to stiff and flat. The sounds of hooting howls and singing crickets morph into a car laying on its horn, and the aroma of dewy night is now the stench of burning rubber. I'm in the middle of the road. There's a car just yards away from me, barreling toward me too fast to stop.

For some reason, in that moment, the only thing that occurs to me to do is to cover my eyes. I throw my forearm up to block the screaming headlights when something collides with me, throws me sideways, and the car goes speeding past.

I spin back and see Beau, standing and staring at me as he gasps for breath. The rest of the world has already vanished again, leaving us alone in a clearing in the woods. For a while, we both just stand there, breathing hard.

Finally, reality overtakes me, makes me lose my balance. "They put him in a coma," I say, my voice throttled. "He might have brain damage."

Beau doesn't budge, doesn't blink. My knees give out. I'm falling to the ground, sobbing, and Beau catches me around the middle as a wail passes through me. He roughly brushes my hair out of my face over and over again, but it doesn't matter. I can't see anything. I can't even force my eyes open.

"It's my fault," I sob, and Beau holds me tighter, pushing his forehead against mine, his hands pulling at the hair against my neck. "It's my fault."

"No," he says. "No." His mouth finds mine, hot and wet with tears, and with every kiss, it's like my pain is flooding through me to him, and there's an endless supply waiting to fill up the space.

I take a breath and open my eyes. "Why did it happen in both worlds?"

Beau shakes his head and pulls me close again.

"I can't do this." It hurts to say. It hurts to look at Beau, to want him and know I'll never look at him again without remembering what happened to Matt. "I can't do this."

Beau stares into my eyes, deep lines creasing his brows.

"I need to find Grandmother," I say. "I need your help." *I need you*.

"We'll find her."

She can fix this.

She'll tell me what to do.

I'll save him.

Two weeks until I leave.

Six weeks until the end.

She can fix this.

The nightmare plagues me all night, only this time Matt's there instead of Mom. And we aren't laughing; we're arguing, fighting, screaming at one another when the car jerks sideways, dives down into the creek. It starts to fill with blood, and I turn to find a deep gash down the center of his head. I press my hands to the wound, but the blood spills through my fingers and it burns my skin where it touches until my whole body is on fire, burning with the heat of his blood.

It's my fault.

A boom of thunder wakes me up. I sit up, sheets soaked through with sweat, and see Gus's snout hovering at eye level.

His front paws are on the bed beside me, back legs on the floor, and he's whining anxiously, shaking with each ferocious crack in the sky. I bury my face in the thick fur of his neck and try to soothe him, though I myself feel terrified.

"Sorry, Gus," I whisper, pushing him aside and getting out of bed. I dig through my drawers for some gym clothes and grab my running shoes from the closet. I dress quickly and sneak downstairs to the key dish in the kitchen, sorting through the coins and buttons and other junk for Mom's car keys. I scribble a note for her and leave it on the island then silently let myself out onto the porch. The rain and thunder have moved off by now, leaving behind a greenish tint to the sky.

I drive Mom's car to the school, parking behind the field house and staring at my phone in the cup holder for a long moment. There's something I've needed to do, and after last night, I know I can't put it off any longer. I grab my phone, scroll to Dr. Langdon's name, and press SEND before I can chicken out.

"Hello?" she answers groggily on the second ring, and I almost hang up. Despite her success, I never particularly liked Dr. Langdon. Quiet and stony faced, she never betrayed the slightest emotional reaction to anything I said, nothing like Alice.

"Hello?" she says again, and I clear my throat loudly, but not on purpose. "Who's there?"

She sighs, and I know she's about to hang up, so I blurt out, "Have you been checking the oven?"

There's a beat of silence before she coolly says, "Natalie?"

"She was right," I stammer. "Grandmother came back and she told me something was going to happen, and it did, and you really need to be careful."

Again, silence fills the line. Dr. Langdon never speaks without thinking, never reacts, always plans. "Where are you, Natalie?
Are you safe? You've made so much progress, and you musn't—"

"I'm fine," I interrupt. "You're the one who's in trouble,
and she's right. I swear she's right. So think I'm crazy if you
want, but you need to check your oven and your stove and anything else hot in your house, okay?"

"What else did your grandmother say, Natalie? Did she
tell you to do something?"

"She's not my grandmother. Check the oven," I snap and
hang up, tossing my phone hard against the passenger seat. I
get out of the car and run to the chain-link fence, pulling myself up it just as Beau and I did on the night of Matt's party.

I don't bother stretching. It's so hot and humid that my
muscles are already warm, my skin already slippery with a
sheen of sweat. I start at a jog around the asphalt track, and
quickly my mind slips into a meditative space I seldom find outside of physical work.

I count my laps—one, two, three, four—until I lose track
of distance and time entirely. There's no end. There's no point
at which I know to stop. It's an eternal run, with no beginning
point for each new lap. Soon it's as if my whole life has been this
run, and I start to feel it through my middle: a quivering veil,
like my stomach's on stage and the curtain's about to drop.

I keep running, and in my mind, I know I'm breaking right
through the veil. The world falls away. For the first time since
my Opening, the world falls away, and I know I'm the one who
made it happen. The earth is no longer flat and paved under my
feet. The damp metal bleachers, the rusty chain-link fence, the

orange and black press box and the unlit floodlights and the goalposts are all gone.

They're still here, but not *now*. They blip back into view, and I try to move myself backward again, seeking out that roller-coaster sensation in my stomach. But though I have a sense that the veil is trembling, I can't do it. I can't move time.

I stop running and bend over, hands resting on my knees, as I try to slow my breathing.

Across the field, someone's descending the bleachers: a waify blond in shorts and a T-shirt. She steps onto the track and waves but doesn't say anything. Megan. Not my Megan, but Megan all the same. She begins to make her way around the track at a steady pace, and I start running again too. We jog at opposite ends of the track, falling into sync, never gaining on one another, like two planets in orbit.

I lose track of time again, and it's only when Megan slows down and heads toward the bottom row of bleachers to sit that I resurface from the depths of my mind. The sun is peeking up, painting the sky a fiery orange.

I finish my lap at a walk and go to sit beside her, wishing she were my best friend. We sit for a while in silence, watching the sunrise. In silence, I can at least pretend I'm with my best friend.

She *is* my best friend.

"I'm sorry," I say suddenly. "About Matt."

She forces a smile but doesn't look at me. "Yeah, me too."

"He'll be okay."

"How would *you* know?"

"I guess I don't know. But I think it."

She wipes at her tears with the back of her hand. "Me

too." She's silent for a couple of minutes, and I think she's done talking and wants to be alone, but then she goes on. "I've been in love with him since I was ten."

"What?" I say, shocked. Is it possible I'd completely missed that in my Megan? When we were ten, I'd hardly given Matt a second thought, but the two of them had been friends for a couple of years already. "Seriously?"

"There's this kid we went to elementary school with, Cameron," Megan says. "He was sort of a redneck, kind of poor and usually dirty. We had this glider thing on our playground, and one day Cameron was on it. He fell off and slid across the mulch, and his pants came down. Everyone saw his butt, and no one would walk there for, like, a week. People would scream 'butt germs' when they went past it."

I stare at Megan in disbelief. I have this same memory. Exactly.

"Matt wasn't friends with Cameron, or anything, but he felt bad," she continues. "People were being so stupid about it just to make Cameron feel bad, and everyone just sort of went along with it just because. Matt was the first person to use the glider after that—I mean, other than Beau, of course, who was *born* not caring about what anyone thinks. Beau's always been popular, but he's not exactly the person people want to emulate. Not like Matt. Anyway, Derek made a big deal about Matt catching butt germs from the glider, so Matt mooned him." She breaks into an uneasy laugh and wipes at her eyes again. "It's the only time he's gotten detention, I'm pretty sure."

I remember all that, I want to say. *You and I were there too.*

You and I made fun of Cameron's butt germs, and felt guilty when Matt finally put a stop to it.

"That's when I fell in love with Matt Kincaid," Megan says quietly.

It's like a dagger in my heart. Not jealousy, at least not toward Megan. If anything, I'm jealous that she loves Matt but doesn't even know me. And I'm jealous that this Megan would tell me about things mine never has. I wonder when her feelings for him went away, if they even did, and how I didn't notice them.

Had I been hurting her, hurting both of them, for the last six years over something it turns out I'd never been sure I wanted? Or is a world without me in it really so different that Megan could have feelings for Matt in one reality and not the other?

"He's going to get through this," I say. "You guys still have centuries of mooning people together ahead of you."

She laughs into her hand, but the tears keep sliding down her cheeks. "I'm not sure that's even what he wants," she says. "He's had girlfriends the whole time we've been friends. It was just starting to seem like . . . and now . . ."

I grab her hand in mine, my Megan no matter what. "He'll have time to figure it out," I say. "And if he gets it wrong, then he'll have plenty of time to experience crushing regret as he watches you grow old with your hot professional hockey player husband."

"God, it's like you've been reading my search history," she jokes, and I feel a rush of pain at realizing how much I miss this.

"I'm super intuitive when it comes to hot guys," I say. "They're my love language."

"Well, you've got your hands full with one, that's for sure." She shakes her head. "Beau Wilkes staring wistfully at an Ivy

League girl. Who would've thought? It's tragic, really."

"How'd you know about Brown?"

"Oh, please. Beau is our resident disenchanted, uninterested, gorgeous, yet undeniably broken one-night-stander, heavily
marked by the scent of Rachel Hanson. You're news, Natalie."
She sees the look on my face, then hurries to add, "Don't get me
wrong. I love Beau. Everyone does. It's just, you seem great, and
I hope you know what you're getting into. Poor guy has enough
baggage to fill CVG Airport."

I shake my head. "I'm not getting into anything. I'm leaving for the rest of summer in a few weeks. Beau's just helping
me with something."

"Right," she says, nodding. "Helping you make out. There's
probably no better coach in the county."

I laugh and, for a second, the heaviness in my chest lifts
away. "So what kind of baggage are we talking about?" I say,
then feel a jab of guilt over my impromptu background check.

"Well, there's his mom, obviously. She's a little bit . . . out
there. And his dad left and *never* visits. I don't think he came to
a single game in five years, not even the two times they went to
State. Apparently he sends Beau liquor in the mail—I mean, the
guy's a recovering alcoholic, and he's practically begging Beau
to take his place now that he's sober. Of course all of this is
hearsay. Probably just rumors."

"I'm not so sure," I say, staring down at my feet, thinking
of Senior Night, Beau slipping into the school to get drunk by
himself and play the piano.

Megan sighs. "And then there's everything with Matt."

"Yeah," I say. "I'm sure that's hard on everyone."

Megan chews on her pinky nail and shrugs. "Yeah, but especially Beau. I mean, the Kincaids totally blame him."

"For the *accident?*" I say, stunned.

"For the drinking. They can't fathom that Matty might make his own mistakes once in a while. Anytime something goes wrong, good old Joyce is quick to point a finger at Beau. The two of them burned the barn down when they were kids, and according to Matt, it was mostly *his* fault, but Matt was afraid what his parents would do. So Beau took all the blame, and Matt had to convince them not to press charges."

"Wow," I say, vaguely thinking that the Kincaids make my parents look like the progeny of flower children and Mother Teresa. I think about the way Joyce and Raymond sat apart from Beau in the hospital the morning of the accident, only sparing glances at him to shoot him daggers. "It's going to be okay," I tell Megan. "It's all going to be okay."

"I'm glad I ran into you," Megan says. We both stand up to go, and it's the same as it's always been—the two of us, understanding one another without too many words.

"Me too."

It's true that nothing has the potential to hurt so much as loving someone, but nothing heals like it either.

"There once was a hunting party," Grandmother said. "Among this party were an old man, his daughter and her husband, and their young son. Though they set off together, it wasn't long before the hunting party was separated. The old man, the woman, and her husband went one way, while their child accidentally went the other.

"They did not notice the missing child until the sun was going down, and then there was nothing much they could do but camp. Luckily, they happened upon a cabin in a clearing, and so they decided to camp there for the night.

"They built a powerful fire and went to bed, the old man on one side of the cabin and the married couple on the other. When the fire had dwindled to sparks, a noise awoke the couple. When they listened, they determined it was a dog gnawing on a bone. Then the noise turned to a sharp rattling, and they got out of bed to find the source.

"Crossing the cabin, they found that the old man had been killed by some kind of animal, his blood pouring from his body onto the bed where he slept. They were frightened, of course, but it was the middle of the night, and there was nothing to be done. The attacking animal had vanished, and so the couple covered the old man's body, fed the fire, and went back to their bed to wait for sunrise.

"But again, when the fire went down, they heard the noise. They leapt out of bed, running toward the old man's body. This time they saw the creature that had killed him: a living Skeleton, who peered up at them before fleeing through a hole in the cabin wall. The husband and wife were terrified. They knew the creature would not willingly let them escape, so they crept back to their bed and made a plan in hushed whispers.

"They stoked the fire back to life, and then the wife said, loud enough for the Skeleton to hear from wherever he hid, 'I am so thirsty, husband. I must go down to the stream for a drink.' And so she left, and the Skeleton did not pursue her. Then the husband built the fire up further and said aloud, 'Where is my wife? Why has she been gone so long? I must go down to the stream to make sure she's all right.' And so he snuck from the cabin too, breaking into a run as soon as he was clear of it. He found his wife in the woods, and together they ran back toward their home.

"But the Skeleton returned when the fire had gone down and found his prey had vanished, and so he took off in pursuit of them, howling terribly. The couple ran fast until they reached their home, where their people were in the middle of a great celebration and feast. Hearing their kindred's cries for help, the people ran out into the woods to meet them, and the Skeleton fled.

"The next morning a group of people set out for the cabin. They found the remains of the old man's body and, in the loft, they found an old bark coffin that held a Skeleton, a man whose friends had left him unburied. To destroy the cabin and the Skeleton, they surrounded it with dry bark and fuel and lit a fire to consume it. As they stood watching the cabin burn, they saw a fox with eyes that glowed like fire flee from the house and dart into the woods.

"The end."

"You're kidding," I said. Grandmother smirked.

"You would know if I was kidding," she said. "I'm hilarious."

"Your stories are about as funny as *The Diary of Anne Frank*."

"That doesn't mean *I'm* humorless. I have a life outside of our time together, you know," she said. "I'm telling you the things you need to know. Later, if there's time, I'll tell you about the time I found a latex glove in my salad."

"No thanks," I said, subduing my gag reflex. "What even happened to the boy?"

"What do you mean? He left the story."

"So he stopped existing? Why even mention him?"

"To show you it was a good thing he went the other way."

"Okaaaaay. And that means . . . ?"

"Look, Natalie, sometimes stories only mean whatever you get from them."

"I hope this isn't supposed to be one of those times."

She surveyed me with heavy concentration. "I guess not. You got nothing, did you?"

"Sorry," I told her with a shrug.

"The nation this story comes from saw the fox as a symbol of sexual love."

"Erotic vampire fox—*now* it all makes sense."

"Listen up," Grandmother said, sharper than usual. "Some people think this story is about youth versus age. The child avoids the pain of life while the adults suffer."

"What do you think?"

"That's part of it," she said. "But it's also about the cost of love. To grow up is to love. To love is to die."

"Charming."

"Girl, if I could get up right now, I'd smack you across the head. Joke all you want, but this stuff's important."

"So what, I should be like the kid? Veer off and forget about love, live utterly selfishly?"

"No," she said. "But you should know what to expect from your life, Natalie. You feel things deeply. Growing up is going to hurt. Only you can decide if the pain is worth the love."

Grandmother taught me that eventually—whether with a thousand tiny fissures or one swift split—love will break your heart. My heart is breaking.

"So tell me about your experiences," Alice says, her eyes wide and pupils dilated. I strongly suspect she smoked pot right before we came, and I kind of wish she'd offer some to Beau, who seems roughly as comfortable as a witch in the middle of being burned at the stake. It doesn't help that things are so tense between us. Since the hospital, we can barely look at one another, barely touch one another.

He glances sideways at me then back to Alice. "Started when I was five or six."

"Okay," Alice says, leaning so far forward over her knees that I'm waiting for her to tip over and face-plant into a stack of books. "Describe that for me—the first time you can remember."

Over the next hour, Alice manages to drag just about as much information from Beau as I got in ten minutes in the closet. But she seems content, and she doesn't stop writing once, not even while she's asking questions, despite most of his answers being four words or fewer.

When she runs out of questions, she starts tapping on her mouth and doing that flip-flopping thing with her head again.

"There's something else," I say, taking the opportunity to speak. "Our friend Matt was in an accident. In both worlds. But in my version, I sort of caused it. And obviously I didn't cause the other one, but it still happened."

"Hmm." Alice draws a spiral on the page as she thinks. "So, like Brother Black and Brother Red."

"I guess," I say. "But my friend Megan—she's different in the other world. At least a little bit. In my world, she's gone off to college already, to train with her soccer team. This Megan hasn't. But she has a memory that I have too."

"Sheesh." Alice rubs at the corner of her eyebrow and blinks rapidly a few times. "This is complicated."

Beau looks over at me, and I warm under this gaze. "Yeah."

"It's still possible it's just the two of you causing the differences," Alice says. "Maybe your existence or lack thereof affects some things but not others."

"But why us?" Beau says quietly.

"That's the million-dollar question." Alice chews on the end of her pen but keeps talking. "*Why* are there two worlds, and why is it *you two* who can pass between them?"

"And where does Grandmother fit into all of this?" I add.

"Is it possible that, in Beau's world, she lives in your house?" Alice posits. "Maybe she's just a lonely old woman whose Closing never happened, and now she's spitting out advice just to have company."

"She doesn't live there," Beau says. "I've seen the family who does."

Alice scrunches up her mouth. "Didn't think so. It couldn't be that simple."

"And Grandmother knows things," I say, shaking my head. "I trust her."

The timer on Alice's phone starts to beep, informing us our session is over. She swears under her breath and flops her notebook on the desk. "You're right, Natalie. Grandmother *is* different. I'm trying to make sense of all this, but we still don't have enough information. Nothing's going to help as much as you speaking with her again."

"Alice, I only have two weeks before I leave for the rest of the summer," I say. "What if it's Matt? What if he's going to die unless I do something? Or have brain damage for the rest of his life? Or what if it's someone else, my dad or—" I can't make myself say Beau's name. I don't want to put the thought into his head that continuously gnaws at the back corner of my mind.

Three months to save him.

"I'm doing the best I can," Alice says, massaging her thin dark eyebrows. "We'll try hypnotherapy again on Thursday. In the meantime, you two need to spend as much time together as possible. Every waking second you should be bouncing back and forth between the two worlds, maybe even looking for a third you haven't accessed yet. Natalie, stay stressed."

"No problem," I say, digging the heels of my hands into my eyes.

"And keep recording your stories. As many as you can. The stories are the key."

"Okay," I say.

One story, one phrase keeps replaying in my mind. It grips my stomach mercilessly, fills me with fear.

It's about the cost of love. To grow up is to love. To love is to die.

Who is going to die?

"We should stop at the hospital," I say on our way back to Union.

Beau and I haven't been speaking. There's a heaviness between us. His eyes dart over to me, and my chest aches under his gaze, the sunlight slanting through the window across his hazel irises.

"Okay," he says.

In the hospital parking lot, it occurs to me that Beau and I are here to see two different Matts. "How should we do this?" I ask.

"Meet back here in half an hour," Beau says.

I stop walking and he does too, holding eye contact. I can't find the words to say it, but I don't want to go inside without him. The waiting room will be too cold, too bare, too scary. The world will feel too dark. The truth—that regardless of whether Matt recovers or not, Beau and I will likely never see each other again after I leave in two weeks—weighs me down. I reach out and touch his side.

He looks down to my hand then back up, slowly, and I'm sure we're about to kiss again when I manage to drag my gaze from his and say, "Thirty minutes."

He turns and walks off toward the hospital's automatic

sliding doors. Before he reaches them, both he and his truck are gone.

I talk to the man at the desk, and one of Matt's nurses takes me back to his room, where his mom is sitting beside his bed. She stands up and gives me a hug. "He'll be so happy to hear your voice," she says.

I look down at Matt's unconscious face. There are four inches of staples along his hairline, and his left eye and cheek are severely bruised. A lump of gauze is taped over his nose, from which thin plastic tubes extend and connect to machines. Joyce pulls back from me and wipes at her eyes. "His back was broken when he was thrown from the car," she says. "They won't know much more about the physical damage until he wakes up."

"Oh." It's all I can get out. The floor seems to be swinging under my feet, all the balloons and flowers and teddy bears stacked along the far wall swaying right along with it. The entire world is a Viking ship ride, and the clear blue water on either side is made up of all the things I can't get to.

"Will you stay with him while I go to the ladies' room?" Joyce says. "I didn't want to leave him alone, just in case . . ."

She trails off and I nod. "Sure."

She leaves the room and I stay where I am, fixed to the rocking floor for seconds I don't count, taking deep breaths and readying myself. Finally I go toward him, mechanically, and lower myself into the chair Joyce pulled up beside his bed.

"Hi, Matty," I whisper, taking his hand in mine. My voice sounds wrong. As wrong as his face looks. As wrong as the quiet hum and beep of the machines and pouches he's connected to. "It's me."

The silence that answers feels like a sky full of dark clouds waiting for the temperature to drop enough to let them break. When they do, tears fall instead of rain. I press my face into the back of Matt's hand. "I'm so sorry," I say.

His skin is cool against my cheek, like his heart's too busy to be bothered with circulating blood all the way to his fingertips. The first time we held hands, that night at the football game in eighth grade, I remember being surprised how cold his skin was. I'd only held Tyler Murphy's hand before and had unconsciously formed the belief that all boys' hands were warm and damp with sweat.

Matt's, though, did nothing against the cutting October wind as we huddled together on that hillside. Despite the cold, I remember thinking how I must've looked lit up from within for all our classmates to be watching us like they were. Eventually, being an extension of Matt started to feel like a cage, but that night it was an honor.

I loved Matt Kincaid, from the very beginning. I may never have felt swallowed up by that love, or surprised by it—of *course* anyone Matt loved would love him back. He's the boy who sees the best in everyone, laughs easily, forgives fast, gravitates toward the shyest person in the room, doesn't gossip or judge when the rest of us do.

That was the same person whose heart I broke, and the same person who'd sobbed to me before he drove away, and suddenly I'm so angry. With myself, with him, with the intersection where he went off the road, and the rest of the world for sitting back and letting it all happen.

"I'm so sorry." I say it over and over again, but it changes nothing, and soon my *sorry*s taste like poison, and I'm crying angry tears because *how could he do this to me?*

How could he do this to all of us?

I close my eyes against the tears, and when I open them, I see Beau sitting on the far side of the bed, his face buried in his hands, his shoulders shaking. Somehow I've slipped into the other world, and he doesn't know I'm there to see it. He thinks he's alone.

He is alone.

I am alone.

I want to go to him so badly. I want to hold him and tell him, *I understand you.*

Instead, I turn and run from the room, wiping tears off my chin and jaw.

Thirty minutes later, Beau walks out into the waiting room, where I'm sitting apart from a few of the younger football players. I can tell by the way they appraise him that we're in his world. He stops to talk to them in low, soft words I can't hear. One of the freshmen rubs at his eyes, and Beau sets a hand on his shoulder, just barely shaking his head. ". . . gonna be fine" is all I hear over the whir of the AC unit.

Beau and I find each other at the exit and walk out into the hot, sticky parking lot. His eyes are dry and determined, everything bottled back up safely inside where no one can see it. But I saw it. I see him. I wish I could hold all of him at once, but the truth is I can't even find all of my own missing parts.

He climbs into his truck without a word. "You okay?" I ask.

He just nods. I touch his hand, and his fingers slowly,

tightly close around mine.

"I'm not either," I say.

Beau comes for me in the middle of the night, as we'd planned, and I sneak out through the closet window. I jog up the cul-de-sac to where he parked his truck, and swing the passenger door open. He's wearing a white T-shirt, and I try not to notice the shape of his suntanned arms, his broad chest, in the dim glow of the cabin light. I'm wearing torn-up jean shorts, and I try not to notice the way he looks at my legs either. I fail on both counts, which leaves me feeling antsy and shaky and guilty on the drive over to the school.

Beau parks around by the back door. He gets out and nudges a big rock full of tiny fossilized trilobites and seashells away from the outer wall, then picks up the key beneath it before putting it back.

"How'd you get that?" I ask as he unlocks the door.

"The key? They gave it to me with my Nobel Peace Prize," he says. "I stole it, Natalie."

We walk down the hall to the band room as silently as possible and let ourselves inside. Beau goes over to the piano and sits, plucking a couple of keys noncommittally.

"This always works?" I ask, staring at his back.

He turns around and barely smiles. "You gonna come sit with me, Cleary?"

I laugh at the ground and cross the room, sliding onto the bench beside him. He's warm against my side and still smiling at me. It's almost enough to drown out the thought of a fluorescent-

lit hospital room humming with monitors and machines pushing oxygen through Matt's body. It feels so unfair for me to
have the thoughts and feelings I have toward Beau right now,
and I tap a key to distract myself.

"Yeah, it always works," he says, focusing on the piano.
"Before I met you, playing was the only sure way I knew how to
grab hold of your world. Football was the only way I knew how
to grab hold of mine."

"You never changed worlds while you were playing?" I ask.

He shakes his head. "Doesn't even feel like there *are* two
worlds when I'm playing. Just the one."

"That must've been a relief," I say, "when you realized
that."

"Used to be." He meets my eyes again.

"Alice thinks I won't be able to cross over anymore in a
couple of months." It comes out as little more than a whisper,
and Beau's eyes dip.

"You think she's right?"

"I don't know. I think Grandmother could help me." It's
not just that I have to save someone's life—though I do. There's
a part of me that believes Grandmother can help me stay Open,
and I actually want that."

Beau's hands start to drift over the keys, and I close my
eyes. The song is beautiful, dark and thick, slow and painful.
Like kissing Beau after I ran from the hospital.

Saying goodbye to Megan.

Watching a new life enter the earth and an old one extinguish.

Growing up, being stretched and stamped and squeezed
through life like homemade noodles cranked through a pasta

maker. As the music enfolds me, I miss dancing.

"What is this song?"

"It's you," Beau says. "But I haven't finished it."

I feel a rising up within my rib cage as I fall through time, and he stops playing. I open my eyes, and we're on top of a hill under the moonlight, a herd of snoring buffalo below us. Beau stands up, and I follow his lead. "Where are we?"

"In the past, I think."

"You brought us back here," he says.

He turns in place, and I follow his eyes to a tree partway down the hill. He starts hiking toward it, and stops with a hand on the trunk. "I wanna try something," he says, smiling crookedly. He holds his other hand out to me.

"Do you, Beau Wilkes?" I trek down to him. For some reason, here—or rather now—there's no anxiety about Matt, about losing Beau's world or finding Grandmother. Here, we exist outside of it all, and I feel calm as I rarely have in the last few years. There's nothing to escape.

Beau pulls me against his side, his arm around my back. His lips move against my temple, and my heart speeds up. "Ready?"

"Mmhm."

He closes his eyes and taps his fingers against my ribs like piano keys, and we start to move forward.

Through time, not space, like we did in my closet. The gentle sinking in my stomach, as if we're being towed upward through warm water. The sun spinning up in the east, shooting down in the west. Clouds shifting overhead, changing color and shape and density, rain falling in curtains then evaporating and condensing above us once more. The grass growing taller and taller and taller until it licks our waists, the gnarled trunk under Beau's hand moving with us.

Animals blur past us for full minutes as the sun, moon, and stars swirl around us. Sometimes people too, though we can't see their features. Wagons and cars and big yellow Bobcats clear the earth, flattening it around us, passing right through us and our tree as if we aren't there. Once the ground is solid mud, we see foundations laid, bricks stacked in the thousands, cement poured, and still the tree stays with us, completely invisible to the lives and objects moving around us like ghosts.

Suddenly I feel as if we've come up against a wall, and my mind recognizes this as *the present*, all its weight and all my fear. The spinning slows, and we see people moving around us in the band room, but too fast to notice us or our mammoth of a tree. When time finally spits us back out, we're still standing next to the tulip poplar. I tip my head back to stare up at the ceiling, which the tree spears through to keep stretching hundreds of feet into the air.

The ceiling isn't crumbling or shattered; rather, it looks like the room was built around it, the tree allowed to grow through it this whole time, pushing through tiny cracks and spreading out overhead, its massive roots digging through the industrial-grade blue carpet. I laugh and look up at Beau, whose serious face tilts back down toward me. "Reminds me of your story," he says. "The girl who fell from the sky."

"I've never seen anything so beautiful."

"You like that tree, Natalie Cleary?" he says. "It's yours."

"You're amazing."

He dips his chin toward his chest almost shyly. I'm looking at a new piece of him, another tiny fragment of Beau I get to have. I want to gather all of them up and spread them out, keep them forever. I cup the sides of his jaw and kiss his cheek. "You make me want to stay," I whisper.

His hand drops from the trunk, and the tree slips away as though it was never there. The ceiling and floor are solid again, and we're alone in the band room. "Then stay," he says, hands gently circling my waist.

"It's not that simple."

"Stay," he says again through a smile.

"*Beau.*"

"Natalie."

To be yourself will cause you to be exiled by many, Grandmother used to say. *To comply with others' wants, though, will cause you to be exiled from yourself. The tension is painful, but there is no choice to make, Natalie.*

That's how I feel with Beau. Like I can't be with him. Like I need to be with him. Like there's no choice to make and the answer should be clear, but it's not.

I untangle myself from his arms. "We should keep working."

"I'll wait if that's what you want," he says.

I think of life without Beau, and Beau with someone else. Both are unbearable thoughts, but I swallow a knot and grit my teeth. "It's not," I lie. "Don't wait."

23

"Oh my God!" Coco shouts, bursting into my room. "Look at this. It's all over the news."

I jolt upright in bed, heart pounding. A second ago, I'd been lost in nightmares, sure my lungs were filling up with blood, and now I can't help gulping down oxygen as Coco shoves her phone at me.

I feel my face flush, expecting to see pictures of the school speared through with a five-centuries-old tree or, worse, more bad news about Matt. Instead, a woman's portrait stares up at me with too-far-apart eyes framed by a brassy pixie cut. "Dr. Langdon?"

"Her house burned down," Coco squeals, yanking her phone back. "She left the oven on."

"Is she okay?" I ask, swallowing a lump in my throat.

"She's alive, but barely. Apparently she woke up in the

middle of the night and she didn't even smell the fire, but something was telling her to check the stove, and when she went into the kitchen the flames were all the way up to the ceiling. They got her and her *cat* out through an upstairs window! She's covered in second- and third-degree burns."

"But she's going to make it," I say. "Right?"

Coco shrugs without taking her eyes off the screen. "I can't believe your counselor's house burned down the same week your boyfriend got into a—" She drops off abruptly and claps a hand over her mouth. "Sorry. I didn't mean to say that."

"It's okay," I lie. *And Matt's not my boyfriend,* I add silently because it feels too cruel to say aloud.

"It's so crazy," Coco repeats, typing rapidly on her phone. Her crystalline eyes flutter up to me. "Why does it seem like you don't think this is that crazy?"

"I do."

"No you don't," Coco says, shaking her red-gold waves. She looks back at the hallway then lowers her voice. "Did you burn her house down or something?"

"Coco," I say sharply. "I didn't *burn* her house down. It's nothing like that, okay?"

"Then what?"

I sigh and close the bedroom door. Mom would hate it if she knew I told Coco this stuff. She'd hate it, and she wouldn't even admit that to me, because she'd be too worried about making me uncomfortable or ashamed. She's like a silverware divider with a conscience, trying to keep us all separate and safe without making the forks feel bad about not being spoons or the spoons feel worried that the forks shouldn't be so poky.

"Grandmother told me," I admit, and Coco's eyes go even wider.

"Told you . . . what, exactly?"

"She told me Dr. Langdon's house was going to burn down."

"No *way*."

I nod.

"And you're sure you didn't do it?" she says.

"What the hell, Coco!"

She holds up her hands. "I don't know—maybe you sleep-walk or something!"

"I didn't do it."

She raises one eyebrow and digs her hand into her hip. "Do you have an alibi?" She looks down at Gus and ruffles his ears. "Did you see Nat leave, Gus?"

"Actually, I was out with someone last night."

Coco claps her hands together and plops down on my bed. "Who? Derek Dillhorn?"

"Ew, no," I say. "He's not from Union."

"Has Megan met him? Did Matt know?"

"Sort of, and yes." The guilt is crushing me now, squeezing every ounce of breath from my body. "We fought that night. He saw me with Beau, and he left. I tried to get him to stay. I knew he shouldn't be driving. I *tried*."

Coco chews on her bottom lip and picks at my quilt. Then she reaches over and grabs my hand. "You know that wasn't your fault."

"I don't."

"Well, I do."

"It feels like you're wrong."

Coco rolls her eyes. "You're just like Mom and Dad. All

the *feelings* in this house could sink the *Titanic*."

"Don't be ridiculous, Coco. Nothing could sink the *Titanic*."

My car's in the shop until tonight, so Beau gets someone to cover his shift and takes me to my appointment with Alice.

"I can't keep losing shifts," Beau says on the drive over. "Now that I'm done with school, Mason needs me to get half of the rent."

"It's the last time." Alice will be furious when she finds out Beau's not joining us for our last two weeks of sessions, but I can't keep asking for every spare moment of his time.

Dr. Wolfgang is in the office again today, smoking a cigarette out the window behind Alice's desk while she listens to the recordings I gave her on Tuesday. She beckons us in, but when Beau follows me, she holds up a hand, stops the recording, and pulls out her earbuds. "Not for the hypnotherapy, Beau," she says. "You wait out in the lobby."

I look at him apologetically, then he nods and leaves.

"Sit, sit," Alice says impatiently.

An hour later, I emerge from hypnosis as though waking from a nap. I see Dr. Wolfgang looking unimpressed as usual, but Alice is smiling and nodding to herself.

"Get something?" I ask her.

"Dance," she says. "You started dancing when you were tiny, and you quit right before Grandmother disappeared, and you didn't think to mention this?"

"Should I have?" I say. "What's that got to do with anything?"

She rolls her eyes and opens the door sharply. "Thank you,

Dr. Wolfgang. Would you send Beau back in on your way out?"

Dr. Wolfgang and Alice have a quick exchange in German. When he leaves the room, she rolls her eyes again. "Miserable old man."

"I thought you guys were friends."

"He was one of my professors. He's a genius, but I hate his guts. He's old, cranky, and impossible to impress. But you should see the size of his—"

"Oh my God, please don't."

"I was going to say *memory palace*," Alice says.

"And that is . . . ?"

"It's a trick for remembering things. You build a house inside your mind. Whenever you want to store information, you focus on where you're putting it. You keep things utterly organized, so you know where to find them." She pretends to gag. "It's not how I've ever worked. It's led to some . . . disagreements while we've been interviewing you under hypnosis."

"Such as?

"He wants to follow the hallways of your little memory hut," she says. "He wants to sort carefully through every room, every drawer, every cabinet, every shelf, in order. *I* prefer to follow the trails."

"Trails?"

"Of light," she says. "I've seen them since I was a child. They're connections that my intuition shows me. Think of it like this: You mention something about your recurring nightmares. You describe them to me, and one detail sort of . . . illuminates. So say it's the orb of darkness that swallows you. That jumps out at me, like it's all lit up, and I start to follow that to everything it's connected to: the nighttime, a growing sense of dread, your Opening, feelings of powerlessness. It can be specific or vague. Either way, I wait until something else jumps out at me before I keep moving."

"And if nothing jumps out at you?"

Alice scrunches up her mouth. "Then I keep waiting until it does. That's why this takes so long. But still, it's easier than starting from the *very* beginning, wasting hours in a room full of memories about birthday parties and balloons and beets. And it worked, didn't it? I mean, minimally, but it worked."

Beau appears in the doorway. "Come in, come in," Alice says, waving him forward.

He takes a step and leans against the doorway.

"We've had a revelation," Alice says, clapping her hands. "Three days after Natalie completed the EMDR process, she quit dancing. Prior to that time, she encountered Grandmother several times a year, and she'd been dancing since shortly before her first visitation, her Opening. There could be a link between your decreased level of physical activity and your losing track of Grandmother."

"Doesn't that seem like a coincidence?" I say.

Her head wobbles. "No," she says firmly.

"And that's because a light string told you so?" I ask.

"Light *strand*, but yes. This is important. I feel it. Besides, think about it: It's a physical activity, a ritual of sorts, but there's also a sort of meditative or artistic quality to it. That's the point of ritual: When you're comfortable enough with an action, your mind is able to disengage from the actual, physical motions and focus elsewhere. When we dream or hallucinate, multiple separate parts of the brain are active. It's possible that dance, which marries physical *and* mental actions, enables you to access Grandmother's world better than simple stress or emotional fatigue would on its own."

Beau looks at me. "Like with the piano," he says.

"What's that?" Alice says.

Beau shifts his weight to his other leg. "I can move between the worlds when I play."

Alice taps her fingertips together. "Perfect. An accompanist."

"But I've never seen Grandmother while I've been dancing," I pipe up.

"Maybe not," Alice says. "But there are so many reasons this could have an effect. For one, it's possible that dancing regularly affected your sleep. After all, this phenomenon starts as a dream state. Completing the EMDR might've cleared out some of your stored, unprocessed trauma, making those heightened dream states unnecessary. But you're still having a recurring nightmare. You're still able to move between your world and a world that exists as a dream state for most of us. I still think pinpointing your trauma is the key here, but deepening your sleep might help too. We don't want to use any drugs that could augment your dream patterns or keep you from waking up when Grandmother appears, but we can naturally exhaust you as much as possible. We'll send you to the studio late at night, and when you get home you can take some melatonin to help you sleep."

"Studio?" Beau says.

"The NKU dance studio," Alice replies. She rifles feverishly through the papers on her desk. "Where the hell did I put my phone? The dance studios have pianos in them already. It's perfect, strangely so even. Two people from two different versions of the same town, with the same gift, accessed by complementary activities. It means something."

"Light strand," I say, and she points one finger at me vehemently.

"Light strand! Light web, really. Which you two will untangle as soon as possible. We'll start tonight. I'll get you a key."

"And what, you'll just sit in the corner and channel Degas?"

"I wish," she says. "But people rarely experience these kinds of visitations with spectators around. The point of this is for you two to combine your abilities, not for me to become the Berlin Wall of hypnopompic hallucinations."

I turn to give Beau an apologetic look, but he's already staring at me, concern evident along his brow. "All right. Tonight, Cleary."

Beau picks me up in the middle of the night again, parking his truck up the street like he did before. There's that same electric feeling that there always is between us when I get in the car, the same lag when he looks down at my spandex dance shorts and bare legs. During the day, the tension between us shrinks to a manageable intensity, but at night it's practically unbearable to be close to him but not touching.

The highway's deserted, and when we reach NKU, the parking lot is too, except for a green-and-tan Subaru covered in bumper stickers bearing political slogans and Rorschach inkblots that all basically resemble a person giving the peace sign. I see Alice's silhouette by the building's front doors, and she lifts her arms over her head, waving at us. Beau parks, and when we get out into the intensely hot night, I feel some relief from his magnetism.

"Hello, hello," Alice says vaguely, fumbling in her pocket. She pulls out a key ring, jiggles one key in the lock, then pulls the door open. She hands me the keys. "Now, the gold key unlocks the studios. It should work on any of them, so just choose your favorite. Be out by six A.M., and make sure you lock up."

"That's it?" I ask as she starts across the parking lot.

She holds her arms out to her sides. "That's it. Make me proud."

The building is frigid and dark, the air conditioning set so high the vents blow my hair and give me goose bumps as we make our way down the hall.

We let ourselves into the first studio we come to. The lights stutter on, illuminating gray vinyl floors, two mirrored walls, and a scraped-up wooden piano beside a rack of sound equipment. Beau walks across the room and sits down at the piano, tapping out "Happy Birthday" with one finger.

"Beautiful," I say. "A true work of art."

He smiles down at the keys and adds his other hand, picking up a slow, quivering song that deepens the chills along my neck. He drops his hands into his lap and looks up at me. "You gonna dance?"

I walk to the middle of the floor and sit down to stretch. "It's cold," I say.

"Want me to warm you up, Cleary?"

"Somehow I think that won't end with me dancing."

"No, probably not."

I stand up and meet Beau's gaze in the mirror. "This is incredibly awkward."

"Why?"

"Because I'm dancing for an audience of one. Who does that?"

"Strippers?"

"Okay, I'll just pretend I'm a stripper. That'll make this so much easier."

He nods. "Or you can picture me in my underwear."

I cover my face and laugh-groan. "I think you're going to have to close your eyes."

"Shyest stripper I ever met," he says.

"And how many strippers have you met, Beau Wilkes?"

"Not too many," he says. "A few dozen."

I groan again, walk over to stand behind him, and cover his face with my palms. I feel his mouth shift into a smile under my hands. "That better?" he asks, starting to play blind.

"I'm going to turn the light off too," I say.

"Fine."

"Fahn."

"Fahn."

"Please keep your eyes closed," I beg.

He grips my wrists lightly and pulls them down in front of him, against his stomach. I lean around his shoulder to look into his face and see his eyes scrunched closed. "Thanks," I say. He presses one of my palms to his mouth, and my whole body warms as I unwind myself from him and go to the light switch. "Keep them closed."

"You're the boss."

When he starts to play, I close my eyes and listen, trying to let all my nerves and discomfort seep out. It's easier than I would've expected—he plays so beautifully it's like the song is a piece of him that's reached outside his body to meet me, and it's drawing me out of myself too, leaving no walls standing between us. The way he plays piano makes me wish I could see him play football too. I bet he's graceful like Matt, but less subdued. I imagine he plays untamed, unfettered, un-self-conscious, the same way he plays the piano. With simultaneous tenderness and abandon, making mistakes that only serve to make those periods of perfection seem more beautiful and real, overflowing with life and possibility. He plays the piano like he's falling and, at any second, his fingers could completely miss the keys. Seeing people do the things they love has always fascinated and inspired me. Seeing Beau doing the thing he loves now actually makes me *want* to dance, to live so big my life swallows the entire world.

I start to move. It's nothing like doing jazz or pom routines with the Ryle dance team. It's like that first ballet class I took. I'm a tree growing; I'm sun warming the earth. An avalanche and a wave glancing off rock, and oil sliding through the palms of ancient hands, and in all that time, I'm also me and nothing else. I'm not my mother's straight-backed walk or my sister's beating hummingbird wings, and it's fine.

It is good. The people I love are in me, little flecks like mica in a creek bed. There are strangers in me too, with my face and hands and feet, a voice that spoke to me while I was nothing but a peanut-sized inkling in her belly; a hand that held mine as we walked down the street. This hurts, but it's good to move and be all the things I am but can't explain. It's good to let my body bear the tension instead of my mind. I try to become the music, to absorb a piece of Beau into my limbs, and soon I'm lost in the darkness of the room, the swirl of the piano keys, the sweat wetting my hairline, my neck, my armpits, my legs as I leap and roll and hinge and turn. I am muscle and sinew, crunch and push, gather and swell. I am roundness, fullness. I am smallness, a tiny important thing tearing through the Earth.

My mind wanders. I fall deeper and deeper into the song, into the dance, into my own memory. The song fades away, and still I keep moving until the last burst of energy thrusts out of me and I feel myself fade and settle like once-disrupted sand falling back asleep on the ocean floor. When all of me has finally stilled, except my overworking lungs, I look up into the mirror and see Beau behind me, standing beside the bench. He's leaning against the piano, eyes visibly soft even in the darkness. "Why'd you stop?" he says quietly.

I run a hand over my neck. It feels like it's been hours since I last spoke, and my heart is still racing. "You stopped playing."

"No, I mean, why'd you quit?"

I cross the room to the far wall, whose top half is composed of windows overlooking the campus, and lean against the barre. Beau follows, splays his hands out on the wooden post. He waits and watches. "It's hard to explain," I tell him.

He doesn't push for more, and maybe that's why, after a minute, I offer it to him. "My mom was a dancer. Not my biological mother—my *mom*," I say. "And my little sister, Coco. She's talented, wants to be in musical theater." Beau looks at me patiently and waits for me to go on. "My dad was into sports, and my brother, Jack, is on the football team. They look like our parents too. I mean, the portrait on our mantel could be an ad for the nuclear family, and then there's me standing off to the side, ten shades darker. Mom used to always tell me: It doesn't matter how things look—we're family. And we are. I know that. But I guess after Grandmother left, I admitted to myself that it wasn't *only* the way we looked that was different."

"So?" Beau says.

I sigh and try to regain traction on my thoughts, which all swam out of me while I was dancing. I feel emotionally stretched out, loose and relaxed, unable to track down my usual knots.

"So as a kid, I felt different from everyone, and the way I combatted that was to make sure no one else noticed, and that meant doing a lot of things I didn't really want to do. But after Grandmother left, everything I'd done to fit in just made me feel sick. I didn't want to be around anyone, other than Megan, because I was so self-conscious that I was pretending, and I didn't know how to stop.

"And then one night, my whole family went to one of Coco's recitals. She and this kid Michael Banks were doing a rendition of the duet from *La Sylphide*. It was beautiful. She was beautiful, completely in control and elegant. I've never danced like that in my life. Dad and Jack were practically asleep, but then I looked over at my mom and she was crying, and the way I felt right then, it was stupid, but I was jealous and hurt and I hated it. And then that night, I went home, and I started Googling Indian reservations in Alabama. I'd thought about doing it a million times before that, but I always felt guilty, like I was betraying my parents. That night I just didn't care. There was a word, something my birth mother called herself the one time she visited me, *ishki*. So I started with that. It means *mother*, in Chickasaw and Choctaw, so I had a pretty good idea she came from one of those nations."

"Did you find her?" Beau asks.

"I don't know," I whisper. "I only really looked at one reservation before I kind of freaked out. There were pictures of people from the tribe, and I guess I didn't expect that."

"Because one of them might've been your birth mom?"

I nod. "But on their home page there was this interview with a girl from the tribe who'd just gotten a teaching job at Brown, after finishing a grad program there. I clicked on it mostly just to get away from the photos, but she was talking about how Brown was such a great place to learn and meet different kinds of people, and how before she went to college she didn't really appreciate her home or her heritage, but that getting some space helped her see it differently, and now she knew she wanted to come back eventually but first she wanted to inspire young people to care about their histories and their traditions. And I want all that—to study something I love and meet people who are like me and not like me and graduate with a plan for how I'm going to make the world better. And I want to stop competing with my siblings and doing things just so people see me a certain way. And maybe someday I'll like board games and window-shopping and movies about sports teams and dance team kick-lines, but right now I just want to start over, somewhere far away where no one expects anything from me and I can just be myself. Does that make sense?"

"It makes sense," he says, "but I think you're wrong. Maybe not about all of it, but about dancing. Maybe you don't dance like your sister or your mom, but anything with eyes could tell that it's a part of you, Natalie. I've never seen you look more like yourself."

"More like myself, huh?"

A small smile pulls at his mouth. "Don't make fun of me. I'm tryin' to be serious." His lips settle into a straight line again. "You shouldn't give dancing up just 'cause you think it belongs to someone else."

I sigh. "What about you and football?"

His head tilts back in a silent laugh. "That's different."

"How?"

"Wasn't my choice."

"Beau, be honest with me. Were you scouted?"

He runs a hand down the back of his hair. "It doesn't matter."

"Why not?"

"Natalie, I only graduated high school because teachers made up my grades so I could play. You think I'm gonna go off and get a college degree?"

"I think you *could*. I also think college athletic departments are every bit as corrupt as high schools', and they'd probably make up your grades there too."

"Maybe," he says. "And in the meantime, Mason would be here, losing the house, and I'd be sitting through class, going crazy."

"Couldn't Mason work more or get a roommate or something? It's four years, Beau, and it could change your life."

"Maybe I don't wanna change my life," he snaps, and when I recoil from him, he settles against the barre again and runs a hand over his mouth then fixes his eyes on me. "I don't want all that. That's not what matters to me."

"Okay," I relent. "What *do* you want, Beau?" He stares at me for a long moment, and I start to feel shaky and full. "Beau, what is it you want?"

"A porch," he says softly. He says it like it's my name, and right then, I think, what both of us want more than anything is something we can never have. "All I really want is to build a house with a nice, big porch that gets used every day."

On Thursday morning, after a particularly unsuccessful appointment with Alice, I head over to the school to get Jack. I pull around behind the field house as practice is winding down, roll down the windows, and close my eyes while I wait. Now that the Jeep is back in working order, I'm back to dropping off and picking up Jack, and now that I'm spending the middle of the night at the dance studio with Beau, the mornings are insufferable.

Life feels too fast and bright right now, but my brain feels foggy and slow. During the day everything hurts less—I don't have the energy to worry about Grandmother, or even Matt, whose mom texts me a steady stream of Bible verses alongside pictures of *Get Well Soon* balloons, with very little actual information. But when I'm with Beau each night, the world snaps into clearer focus and I'm terrified again. Terrified and awake and a little bit on fire. I spend the whole time we're together worrying he's going to kiss me again and then, when he doesn't, feeling devastatingly disappointed.

The clash of shouts on the field draws me back to now. I open my eyes and scan the field until I see the two boys—Jack and someone else—pummeling each other on the ground while the rest of the team tries to pry them apart. I jump out of the car and sprint straight for the gate, but by the time I get there, Stephen Lehman has already pulled Jack clear of the other guy and Coach is shouting at them both, pointing off the field. "What happened?" I ask, voice tinny, as Jack stomps right past me and gets in the Jeep, slamming the door. I fling the door back open. "What the hell was that, Jack?"

His chin is smeared with mud and grass stains, but he has no visible injuries. Even so, his face is all screwed up in anger, and he doesn't look like my little brother. "Nothing," he spits, slamming the door again.

I stalk around the car and get in. "What's going on?" I say more softly. I reach over to him, but he swats my hand away, and turns toward the window.

"Don't tell Mom and Dad."

"Fine, then talk to me."

"If you tell them, I'll tell them about that guy who picks you up in the middle of the night."

"Jack, that's not . . ." I shake my head but don't go on. My phone's buzzing in my pocket, and when I slide it out I see MOM on the screen. Jack swears and drops his forehead against the window. "Your coach must've called them." Jack doesn't reply, and I answer the call.

"Is he okay?" Mom says.

I glance sidelong at Jack, face impassive and eyes unfocused. "Physically," I offer. "Yeah, he's fine."

Mom sighs, a mix of relief and blossoming concern. "Okay," she says. "Okay, well, I can't leave work right now, but Dad's going to take off early. He'll be right home." Jack's eyes flick to mine when he hears her words through the speaker, then away again miserably.

When I hang up, I stumble over an apology. "I'm sure they'll understand if you tell them what happened."

Jack says nothing, doesn't look at me. As soon as we get home, he storms inside, and I follow him up to his room, but the door's already shut, his and Coco's whispers spilling through the cracks around it. I stand with an ear pressed to the door until I hear the soft squeak that escapes when you hold tears in. Jack, definitely. There's nothing scarier than hearing someone you love cry, and the smaller the sound, the deeper it can burrow into you.

". . . . just don't want this sometimes," Jack's saying.

"Don't want what?" Coco murmurs gently.

"Don't want to *be*."

I step back from the door and lean against the wall, mind spinning and dark splotches floating across my vision.

Three months to save him.

There's nothing scarier than hearing someone you love cry, except imagining a world where that sound stops. Suddenly I can't breathe. Can't be here. There's nothing scarier than loving someone.

Beau and I sneak out to the studio every night until my next appointment with Alice, and every night's the same. We're jittery and tense on the car ride over, every inch between us thick with our heartbeats. We talk and flirt while I stretch in the center of the studio floor. Then we turn off the lights, Beau closes his eyes, and I dance. Every song is beautiful, but none is mine. I wonder if I'll ever hear that song again, or if telling Beau not to wait for me means he'll never finish writing it. Toward the end of our time in the studio he always ends up watching me while playing, but by then I also feel comfortable and relaxed. Then, once we get into the truck, the tension falls again with a renewed fervor.

Every glance across the dark cab, every moment of eye contact, of almost touching, is overwhelming. Every early morning when he drops me off and we whisper goodbye, I run back to my house, push Gus off my pillows, and collapse into bed feeling wired.

But when I sleep it's deep and dark and warm and dreamless. I only have a week and a half until we leave for our trip, and while our nights at the studio don't seem to bring me any closer to Grandmother, I covet them. Every moment with Beau drowns my fear out, but when I wake up from my late-afternoon nap, and the buzz of spending the previous night with him has faded, dread fills me to the brim.

Someone is going to die.

Someone is going to die, and here I am worrying whether Beau and Rachel are back to Whatever They Were since I told him not to wait for me and we don't see each other outside of the studio.

My Tuesday appointment with Alice goes horribly. I can't

think clearly, and Alice is irritated by my long pauses and short answers. When she asks me to talk about my relationship with Mom, and I respond after thirty seconds with "She's nice," Alice slams her notebook shut though we still have half an hour together.

"I can't work with this, Natalie."

"Work with what?" I say, at least as annoyed as she is.

"Every session, your emotions cyclone around you like tornadoes, and all you'll give me is *she's nice*. You have to really cut yourself open for counseling to work, and you won't. You're trying to kill your feelings to make life easier. You've given up. And don't get me wrong, I appreciate all the new insight you've lent to this. But if you're really so convinced Grandmother is a prophet, or deity, then you know someone's going to die soon if we don't crack this. This may be about science for me, but a girl with your already fragile psyche is going to fall to pieces when she lets someone she loves *die*."

"I do *not* have a fragile psyche."

Alice stands up and opens her office door for me. "You're shutting me out. You're too afraid."

I don't budge. "Afraid of what?"

"You want a counselor, Natalie? Is that what you need? Fine. I should've cut my schooling in half if all I was going to do was psychoanalyze teenagers, but if that's what you need, I'll be your child psychologist for sixty seconds. Here's my diagnosis: You are suffering a typical, run-of-the-mill, naval-gazing, *who-am-I* existential crisis. You were separated from your biological family at a young age, and you've had abandonment issues ever since. Though your adoptive parents are incredibly supportive and loving, and yes, as you said, *nice*, you didn't see yourself reflected in either of them as a small child. Thus you learned to look into yourself, overthink and imagine and fantasize, about your identity. Most likely you would have this natural disposition and these feelings of isolation regardless of whether you were raised by your birth parents or adoptive parents, but your obsession with self-knowledge is compacted by the assumption that your biological parents gave you up for the same reason that you don't recognize yourself in your adoptive parents: because you are missing something. So while most children form their identities out of their likes and dislikes, their interests and relationships, you spent all your time trying to develop an identity from scratch. And what foundation do you build it on? Emotions. Now the problem for highly emotional people is that feelings are unstable and unreliable. They come and go. They change swiftly. Sometimes, in certain seasons of life, they seem to be absent entirely. Not much to build on, is it? Shall I go on?"

"Alice, I—"

"The more negative interactions with others you had as a child, the more you reinforced the belief that you were missing something, and thus the more isolated and alone you felt. The more you *convinced* yourself you weren't like your peers. And in one essential way, you're not like them. Most of your classmates never worried about who they were when they were ten years old. Don't get me wrong, eventually they will—probably in six months when they're on their own for the first time. But right now most of them are just living their lives. So why aren't you? Because you have conditioned yourself to spend the vast majority of your time trying to *know* yourself. You are incapable of letting any feeling go unnamed. Your quest for self-awareness has resulted in crippling self-consciousness. You aren't able to describe your mother to me in any word other than *nice* because you are at once desperate to be seen and afraid of being seen. You are afraid of unveiling any piece of yourself you don't like or you find shameful. I can tell you, even if I *had* cut my schooling in half, I'd still be confident enough to bet money that *that* piece is made up of resentment and jealousy. You disdain yourself for feelings you believe to be unique to you, which only further encourages the thought pattern that whispers in your brain at night: *I am not good enough. I am not good, period.* Maybe even, *I'm bad. There is something in me that cannot be fixed.*"

Something's searing though me, and it's hard to breathe or even see straight. I want to tell Alice to stop, but my throat feels closed and my chest too heavy to get in the breath I need to make words. She goes on.

"No matter how many times your mother and father encourage you to feel comfortable asking questions about your origins, you still feel guilty for wanting to know, and thus refuse to search anywhere but within yourself. You seek out relationships with people you hope will reflect yourself back to you and validate the person you *think* you are, the person you don't believe your parents accurately see. When you realize that no one can fully see your soul, you become disillusioned. You become hopeless and despairing and you retreat further into yourself, believing you cannot go on living until you have a firm picture of who you are.

"It doesn't help that, for years, you had Grandmother, an entity that seemed to know everything about you, only to have her abandon you when you most needed confidence in your identity. And the worst part, for me personally, as I watch this incredibly slow-moving train wreck, is that I—a scientist—am more aware of the quintessential and unnamable thing that makes Natalie Cleary Natalie Cleary than you are. What's tragic is you're self-destructing purely by inaction even though you are a smart, strong, emotionally resilient, competent, and capable young woman who should be out conquering the world and falling wildly in love and saying *yes* to every opportunity while, might I add, helping me dismantle the patriarchy controlling the world of scholarly scientific journals by uncovering the truth about Grandmother."

I'm dizzy now and shaking, my eyes damp, but the pressure on my chest has lightened. I feel empty, like a flimsy outline. "I'm trying."

"Listen to me." Alice crosses the room and roughly takes my hand in hers. "I'm older than you and, no offense, way smarter. You're not missing something. You're not broken. Your grand identity will not be revealed to you like a bolt of lightning. It's okay to be scared. Your big feelings are powerful. But it's not okay to hide, especially when what you want more than anything is to be known. Don't shut down. Stick this out. Woman up, tell your parents what you're doing, and stay until we finish this."

I drop my face into my hands. It's hard to look at her right now. I feel transparent, horrifyingly naked and not in the comfortable way I do when I'm with Beau. It's more like I'm in a room made of mirrors and stark light. "What if I can't, Alice?" My voice comes out quivering, and I realize how afraid I really am. "What if I do everything I can and it's still not enough, and I lose Matt or Beau or Dad or Jack? What then?"

I look up at Alice. Her face has softened; she almost looks like a different person. "I don't know, kid," she says. "But the only promise you ever get is this very second, and if you leave Union now, you may never see Grandmother again. You may never again see the parallel-universe-traversing boy who's in love with you, and you may never again see whoever's about to die. And even if you're the one calling that shot, it's going to hurt like hell."

"My mom's not going to go for it," I tell Megan when she calls the next afternoon. I've just woken up after another long night at the studio and a break during which I drove Jack over to the football field in my pajamas before coming home and dropping back into bed. I'm in desperate need of a shower and sheet-washing, but I can find the energy for neither. "She's not going to let me miss this trip. She *lives* for this trip. In her mind it's a sacred family pilgrimage. The rest of the year is just filler."

"Well, she's got to come to terms with you doing your own thing eventually," she says. "The Cleary family cannot always be one big, happy, five-limbed starfish that goes everywhere and does everything together. Case in point: College. Marriage. Jobs."

"College, marriage, and jobs will come and go—in the end, only this trip will remain."

"Trust me, your mom will drown in happy tears when she finds out you willingly went to see a counselor," Megan insists.

"Plus I'm coming home for a weekend before school starts, so if you stay, we'll get to hang out. Please do it. When your mom gets home tonight, just *ask*. If for no other reason than we'll have another weekend together. And you might save someone's life. And Beau Wilkes."

"Oh, is that all?"

"I'm trying to think of something better, but that's all I've got. Hey, by the way, have you heard anything new about Matt?"

"No," I say, stomach tightening. "Joyce told me she'd call when the doctors decide when to wake him up, and every time I ask how he's doing she replies with an idiom not even Google has heard of. Like, *when the clouds part, the patient cow yields the best milk, keep praying*." We're both silent then, and I busy myself with the familiar stray threads on my quilt. "Is Alice right? Have I been hiding instead of living?"

Megan sighs softly. "I don't know, Nat. But if you were, who could blame you?"

My throat tightens, and I nod as if she can see me.

"Let's talk about something happy. Tell me about Beau or something. How are you feeling about him?"

"I'm bad at talking about my feelings. Clearly. I just got thrown out of a therapist's office."

"I'm not asking as your counselor," she says. "I'm asking as your best friend. That's basically like talking to yourself. If I were there, I'd know from looking at you, because I *do* see your soul. But we're apart, and now I'm reduced to the communication methods of the rest of the world, so you have to tell me. *Feelings*, et cetera. Short response. Go."

"Um, warm?"

She laughs. "I'm sorry. That's a good answer."

"And nothing is funnier than a good answer about your feelings!"

"No, it's really good. I'm not trying to make you feel bad. It's just—of course you'd go straight for temperature."

"Ugh, this is hard." I know what I feel, but saying it aloud feels risky, as if I'm daring the world to come at me. Like talking about a nightmare or wearing all white to a barbecue. Once you say something, it's just out there, where the Universe can use it against you. "God, I *am* a slow train wreck of inaction, or whatever she said. Alice is right."

"You're going to counseling, aren't you?" Megan says. "You're getting hypnotized and you're staying up all night dancing and you're fielding text messages from Matt's parents and you're trying to be there for Jack and I wouldn't put it past you to send a decoy on vacation so your mom can have her perfect trip while you stay home and kill yourself trying to save someone's life. Sure you're scared and you have trouble opening up, but you're not a slug, Natalie. And you're putting yourself out there with Beau. That has to count for something."

"Beau and I literally come from different worlds," I say, frustrated. "So why am I putting myself through this? I mean, on the one hand I can't even tell my best friend how I feel about him, and on the other, I can't make myself stop *going* there with him."

"Nat," Megan says, the pounding of her feet against the treadmill slowing. "We don't have to talk about this."

"He does make me feel warm," I say. "And safe. He's . . . even. I doubt I could ever shock him. And he knows about Grandmother and the two worlds, and that makes me feel un-

derstood. Like, less alone than I've ever been. Like we're somehow two parts of the same thing." That's what I've been scared
to say. That's why I'm afraid to want him, and also why I can't
make myself stop. "I don't know. He's *gentle*. He's so gentle that
I feel like crying when I think about it, and I don't really understand that but it's the truth and I don't want to lose him but I'm
going to, and somehow, even with the guilt about Matt, it's *still*
worth it to me to spend every minute I can with him."

Megan's silent for a long moment before she murmurs, "I
changed my mind."

"About what?"

"Denial," she says, "I don't want to live there after all. I
want to feel everything so much it hurts."

I take a deep breath and fumble over my words. "Did you
ever think you and Matt might . . . *you* know."

"Might what?"

"Date."

She snorts. "You mean throughout the years of him staring
at you like a desperate-to-please Labrador puppy? Yes, naturally. The biggest turn-on in the world is someone who's obsessed
with your best friend."

"I'm serious, Meg. You've really never thought you guys
might work?"

"In a group project or flag-football scenario, yes. But in
a romantic relationship, only if you died shortly after having
Matt's baby and, in my resulting psychotic break, I began to
wear your old clothes and only eat your favorite foods and continue your life *à la* Stevie Nicks's marriage to Kim Anderson,
and even in that situation I don't think I'd make it as long as

Stevie before returning to writing songs for mothers and wives rather than being a mother and wife. Hey, speaking of psychotic breaks, any reason why you're trying to set me up with your ex-boyfriend who's in a coma?"

Despite the way the word *coma* slices through me, I laugh in relief. "Sorry. I don't want to live in Denial either. I want to live in a world where you get everything you've ever wanted. And cheese fries. I want cheese fries."

"Always."

Thursday's hypnotherapy is a bust, and Alice won't speak to me when it's over. "I'm going to ask my parents tonight," I tell her as I'm leaving. "About missing the family trip."

"We'll see," she says sharply.

"I just need a little more time. It's more complicated than it seems, but I'm going to ask."

"Everything on this entire planet is complicated," Alice says coolly, and with that, I nod and leave.

I hate to prove her right, but when dinner comes and we're all peacefully sitting around the table, I start to feel like there are hands grasped around my trachea. It doesn't help when the trip comes up in conversation naturally, and Mom starts giddily describing all the pre-trip research she's done. I promised myself I was going to ask to stay home, right after dinner, but now the thought of actually doing it makes me visibly shake.

Then, halfway through the meal, Coco sets down her fork and clears her throat, immediately summoning all of our attention.

"I don't want to transfer," she announces. "I want to stay at Ryle."

Mom sets her own fork down and stares at her, mouth agape, but Dad just half shrugs and keeps eating. "If that's what you want, baby," he says. It's what he's always called Coco, but now it elicits an eye roll. Mom shoots him a *We have to talk about this before we say such things!* look, and he clears his throat exactly like Coco just did. "Any particular reason?"

She shrugs and toys with her hair. It's like watching a *Twilight Zone* version of tennis in which hereditary mannerisms are being volleyed back and forth. "I just don't."

"Coco, you've worked so hard for this," Mom says. "A performing arts school—"

"You let Natalie quit dance," Coco says, and now even Dad looks up.

"You want to quit altogether?" he says.

"No . . . I just don't want it to be my whole life, is all."

Jack officially checks out of the conversation when he starts dropping linguine noodles under the table for Gus, who's always on top of our feet while we eat. Mom sighs and runs her hands through her hair before addressing Coco again. "Well, your father and I will have to talk."

Per usual, Mom's fighting for a serene expression, though it's obvious that internally she's sobbing and wondering what anti-dance god has cursed her family.

At the end of dinner, Jack ambles off to play video games, and Coco goes to pack for a sleepover at Abby's, leaving me to help Mom and Dad carry the dishes into the kitchen. When the dishwasher's loaded, I lean against the island, send a prayer to Grandmother, and force out the words "Can I talk to you guys for a second?"

"Sure, honey," Mom says. They must think it's bad because Mom leads the way to their bedroom. The rest of the house is clean and quaint, carefully designed to look homey without being cluttered, warm without being stifling, and country without being hick, but Mom and Dad never bothered giving their own room the same attention. It's clean but not neat, the dresser covered in mail and the plaid chairs beyond the bed loaded with clean laundry. The walls are the same eggshell color they were when Mom and Dad bought the house, and the bedding, curtains, side tables, and lamps are so unintentionally mismatched that the aesthetic can't even be called "eclectic." When Mom picks up new pieces from estate sales and antique stores, the furniture being replaced typically comes up here to die. If Pier 1 Imports sponsored a production of *The Lion King*, this is where the hyenas would live.

As I follow Mom and Dad around the bed, I think about Beau's credenza, the singular bright spot in a room I *know* I'd find depressing if not for the person who lives in it. Unlike Mom, I've never happy-cried over pretty furniture, but seeing something Beau made with his hands—that wouldn't exist without him—turned me into goop. I think right then he could've told me he was the one who spread out the stars and I would have been neither surprised nor any more impressed than I already was. Thinking about that night makes my insides feel warm and mushy and a little achy all over again. It's not *why* this conversation's so important, but it is helping me go through with it. I want those three extra weeks. I want them so badly.

Mom perches on the edge of the bed and pats the blankets beside her. I sit down, and Dad eases into one of the chairs across from me.

"I've been seeing a counselor," I say.

"You have?" Mom says. "Dr. Langdon?"

"No, not Dr. Langdon. She works at NKU. I found her online, and she specializes in . . . my issues, I guess."

"How are you paying for it?" Dad says.

"It's free. I mean, it's helping Al—Dr. Chan with her research, so it's sort of a trade."

"Oh." Mom nods encouragingly. "That's great, honey. Isn't that great, Patrick?"

"It's great," Dad confirms, but his eyes are discerning, and I know he senses there's more to it than what I've said.

"We've been making real progress," I go on, "but we're not finished, and . . ." I gather my courage and push forward. "And I want to keep seeing her for as long as I can."

"Would she be open to that?" Mom says. "Long-distance sessions? Maybe video chat or something?"

"No," I say.

"Maybe she could recommend someone near Providence then."

I sigh and crack my knuckles. "Actually, I had another idea."

When I've spit it all out, at least the parts that leave out eerie warnings and alternate realities, Mom and Dad just stare blankly at me. To my surprise, Dad speaks first. "Well, sugar, sounds like you've made up your mind."

Mom looks up at him, her face frozen in something that resembles terror. She swallows audibly and tries to compose herself. "Honey, I thought you loved this trip."

"I do," I hurry to say before Mom's spirit can wilt. "And I'll be really, really sad to miss it. But this is really, really important to me. If I'm going to go to Brown, I feel like I need it."

"If?" Mom's voice cracks. "What do you mean, *if*?"

Dad clears his throat again. "You're going to Brown, Natalie. It's settled. We didn't take out a small fortune of loans for nothing."

"That's not what I meant. I just . . . There are things I need to resolve before I go. Please just trust me."

"Honey, we *do* trust you," Mom says, running her fingers frantically through her hair. "We let you go to parties, you don't have a curfew, we do our best not to pry even though it kills us not knowing where you are every second of the day because we know you're a good kid and you're smart and if you make mistakes, you'll come to us. This isn't about trusting you. It's about our family, and this trip's important to us."

"I know," I say. "It's important for me too, and I hope I'll never have to miss another one. But I'm going through some things right now—"

"You can talk to us," Mom says, shaking her head.

"I can't," I say, and Mom looks utterly crestfallen. Her eyes gloss over at the same instant they dart toward Dad's. He's just staring at me, reading me like I'm a horse, as he probably has been all summer. "It's not you guys. It's me. I'm not ready to talk to you about some things, and I need that to be okay."

Mom wipes her eyes with the heel of her hand, and Dad comes to sit beside her, pulling her against his side. "That part is okay, sugar," he says. "Just give us some time to think about it." Mom nods along, and I lean against her side.

"I do love the trip."

"Except the board games," Dad says. "You hate those."

"I never said that," I argue.

"You didn't have to. You're our kid. We've got your number."

Mom and Dad give me the okay at dinner on Monday, four days before the trip.

"Under one condition," Mom says.

"Anything."

"You have to stay with someone," Dad says. "Adults. We don't want you here all alone while we're across the country."

"We talked to Megan's parents," Mom adds. "The Phillipses are happy to have you."

"Megan's not even home," I remind them.

"Not the point," Dad says. "You need some semblance of supervision."

I don't point out that Megan's parents are the definition of "hands-off." Megan's been joking that they probably haven't even noticed she's gone yet. "Okay," I quickly agree. "I'll stay with the Phillipses. That's perfect."

"Good. We'll be back on the twenty-first," Mom says. "We'll have to make the most of our last week together."

I get up and throw my arms around them both. "Thank you so much."

"We're just happy you're taking care of yourself, honey," Mom says. "If three weeks apart can make a difference, then so be it."

"I promise you it will," I say. Three more weeks to work, three more weeks *with Beau*. As sad and strange as it will be to miss the trip, this is the best parting gift my parents could have given me. I'm going to find a way to make these three weeks stretch and last, use every second to make a memory I can hold on to. "Thank you."

Dad stands behind Mom's chair and squeezes her shoulders. "It'll be good practice for us, for while you're at Brown. Where you will be going. No matter what."

Beau comes to pick me up that night, same as always, but this time he's still covered in grease from work and his eyes are bloodshot.

"Hey," I say, climbing in beside him.

"Hey."

"You look tired."

"You look beautiful."

I turn my smile down toward my lap. "I have news."

"Yeah, what's that?"

"I'm skipping out on family vacation," I answer, meeting his eyes. "I have a few more weeks here."

"Really?" The barest hint of smile climbs up the side of his mouth, and I want to do whatever it takes to make it stay. "We gotta celebrate."

"Oh, we do?"

He nods. "However you want. It's your night."

"Anything?"

He nods. "Name it."

I glance out the window, considering asking for the moon or the stars, but tonight the small things Beau can give me are bigger and brighter than the lights in the sky. "Cereal," I announce, and Beau laughs and pushes my chin down with his thumb.

His voice lowers, softens, filling the car with heat. "You wanna come over for cereal, Natalie Cleary?"

"I do, Beau Wilkes."

We drive in silence, and when we get to Beau's house, we see his brother's Buick parked outside, headlights on and glowing across the unkempt, weed-ridden lawn. Beau leads me inside, the screen door whining, and the man I saw fall-down drunk a couple of weeks ago sits up on the dull brown couch, lifting a beer bottle into the air in greeting. "Who's this?" he says.

"Mason, this is Natalie," Beau says. "Natalie, this is my brother."

"Nice to meet you," I say.

Mason furrows his brow over his already squinty eyes. "Natalie." He nods sharply. "Why don't you go get a beer out of the fridge and come tell me what a girl like you is doing hangin' out with my brother?"

"I lost a bet," I say, following Beau straight through the living room.

"No doubt," Mason calls after us. "When you get sick of him, I'll be here."

"Left your headlights on," Beau calls back.

We don't go to the kitchen, and instead head down the unlit hall toward Beau's bedroom. He crouches in the corner between his bed and the Holy Credenza, twisting on the lamp sitting on the floor. I stand in the doorway, chest heavy, as I watch the sharp lines of muscle shift across Beau's back under his shirt. He sits back on the bed and says, "You gonna come in?"

I close the door behind me and sit beside him, staring into the browns and greens and golds of his eyes before my gaze travels down over his neck and shoulders, his chest and stomach, his legs. I look back up and he leans forward over me, his hair falling against my face, his mouth hovering over mine. Slowly, he brings his hand to my cheek. "Hey."

I cover his hand with mine. "Hey."

Beau shifts closer to me and gently tips my chin up so we're breathing into one another, our chests expanding to press against each other with each inhalation. I close my eyes, and his mouth trails down to the hollow of my throat, his tongue brushing my skin. "Beau," I barely whisper.

He lays me back against the bed and lies over me, his hand skimming down to my hip. "Beau," I say again into his mouth. His bottom lip catches my top for an instant, making him smile.

"Natalie," he whispers back.

I lift my fingers up to his neck, and he shudders under my touch. He turns his mouth into my palm and kisses it gently, and my hand slips down to curl around the collar of his T-shirt as he lowers himself until our bodies are aligned, warm against one another, our mouths barely touching. Every space between us aches. Every part of him feels warm and magnetic over me.

We're both breathing heavily, and I run my lips over his, parting them and leaving another space between our open mouths. "Say my name again," he says, faintly smiling.

"*Beau.*" He kisses me. Deeply, softly, warmly. My hands slide up his back as I lift myself closer to him.

"You feel so good," he says against my ear. I pull his belt loops closer to me, and he groans. I can't think clearly, and I'm fighting an urge to whisper that I love him. The words replay in my mind as he kisses me more fiercely, and I don't know if it's a habit from making out with Matt or if I really do love Beau Wilkes already, but I know I don't want to run. I know when I'm with him, I want to hold back all the darkness for him, like I feel he does for me.

"Natalie," Beau murmurs into my hair, his mouth moving down to burrow into my collarbone. "I want you."

A door slams shut somewhere in the house, and I sit bolt upright, my head colliding with Beau's. He swears and clutches his head.

"Oh my God, I'm so sorry," I say, clamping a hand over his. He shakes his head and looks over his shoulder to his door, through which we can hear voices. "Who is it?"

Apart from the stern lines between his eyebrows, his expression is wiped clean. "I think it's my mom."

He stands up, pulling his rumpled shirt back down over his stomach before running his hands through his hair and smoothing out his face.

"Beau!" a shrill voice calls from down the hall.

He looks over at me apologetically.

"It's fine," I say, standing and smoothing my tank top and hair. The corner of his mouth tweaks up, and he crosses toward me, pulling my hips against his. He kisses me on the mouth and then the forehead before leading me into the hallway. We step into the living room, and the woman on the far side of the couch squeals.

"Hey, baby," she says with a sloppy grin, holding her arms out for a hug. She's thin with bleached-blond curls and leathery, overly tan skin, dressed in jeans, cowgirl boots, and a tight denim jacket.

Beau looks between her and the burly, bald man standing behind her. "What're you doin' here?" he says to his mom.

She glances at Mason on the couch then back to Beau. "That any way to talk to your mama?"

"What's *he* doin' here?" Beau tips his head toward the man, who snakes an arm around Beau's mom's waist.

"Tell him, Darlene."

She holds her left hand up in front of her chest and brandishes a diamond ring. "Bill and I got back together, and—well, baby, we're married!"

Beau stares at her blankly, and Mason takes a long sip of beer, eyes fixed on the coffee table he has his feet up on. This is when Darlene notices me, leaning around Beau to get a good look at me, her lips pursed. "Hi there," she says to me, then turns to Beau. "Beau, baby, why don't you be a gentlemen and take your friend home. It's time we celebrate, as a family."

Beau stalks right past her to the front door without a word, and I hurry after him, turning back to say, hastily, "Nice to meet you all," before chasing him down the steps and to the edge of the moonlit cornfield. He has both hands twisted through his hair, and he's breathing heavily.

I touch his shoulder and he spins around. "That guy's scum," he spits. "What the hell is she thinking, gettin' back with him?"

"I'm sorry," I say helplessly.

He drags his hands down his face. "Come on. I'll take you home."

When we get back to the top of my cul-de-sac, Beau's still fuming silently. I wonder what happened between him and his mom, or him and Bill, to make him this upset. "Are you going to be okay going back there?" I say softly.

"I'm not goin' back there."

"Where are you going?"

He shrugs. "I'll sleep in my truck."

I pull his face toward me, and he nestles against the space between my neck and shoulder. "Come inside," I say. "We can sleep in my closet."

He tightens his arms around my middle. "I won't sleep if I'm layin' next to you, Natalie."

Heat spreads all through me, and my insides start vibrating again. "Then I'll stay in my room," I say. "We'll have a door between us."

"You think I'll sleep better layin' ten feet from you than I will in my truck?"

"Don't you?"

He laughs, and drags me onto his lap, his hands soft on my hips. "How tired do you feel right now?"

"Like I haven't slept for four days, and someone just stabbed a shot of adrenaline into my heart."

"That's how I feel when I'm at home, miles away, and I think about you." He brushes a few stray hairs away from my lips and kisses me. "Goodnight, Natalie."

25

"Why are you glowing?" Alice says flatly when I come into her office.

"I don't know," I reply. "Maybe because my parents agreed to let me stay until the end of the summer?"

Alice eyes me skeptically. "You're screwing the guy from the other world."

"I am *not*."

She holds her hands up in front of her. "Whatever, *making love*, I don't care. Just don't let it get in the way of everything else."

"I'm not, and it won't." I will my blush to fade as I plop down across from her.

"I wonder what would happen if you got pregnant," she says, eyes growing distant with thought.

"*Alice*, I'm not having sex with Beau."

"I'm just saying, do you think the baby would disappear after your Closing? Do you think it would be like you two? Which world would it belong in? It's actually not a bad idea . . . are you open to getting pregnant?"

"Are you open to me leaving and never coming back?"

She waves a hand dismissively. "Don't get all bent out of shape. It was just a thought. Anyway, good job buying us time. But three weeks is still not much."

"It's not," I agree. "Maybe we should get to work."

"How's the dancing going?"

I shrug. "It feels great. Sometimes we seem to travel forward or backward in time, but I haven't seen any clues that there's a third world."

"She's hiding somewhere."

"Yeah," I say, "or somewhen."

Alice's eyes dart to me. "What'd you say?"

"I just meant she could be hiding in some other *time*," I clarify. Alice stands abruptly and shoves a pile of books out of the way, grabs her purse, then heads toward the door. "Where are you going?"

"Something came up," she barks. "I'll see you Thursday for hypnotherapy, okay?"

"Alice!" I call after her.

"Thursday!"

My phone vibrates in my pocket, and I fish it out to see Joyce's name onscreen. My heart stops, but when I open the message, it's just a picture of a bundle of flowers with a little note from the coach and Mrs. Gibbons. *That's so nice!* I type back while swallowing the latest wave of anxiety. Every new message like that is just one more false alarm, one more reminder that Matt's life is hanging in the balance and I'm no closer to figuring things out.

When Beau comes to get me that night, he looks more haggard than I've ever seen him. All day I've hardly stopped replaying our time together, haven't stopped counting the seconds until we're together again, but seeing him now, after a night in the truck and a long day at work, I know these excursions are pushing him too far. He needs rest. "We should take a couple of nights off," I suggest.

"All right." He reaches across the truck to pull me into his lap, awakening an electric current under my skin.

"That's not what I mean," I say, staring down into his parted lips. He starts to kiss my neck, and my breath becomes heavy, my fingers splaying out against his chest. "Beau, you need sleep. And you're going to have to go home eventually." It's not what I want, but it's what he needs.

He sighs, sets me back down beside him, and his eyes go to the steering wheel. "I know." He runs his hand over his mouth and shakes his head. "You're right. I need to go home."

"I'll miss you," I say quietly. "Would you come to dinner here tomorrow?"

He drops his head back against the headrest and lets out a long breath.

"What?" I ask.

"Probably not a good idea. Parents don't like me."

"Mine would." I can't share everything with them, but I could share Beau. I want to.

"And what makes you think that?"

"Because I like you," I say. He laughs and his face drops, the corners of his eyes crinkling. For a moment, he looks just like a little boy. "Do you like me, Beau?" I tease, shaking his elbow.

He looks up and knots his arms behind my lower back, easing me against the seat and climbing on top of me. "What do you think?"

"It doesn't matter what I think," I say. "It matters what you think."

"I'm not good with words, Natalie."

"Try."

"You remember that night on the football field?" I nod. "I want you more now than I did then, and I didn't think that was possible."

"You like me."

"I like you," he says softly.

"You want me," I whisper.

"Everywhere," he says, "all the time."

It's the same look he gave me when I asked him what he wanted in the dance studio: serious, almost sad. I reach up to trace the lines of his face, committing each to memory. "I want you too," I tell him. "Everywhere, all the time."

His eyes dip, his arms tighten, and his voice drops into a whisper. "Natalie . . ."

"You need sleep."

"I need you."

A momentary battle rages inside my head, and then I make one of those choices that isn't *really* a choice. "Let's go inside," I say.

We hurry to get out of the car, leaving it parked on the street, and take off down the dark cul-de-sac, humidity sheening us in sweat by the time we reach the porch. I climb up first to let myself in through the open window, and then turn back. I can't see Beau in the yard below, so he must already be on the porch railing. I wait for a few seconds of silence, but he doesn't emerge over the side of the porch roof.

"Beau?" I hiss into the night, disrupting the cricket song. I listen for an answer, but none comes. After the longest minute of my life, I scramble back onto the porch roof to see what's taking so long. I lean out over the ledge and gaze down into the yard, but I find no sign of him. "Beau," I whisper again, a bit louder.

No response but the hoot of an owl.

I scurry back down to the porch railing and drop down into the yard, scanning the cul-de-sac. "Beau?" I say again, louder still. My heart is wild. Something's wrong.

He must've slipped back into his world.

I jog up the street to the curb where he left his truck, but it's gone. I spin in place, searching for any of the flickers of change that have become my norm. "Beau," I call again. *"Beau."*

I close my eyes and try to grasp at the fragments of song drifting through my mind.

I feel nothing. Hear nothing.

"There once were four ghosts," Grandmother said, "and they lived in four houses beneath the ground, each one deeper than the last.

"There was a woman from a nearby tribe, whose father had died, and she went to his grave and lay on it and wept for four days. But on the fourth day, she heard a voice from below the earth. 'Crying woman,' the voice said, 'Come downward.'

"So she jumped up and followed the voice of the ghost downward through the earth until she reached a house called Hemlock-Leaves-on-Back. She went inside and saw there an old woman in the corner, near the fire. The old woman said, 'Sit down and eat.' Then she passed the crying woman dried salmon.

"But before the crying woman could take the food, another person came in and led her to the next house below, Maggots-on-Bark-on-Ground. Here again she saw an old woman beside a fire, who appeared identical to the woman in the first house. This old woman also offered the crying woman something to eat, and again, before the crying woman could take it, another guide appeared and said, 'Come to the house of the Place-of-Mouth-Showing-on-Ground,' and the crying woman followed.

"As before, she saw an identical old woman preparing meat beside the fire. As before, the crying woman was interrupted by another guide before she could take the food. 'Come to Place-of-Never-Return,' the guide said, and led the crying woman deeper into the earth and to the next house.

"When she entered this time, though, the crying woman saw her father sitting beside the fire, and he became angry at the sight of her. 'Why have you come here?' he shouted at her. 'Whoever enters the first three houses may return, but from this place there is no return! Do not accept the food of the ghosts, and return home at once! We will sing, so the tribe will hear and come for you.'

"Her father called to the guide who had brought the cry-ing woman there and begged that he return her at once to the land of the living. And so the guide carried her back up to the grave tree on a board, where she lay like one dead, and he sang as her father had said, and the tribe heard the song and came to the tree where the man was buried. But though they saw the board and heard the singing voice, the people could not see the girl lying beneath the tree."

I waited for a long time, though by then, I was fifteen and knew one of Grandmother's endings when I heard one. "That's it?" I said finally.

"That's it," she told me.

I sat in bed, turning the story over in my mind, trying to make sense of it. Several times I thought I'd caught the mean-ing, but then it would slip away again. "Sometimes," I told her, "when you tell these stories, I *feel* them."

"How so?" she asked, narrowing her dark eyes.

"Like, I almost remember them. Like they happened to me. Like they're more real than my actual life, only I can't quite pin them down. Does that make any sense?"

"No," she said bluntly. "But I know what you mean. I feel that too."

"The world doesn't feel right," I said, yawning. Sleep was overtaking me, and my mind began to chatter half-formed thoughts, things I couldn't fully understand.

"We're hostages, Natalie," Grandmother said softly.

"Hostages?"

"We're living on our own land, but it'll never be ours again. We answer to a government that doesn't acknowledge that we're many nations—nations they bought from people who had no right to the land in the first place. We're surrounded by people who forget we exist except when they read about our downfall in their history books, as if we aren't still here, occupied, waiting for an ending that, after five hundred years, we know will never come. Trying to learn how to live in and belong to two worlds at once. There's a separation between us and everything around us. We can't get close enough to it, no matter how hard we try. You and I, we feel that distance every moment of every day. In a way, we're ghosts already. These stories are the thread that connects us to the world that came before us, a world we'll never see but always dream about."

"Well, that's a cheery outlook."

She shrugged. "Sometimes the most beautiful moments in our lives are things that hurt badly at the time. We only see them for what they really were when we stand at the very end and look back."

"You're particularly cryptic tonight," I said.

"I feel particularly old tonight, Natalie. Age makes one think."

"About?"

After a long pause, she said, "Regret."

I watched her eyes glaze over in thought. "Grandmother?"

"Hmm?"

"Do you know my mother?" I asked. "My biological one, I mean."

"Of course," she said. "I know everyone you know, and many people you don't."

I steeled myself before asking, "Do you know . . . why?"

Grandmother fixed her eyes on me and rubbed at her chin. "Why she left you?"

I nodded.

"I understand her decision as well as she does, but these things are rarely simple."

"She was young."

Grandmother nodded. "And poor."

"And unhappy."

"Very," Grandmother said.

"Will I ever meet her?" I asked. "Does she think about me?"

"She thinks about you every day," Grandmother assured me. "And someday, you may very well meet her."

"But you can't say for sure?"

Grandmother hesitated, then shook her head. "The future's rarely certain, Natalie. All we ever have is the present."

But my present might already be over. He could be trapped in my past.

Beau doesn't show up for dinner. My calls don't reach him, and he doesn't come to take me to the studio either, so I lie in bed and worry. To make matters worse, Joyce Kincaid just sent me a picture of Matt in his hospital bed, and, for one millisecond, I think she's telling me he's awake until I see her caption: *Thought you might miss seeing his face.*

I don't. Maybe I should, but there's nothing comforting to me about Matt's pale skin or the tubes in his nose or the bruising along his temple. Every time I close my eyes, the image resurges until, despite my fatigue, I get out of bed and pace.

I hate driving at night, probably because of both my night-mares and my steadfast conviction that a murderer's hiding in the backseat, but I grit my teeth and decide to drive to NKU anyway.

I navigate my way through the unlit building to our studio and force myself to stretch quickly, straining my mind for the sounds of Beau's fingers settling against the piano keys. He's here. I know he's here. I can almost feel him. I close my eyes and try to catch his smell in the air, the twang of his voice, the line of his shoulders.

But I can't. He's here, but we're separated by worlds, and it feels so wrong—I'm so terrified it could be permanent—I can't take being here any longer, and I head home, heart thumping like a jackhammer and breaths coming spastically all the way there.

When I tell Alice in Thursday's session about Beau's disap-pearance, all I can get out of her is one of her infuriating *hmm*s.

"*Hmm* what?" I press.

She shrugs. "Honestly, I hesitate to say too much. We should let this work itself out before we panic."

But I know what she's not saying. *What if I've had my Clos-ing? What if Beau's had his Closing?*

Friday comes, and Mom and Dad have the rental minivan fully packed. All that's left is to say our goodbyes before I go set-tle in to Megan's old bedroom. Mom and Dad want to follow me over, to talk to Megan's parents and make sure I have everything I need, but Jack and Coco opt to stay behind at the house and wait for them to get back, so I give them each a hug in the kitchen.

Gus is intensely whiny, stressed by the commotion of packing—a sure sign that he's about to get dropped off at the "doggy motel." I kneel down and wrap my arms around his tree-trunk neck, nestling my face into his downy fur. "Be good," I tell him, then stand up and face the twins.

"Keep me updated, okay?" Coco says. "About Matt and everything."

"Yeah," I say. "Though to be honest, you could probably get more news from Abby." Coco's gaze falls, and I can tell something's wrong. I glance around to see if Mom or Dad is eavesdropping then drag Coco down the hall by the elbow. "What's going on? Abby didn't like the body spray? Probably should've gone with edible body glitter."

She sighs. "It's nothing."

"Coco, tell me."

"She's a bitch, okay? She's awful."

"Your best friend?"

Coco shakes her leg impatiently. "She's just . . . she said some things."

"Things?"

"Stupid, bitchy things."

"Coco, if someone's bullying you—"

"They weren't about me," she interrupts, and the situation slowly crystallizes for me. "She said Matt's accident was your fault. She doesn't even think that. I *know* she doesn't, but she was saying it to some of the juniors to—I don't know—impress them."

I glance toward the living room, where Jack's sprawled on the couch staring into space. "And Jack's fight?" Coco nods once slowly. My vision starts to splotch, and I dig the heels of my hands into my eye sockets. "You guys don't need to get into fights or end friendships over all this."

Coco crosses her arms. "You don't get it. Abby's changing, or maybe I am. Either way, I'm so done with this gossipy little school. And it's even worse for Jack—and *no,* not just because of you and Matt."

"Coco . . . you *just* told Mom and Dad you wanted to stay at Ryle."

In a rare moment for Coco, her eyes betray the hint of tears. She shakes her head until they subside. *"Jack,"* she musters.

"You ready?" Mom appears at the end of the hallway, clapping her hands together, and Coco's eyes shoot me the *don't tell* look as she discreetly shakes her head.

"Let me get my bags from upstairs," I stammer, and Mom gives us a suspicious look before heading back into the kitchen. I pull Coco into a tight hug. "You fit here. You and Jack fit with me," I whisper. "I should've been there for you, and when you get back . . ." She nods, and I peer down the hall at Jack again. Mom's buzzing past him back and forth, checking for everything she could've forgotten. I decide to risk furthering her suspicions and go sit beside him. "Hey."

"Hi," he mumbles.

I lower my voice. "Remember when I was the worst?"

His eyebrows flick up, and he struggles against a smile. "When was that?"

"At least all summer," I say, "but possibly longer."

He finally looks at me, and despite the way his chubby cheeks have started to hollow after his recent six-inch growth spurt, he is unmistakably a stretched-out version of my baby brother. Coco's always been the more assertive leader of the two, and it surprises me to see goofy, laid-back, go-with-the-flow Jack looking so grown up and downtrodden.

"I'm sorry," I say quietly.

"For?"

I look over my shoulder to watch Mom slip into the laundry room. "Coco told me about the fight."

He rolls his eyes and sighs in annoyance as he cranes his neck to look for Coco. "Jack, it's fine. I won't tell Mom and Dad. I just wanted you to know that . . . you're wonderful, and I love you, and I don't want you to pick or finish fights on my behalf, and I'm sorry I haven't been around much, and also you were wrong about the carburetor, so there's that."

Jack snorts a laugh. "You're weird."

"Are you sure? Because no one's ever told me that before."

"And you're not the worst."

"Likewise," I say. "You're very not the worst."

I stand to go, but when I walk behind the couch, a sharp lift in my abdomen doubles me over, and when I cut my eyes back to Jack, he's gone. The house is dark, the windows along the deck a glare-ridden midnight blue, and a soft yellow circle glows on the kitchen table, just under the hanging stained glass lamp over its center. I feel swayed by a slow motion, like the world's swirling around me at half-speed.

My mom sits at the end of the table alone, her face pressed into her hands and her shoulders shaking. She pulls her feet up onto the chair and hugs her legs to her chest, letting her forehead dip against her knees. She looks young, a lot younger really, or at least like she's dyed her hair.

Oh, God. Why is she crying? Who is she crying for?

I don't want to see this. I can't. I stumble backward down the hall and run up the stairs, time jolting back into place as I push back my bedroom door to find my hideous Raider staring at me from behind one eye patch. The floor is bare, apart from the cardboard boxes stacked in the corner, but I still feel too crowded to breathe.

I try to focus on anything other than the pain in my chest and the multicolored dots popping across my vision: *The nights Megan and I spent watching thunderstorms from the garage, searching the sky for shooting stars from the roof of the porch. The hours I slept in Beau's arms on the floor in the closet. The stories Grandmother told from the rocking chair. The bus stop where I waited in the dark, in the sweltering heat and burning cold on school mornings.*

Still can't breathe, can't calm down.

The sledding hill in the backyard, and the creek at the bottom that nearly gave me frostbite. The sprinklers we ran through in summertime. Sneaking downstairs with the twins on Christmas Eve to see whether Mom and Dad had put our presents out yet. The series of clues Mom spread throughout the house that led me to the garage, where my birthday present, a Saint Bernard puppy in a blue bow, waited for me.

And the night I climbed through the window and looked back to find that Beau had vanished. The slow passage of minutes ever since then that I've spent waiting.

I'm in a house full of ghosts. I can't take the thought of adding another. I bring my hand to touch the wall. "Grandmother," I whisper into the emptiness. "If you can hear me, *find* me."

Megan's mom is an anesthesiologist, and her dad's an architect who loves hunting, so their house is not only enormous but remote, hidden down a long gravel road and a beautiful perimeter of forest. As a kid, its spaciousness and its white columns reminded me of the White House, but the floor plan is surprisingly open and modern.

Mr. and Mrs. Phillips escort us all down to Megan's room, which takes up the majority of the basement, its sliding back doors stepping onto a big patio that overlooks a manmade fishing lake. The room has a distinct princessy feel that Megan neither had anything to do with nor ever worked to change or keep up. The floor, usually covered in clothes and paper and books, is now spotless, and I feel a twinge of sadness.

"Can't believe we agreed to let you skip out on us," Dad says from behind me.

"You guys thought it was a good idea," I remind him. "Independence and mental health and all that."

"No, your *mom* thought that," he says. "She's the fun, laid-back one. I'm the disciplinarian."

I snort. "Yeah, that sounds like you. You should consider changing the title on your business cards from Horse Whisperer to Horse Fascist."

"You know what, that has a ring to it. Not a bad idea, sugar cube." He kisses the top of my head, and Mom releases a little whimper.

"We'll give you a minute," Mrs. Phillips says, then slips back up the stairs with Mr. Phillips.

Mom pulls me into a hug. "It's only for a few weeks," I remind her.

"And then you'll go off to college," she says. "You're too grown up. Stop that."

"Trust me, I tried."

Mom laughs, and snorts back her accumulating tear-snot. "We really are so proud of you."

"Thanks."

"Call us, sugar," Dad says, nudging my chin with his hand.

They leave, and I dissolve onto the bed. If only Beau were here, I wouldn't feel so scared or empty. If only I knew where Grandmother had gone.

26

Joyce Kincaid calls me Saturday morning to remind me about the benefit tonight. They've combined it with Raider Madness, a portion of the proceeds going to Matt's medical expenses and the rest to the football team.

"I just hope that, wherever he is, he knows," she sniffles. "That he sees how much everyone cares. And I'm so happy you could stay through all of this. It would mean so much to him."

"Yeah," I say, "I'm happy I could stay too."

Truthfully, I'd been desperately trying to convince myself I didn't have to go to the benefit, while driving myself insane with the thought that, very likely, Beau would be there, if in another universe. Even standing on the other side of an impassable veil from him sounds better than the last couple of days without him. When I hang up with Joyce, I slip out the back of

Megan's room onto the patio. The air is cooler than I expected, and dark clouds hang in low clumps over the pond and the woods. Everything's completely distorted by fog, but I set out anyway, taking my phone with me. I try to get ahold of Beau again, but the call won't go through, and I'm left trudging aimlessly through the forest, straining my mind in an attempt to open his world again.

My phone starts buzzing in my hand, and I nearly drop it before accepting the call and planting it against my face just as I process the name onscreen.

"Rachel?"

"Well, hello to you too," Rachel says, apparently indignant at my surprise.

I sigh. "Is there a reason you're calling, Rachel?"

She lets out an even longer sigh. "Look, I'm sorry about what happened between me and Matt. He was wasted, and I guess I was . . . curious."

"It's fine," I say sharply. "Is that all?"

"God, Natalie, I'm trying to apologize."

"You don't need to." The anger in my voice makes my words unconvincing, even though I honestly don't know who I'm upset with anymore.

"Fine, whatever," Rachel says. "I was just calling—I just wanted to know if you wanted to ride together to Madness tonight."

"Why?" I say, genuinely confused.

"Because no one else gets it," she replies fiercely. "Because I don't want to spend another freaking second listening to Molly Haines sobbing like she knew him. I don't even want to go tonight, but now that it's for Matty . . . I just thought if *you* went . . ."

She trails off, and I'm so surprised I don't know how to answer.

"Hello?"

"Okay," I say.

"Okay what?"

"We can ride together. I don't really get why, but fine."

"Fine," she says. "You can pick me up at nine. I don't want to be there all night."

"Wow, really? Thank you so much."

"And people think *I'm* the bitch," she retorts.

Rachel lives in a trailer park out past Derek Dillhorn's Mc-Mansion neighborhood, like the city planners thought it might be a good idea to remind poor people they were poor and rich people they were rich. It's a complete grab bag as far as upkeep. Rachel's house is one of the nicest, with a neat yard she's probably responsible for tending since both her mom and sister work night shifts and sleep mostly during the day.

When we were kids, we loved to have slumber parties over there on nights Janelle, her sister, was in charge because there were no rules. As we got older, though, the invitations to Rachel's house stopped coming, and it's been ages since I've been here.

She's waiting out in the yard, another thing she used to do when we came over, to make sure no one knocked or rang the doorbell while Mrs. Hanson was sleeping. Watching her walk up to the Jeep, I feel an ache of regret. Not that I feel bad for her—I don't—but I remember all the reasons I love her. All the reasons we used to be friends. She may be a bitch, but she's a genuine bitch with heart. She's a fighter, keeping everything together for her family, and working hard to graduate, despite the fact that Mrs. Hanson's been telling her she was pretty enough not to have to since we were ten years old.

"Never thought I'd see an Ivy League girl in my driveway," Rachel says as she plops into the passenger seat. "So, what made you decide to stick around in the boonies for the rest of summer?"

"Stuff," I offer.

She runs her hands through her hair. "Sounds important."

We lapse into silence as I pull out of the neighborhood and turn back toward the school. We're still ten minutes off when Rachel's eyes snap to the passenger window. "Pull over," she says anxiously.

"What—why?"

"That's it, the memorial!"

"Memorial?" I say, scouring the side of the road up near the next intersection. "For Matt? He's not *dead*."

"Shrine, vigil, whatever you want to call it—just pull over."

I slow down and rumble to a stop beside the poster stapled to the telephone pole that reads PRAY FOR MATT KINCAID #4. Teddy bears and notes and flowers and jerseys sit in piles around the sign, and Rachel jumps out and runs to them before I've turned the car off. I step out and follow to where she's kneeling in the gravelly shoulder, two fingers pressed to the sign.

"What are we doing here?" I ask softly as I approach.

She opens her eyes and sighs in annoyance. "What does it look like? I'm praying. What, are you too sophisticated to pay your respects?"

"Rachel, can we cut it out with your whole snobby Brown bit?" I say, sitting down beside her. "I'm really not in the mood."

She glances at me sidelong. "Why *did* you stay? I mean, was it because of Matt?"

I run my fingernails over the sides of my scalp. "I don't know," I say. "Maybe partly. But mostly, I'm just trying to figure out what I'm supposed to be doing right now. It didn't feel like a good time to leave."

She drops onto her butt and pulls her thighs up to her chest, resting her chin on her knees. "You're lucky."

"Why?" I ask, suspicious.

"Because you're one of those people who's *supposed* to be doing something, while the rest of us just do what we do, you know?"

"No," I say. "I don't think there are people like that."

She gives a brittle laugh. "Natalie, you've wanted to go to Brown since you were fifteen. That year, all I wanted was for Janelle to invite me to her parties and to go to homecoming with Derek. I thought I was just enjoying my life, you know, while you were trying to get away from yours. But everything I've ever wanted was wrapped up in high school, and now it's like there's just *nothing*. Nothing except Matt in a coma, and all my friends going off to UK. And you, getting the hell out of here like you've always wanted."

"It's not you guys I wanted to get away from," I say quietly. "You know that, right?"

She gives me a disbelieving look then glances back at the poster. "At least you want something, even if it is just to leave. I have nothing to want, except for everyone to come back. Nothing, forever."

"What about dance?"

"I never wanted to *dance*," she answers. "I wanted to be on the dance *team*. That's different."

"I don't know if I want to go to Brown." It comes out like a balloon deflating, but there it is, hanging in the air for the first time ever. "I want to be smart. I want to know the truth, and to matter.

"That's stupid," she says.

"Excuse me?"

"It's stupid," she repeats bluntly. "You won't *matter* because you went to Brown. You already matter."

"Rachel," I sigh. She doesn't understand—and how could she?—but she opened up to me, and today, right now, I want to try. "Look. When I was fifteen, I lost someone who was really important to me. She knew me better than anyone, than even my family or Megan or Matt. Like, she totally got me and was more like me than anyone I've ever met, and once she was gone, I stopped feeling like I knew who I was, and I especially stopped feeling like I fit in. I went back to feeling like a five-year-old kid who had to prove she was just like everyone else. That's why I quit dancing—I felt like it was feeding into that feeling, and I wanted to learn how to be myself, unapologetically. And I want to know about my heritage, because I've still never really looked. *That's* why I chose Brown. Because it's far away, but not *too* far away, and they have Native American and Indigenous Studies *and* dance, and yes, because it's Ivy League. It's a little easier to explain wanting the supreme college experience than all the other stuff."

"You could've explained that, if you wanted to." Rachel appraises me with the same look she used all those years ago when we first met. "Well," she says finally, "Brown won't make you become yourself either. You just *are* yourself, whether you want to be or not."

"And just because you don't know what you want yet, it doesn't mean there's nothing to want."

She rolls her eyes, but then a smile lifts up her mouth. "Whatever." She pushes against her knees to stand and dusts off the back of her jeans. "We should get going."

I nod. "Just give me a second?"

"Sure." She walks back to the car to wait for me.

I turn to the poster, unsure of what I need from it exactly. I touch my hand to it like Rachel did and close my eyes. "Help me," I whisper.

I open my eyes, and something flutters across my vision. My heart starts within my chest as I try to catch hold of the change. The poster is gone, a new stone sign appearing in its place. The paraphernalia littering the shoulder is gone too, replaced with a mound of purple and yellow wildflowers, but before I can read the new words on the sign, they change again. Not back to Matt's name and number either, but to a wooden cross with words etched into it that vanish before I can process them, PRAY FOR MATT KINCAID #4 reappearing almost instantaneously.

Oh God.

Alice must be right.

There are more than two worlds.

Either that, or I just moved through time again. Maybe the poster will be replaced someday. Maybe it used to say something different. All I know is there are at least two other signs occupying this exact space.

Just then Rachel honks the Jeep's horn and shouts, "Hey, Nat, it's hot, and God can hear you fine in the car, okay? Come on."

Before Grandmother disappeared and before there were more than two worlds and before my childhood love was in a coma, Raider Madness used to be one of my favorite events of the summer. I remember all the excited nerves jostling around inside me freshman year as Mom drove me over. The carnival-style night ends with an open football practice, and it was Matt's first year on the team.

I wondered if they'd give him any playing time, or if Devin Berskhire, the senior QB, would be out strutting across the field the whole time. I actually *worried* that Matt would get to do a few plays and mess up. Not because I cared whether or not he was good at football, but because I knew how embarrassed he'd be, and the kinds of things his dad would say to him later. It's weird to think that Matt was only weeks away from escaping Raymond's constant criticism, and now . . .

The things that used to scare me seem so small now. An increasingly familiar pain pushes against me, an ache to have Beau here. I can't help thinking everything would be okay, or at least better, with Beau here.

Rachel and I make our way through the parking lot, snagging a fair amount of stares and whispers. Rachel responds by baring her teeth. "Goddamn gossips," she says. "Staring at us like, what are those two girls who've both made out with Matt Kincaid doing standing beside each other?"

"It's not you," I say. "It's me."

"Well, *that's* not egotistical."

"It's a fact. I'm the one who made out with someone else

at Derek's, then argued with Matt in the street before he drove off. They all think it's my fault, and they're not exactly wrong."

Rachel stops walking and snorts. "Oh my God. You don't honestly buy that?"

"Don't you?"

She sort of glances around then grabs my sleeve and drags me behind an inflatable obstacle course. "Look," she says. "Matt told me something. And he really didn't want me to tell anyone else, but if it'll help you get over this phase, then I guess it's worth it."

"Go on," I say.

She crosses her arms and looks down at her sandal, which she's twisting against the ground. "Matty's an alcoholic."

"*What?*" I say. "No, he's not."

"I mean, that's the short version, not his words, but yeah," Rachel says. "He told me the night of his birthday party. Or . . . the next morning, actually." I stifle a groan as she looks back up at me. "He started drinking more when you guys broke up, and I guess it got out of hand. Lately, the guy hasn't been able to take a sip without finishing the bottle."

I shake my head in disbelief and slump against the moon bounce. "How could I not have known that?"

She shrugs. "No one did. We all just thought he was partying, like the rest of us. He only told me because he felt bad that we almost screwed and he barely remembered it. He was really ashamed. It wasn't the first time he blacked out, and he knows he's a dick when he drinks too. He just hadn't figured out how to let go of it yet."

"Oh my God."

"Yeah," Rachel says, though she doesn't know the half of it.

She doesn't know how the Other Matt refused a drink that fateful night of the party, how Beau tensed when I even offered it.

Nah, I shouldn't, he'd said.

How, after Matt and I fought by his car, Beau dragged him off me and threw him down in the street.

And then that morning, in the hospital, when Beau sat apart from the Kincaids, Joyce's upper lip raised in a near-snarl like she blamed him for the accident. The Other Megan affirming, that yes, in fact, Joyce *did* blame him. Not for the accident. For the drinking in general.

It's all making sense. Matt may have just become an alcoholic in our world, but he'd already been one in Beau's. A golden boy with a predisposition to addiction, regardless of his circumstances.

"Are you all right?" Rachel asks, gripping my shoulder. That's when I realize how lightheaded I feel. Rachel steadies me as I slide down the side of the inflatable castle to the ground.

"It wasn't my fault," I say.

"No, it wasn't."

"It's raining."

"You really are a genius." But I barely hear Rachel. I'm distracted by the faint shadow of a person moving across my line of view behind her.

Rachel turns around to see what I'm staring at then looks back to me, clueless. Completely unaware that I just watched a platinum-blond version of her wandering around the carnival alone. The other world is there again, within reach. Just like at

the hospital, when I saw both Joyces. It's like the two are colliding, then bouncing off one another, sometimes overlapping
and other times separated by an impassable amount of space.

"I have to go somewhere," I tell Rachel. "Can you get a ride
home?"

"I mean, everyone's treating me like a leper since Matt and I
hooked up, but sure, I guess I can suck it up and get in a car with
someone who smiles to my face and trash-talks behind my back."

"I'm sorry," I say. "It's important."

She sighs. "Fine, Brown. But you'll owe me one."

"Oh? For driving out to your house and bringing you here,
I'll owe you one?"

"Basically."

I grab her in a hug, and she stiffens for a second before
reciprocating. "Thanks," I tell her. "For everything."

"Whatever."

I drive along the stretch of gravel past the Kincaids' barn all the
way to Beau's house, rain nearly blinding me despite the rapid-fire
swishing of the windshield wipers. I step out of the car amid a
clap of thunder and scan the little house and yard in front of me.

It's the unused rental property with cracked windows and
an unshorn lawn, not Beau's. I let myself in and meander down
the damp and humid hallways to the empty room that should
be his. I sit down in the corner where his bed should be and focus all my energy on trying to reach him, calling his name and
imagining my stomach rising and falling as though I'm floating
over immense waves.

I don't feel him. He's not here, not even in a different here.

I leave the house again, the screen door swinging closed behind me, and bend my head against the rain as I dash toward my car and click the key into the lock.

"Hey," says a voice muffled by distance, and I look up, turning in place. I feel him seconds before I see him, standing at the far end of the driveway and cornfield, his hair and clothes soaked through along with the paper bag he's holding down at his side.

Despite all that, Beau looks happy. Quiet, content.

"Hey."

He lifts the bag up. "Been lookin' for you."

Tears of relief form in the corners of my eyes as I start slowly toward him. He ambles toward me too, and when I break into a jog, he tosses the bagged bottle aside and starts running to me through the rain.

I am so relieved.

I am so near to happy, so close to feeling safe.

I throw myself against him, and he lifts me up, arms enfolding me, mouth on mine as rain slides between and around us. "You're shaking," he says, looking into my eyes.

I shake my head. I can't speak without crying. I can't tell him that I know everything—that it wasn't his fault Matt had a problem, even if the Kincaids blamed him. All I can say is "I thought I lost you."

"No." His hands glide up through my sopping hair to grasp the sides of my face, and he kisses me roughly before shaking his head. "No."

The rain's falling hard, slapping the corn and the grass and the gravel mercilessly, and I can barely hear his voice. "Matt's an alcoholic," I say.

Beau's eyes drop. "I know."

"Why didn't you tell me?"

His gaze barely lifts, a pained smile tightening one corner of his mouth. "Where do you think a golden boy like Matt Kincaid learns to drink, Natalie? You think he just stumbles on a bottle of whiskey in the woods one day? Surely not from the loser kid of the alcoholics next door."

"You drink to help pass between worlds," I say. "You can't blame yourself."

He shakes his head, still avoiding my eyes. "Natalie, you and I both know I drink for all kinds of reasons," he says. "And you know what's messed up? I can stop when I want, right in the middle of a drink, with a shot glass against my mouth—doesn't matter. I've lived with enough addicts to know that's not how it works for them. I never thought—I expected it to be easy for Kincaid, like it was for me. Easier, even. I thought, hell, we lose a game, he's mad at his parents, he needs to blow off some steam, whatever—we can drink it off. It's what I've done whenever I've had a problem since I was fourteen and my mom left us the first time. I didn't know what it would do to him—what *I* was doing to him."

He tips his chin down and scrunches his eyes shut, shaking his head to draw back emotion. "I didn't know."

"Beau." I take the sides of his face between my palms. "Matt's an alcoholic in my world too. And it's not because his best friend is Beau Wilkes. You don't even exist to him. It's because he has a certain personality type. It's because we all took it too lightly. *None* of us knew."

I tip his face upward, but his focus stays low, avoiding me.

"What happened—it wasn't our fault in either world. And Matt's problems . . . you're not the reason he has them. They were *always* going to come out eventually."

Finally he raises his gaze to mine, brow furrowed. "I told you. It wouldn't matter. My fault or not, I wasn't trying to stay away from you, Natalie. It's getting harder to find my way back to you, and I'm losing track of time. Big chunks of it."

My heart stalls in my chest. I thought I'd found the key, unlocked the answer. I thought I could make Beau stop blaming himself and then he'd stop disappearing, and all along, it was out of our control. I swallow a fist-sized knot in my throat. "What do you think it means?"

He slides his hands around my hips and glances down before meeting my eyes. "We're running out of time."

I fight back more tears. I've been crying too much lately. I'm so tired of crying. I push up on tiptoes and kiss the space between Beau's eyes, as if to smooth out the furrow there. "Don't let go."

And he doesn't.

Not as we make our way inside the abandoned house, creaking with the swell of humidity and the drop in air temperature. Not as we lie down on the floor where his bed should be. Not all night as we entwine around one another.

He holds on to me with every part of him all night, hardly blinking, until suddenly, he disappears from my arms.

"We're running out of time," I tell Alice. I finished explaining everything that's happened at least two minutes ago, but she hasn't said a word. I've seen Beau for a couple of hours the last two days, but both of those visits ended with him disappearing from me—Sunday evening as we sat on the bleachers of the football stadium watching the sun fall, and Monday morning as we lay together in his bed, fingers twirled through one another's hair. "What happened when you ran out the other day?" I ask. "Did you figure something out?"

She sighs. "Not exactly. I thought I had something when you mentioned Grandmother hiding in another time, so I went down a rabbit hole on time-travel philosophies."

"And came up with nothing?"

"A little bit more than nothing. Albert Einstein thought

time was an illusion, a sort of fourth coordinate to show where you are, relative to how fast you're moving. So maybe that's what's happening when you and Beau see the future and the past—you're rapidly moving forward or backward, but not along length or height or width. That could be why, when you're slipping through time, nothing around you interacts with you as if you're solid. You might be traveling so fast you could walk through the cells of a wall."

"But we're solid to each other," I point out.

"Yes, and you also said Beau couldn't get back to his world the night you met. I believe he used the word *grounded*. Perhaps when you're together, you're tethered to each other. And since neither of you appears to be *fixed* in the space-time continuum, theoretically one of you could pull the other along at the same speed. And perhaps there's a looser form of tethering that occurs with animals. Thus Beau's hamster's epic journey and your flip-out with your dog. It's as if the animals are somehow trying to decide where in time they belong and thus bouncing back and forth." She opens her desk drawer and digs out a Slinky, flipping its metal spirals back and forth between her palms as she thinks.

I raise an eyebrow. "Any particular reason you, an adult research psychologist, keep that in your desk?"

"It helps me think," she says matter-of-factly. "A physical action to busy the hands. Anyway, I was high while doing aforementioned research, which meant I was messing with this thing, and it sort of struck me." She flattens the Slinky between her two hands. "What if this Slinky is all of time, and it *all* already exists—past, present, future—but the human or animal experience is, essentially, moving along a series of moments in just one direction? We can't see, hear, touch any moment but the one we're currently experiencing, but they all exist simultaneously.

"That's why you saw an earlier version of yourself when Beau first showed you how to move time. That Natalie continuously exists just as the You of two minutes ago and two minutes from now continuously exist. But technically human perception should only allow you to see one of them at a time, rather than the million Natalies leading from the parking lot to this office, or the billions of Natalies and Beaus stretched across the highway from Union to here. It's like you're moving forward through a flip-book, but there are always other versions of you who are further behind or ahead of you."

"I think you broke my brain. I don't get it."

Alice stretches the Slinky apart, pulling the metal coils taut, then points toward one near the middle with her pinky. "Each of these rings is a moment, and right now we're both experiencing this one. But then, say you start slipping backward along the Slinky. You're flipping through every moment that occurs in your current physical space: moving *through* the Slinky. When the time slip passes, you snap back into place right after the last moment you experienced chronologically, even if by then the You that didn't experience the time slip has moved to a different physical space."

"I'm moving through a time Slinky," I say flatly.

"To be more exact, you are moving through a wormhole that runs through the time Slinky, that lets the version of you in *this precise moment* move to another moment."

"And that's possible."

Alice's head wobbles. "Oppenheimer—you know, the atom bomb guy—proved black holes were physically possible."

"Wait—the 'I am become Death' guy?"

"The very same, though he was actually *quoting* from the *Bhagavad Gita*. Anyway, Einstein seemed to think wormholes were another logical step. But he also posited that a wormhole wouldn't last long before collapsing."

I sit forward. "You think there's a wormhole in Union, Kentucky?"

"Of course not," she says. "If there were, we'd all be experiencing time slips. I think there's a wormhole . . . in *you*."

I must be gawking. The idea that an eighteen-year-old girl who's afraid of the dark might actually encompass a hole in time is almost funny. In an I-want-to-sob-in-the-shower kind of way.

"Think about it," Alice hurries to add. Her sudden giddiness is in direct contrast to the desolation I feel in my abdomen. I imagine a tumbleweed rolling through my rib cage, then getting caught by the pull of my inner black hole and soaring off into darkness. "If all time is *actually* simultaneous—and the passage of it is an illusion—then maybe people like us have wormholes in our very *consciousness*. The other moments always exist, and an anomaly in our perception allows us to interact with them—which makes sense since this all started with a dream state. As soon as your consciousness stops traveling, it tries to snap back to where it *should* be on your time stream.

"It's trying to wake up and perceive time as the human brain is meant to—in a linear fashion. Even if you could find the right *time* where Grandmother's hiding, I doubt you'd be able to keep yourself there. I'm guessing the Closing is the point at which your perception gets locked back into place and starts moving along your moments as it should—exclusively forward, at a steady pace."

"There has to be a way, though. If Grandmother can do it—"

"Theoretically, there is," Alice says. "I don't know that I'm on the money with all this. But assuming I am, I'm still convinced that hypnotherapy's the key. Pinpointing that trauma, and using it to stimulate the brain activity that creates the visions—*time slips*—is our best bet."

"What about Beau?" I say. "How does he fit into all of this? Is he a wormhole too?"

"Well, that's the thing that doesn't add up." Alice stands and picks her way over to the whiteboard that's wedged between the bookshelves. She draws a line on the board then starts scribbling branches stemming out from it until it looks like a sideways tree. "This is a totally different theory of time— what I call the 'many worlds interpretation.' In it, every decision or action has alternate possibilities. Parallel realities. This is the theory that allows for our Union to coexist with Beau's, with the division having at some point been created by a decision or series of decisions." She circles the last two branches she drew. "Hypothetically, even the smallest decision could create two different outcomes."

My stomach contracts and my shoulders tighten. "Like maybe my parents didn't decide to adopt me."

Alice jams her mouth shut. "Or maybe your birth mother decided to keep you. Or maybe someone offered your mom a different job and in Beau's world, you live in Timbuktu. Natalie, it could be anything—there's no way to know that hitting the snooze button on your alarm clock one extra time couldn't have been the point at which these two worlds split. The point is—the two theories don't strike me as altogether compatible. We're still missing something important."

"Couldn't both theories be true? I mean, what if it's just one enormous, windy time Slinky with a zillion arms?"

"I have no idea. Believe it or not, I haven't spent a ton of time studying time travel. I've made some calls to supposed experts, but if we're being realistic, we probably know more than them at this point. They're operating on math-based theories, with no experiential element."

"And *we're* following trails of silver light and your gut." I drop my face into my hands and grip my hair near the scalp. "I don't even care. I don't need to understand how all this works, or even understand why. I just need to find Grandmother and figure out how to save Matt, or whoever else might be in danger, and we're no closer to that than we were last week."

I close my eyes until I'm sure no tears will come, then look up at Alice again. She's back in her chair, her mouth screwed up and fine lines drawn between her brows. She leans forward and awkwardly covers my hand with hers. A few seconds pass, and she lets go and comes to sit beside me. "We'll keep trying."

"Someone's going to die," I whisper.

Alice sighs and leans her head back against the couch. "Maybe," she says softly.

We stay like that for the rest of our time together, and that's how I know: We've both given up.

When I stand to go, she grabs my elbow. "You'll be here

Thursday." It's somewhere between question and statement.

"Probably," I manage.

For the rest of the day and most of Wednesday I call Beau at thirty-minute intervals, but still I can't get through to his burner phone. I spend my time pacing in Megan's room, hiking listlessly through the woods, stumbling through painful small talk over the dinner table with Mrs. Phillips, and driving out to Beau's house to sit in the room that should be his.

Around midnight, I'm lying in bed when my phone starts to vibrate beside my ear. "Hello?" I answer, immediately alert.

"Natalie." Beau breathes my name out like a sigh of relief.

"Thank Grandmother," I say.

"I missed you," he says. "I thought maybe . . ."

He trails off, but I know what he was going to say. "No, not yet."

We haven't seen each other for the last time yet.

"Can I come there?" he asks.

"To Megan's?"

"I can't be at home right now."

I debate it in my mind for a minute. I don't want to be disrespectful to Megan's family, but so much more than that, I don't want to lose any time with Beau. "Park down on the street and come to the back door."

"I'll be right there."

"Can we stay on the phone?" I ask. "Just in case."

"Yeah," he says. "We can do that."

I don't hang up until he's standing in front of me on the

other side of the glass door, his phone to his ear and that heavy smile across his face as he raises one hand. I toss the phone into the chair and slide the door open, pulling him against me. He nestles his nose into the side of my face.

"You're here."

He turns me around so my back presses against the half-open door and his fingers rest on the waistline of my shorts. "I'm here." He stares at me hard through the dark, and everywhere his eyes touch me, I feel heat.

"Do you think if we had more time, it'd stop feeling like this?"

"That depends," he murmurs.

"On?"

"On how *this* feels."

Before I can reply, the lamp beside the bed winks out, and the empty layers of sheets surge upward around a body that wasn't there before. "Oh my God," I gasp, then clap my hand over my own mouth.

Beau glances over his shoulder toward the softly snoring person in the bed: the Other Megan. "Come on," he mouths, pulling me outside and sliding the door shut.

We move off down the patio to the wooden lounge chairs and little table where Megan and I used to sit on Saturday mornings, drinking coffee and eating sugary cereal to stifle mild hangovers. "What am I supposed to do?" I ask Beau. "Even if she disappears, I could go back in there, fall asleep, and wake up spooning a version of her who's only met me for, like, five minutes."

Beau rubs the pinched spot between his eyebrows. "This is getting a little crazy."

"No kidding. We really can't go to your house?"

He stares at the ground and runs his teeth over his bottom lip. "It's not good there."

I touch the side of his face, his skin warm and sleek with sweat. "Okay."

We sit down in the dewy lounge chairs, heads leaned against the side of the house. "I wish we could find out," Beau says.

"Huh?"

"How it would feel later," he says, "if we had more time."

I sigh and pull his arm around my shoulder. "Probably you'd get sick of me shouting out what I think's going to happen in every movie, and I'd get sick of you drinking and leaving your clothes wherever you took them off. I'd hate how messy you keep your room, and it'd drive you crazy how I can't do anything without planning every detail first."

Beau laughs.

"What, you think I'm wrong?"

He looks over at me. "I think that's a lie and you know it."

"Okay, fine. You tell me what would happen."

"We'd get married," he says.

"Oh? In my world or yours?"

"Both," he says. "Then someday, ten or fifteen years from now, you'd have a baby."

"What would we name him?" I say, playing along.

"*Her,*" he says.

"What would we name *her*?" I say softly.

"I don't know. Maybe Natalie Junior," he says. "She'd look just like you."

"But she'd throw like you."

"And she'd be smart like you. You two would talk about all the things I don't get, and that way you'd never get bored with me."

I laugh into his neck. "And you'd coach football so you wouldn't get bored with *me.*" His face lights up. It makes me want to say the sentence over and over again. "Beau Junior will be on the team, obviously."

"We can't name our kid Beau Junior. He'd get called BJ. You want our son's nickname to be Blow Job, Natalie?"

"Oof, good point. So what would we name him?"

"I don't know." He smooths my hair and kisses my head. "Probably just name him Natalie, too."

"You're just saying all this because you know I can't hold you to it."

"No," he says. "I'm sayin' it because I might not get another chance."

I twist my fingers through his hair, press my lips to his cheek. The words tangle in my throat, being born and dying a thousand times. *I love you.*

On Thursday I climb out of the haze of hypnosis, and the first thing I see is Dr. Wolfgang's smirk. My immediate thought is that I've just divulged something humiliating, but then I find Alice wringing her hands, eyes wide.

"You guys find something?"

"I always find something," Wolfgang croaks. "This is the point of using a map."

That last bit comes off snidely, and his eyes flick to Alice,

but she doesn't seem to notice. She swallows and says. "Thank
you, Frederick, we can handle it from here."

He mumbles something to himself in German but packs
up and clears out all the same. When we're alone, Alice goes to
close the door and sits down in her chair, staring at me.

"Well?" I say, uncomfortable and anxious. "Are you going
to tell me?"

She grabs the voice recorder off the desk and passes it to
me. "Go on."

It takes me a minute to gather myself. Whatever's in this
recording, once I hear it, there's no forgetting it. But if it's the
key to getting Grandmother back, I really have no choice. I
take a deep breath and press PLAY.

At first, all I hear is my own even breathing, how I imagine
I must sound when I'm asleep.

A sharp gasp interrupts the rhythm, as if I've been startled
awake.

"Mommy?" I hear myself say, only my voice is higher and
smaller, somehow younger. *"MOMMY!"*

I start to scream—the me in the recording—bloodcur-
dling shrieks.

Suddenly, I'm not just hearing the sound anymore. I'm
making it. The me in the room. I'm seeing it. I'm feeling it.

All of it.

I'm not in the office. I'm in the car, strapped into my car
seat, as we smash headlong into something and spin sideways,
flipping, my stomach looping inside me like we're on a roller
coaster. We hit the ground, the windows shattering on impact.
Glass everywhere. Pain. The dark of night. Thunder screech-

es overhead, but I barely hear it. Silence drapes itself over the whole world, muffling my ears, the sound of my own voice, screaming, "Mommy, Mommy!" as the creek water and rain rush into the car.

"STOP IT," comes another voice.

Not from my memory. It's Alice's voice, and I snap back into the office, mind reeling.

"Wake her up," Alice is saying from the voice recorder. "Right *now*, Frederick."

The recorder turns off as it reaches the end. I look up from the hunk of plastic shaking wildly in my hands to Alice, whose face is ghostly. "My dreams."

She nods. "They're not dreams," she says. "It's a memory."

"She fell asleep," I whimper. "She fell asleep at the wheel, and we wrecked." Alice's features remain stony as the memory keeps replaying in my mind, fragmented and dark, cold and wet, panic overtaking me. It shouldn't be so scary—it was a long time ago. I shouldn't feel this way, like nothing can make me safe. A wave of dizziness hits me, and I can't remember how to breathe. I keep inhaling but the air won't make it to my lungs. My chest aches all the way down through my arm.

"Natalie," Alice says, her voice rough but somehow comforting in its solidity. "Take deep breaths. Focus on your breathing. It's all going to be okay, I can promise you that. What you're experiencing right now is temporary."

I barely hear her. I can't breathe. I'm going to die. Whatever's wrapping around me, suffocating me, it's inescapable.

"Natalie," Alice says more harshly. She grabs my hand in hers. "Hold on to my hand as tight as you can."

I'm so dizzy, so lightheaded and empty of breath.

"Grip my hand, Natalie."

I tighten my fingers around her hand.

"Tighter," Alice says. "As tight as you can, and inhale. Breathe in."

I obey, fighting the stuttering of my lungs as I fold my hand over Alice's.

"Good," she says. "Now relax and let your breath out. Can you do that?"

I can, and after a few more cycles, the dizziness and pain subside. Alice squeezes my hand lightly and gives me a weak smile. "If it's too much, we could bring in an EMDR therapist," she says quietly. "You don't have to keep feeling this."

I free my hand from hers. My breath still comes heavy, but the crushing feeling has lightened. "Two more weeks," I say. "That's all."

"If you're sure," Alice says, sitting back.

I do my best to keep my mind on this crammed office, my eyes on Alice's face, my heart rate detached from that memory as I ask, "Why wouldn't she tell me?"

"Who, Grandmother?"

"My mom," I say. "I've had this nightmare my entire life. She knows about it. Why wouldn't she tell me?"

Alice sighs and tilts her head. "Natalie, the one time I ever had sex with a man, when I was nineteen, I got pregnant."

"I didn't realize you're—"

"Definitely gay," Alice says. "But that's not the point. The point is, that guy didn't want to be a dad, and I didn't want to have him in my life forever, and I was in the middle of undergrad at Stanford, and . . . all signs pointed to abortion. Except that I really wanted to have the baby. I was a lesbian, feminist scientist, but deep down, I knew I'd also always wanted kids. Anyway, I ended up convincing myself I wasn't ready but by then I was pretty far along. I lined up a family to adopt the baby, and I made excuses not to go home on breaks. When my son was born, I handed him over, and I never told my family he existed."

I shake my head. "Why are you telling me this?"

"Because the reason I kept it from everyone wasn't that I thought they'd be disappointed in me. It was because my heart was broken. I know now I was suffering from postpartum depression, but that wasn't all. I regretted my decision. And I can tell myself that my baby was better off with parents who were adults, who had steady income—he probably was—but there's no way for me to ever know that for sure."

Alice takes a shuddering breath, and her voice tightens. "I've regretted my decision for thirteen years now. Nothing has ever hurt me like the fear that I'd made the wrong choice for my kid. And sometimes, we don't talk about things because we don't want to be comforted. We don't want anyone to tell us it wasn't our fault, or that they forgive us, or that we did the best we could. We want to hold on to that pain because we think that's what we deserve. We worry that if we let it go, we're dishonoring it. And, when I look at you . . ." She presses her fingertips over her mouth, bobbing her head as she fights back tears.

I don't want to comfort her. I want her to cry. I want her to cry like I've cried, like I want my birth mother to cry. It scares me how I feel, now that the anxiety has faded: furious, boiling, explosive.

"You have to understand her," Alice whispers.

"She could've helped me," I say. "She could've helped me, and she didn't."

"Hey, honey!" Mom's voice comes over the phone bubbly and excited, which only upsets me more. "We were just missing you!"

It takes me a second to steady myself as I pace along the patio behind Megan's room. "I know," I choke out.

"What?"

"I know about the accident."

A long exhale follows the silence. "Baby, I'm so sorry."

"You're *sorry*?" I'm so frustrated that all I can do is laugh. "You've known the whole time. Why I was having the night-mares, why I was afraid of the dark, why I was having *panic attacks*. At any point in the last *fifteen years* you could've helped me, but you were so worried I'd find out it was your fault that you just let me suffer. You could've taken the suffering away, and you didn't."

"You don't understand," she pleads. "I was trying to protect you from unnecessary pain—"

"Protect me?" I shriek. "Why even bother sticking me in counseling if you weren't going to tell me what was causing my problems?"

"I didn't know if the accident had anything to do with it!" she says, voice shaking. "Your counselors were all so sure it was about—"

"God, I'm the only person who's not entitled to know anything about my life, aren't I?"

"Natalie, that's not fair. I'm your mother. It's my job to—"

"To lie to me? Admit it, Mom, you were protecting *yourself*."

"Baby, please," she whispers. "You don't understand. I thought about telling you, a million times, but I didn't want to make you relive it if it wasn't going to help you. The EMDR—it *worked*. I didn't think . . . I didn't think you needed to know—"

"Stop trying to justify yourself."

"Natalie, I'm your mother!"

"I don't *have* a mother," I scream.

I can't do this, can't finish this conversation. My mind is swimming. My breathing is spastic. The weight pushes down on my chest again. I hang up and throw my phone toward the woods. Almost immediately, it starts ringing from the brush where it lands.

Sheryl Crow's and Stevie Nicks's voices slow to a warbling as my mind spins, my lungs heave, and my vision splotches. The moment I realize I can't feel my legs, the darkness surrounds me.

"There once was a man named Abraham, and God spoke to him freely," Grandmother says.

"Like you talk to me," I say.

"Sort of like that," Grandmother says. "Maybe more like Megan and God talk, in quiet thoughts and deep, intense feelings. Anyway, they talked all the time, and Abraham knew God's voice so well that when God spoke, he heard him precisely. And Abraham knew God's heart so well that when God told him to do something, he trusted him implicitly, like a child trusts a parent before she realizes adults can fail."

It hurts to think about.

Why does that hurt me?

I'm safe, in my bed, down the hall from my parents, but something's not right between us.

The recurring dream. It hits me like a wall of wind. *The dream about the car accident isn't a dream. It's a memory.*

I lift my eyes to Grandmother's chair in the corner and see there's no door beside it. "I'm dreaming right now," I say. "This is a dream too."

"No." Grandmother shakes her head, a gray-streaked section of hair falling across her forehead. "This is a memory, inside of a dream."

"A memory," I murmur to myself, sinking down in my sheets.

"You were fourteen when I told you this story."

"That's right," I say, though my mind's still foggy. "The story didn't make sense to me then."

"Does it now?" she asks.

"I . . . I don't know," I manage. "At least the part about trust, and how parents can fail. That makes sense."

"Ah," Grandmother says, folding her hands in her lap. "So we're here already."

"Where?" I ask, trying to shake the fog from my head.

"At the part of the story where your trust is broken," she says.

"You knew?"

"Girl, how many times have you told me I know everything?"

"All the stories," I say. "They didn't mean anything when you told me them, but they all apply later, don't they? Like prophecies."

"Like prophecies, yes," she says. "But not prophecies. Like parables, but not parables."

"You're even behind a smoke screen in my dreams," I say.

"That's your fault, isn't it? You can't blame me. I'm not really here."

"How does this work—a memory inside a dream?"

"Exactly like the nightmare, I assume. You're remembering a story I told you and conflating it with the current events of your life to parse out meaning."

"Now you sound like Alice."

"Well, you've got a little bit of her stored up in here too. You keep everyone you love close, Natalie. You keep bits of them within you. You let every person you meet affect you."

"I wish I didn't let them affect me so much."

"You must be feeling uprooted now that you know the truth about the accident," she says. "Like your family is no longer a safe place, and if they aren't, what is?"

"If you say so, I must. Since you're just a product of my consciousness."

"You've got some nerve, girl," she says.

"I learned from the best. Before you left me."

Grandmother's knowing smile falters. She leans over her knees toward me, reminding me of Alice. "I'll never leave you. Don't forget that," she says.

Did she actually say that? I try to remember. I don't think she did, but still, it feels so real I believe her, this dream version of Grandmother. I must really think that, deep down, or at least want it, to be able to conjure up those words from her now.

"Now sit back and let me tell you this story," she says.

"Again," I point out.

"Again. One day God spoke to a man called Abraham. 'Abraham,' he said, 'take Isaac'—or Ishmael, depending on who's telling it—'your son whom you love more than your own life, and go to Moriah, where you will sacrifice him on a mountain.'

"And hearing and knowing God, Abraham obeyed, taking his son and two servants on a journey to Moriah. When he saw the mountain God had chosen, Abraham told his servants to wait at the bottom while he and Isaac went to worship. 'Then we will come back to you,' Abraham told his servants, for he knew God would not lead him into danger. He wouldn't cause Abraham pain.

"As they climbed, Abraham chose wood to build the sacrificial fire. He passed it to Isaac, who said, 'Father, where is the lamb to be offered?'

"'God will provide,' Abraham told his beloved son, and they kept climbing. When they reached the summit, Abraham strained his ears, listening for God's voice, but when he heard nothing he built the altar and bound Isaac to it. Though he began to be afraid, he still trusted that God loved him, that he would not lead him to slay his son without reviving him again. And so he raised his knife over Isaac's heart, and finally he heard God speak again.

"'Abraham, Abraham,' God said. 'Set down your knife. Do not harm your son. I've seen your heart, and I know you withhold nothing from me. You know my face as that of your father. You recognize my love for you, as you know your own for Isaac. You know what you would do for your child, and you understand that is what I'd do for you.'

"Abraham released his son then, and when he looked up to the bramble, he saw a ram with its horns caught in the brush. Together, they sacrificed the ram, which had been sent to take Isaac's place. From then on, they called that place God Provides."

"Why did they have to sacrifice *anything*?"

"It was a symbol," Grandmother explains. "Of an innocent dying on behalf of someone else—the greatest act of love. A choice to die so someone else doesn't have to."

"Your stories are full of symbols, aren't they?"

"Every great story has sacrifice," Grandmother says.

"Don't you think saying that goes against your 'we can't apply Anglo-Saxon context and standards to Native stories' mantra?"

"Yes," she says. "But I never said that. *You* did."

Someone's saying my name. A low voice that lilts and drawls. Hands squeeze my shoulders, push my hair from my face. "Natalie, wake up."

I blink against sleep to see full lips, dark hair, and hazel eyes, all shaded by darkness, hovering over me. My head is inexplicably throbbing, and the hoots of owls and rustle of nightlife surround me. "Beau?"

He helps me sit up. "Where am I?" I ask before I can register that I'm lying on the cool cement of Megan's back patio.

"I've been calling you for hours," Beau says, gently cradling the back of my neck. "What happened? Are you all right?"

"My phone," I say, fighting back the lingering confusion. "I threw it in the woods."

His eyebrows flick up in surprise, but his usual soft, heavy smile is missing, his shoulders hunched and tense.

"What's wrong?" I say, touching his lips.

His eyelids dip. "Kincaid's awake."

"Both of them?" It's little more than a whisper.

"I don't know," he says. "I've been losing track of time more and more. No one else seems to notice, but it's like I'm missing for hours at a time. I woke up standing in my room with my phone in my hand and a voice mail from Rachel."

"Have you seen him yet?"

He shakes his head. "I wanted to find you first."

What happened to me? Where have *I* been for hours? I wrap my arms around Beau and press my forehead against his heart. "What's happening to us?"

He strokes the back of my head. "I don't know."

Maybe our Closings are happening, but there's more to it than that. All these things are connected—Grandmother's stories, her warning, our two worlds, and our missing time. "I'm scared," I tell Beau, and he kisses me, his way of both comforting me and admitting he feels my fear too.

He lets out a long exhale. "There's something else." I pull away from him so I can see his eyes while he tells me. "I don't know what it means," he says, shaking his head. "But I saw your family."

"What? When? They're not here. They're—"

"I know." He nods. "They must've been my version. At a gas station, lots of stuff in the backseat, like maybe they were just passing through. Your brother was wearing a St. Paul's sweatshirt. Think maybe he goes there, or went there, or—I don't know."

"I don't understand—I wasn't with them?"

He shakes his head again. "Waited until they left, just to make sure you weren't in the bathroom or something." I feel nauseous and dizzy again, like my body's spinning but my brain's stationary. Beau touches my shoulder to steady me. "Natalie."

"It's okay," I tell myself. It doesn't feel okay. It feels bad; it feels like the very sort of thing the word *bad* should be reserved for. "It's okay. We can figure this out later. We should just get to Matt." He doesn't budge until I start staggering to my feet, and then he helps me up and leads me around the house. "Beau?"

He stops in front of the truck.

I force the knot in my throat down. "How'd they look?"

Beau pulls me forward so his lips rest against my forehead. "Happy," he says. "Your family looked happy."

I close my eyes tight. "Good."

We ride together to the hospital, though we don't know which worlds we'll be able to find when we get there. I take his hand as we cross the parking lot. "Which world is this?"

He closes his eyes for a second then looks at me. "I can't tell. It's getting harder."

What could that mean? What could it mean that two distinct versions of the same place are no longer so distinct? What could it mean that Beau's losing hours at a time? What could it mean that in his world, I'm not with my family, but I'm also not with him?

We go inside anyway, and when Rachel, dark hair and puffy eyes, springs toward me in the waiting room, I know which world we're in.

I also know that something's wrong.

Rachel grabs me tightly and immediately starts to shake and sob against me. "Rachel," I say, my voice broken, almost angry. Her weeping doesn't let up, and I push her back harder than I mean to. "Rachel, what happened?"

She looks at me, her mouth agape and twisted, her forehead wrinkled and cheeks wet.

"*Rachel,*" I demand. Beau's standing a few feet behind me, stock-still and expectant. "What happened?"

"He . . ." She closes her hands around the hem of her tank top and squeals throatily, "He's gone."

"*Gone?*" I breathe.

She folds over, racked with sobs. "He's gone," she chokes out. "The doctors said there's no brain activity. He's on life support now, but they're going to . . ." She can't finish. She sinks to the floor and reaches a hand up to me as she sobs, but I can't take it.

I can't move.

I can't.

I can't anything.

Behind me, Beau turns and storms back toward the automatic doors, pounding a hand flat against them and kicking them as they open too slowly, then stalking out into the night.

Still I remain frozen.

This is how it feels when the world ends.

When you know, for certain, that there's nothing left for you to do, that you could stand there until it all disappears.

I failed. I didn't save him. My best friend. My broken best friend. The person who has hurt me most, who I have loved deeply, from whom I always expected an apology and I meant to forgive. All that's over now.

It's all over.

I don't know how long it takes me to move. I know Rachel is still on the floor crying. I know Matt's parents are still back beyond those doors I'm not allowed to pass through.

I know Matt is still lying in bed hooked up to machines, some keeping his lungs moving, others documenting his absence of thought.

The world is still over.

When I'm sure of all that, that's when I finally leave. Because there's nothing else to do aside from standing in this one spot until I'm fossilized.

Beau is sitting in his truck, and when I get in beside him, he lifts his phone from his lap. "I talked to Rachel," he murmurs. "The other Rachel." His eyes slowly trail over to me. "The other Matt's fine. He's awake, talking. Doesn't remember much."

"That's good," I say, voice trembling. I wish I meant it, but I don't. It's not good. I wish I didn't hate that Other Matt for living when mine will die, but I do. I wish I didn't hate everyone in that world for having him when everyone in mine can't. Or feel angry that we'd never make things right between us. Those things shouldn't matter after a person's dead. Should they?

"It's me," Beau says. "Destroyer of worlds."

It's not true, but I can't make myself say it. "I want to go somewhere safe." Somewhere the pain in my chest can't follow.

"Okay, Natalie Cleary," he says quietly. "I'll take you somewhere safe."

We drive away from the hospital, away from Union, deeper into the country, out toward the salt-lick-turned-state-park where they found woolly mammoth fossils in the 1700s. We drive away from life and streetlights until the narrow road corkscrews back and forth through the moonlit hills and Beau pulls off at a dilapidated redbrick house with a half-collapsed front porch and big rectangular windows framed in crumbling white paint. We get out of the truck silently, the floorboards of the porch whining as we cross them into the dark house.

We walk from the hallway into an old living room where squares of silver light shine from the windows toward the old brick fireplace. The floor, though old, is smooth, polished, the wallpaper mostly scraped off.

"Doesn't look like much," Beau says quietly, like he's afraid to disrupt the dust. "But the foundation's solid."

I look back to where he hesitates in the doorway. "What is this place?"

He ambles toward me and takes my hand in his. Slowly we begin to move through time, as though being towed upward through calm water. Reds and golds then blues and greens pop and flicker against the windows as Beau carries us into the future. I watch another version of him travel full tilt through the room, replacing bricks in the fireplace and baseboards and wainscoting, patching holes in the drywall, painting the room a soft peach, and shoving a beat-up piano up against the wall as the sun and stars take turns splashing us. Wildflowers sprawl out from the window across the yard and die beneath frost, only to regrow. Wisteria clumps up around the windowsills, blossoms opening and closing like heartbeats.

Tears rise in my chest. I'm flooding with them as the house becomes brighter, fresher, more and more a home. Time-slipping feels different this time, though, less substantial and more like a dream—the *shadow* of a future. "Beau, where are we?"

Whitewashed slats appear in a pile on the floor. The blur of a bear-sized person hammers and fastens and screws the beams together. They become a rectangle, a box. They become a crib.

"You wanna hear a story, Natalie Cleary?" I nod, and he folds his arms around me. "We live in the same world," he says softly, slowly. "After school, you get a job teaching over at NKU. I coach a high school team, or maybe middle school. We live in an old house with a big yard, and one day, I talk you into marrying me." He rests his chin on top of my head. "You wear flowers in your hair at our wedding, and Mason gets so wasted he throws up during his speech, but we're so happy, we just laugh."

"You finish my song," I say.

He shakes his head. "I finished that weeks ago," he says. "Pick something else."

I tighten my eyes against the tears, my arms against Beau's back. "The porch," I say. "Every night, you and I sit outside until the sun goes down. And a piano. I surprise you with a piano."

"And you dance whenever I play it."

"Where?" I ask, laughing.

"In the sunroom, of course," he whispers.

"Oh, of course. And does time move when you play and I dance?"

His hands enfold my jaw, and he kisses my forehead. "No, Natalie," he says. "Time doesn't move. It stands still."

"We never run out of it," I say.

Beau looks down at me, thumbs swiping away twin trails of tears on my cheeks. "And it's enough for you?"

I swallow the painful knot in my throat. "It's more than enough."

And for a moment, I let myself believe it's real. Beau restores this house for me. I come home to him every night, fall asleep, and wake up with my legs tangled with his. I go to all the games he coaches, and watch him kiss our kids goodnight, and someday notice his hand is wrinkly in mine. I'm the one who gets to see every part of him and who watches his softness cover the hard world. Still, we move forward, forward, forward, and for two beats of my heart, I'm sure I see an old, bent woman standing on the porch, looking through the window. Dark hair falls down around her hunched shoulders, and the pink light of early morning splays its fingers out around the crown of her head, silhouetting her face, but I still think I see her barely smile as her hand lifts up and presses against the dew-splotched windowpane. Before I can say a word, Grandmother disappears again, so thoroughly I can't be sure she was ever there.

"You asked me what I want," Beau says. I turn back to look up into his face, and into him. His hand comes up to cradle the side of my jaw.

Time slips back into place, and it all goes away. I want it too. I want it so much it hurts.

"You're wrong, Beau," I say. "You're not the atom bomb. You made all this. You made the world."

The nightmares plague me endlessly. In these, I'm the one driving and Matt's beside me, where my toddler-sized car seat should be strapped in. Bright headlights flash up over the windshield, making the heavy rain glitter like diamonds for that silent instant before the car goes off the road.

My ears are ringing so much I can't hear my own screams, and Matt is silent, eyes glazed, yards of tubing coiled in the backseat and stretching into his nostrils. "Matt," I shriek. *"Matty."*

I wake panting, my heart thundering, and when my eyes snap open, my whole body clenches painfully as I see the black orb floating overhead. "No," I hiss, scooting backward away from it. "No, no. *No.*"

It's starting: the end.

The orb drifts toward me, and I tumble out of bed, running to the dresser where my car keys sit. I don't know what I'm thinking; all I know is I have to get away from that orb. I have to outrun this. I stuff my feet into the boots by the door and flee from the room, circle the house at a sprint, and jump into the Jeep.

"Grandmother," I'm whispering under my breath. "Don't let this happen. Don't let this happen."

I start the car and back down the long driveway haphazardly, jerking onto the country road beyond.

How do I stop this?

At first I head toward Beau's, like if I can see him, tangle my fists in his hair and shirt, he can't be taken from me. The Other Matt can't be taken from me. Life as I know it can't be pried from my grip.

But as I near the turnoff for the Presbyterian church, sweat breaks out along my hairline, my hands start shaking against the steering wheel, and I know exactly where I'm going, where I've been going this whole time. I pass the church and the high school, and still I keep driving, my mouth dry and heart speeding.

I try to think about nothing. I try to think about anything but my destination and the dread coiling in the lowest part of my stomach or the creeping sensation along my neck. I see it up ahead, and a burst of adrenaline shoots across the back of my tongue, metallic and cold.

Don't think about it. Don't go there. Don't remember it.

I pull off to the shoulder, the headlights lancing over Matt's memorial, startling me anew. I leave the lights on as I step out of the car, the only illumination besides the red glow of the stoplights strung across the road. It's an intersection of two narrow country lanes with poor visibility due to the wall of trees on both sides of both streets. It used to be a two-way stop, but they changed it to a four-way and later added the stoplights after one too many accidents happened there.

My accident.

I run to the memorial, feeling all the way as if I'm being chased, hungrily pursued by the black orb, by a closing door trying to shut me out of Beau's world, and Grandmother's too.

But this is where it all started. Somehow I know that. Somehow I believe I can stop this.

I drop to my knees in front of the poster, my eyes pushing against the dark. I think about Beau's hands sweeping over the piano and visualize my movement, but I can't make the veil inside me drop so I can pass through.

"PLEASE," I scream into the night. My eyes bounce down the bank to the mostly dry creek bed, my ears tuning in to the trickle of water over stones and the buzz of mosquitoes skating across the surface.

It's like I'm back in the car, flipping endlessly, stomach lurching, tiny voice screaming as we careen into the water and the windows explode in a fine mist of glass. I find myself gasping for breath, reaching for something to steady myself as there are several sharp tugs at my stomach. When my hand touches the poster but instead finds cool stone, I realize I've finally broken through.

I don't know to which world—Beau's or Grandmother's or some other entirely. A world in which purple and yellow wild-flowers grow thickly around the telephone pole and beyond.

All I know is it isn't my world. It can't be mine.

Because below REST IN PEACE, the name engraved on the stone is NATALIE LAYNE.

I'm dead.

Somewhere, sometime, I'm dead.

There's an epitaph too, but the letters jumble in my mind, unread. Rain clouds break apart overhead, and I feel myself gagging in front of the poster and run a few feet before the bile shoots up my throat and hits the slick, muddy grass between my boots. I shouldn't drive, but I can't stay here. All I know is I can't stay here. I stumble back to the Jeep and turn around to drive back toward the high school, Beau's house, my house, Megan's house.

I find myself on the stormy gravel road, crossing the little bridge that leads to the Kincaids'. Next thing I know I'm outside Beau's house—and it *is* Beau's house, and the lights are on, but his truck isn't there.

Still I don't leave. Where will I go? Where will I be safe
when I know that somewhere I'm dead, my body rotting beneath the ground, and that maybe tomorrow morning I'll
awake and that orb will have descended around me, cutting me
off from the two people who can understand all this.

I turn off the car and that's when I hear the screaming.
Two hardly familiar voices shouting furiously at one another:
Beau's mom, Darlene, and her new husband, Bill.

Their words are impossible to decipher, muddled by the
linoleum siding and drywall between them and me, but I can
tell it's serious, brutal, angry, and I don't know what to do.

I start the car and drive away, backsliding again into my
thoughts and my terror, until I find myself parked outside Megan's house, my whole body trembling like a sapling in a tornado and my face striped with tears and snot. I wipe my nose
across my arm as I get out and circle around the white, col-
umned mansion to the basement patio and let myself inside,
out of the rain.

The orb is gone, but I know it will be back. The second
I fall asleep it will engulf me. I sense it. This is the end, and I
won't have any answers. I'll have no peace.

I kick off my boots and pace. My legs and back ache, so I
sit on the edge of the bed, trying to empty my mind but stay
awake, to not think and not sleep. Hours pass and I've managed
to conjure a mindless numb, but when I hear the knocking on
the glass door, "Thank God" escapes me, and I realize I've been
holding my breath, waiting.

I hurry to open the door, but Beau hesitates, swaying in
the doorway with his face turned down. Something's wrong:

he's sopping wet, his hair dripping along the outside of his downturned face. I take his hand, and he squeezes mine in his, almost painfully. "Beau?" I whisper.

I touch his face, and he flinches under my fingers. I tilt his chin up to me.

"Oh my God," I breathe. His lip is split and, though no longer bleeding, still smeared in red. His left eye socket is garishly bruised, the top of his high cheekbone starting to swell. *"Beau."*

He finally looks at me, and I feel my heart breaking in my chest.

"Why are you all wet?" He half turns away, face hanging again. "Beau, what happened?"

"Bill sold my truck," he says.

"What?" I ask. "How? It's not his."

"He's an addict. They're all goddamn addicts," he says. "It was in my mom's name, but she didn't know he was doing it. Someone just came and took it. Then Bill came home high. My mom was mad, and they started to fight."

He stops talking for a second, his bottom lip trembling. I don't say anything; I'm waiting on the edge of a precipice, afraid any motion will shut him up, shut him down. Finally he goes on. "He started hitting her, and I pulled him off her, but . . ."

I press my fingers to Beau's split bottom lip, and his eyes find mine. "She told me to leave."

"I'm sorry." I stretch my arms up around his neck. "I'm so sorry, Beau."

I pull him closer, and he's tense and stiff in my arms for a second before his eyes close and he starts to shake, his face pressing into my neck, my chest, his hands gripping my hips as he silently cries. "I'm so sorry," I say again, cradling his face as I kiss his fore-head, his cheeks, his black eye, and neck. "I'm so sorry."

I pull Beau inside the rest of the way, and clumsily close the door behind him as he kisses me roughly, ignoring the slice through the side of his lip and his soaking clothes between us.

Cool rain and hot tears, mine and his, slip down our faces, catching between our mouths as we wind ourselves together. He lifts me and carries me to the bed, and I hear myself say, *"Don't let go."*

He shakes his head against me. "No."

I want to tell him I love him. If I don't get to tell him about the headstone with my name on it or the black orb floating over my head or the panic attacks or the end looming over us—it will be okay. But if I don't tell him I love him, I'll regret it far past the end.

I need him to *know* he's loved.

I need him to feel safe, like he makes me feel safe. I need to wrap my love around him and leave it there, even after I'm pulled away from him forever.

"I love you."

He lifts his face away from me, and his rough hands push the hair back from both sides of my face before he presses his wet nose and mouth against my cheek. "I love you, Natalie Cleary." It's no more than a whisper. It takes no longer than a heartbeat.

"I love you," I tell him again.

"I love you," he breathes, lifting me against him and hold-ing me there, the muscles of his body and mine both tense against one another. I skim my hands up the back of his soaked shirt and along his damp skin. He sits back, letting me sit up too as he peels the thin gray shirt off and tosses it on the floor.

My heart is pounding, but I don't feel nervous. I feel only the crushing heaviness of a future without Beau, where I'm not there to pull him inside and protect him from all the darkness and pour light into him through kisses and touches and whispered words.

His fingers graze the hem of the tank top I'd planned to sleep in, the front already cold and damp from the water squeezed out of his shirt between us. His hands are so careful, his eyes heavy, as he lifts the shirt from around my waist, up over my shoulders. For a minute, we sit there looking at one another, his hands soft on my bare waist, and then he slides me closer to him and folds his arms around my bare back, placing his lips against the space between my neck and shoulder as our chests connect. His skin is softer than I would've expected, unevenly tanned by the sun and etched in muscle.

He takes my chin in his hand and brings my mouth back to his, a deep yet delicate kiss as his rain and sweat scents curl around me. I slide my hands around his back, feeling every new inch of him. I pull back as my fingers graze something rough and raised up along his spine, between his shoulder blades. "What's that?" I whisper.

"Just a scar," he says.

"What happened?" I ask, gingerly touching the raised streak again.

"Car accident," he says. "I was five. My dad was drunk. Nearly died."

My heart stops in my chest. I feel all the blood drain from my face and my hands. I swallow the lump rising in my throat as the weight of the whole night crashes down around me.

"Where?" I ask, though I already know the answer.

"Where?" he repeats, clearly confused.

"Beau, *where?*" I choke out.

He shrugs. "Same place Matt wrecked, actually."

30

I lurch off the bed and grab my shirt off the floor, pulling it back down over my head and turning to search for my boots. Beau grabs my arm, but I break away.

"Where are you going?" he asks as I step into my shoes.

My voice quavers as I wipe my eyes with the heel of my hand. "I have to find Grandmother."

"Right *now*?"

I nod and rub at the tears on my cheeks as I turn back toward the door. Beau gets off the bed and snatches up his shirt too. "I'll go with you."

"*No,*" I say more harshly than I mean to. "I don't—I don't know if she'll come if you're there. Stay here. Please stay here," I beg. "Don't leave, okay? Just stay here and wait for me."

He holds my eyes for a long moment. "Okay."

I cross back to him and stretch up to kiss him one last time before I leave. When I pull back, I walk to the door, slide it open, and look at Beau one more time. "I love you," I say.

"I love you too, Natalie Cleary," he says quietly, and then I dart out into the rain.

I know where I have to go—the only place where I stand a chance at finding her, the truth, at understanding Beau's and my entwined fates—but first I have to make one last detour.

I get into the Jeep and speed back toward the intersection adorned in teddy bears and flowers and notes. I leave the car running, the windshield wipers dancing spastically, as I run through the rain to the memorial sign. It's so hard to tear through the worlds, but when I do I find the same haunting words as before: REST IN PEACE, NATALIE LAYNE.

I let go of that world and it snaps away from me immediately, dropping the PRAY FOR MATT KINCAID #4 sign back in its place as my stomach slings back to my center. I feel for other worlds, but, despite my oncoming panic attack, the walls holding me here are more solid than ever. I scream in frustration as I mentally try to push at the curtain around me, and suddenly time starts ticking backward again. I'm sailing backward in time, the sun rising and falling, the cars speeding past backward, so fast that I almost miss the moment the sign in front of me changes.

Almost.

But I don't.

Matt's sign disappears, but there in its place is another: a wooden cross pounded into the damp earth and ruined by time. Burned into it is a date—fourteen years ago—and two words: BEAU WILKES.

I back away, horrified, fingers clamped over my open mouth as I wheeze and wail. Then it's gone. Both night and rain have descended on me again, and Matt's poster is where it should be, but still I'm gasping for breath, half-screaming my sobs as I run back to my car and jump in.

I race toward home, mind reeling. I reach the stone sign guarding the neighborhood's entrance and turn down my cul-de-sac and park in front of my house.

The basketball hoop's there. The shutters are green. This is still my world. I get out of the car and walk slowly up the yard to stand under the cover of the tree, staring up at the window of my closet.

I try to grab hold of time, to pull it upward around me and let myself fall through it into the past.

It gives in. Unlike trying to breach that ever-strengthening wall between Beau's world and mine, it feels easier than ever before to draw the sun around the Earth, watch it splash over the far side of my childhood home over and over again until finally there's a rental van sitting with its back open. The light hangs bright in the sky, and my family speeds from the house and garage to the van on a half-dozen different trips.

I keep going. Falling, falling, falling through time.

The van is gone. Rain shoots back up into the sky, clouds dissipate, the sun rises and falls. The cars in the driveway move backward and forward, disappearing at the mouth of the cul-de-sac and reappearing. I see Beau's truck for an instant. I see him and me walk backward toward the truck and lie down inside it together. I see him right himself again, pulling me with him until my back is pressed against the side of the car. I see us argue. I watch myself stomp backward toward the porch and scramble back up it and into my window.

I keep going.

It's so simple, what I have to do to find Grandmother. It's been so simple all along, and I didn't see it.

Time still whisking past me, I finish crossing the lawn and pull myself up onto the porch roof, sunlight then moonlight then sunlight splashing my back as I go. I hop down into the closet and see myself speeding backward between there and the bedroom, undressing in the morning and climbing backward into bed as it becomes night again.

I walk into the bedroom, my heart almost in my mouth, and everything keeps moving as I go to stand beside the rocking chair. Time keeps passing through me, the world rewinding until I see an earlier version of me kneeling in front of the rocking chair, and my mouth goes dry.

It doesn't make any sense. Grandmother should be here. I know she should: This is the night three months ago when she came to me to warn me. When she cried, I went to her and knelt there, just like the girl in front of me is doing, only Grandmother's not here. The chair is empty.

I take another step forward and time slips through me again, this time moving forward in one abrupt jolt, as though I were just dragged upward through a mile of water in the blink of an eye, and the room changes: every detail, but only very subtly.

A bed like mine sits right where mine should, a similar quilt draped over it. The orange and black walls shine in the moonlight, but the shades aren't quite right, and the rocking chair in the corner has tiny roses carved into it. It's my room, but *different*.

And there she is: Grandmother, sitting in the slightly off rocking chair, Earlier Me crouched at her feet.

I stop time's movement to appear in my own bedroom, behind my own kneeling self, staring at the ancient woman I've always thought was God.

Her eyes, dark brown hazed by milky film, shift up from the Earlier Me, and her mouth drops open. *"You,"* she breathes, "already—*you're already here.*"

I watch as Earlier Me starts to turn over her shoulder—just as I did months ago.

"Don't be afraid, Natalie. Alice will help you," Grandmother tells her. "Find Alice Chan. She can help you."

Before her eyes can process me, the earlier version of myself vanishes, leaving me alone with Grandmother. She stands from the rocking chair, her raspy breath the only sound.

"Who are you?" I demand.

Her cracked lips break into a sad smile. "Natalie," she says slowly. "I'm *you*."

"How is that possible?" I ask.

She flashes a sad smile again. "How is any of it possible?" It's what Beau said when he told me he saw the two Unions too.

"What do you want?" I say, feeling desperate. "I couldn't save Matt. You didn't tell me it was him, and I couldn't save him. He's on life support."

Her dark eyes—*my* dark eyes—fall to the floor. "I know," she says. "But I didn't come to save Matt."

"Then who?"

"What do you really want to know, Natalie? Ask me the question that's been weighing on you."

The answer surges to my lips, though I'm less and less sure I want the answer. "Why are there two worlds—why Beau and me?"

"There aren't two worlds," she says simply.

"What are you talking about?"

"You're slipping in time, Natalie, seeing other moments in your physical space. Hypnopompic reach forward, and hypnagogic reach back."

"Alice already figured out the time slips," I say, impatient. "What I don't understand is . . ." I hesitate, gathering the courage to say it aloud. ". . . why there's a cross with Beau's name on it in the same place there's a memorial for me."

Grandmother takes a deep breath. "Oh, sweet girl. I know you better than anyone. I know when you're lying. You do understand. You just don't want to."

"There's no way I'm this annoying in the future."

"Young people always think old people are annoying," she says. "But we don't care, because we think *they're* annoying."

"Stop," I say. "Just tell me what's going on."

"Beau died, Natalie. That's truth. If you look at time in a straight line—no detours, no do-overs or rewrites or wormholes—Beau's father made a left turn into oncoming traffic. He was drunk, and our mother had fallen asleep at the wheel. He saw her coming and sped up to miss her. She woke up and yanked the wheel left, but neither of them was fast enough. The passenger sides of the cars collided. You survived, and a five-year-old boy named Beau Wilkes died."

Full plump tears roll over my cheeks. "You're lying," I squeal between my fingers. "He has a future. I've seen it. I've *been* there." To the house. Our house. Our wisteria. A crib.

"I'm not," she says softly.

"Why can I touch him then?" I shout. "Why is *my name* written at the memorial too?"

"Because it's not the *whole* truth," she says, looking down at the floor again. "With time, sometimes there *are* do-overs. There are wormholes. I believe Beau's world exists to *you* because you have the power to change things."

"*What* things? What are you talking about?"

"Beau's death is in the past," she explains. "It happened. But when you tore loose from your position in time, time tore in the process, triggering the slips. And when I was your age, I met Beau Wilkes, despite the fact that he had died years before. I discovered what I thought to be another world. I fell in love with the boy who lived in it, and my whole life changed. I wanted to spend every day with him more than I wanted to hide or to run from what was happening. Loving him changed me. And then I found . . ." She pauses, mouth tight. "Well, the same thing *you* found: a cross with his name on it, marked with the date of our accident. I kept pushing against the barrier between our worlds and against time, trying to see through it for some explanation. Getting to Beau's world had been getting harder for me all summer, but I stayed there, kneeling in the mud until I could slip through time again. When I got traction, I was staring at my own name, not Beau's. No date, but that didn't matter. I knew right then, just like you knew, somehow we both must've died on that night. I looked it up, found a news story about that night, the accident that ended Beau's presence in our world. The same accident that, in his world, left our mother crying at the kitchen table, sent our whole broken family moving out of that house and its darkness.

"And just like you, I thought there must have been some kind of fork in time, Beau surviving on one side, I on the other.

I planned to tell him, but I never got the chance. That night I woke up with a black orb over my face, and his world closed to me, permanently. Like I'd been locked back into linear time, no slips, no alternate realities. Or more like the split between our worlds was sewn shut.

"I went away to college, devastated. Every time I came back, I tried to get back to him, but I couldn't make time budge. I couldn't find his world. After school, I moved back to Union and started working with a professor at Northern Kentucky University who studied experiences like mine. With all of her subjects we found the same thing: a cataclysmic event preceding their time slips, some hint of an alternate world—a world in which that event had been changed or prevented—and a black orb marking the end of it all. I think that's how it always is for people like us, who can move time. There's a reason, some *thing* we could fix or change, if we only knew how.

"Maybe someone, in some time, has managed to do it. But if anyone were to actually change or fix that thing, their whole past would be rewritten, leaving them with no memory or evidence of how things used to be. It's possible Alice and I helped someone make that different choice, but that probably would have erased our memories of ever having known that person. We do, however, remember those patients whose mysteries we tried and failed to help solve before their time ran out. Either way, it became obvious that we only have a certain span of time in which we can access and change the past: None of the subjects were successful in moving time or breaching alternate realities after their Closing. As if tears in time are self-healing, allowing those ripped from its natural course to traverse freely until they are locked back into a linear track.

"I knew all of this meant there was no getting to Beau. But even when I went away to graduate school, I couldn't get him out of my head, what had happened to him and whether there was some way to undo it. He'd been losing track of time before my Closing happened, as if the resealing of time was making him less and less real. That was the first hint for Alice and me that Beau's world had collapsed alongside the wormhole within me—that the Opening was, in effect, the beginning of an alternate timeline, and the Closing was its end. All of our later subjects found that, leading up to their Closings, the same thing happened to those they'd met in their alternate realities. They lost time, like Beau. More and more of it, until there was no more to lose. It may be conjecture, but it's conjecture in which even Alice Chan was confident: *We* are the door to Beau and his world, Natalie. When that door closes, he's gone. When it closed inside me, he was gone.

"I did my best to move on. I married my grad-school boyfriend, did work that I cared about, poured myself into meaningful friendships. Still, I didn't want to accept that Beau was gone, so I kept searching for a way to get to him. Eventually Alice realized I'd been going about it all wrong. Unable to move time anymore, I was never going to find Beau. My only hope was to *be found* in time. So I bought my parents' old house and fixed it up, returned my childhood room to its original state to the best of my ability—so it wouldn't scare you if you showed up here—and waited."

"Waited?" I hear myself whisper.

"For you," she says. "To find *me*. In the meantime, I started teaching at the University of Cincinnati. I commuted so I could keep working with Alice and her new subjects, who revealed another piece of the puzzle: the physical sensations of time travel. When moving forward in time, subjects felt a pull in their abdomens, like they were rising upward. When moving backward, they felt as though they were falling. Pretty obvious, really, but what we hadn't documented before was that the physical sensation of entering the Other World *always* matched that of moving forward, while the feeling returning to your own world matched that of moving backward."

I shake my head. "I don't understand. What does it mean?"

"Time is an illusion, Natalie, relative to the person experiencing it. There's the overall timeline of the world—dinosaurs, Ice Age, Middle Ages, Elizabethan Era, et cetera—but then each person experiences their own unique time stream as well. For most people that's just a tiny section of time within that overall timeline. For people like us, it's different. Our time streams can include excerpts from outside our linear lives. Think of arriving at our Senior Parade. Five minutes into our future, we were going to see buffalo where the school should be. *That* was our future, a moment occurring decades, if not centuries, in the past.

"Sometimes, you move through time and see everything changing before your eyes. Other times you lurch, or *slip*. That's what used to happen to us as a little girl. Our body would wake up in the middle of the night, but our dreaming consciousness would lurch to a different time: a hypnopompic hallucination. You didn't see yourself passing through every moment. You simply arrived, in *my* present, like you were locking on to me. That's what you do when you go to Beau's world. You jerk *forward*, as if you're stepping over ripples in time to a point in the future."

"Forward?" I say.

"You feel it, don't you? The same sensation as passing into the future?"

"Beau's in the same *year* as me, same day even—how can that be a future?"

She exhales. "We'll get to that. Anyway, shortly after we made the discovery, Alice passed away. I was alone by then, my husband gone, and I almost gave up on you ever coming. Then one night, while I was sitting in my rocking chair, you found your way to my present. I knew from looking at you that you were around eighteen, probably already in the summer we met Beau. You only held time there for a minute before you lost your grip again—your Closing was close, after all. I was so caught off guard. I tried to comfort you, but I didn't even know if you could hear me."

That was the night of Matt's accident, the last time I saw Grandmother. Though for her it was the first. The fear of that night, of tonight, crushes against me even as I remember.

"I spent years waiting for you to find me again. I thought if I could just see you one more time, I could at least steer you to Alice sooner. When I saw you next, though, we were further back in your own time stream. You were so little, and I didn't want to scare you—I didn't want to *push* it, so I just told you a story, one of the hundreds I've spent my life studying and teaching. It was the most natural thing in the world to tell you those stories, because I knew what they meant to me already and what they would mean to you someday. That night you listened, and then, after forty minutes, you were gone again.

"But a moment later you reappeared, and you held time there while we talked. It started skipping, like a scratched disc. I'd tell you a story, and then you'd lose traction. Those visits were far apart for you—six months or a year each. But for me, only minutes passed between them, as if your dreaming mind kept bringing you straight back to my time whenever it could, picking up where we'd left off. I watched you grow up in a matter of days.

"And as I said, I knew by then I'd never get to Beau again—has Alice explained the many-worlds interpretation to you yet?"

"I . . . I think." My voice comes out as little more than a squeak. "She drew time with a bunch of branches. Each was a different world, I think; I mean, we're talking about Alice, and she was in a science trance, so I'm not sure."

Grandmother cracks a sad smile and nods. "We believe that those branches are wormholes. As such, they have an expiration date. An alternate future may be initiated, but unless the person with access to the wormhole *chooses* that future, it will collapse. Imagine an envelope that's been sealed shut. You run your finger across the top of the envelope, and that's time: one straight path. Then you take a letter opener, and you slice open an inch across the top.

"Now, when you run your finger over the envelope, there's a portion where there are two separate paths, forming an ellipse. That's the time between your Opening and your Closing. Say you run your finger partway up one—the current version of the world—and then decide you want the other one instead. You jump back to that initial split and change the course of events to take the other path. When we arrived at the Senior Parade, the venture into the past was a part of our future, just as Beau's world—his alternate version of the present—is a part of your future. It's the present when you look at days and years, but it's *your* future because his version of events hasn't *truly* happened yet, not for anyone but you."

"I'm still lost," I flare. "None of this makes sense."

"That split in the envelope—those fourteen years between our Opening and Closing—that's the time during which we can choose a different timeline, Natalie. You can choose for things to continue as they did for me, with Beau's world collapsing. Or you can go back to the moment when time was first torn, and change things. You can choose Beau's course of events. After your Closing, whether through action or inaction, you've chosen which path will survive. For me, that means Beau died. He died when I was four, and in a way he died all over again when I was eighteen and his world, his possibility of a future, collapsed.

"But you . . . you can still see it. A future where . . ." She meets my eyes, shaking her head as tears bloom along her lashes. "Where you go back and you choose him."

My mind reels with questions and mental diagrams and so much panic as I try to make sense of what Grandmother is saying. Again and again, my body replays the sensation of passing into Beau's world, and every time I feel the same thing: the upward motion, the feeling of being lifted quickly, the same when I swim forward through time. What does it mean that Beau's present is my future? What does it mean that his version of the last fourteen years hasn't truly happened yet, but that it will?

Grandmother's shoulders are shaking from the effort of

holding tears in, or maybe it just looks that way because time is pulling against me even now, trying to drag me back into my present. It settles in me then, the thing Grandmother can't bear to say aloud, at least not as plainly as it hits me. "You think seeing his world like that means that I'm going to go back," I murmur, "that I'm going to change what happened the night of the accident, and that will create Beau's world."

But we're not *both* in Beau's world.

He saw my family in his world. All of them except me. *Happy*, he said, *they looked happy*.

And I saw my name on a piece of stone there too.

"You think he survives instead of me," I whisper.

Grandmother buries her face in her hands as she starts to cry. "I can't get back," she says. "I can't go back, or I would. I can't tell you how many times I've tried. I thought maybe I could stop the accident altogether, but, Natalie—the tug and pull, the physical evidence of time travel—when we saw that headstone with our name on it, we were in the future—not the natural one but the chosen one. We *felt* the pull. I don't think you can stop the accident completely, but you can change it."

"You think I choose—" My voice breaks, and a sob wrenches my words. "To die."

She looks up at me. Despite her thick wrinkles and age spots and cataracts, she looks young, tiny. Like Little Me in home videos, a puny frame in too-big clothes. "I think you do what I couldn't," she whispers.

I open my mouth but can't make any sound come out except a high-pitched groan. "The orb," I finally say. "I saw it tonight."

She nods but can't look at me anymore. She slumps to the

ground and curls her thin arms around herself. "It's tonight. It feels exactly like the first time. Like it's all being sewn up. The tear in time is closing tonight."

The first time.

Today I got in the first real fight I've ever had with my mother. I fainted for the first time. I lost a friend for the first time, my first boyfriend. I thought about my own death for the first time when I saw my name written somewhere it shouldn't be. And I told Beau I loved him for the first time.

And the second.

And the third.

I had meant to make love with him for the first time.

Now, he's waiting back in Megan's bedroom as his world crumbles. I feel the imminent fall in my stomach. Something's trying to cement me back where I belong, and when it does—*if* it does—Beau will be trapped under the rubble of a world that never happened. "I haven't lived yet," I say because I'm help-less. Because all I have to protect me now is words. Because it's an impossible choice to bear, but I don't *feel* there's a choice to make, and I think saying that I don't want to do this is the closest I can get to not doing it.

Grandmother reaches a hand up toward me. I take it as I lower myself to the floor in front of her. "It should be me," she says. "I could do it and have no regrets. It's what *I* would choose, but that doesn't mean it has to be what you choose. I can't ask that of you. I know you haven't lived yet. I know the life you can have, and how full it will be even without Beau, all the people you'll affect, and those who will change your life forever.

"I know all the stories you should know someday. I know both of your mothers, and how much they both love you. I know secrets about Coco that would make your toes curl in delight, and I know Jack's kids and how much they love him. I have all the answers, and you have none."

She squeezes my hand. "All you have are the stories I was able to tell you and the love in your heart for Beau right now. I know all that, Natalie, and I'm still here, asking you to do something I should *never* ask of someone your age, especially not someone I love, whose every heartbreak and joy I've also known. I'm asking because it's what I wanted to do, and you have the choice now."

"I don't have a choice," I lash out. "You *know* I don't. You practically raised me for this. You spent years drilling it into my head. You taught me that to love was to die."

"Oh, honey. You misunderstand. I didn't tell you those stories just to change your mind. I told them because I remember how badly it hurt, not being able to see the truth, feeling like I was going to be swallowed up by the dark. What is love," she says, "other than putting someone else before you? Our birth mother gave us away because she hoped we could have a better life away from her. Our parents kept the car accident from us because Mom suffered from PTSD for years. She worked so hard to make the pain manageable for herself, but she also protected us from that pain. Love is nothing *but* putting someone else first. I didn't teach you that so you'd save Beau. I told you so you'd see how this whole world was made for you, how it warms when you smile and aches when you hurt. I told you so you could stop being afraid."

"If that's true, then there has to be another way," I snap. "How can you tell me the whole world loves me and in the same breath tell me I have to die? I want to know. I want this secret knowledge you have that has you so confident that *this is it,* that you're willing to ask me to go to the past and lie down in the road in front of my own car to kill my child self. Because I don't buy it. There *has* to be another way."

"Why?" Grandmother challenges. "You've seen evidence of exactly two presents. I've seen evidence that Beau died that night in our world. Beau's seen evidence that you don't exist in his. You've looked at your own memorial in the same place as his. So *why* does there have to be another way?"

"Because this is happening," I shout. "This doesn't happen every day, Grandmother, or at least not to everyone. There has to be a better reason for why I can change things. Why Beau and me out of everyone in the world? Why do we get a second chance? What makes us special?"

"Maybe nothing," Grandmother says. "Maybe chance. Or maybe someone thinks the choice is just the kind of gift you would appreciate."

"Or maybe it's because the world would be better with both of us in it," I counter, "or because things are broken and when we're together, they're less broken. Maybe it's because we're connected or we fit or we're right together, and if time is really flat, then maybe it saw all of that. Maybe, even though Beau died, time itself saw every possible world where we could love each other and that was as good as us having loved one another. Because we could've loved each other anywhere, in any world, and maybe the reason we can change things is because the thing between us is big enough to reach through every branch in time. Maybe our love couldn't die, even when we did. Something's pulling us together, Grandmother. Something brought him *back from the dead* to me. Even if I go back to the night of that accident and die, why would death and time be any stronger this time? It has to mean something. It *has* to mean a future."

"Maybe there is another way, Natalie. But I'm not going to promise you something I can't give you." Her words are stretched taut and shivering with tears, her voice wild and round, a meniscus about to flood the lip of a glass. "I'm not going to tell you that you get a future with Beau because I don't know that. I *won't* be the one to tell you that you can have it all, no matter how badly I want Beau to have a chance to live. I want to believe in that future, Natalie, but I don't. You say you saw it? Well, I never did. Even if you *can* make a future, who's to say it's really *you* in it? I mean, look at us. We're the same person, but we're living different lives. If you can create a world with you and Beau in it, it's still not quite you, just like you're not quite me."

It feels like she's dropped a weight on my chest. "Then lie to me," I beg. "Because I'm doing this, and I need you to tell me it's going to be okay. I need you to lie to me."

When her mouth shifts into a smile, tears break and slip down her cheeks. "It's not a lie," she whispers. "It will be okay."

I shut my eyes against the tears, and Grandmother's stories flash through my mind, a warm current of electricity woven throughout my life, like Grandmother Spider's web and Alice's trails of light, guiding me and teaching me everything I know about love. But that whole web hurts, like it's growing through my veins, all the life I want to live pulsing alongside the one I want to give Beau. The things I want to lay out in front of his eyes and place in his hands and sing into his ears and the places I want him to be carried, the thousands of golden sunsets on that day-warmed porch.

"I saw it," I rasp. "I saw how all of it would be." How we would fit, what would be built between us. "I was there. What do I do with that?"

"Sweet kid." Grandmother reaches out and swipes a piece of tear-dampened hair away from my eyes. "I may have never seen it, but it never left my heart, this whole time. You take your hope with you to the end, just like I'm doing."

I look up into her face, searching for her meaning, and she presses her finger to her lips, eyes dipping toward the ground. When she speaks again, her voice is hoarse and rough. "I'm dying." Her confirmation is little more than a squeak, and she takes a long second to build her voice back up. "This isn't about me anymore. It's about you, and what *you* want."

"Dying?" I whisper. "How?"

She closes her eyes. "I won't tell you that. I don't want to ruin any surprises, or give you any fears. Everyone dies, honey, and you already know that now, at eighteen."

"And even Jesus was scared to die," I remind her.

"He was."

"You can't tell me anything? Give me any hint?"

She folds her hands together to steady her trembling. "I can tell you that the pain of living is worth it. That if you live, your life will be as full of love as it is darkness, and for every moment of pain, you'll have one of joy too. The one thing you won't feel is what you feel now with Beau, and that doesn't make your life any less worthy of being lived. But then again, worthiness isn't a factor in whether we're alive or loved.

"You have the choice to either appreciate the impossible and unwarranted gift of being alive or to give it to someone else. To use your love to remake the world. Whether you give it to Beau or keep it, Natalie, the world's going to keep right on being terrible and beautiful all at once."

I've been so afraid of those terrible things, of everything falling apart and of never knowing who I am or finding the place I belong. But here I am, looking at myself at the end of time, and she was never alone, not really. God, it's a painful sort of relief, seeing that some version of me has already lived and that all those fears eventually fell away, unrealized. I still want the whole picture all to myself, to get to the end of my world and slip quietly from there, but there's no real choice to make. I don't know for sure what will happen when I go back to the night of the accident, but I know I'll go. Not because Beau's future is so big or because mine is so small, but because love is giving the world away, and being loved is having the whole world to give.

"How much time do I have?" I ask.

"Hours," she says. "Minutes. I don't know, Natalie. Not much."

"I'm so scared."

She pulls me into a hug and smooths my hair away from my face, exactly as Mom has a billion times. *Mom.* The last thing I said to her was *I don't have a mother.* There are so many things I need to do. See my parents, Jack, Coco. Tell my mom to stop carrying around her guilt and promise her it'll be made right. Say goodbye to Megan, tell her how much I love her. Comfort the Kincaids, who will have their son back, if this works. Thank Rachel for loving me brutally, enough to hate me for leaving her behind.

And I need to be held by Beau. To make sure he understands how deeply I really do love him. How kind and gentle and soft he is. How safe and cared for he makes people feel, and how much brighter the world is for all he does and gives. How good he is, and what kind of life he deserves despite the one he's been given.

But there may not be time to say these last words. I can't risk it. This is my only chance. I'll never get to tell him how I think that if it were an option, I could love him well until I died.

I guess I *will* love him well until I die. I have to believe the world will pick up where I leave off. I have to believe that, whether I'm there at the end of the world with Beau or not, love is bigger than death.

"I'm scared too," Grandmother whispers in my ear. "But we're so brave, girl."

I give a phlegmy laugh. I'm minutes from death and non-existence, and I'm laughing. Suddenly, I'm laughing hysterically, and Grandmother's laughing too, and we're both rocking on the floor of our bedroom, tears of laughter streaming down our faces, snot dripping from our noses.

She regains composure first, gritting her teeth, smiling forcefully, and nodding at me. "You can do this. I should know. I was a surrogate mom *twice* for Jack and his husband." She responds to my surprise with a dramatic wink. "We can do anything."

I nod because I can't speak. Harsh sobriety has set in, and yet my head and breastbone feel as light as balloons, like all the weight of anxiety is gone now that the choice has been made, and I'm full of something bright and warm, a gift for the boy I love. I stand up, and Grandmother stands too, then pulls me into a bone-crunching hug. She steps back but grips my upper arms with surprising strength. "Because of you," she says, "a whole new world's about to get born."

She lets me go, and I walk toward the closet door, catching its frame in my hands and pausing. I look back to where she stands, back straight, hands clasped in front of her stomach and chin tipped up. "Grandmother," I say.

"Yeah, honey," she says.

"Do you think . . . I mean, is it possible . . . that there *is* a God?"

She smiles that same smile I recognize from childhood, the mysterious one that makes our eyes sparkle. "Girl," she says, "how do you think *any* of this is possible if something didn't want it to be? Something tore a hole in time just over our bed all so *you*, lucky bitch, could know what it is to *love*. Someone tore up a tree and let us look through and decide to fall."

"You think God loves me like you do?"

"I think He or She or It loves us like we love Beau. I think God loves us fucking well, Natalie Cleary."

Tears flood my vision. I nod once then turn, walk into my closet for the last time, slip through my window, hop down into my beautiful, blue-green swamp of a yard, and get into my car. Before I pull away, I see Grandmother standing in the closet, silhouetted by light. She leans forward over the windowsill and shouts to me, loud and clear, "Her name was Bridget. Our *ishki*'s name was Bridget, and she never stopped caring."

Bridget. I whisper her name to myself twice, and then I fold it in my chest with everyone else who's a part of me, all the people some version of me has already known and those who—I have to believe—some version of me will meet someday. Then I drive back to the intersection and pull onto the shoulder one last time, chills alive over every centimeter of my skin. But I'm not panicking, despite my fear. I'm not dizzy, despite the swelling lightness in my chest and head. I'm staying, I think, I'm staying until the end and for whatever comes after.

I want you to understand something, Natalie. No matter how hard it feels, you don't need to be afraid to move on. There's always more to see and feel.

32

I stand in the middle of the road, facing the direction from which I know I'll see the car from my nightmares come, drifting mindlessly across the yellow line. For now, the rain has let up, and the night is still. This time, when I think of that song I first heard Beau play, it comes to me—a measure of it, at least—and I take time by the hand with no more than a gentle tug, sending it unwinding backward right through me.

Night turns to day turns to night in flashes, like a yellow-gold strobe light. Cars zoom past as blurs of color on either side of me, whipping my hair around my face, shaking my clothes out until they're dry.

I don't know how I'll know it's time, but I believe I will.

I watch several accidents reverse until I see a maroon blot against the creek—a pile of crushed metal unfolding again and pulling back onto the road, parting ways with a black pickup. I go just past that before I stop focusing on Beau's song, on the wheel of time, and let the world fall back into its rhythm.

Neither Beau's dad's car nor my mom's are in sight, but a shiver trickles down my vertebrae, letting me know—as Grandmother must have known when I told her of my impending Closing—that this is the same night. I feel the night air itself thick with expectation, like the still woods and the mute crickets and the barometric pressure and the floating clouds and ancient rocks are all holding their breath, preparing to weep for me.

At the end of all this, the end of the world, I stand on a yellow line of paint and look up into the night sky, searching the stars. "Are you there?" I whisper.

I feel nothing but the warm breath the night's held on to since the Sun's last setting, the soft glow of the Moon, the distant heartbeat of Thunder, the lick of Fire, and the flash of Rainbow, and while none of these is the voice of my father or the face of my mother, I know—with certainty—that I am somebody's child, that I am deeply loved. And when the headlights reach around the bend at the end of my line of sight, that's enough.

It's enough when I glance over my shoulder and see the truck rumbling from the opposite direction, bouncing drunkenly between the shoulder and the median.

It's enough when I face the glare, peer through it to the maroon car beyond, and step into the middle of the lane. Because I found myself in the stories Grandmother told and in the hearts of those who loved me.

I start walking toward the end, heading off my own accident. All the while, time shudders around me. It pulls against me, like a river current trying to drag me back to my own time. I find a stone in the road, and I take it in my hand. There's not much time until I'll be whisked away from all this, certainly not enough time to redo this if it doesn't work. I have one chance to make any sort of change, and so I dig my heels in with every step and keep moving. In a way, I become the dark and mysterious mass from my dreams, moving toward myself.

I think of the blueness the girl fell into in Grandmother's story, endless possibility. Even that can be terrifying. I have to believe in whatever lies within the blue, that within its primordial goop there's another Beau, another Natalie, another summer containing all time, when we'll stop asking who we are and let ourselves be savored fiercely by the world. And if there is no other Natalie on the other side of this, I have to believe there's at least a long and exceptional life for the person I love. The tears start to fall; my speed increases.

Goodbye, Sun. Goodnight, Moon. Thank you, Thunder. I love you, Fire. Goodbye, Rainbow.

And Mom, who stroked my hair when I woke from nightmares drenched in sweat.

And Dad, who squeezed my neck on the deck overlooking the mist, as he told me he'd always listen.

And Matt, who loved me first.

And Megan, who loved me best.

And Rachel, who loved me fiercely.

And my Bridget, who loved me selflessly.

And Beau—Beau Wilkes, who loved me until the end.

I stop walking as the lights bear down on me. They swell.

Brighter and brighter and brighter still, until they're a pool of clear blue. A beautiful, perfectly broken new world I would die to see. For a moment, I imagine the dark outline of a hunched woman, her smile and her wrinkly hand lifting. She was there. The Grandmother I know said she never saw Beau's and my future, but she was there. She stood on our porch and looked through our window. And maybe she'd come there to look at the past with the Beau she'd already lost, while I stood there looking toward his future without me, with someone else. But maybe, just maybe, she—that old, crooked version of me—had just come home from the grocery store. Maybe she was standing on the porch her husband had built for her, weighed down by bags of beer and cereal, when she thought she saw something familiar in the window. Maybe she stopped and felt her insides shiver because, for an instant, she could've sworn she saw herself, sixty years younger, standing in the living room with arms coiled around the love of her life. Maybe she lifted up her hand to say, *I'm here. I'm still here after all this time.*

I had meant to throw the stone in my hand at the hood of the car, but it's becoming hard to see. Time is whipping against me, every breath a fight to stay.

Now, now is the moment I have in life—no future, no past. Now is the moment I have to choose how I live, and now is quickly collapsing. I let the stone fall out of my hand as I lift my arms up over my head. *I'm here,* I think. Maybe that will be enough to undo everything, but if not . . . if not, I'm still a happy kind of sad. "I'M HERE."

The headlights grow. And then they consume me, fold me in their endless arms, and I feel nothing.

Nothing but warmth.

Though I see a dark orb swelling behind the car, beyond the light, trying to catch me and tear me back into place before time falls shut.

Though I hear the screech and thud, even the sharp intake of breath from behind the glass.

Though I hear the door swing open and the desperate breathing.

And very last, the last thing I'll ever hear, my mother's words: *"There's no one there. I swear I saw a girl. There's no one there. She's—"*

And that's when I'm lost, and in my place, the world gets born.

33

There once was a girl who fell in love with a ghost. When she looked through him, she saw the world as it was made to be: warm, lush, aching with growth and quaking with tenderness. Through the boy, she saw the web of time, and how every moment—past, future, good, and bad—had conspired to tell their love story.

She loved the ghost boy so much that she thought the feeling alone might be enough to fix everything that had ever broken. In her. In him. In the whole world.

And because she loved him like this, she finally understood how deeply she was loved.

She knew she would do anything for the ghost boy. She would fold herself around him to protect him. She would drink out all the darkness from him and pour out all her light on him. She would rebuild the whole world for him.

One day, a voice spoke to her from above. Perhaps it came as a quiet whisper, carried on a gentle wind. Some say it was in the rumble of thunder or the crunch of stiff summer grass. Still others describe it as the delicate flutter of moth wings.

"My child," the voice said. "It is I, Love, the maker of worlds. If you want the ghost boy to live again, bring him out beneath the moon tonight, and I will send Death down to trade your life for his."

The girl loved the ghost boy so much that she felt only the smallest hesitation. There's little to fear when you love. There's nothing to fear when you *are* loved. So the girl took her ghost lover out into the valley beneath the moon that night and found Death's own knife waiting for her. It was strange, that Death was not chasing her, coming to collect her, or swallowing her whole.

Instead the girl was standing beneath the stars, the soft breath of the grass warming her ankles, the heartbeat of the world thudding gently, devotedly against her feet, and the crickets singing a lullaby. She looked into her ghost boy's eyes, and the softness of his smile filled her heart so quickly that it began to break as she brought the knife toward her chest.

The sky split open then.

The stars fell like silver rain.

The world stopped turning. The Universe held its breath.

The voice came again. "Stop. Set down Death's knife. I've seen your heart and that you withhold nothing for yourself. You know my face. You recognize my love for you, as you know your own for the ghost boy. You know what you would do for him, and so you understand now that, for you, my beloved, I would fix the whole world."

Then the moonlight fell down too: a brilliant sheet of white that cleansed the whole valley and left the world utterly dark, perfectly quiet as it was in the beginning, before all things. And in the dark, the girl fell into a dreamless sleep.

When she awoke next, the sun was starting to rise. Birds were singing. She remembered nothing, not the night before nor any night that came before it.

It was the first day of her life, and when she looked up the side of the valley, she saw a boy watching her. He looked familiar and unfamiliar at once, like someone whose vague notion she'd seen in a dream.

"I missed you," she heard herself call to him—though was it possible to miss someone you didn't know? Her chest hurt then, an immeasurable burst of pain.

"Every day," he answered softly. "All the time."

He came toward her, the early sunlight glinting off his skin and hair and eyes.

THANKS

If you've finished this book, you probably suspect by now that I've been treated better by the people around me than any person can reasonably expect in this world. My heart is full and my words fall short. Here are some people I want to thank:

The First Nations whose stories are seen here: Iroquois (The Woman Who Fell From the Sky), Natchez (Adoption of the Human Race), Sioux (Teton Ghost Story), Seneca (Brother Black and Brother Red), Caddo (The Flood), Creek (The Yamasee and the Flood), Onondaga-Iroquois (The Vampire Skeleton), and Kwakiutl (Ghost Country). There are several beautiful variations of each of these stories, and I highly recommend that anyone who's unfamiliar take time to sit with them, whenever possible, with the interpretation of a scholar from each tale's respective nation. This book wouldn't be the same without these mesmerizing and unquantifiable stories, and I'm forever changed by what I discovered in them.

Gramma and Grampa, for beginning a tradition of gentleness and love that still defines our family; you are the people I want to be when I grow up. Mom and Dad, for reading to us in the hallway between our rooms so many nights, and for always doing the voices. To my brothers and sisters-in-law, thank you for being the kind of people who fight through the hard things and appreciate the good.

K.A. Applegate, for my first book crush (a boy who is literally trapped as a hawk for the majority of the series). Lois Lowry, for teaching me that words can forever change your world. J.K. Rowling, for smart girls, tender boys, deep magic, and love that casts out fear. Madeline L'Engle and Kurt Vonnegut, for an addiction to Weird.

Ms. Hanke, for that first writing assignment. Ms. Neugabauer, for that detention. Ms. Richards, for not punishing me when I turned in the choose-your-own-adventure story in which all roads led to you locking us in the flame-engulfed classroom and picking us off with arrows.

Rhoda Janzen, for giving me someone to look up to and up to, and for telling me I could do this, and I should. Beth Trembley, for teaching me how. Heather Sellers, from whom I first heard the phrase love you into the world. Sarah B., Peter S., Pablo P., Stephen H., Steven I., Martha G., Jesus M., Dean Reynolds, and the rest of the Hope College faculty, for creating the perfect little adult-incubator, despite the frozen lake next door.

Daniel Nayeri, who unwittingly encouraged me to keep going on at least two separate occasions, and John Silvis for his beautiful NYCAMS program, may it rest in peace. Or alternatively, someday be resurrected.

Bri Cavallaro and Anna Breslaw, for talking me up/down/all around: you are beautiful and rare gems. Candice the Queen, for reading an early draft of this book plus, I think, three alternate endings, and helping me admit which was the right one.

The online YA community, book bloggers, and Sweet Sixteens: I'm so impossibly lucky to have been embraced by you. Don't play dumb. You know who you are.

Noosha, for being my first fan, my best friend, a life-changing love. Megan, for being my sister, my warmth, the person to whom I'll never say goodbye.

Lana Popovic, my incredible agent, for reading my first book in 23 hours and this one in 36, for always making time, for dissecting my manuscripts and operating on them; for your sass, feist, smarts, and love. And for getting me to watch Fringe.

Liz Tingue, the editor I wanted to make mine, whom I now get to call mine, in the least creepy way possible. You saw the spark in this wild, weird, sprawling, and sometimes slow book. You knew what this story wanted to be, and you believed it would get there. Thank you for speaking my language, for loving Beau and Natalie, and for being the hilarious, glittering, genius bombshell of a human being you are.

Marissa Grossman and Jessica Harriton, whose capable yet elegant hands helped knead this story into shape and then pack it into mailers.

Anthony Elder, for giving me a cover that could make hardened criminals and jaded dystopian heroines fall to their knees weeping.

Ben Schrank, for essentially handing me my dream on a glowing, LED platter, and occasionally favoriting my tweets (can't wait for anthropologists to study this sentence in the year 3000) just to remind me He's Always Watching from the clouds.

Jennifer Dee, Rachel Lodi, and Anna Jarzab—you know what you did. You are each uniquely amazing.

Krista Ahlberg, Phyllis DeBlanche, Shari Beck, Jenna Pocius, the rest of Razorbill/Penguin team, and every penguin, for being incredible, hardworking, resilient, and adorable.

Everyone who picks up, reads, borrows, buys, or lends this book: if you love this, I hope you know it's yours. If you don't, I hope you find $20 in your dirty laundry to make up for it.

For everyone I've missed: frankly, you deserve better.

Finally, thank you to Joey, who stole my heart at seventeen, when I was young(er) and stupid(er), and daily gives me a steadfast, quiet love I never knew I needed until I had it. You make this whole world soft for me, and I love all of the yous I've known, will know, will never meet. I love you in every moment.

And to the Love who dreamed the world, who gave me breath, and who gingerly passed me this idea page by page: thank you for that time you wept, and for loving me well.